BEAUTIFUL BODIES

BEAUTIFUL BODIES

Laura Shaine Cunningham

BLOOMSBURY

A Note on the Author

Laura Shaine Cunningham is the author of five books including
the acclaimed memoirs *Sleeping Arrangements* and
A Place in the Country. She lives in New York.

First published in Great Britain 2003
This paperback edition published 2004

Copyright © 2002 by Laura Cunningham

Bloomsbury Publishing Plc, 38 Soho Square, London W1D 3HB

A CIP catalogue record for this book is available from
the British Library

ISBN 0 7475 6818 9

10 9 8 7 6 5 4 3 2 1

All papers used by Bloomsbury Publishing are natural, recyclable
products made from wood grown in well-managed forests.
The manufacturing processes conform to the
environmental regulations of the country of origin.

Printed in Great Britain by Clays Ltd, St Ives plc

www.bloomsbury.com/laurashainecunningham

This book is dedicated to my mother Rosie

Contents

Chapter One

In which Jessie Girard ponders the possibility of love, buys food for a party, and suffers "hostess regret."

Raw Space

She was out, at night, in New York, laughing on the near-empty street, laughing like a crazy person, which perhaps she was. She didn't feel the record-breaking cold; she was wearing an extra mantle. She was afraid to name the feeling, but she recognized it. Only love could warm you like this, lying soft and unseen, like a cape across your shoulders. She felt wrapped in cashmere and wondered for an instant if all the conspicuous consumption of good woolens and fur that she'd just walked past in the brighter lit shopping district of SoHo was an attempt to substitute for this sensation, when it was missing.

The five-below-zero temperature created an optical illusion as Jessie walked toward her loft. Her vision altered—she looked out at her street as if through too-strong prescription glasses. The buildings appeared sharp and overly outlined, so distinct that they seemed to move toward her, doubling in dimension, like a 3-D effect in novelty films she'd seen as a child. She felt keen, sharpened herself: everything had just changed for the better. Oh wasn't it wonderful? She laughed again, almost "hearing" his voice as she conducted both sides of a conversation that played on in her mind.

3

How could she have forgotten love? What had she been doing, thinking, that this could have been lost to her for so long? She felt as if she had been shaken from a dreamless sleep that had lasted nearly a decade.

It had been at least that long since Jessie had nourished delusions of domestic nirvana. She'd been divorced from her childhood sweetheart for years, divorced also from the goal of a marriage. She had edited out a wedding as the hoped-for ending (although from time to time, the image did pop up, like one of those gimmick greeting cards: bride and groom, atop the cake). For years now, she had mentally cried "No" at the unbidden nuptial apparition. She knew better, she thought. When she wanted male companionship, Jessie imagined the comfort of a standing body hug, the clinch at the sink, a warm belly at her back in bed, for better sleeps. Someone to say "I have a cold" to, split an entrée, walk her home from a distant party. Maybe down the road, a friend. A traveling companion to see the world with, when her work was done, if it ever was. . . . Yes, she sometimes thought she might like to share her life, but she'd considered herself content to go it alone.

And now, a man had taken her by literal surprise and left her in, of all things, a state of grace. She had forgotten even the possibility of falling in love. The "falling" part was apt—she had in fact tumbled backward onto a bed.

As she walked up her block, the memories of the past few days insulated her from the bitter temperature (the date later proved to be the coldest night of the year). How on earth could she have forgotten sex? It had been three years, her longest intermission . . . but *still*. . . .

She was still laughing at the jokes they had shared—"I can feel my bones creak." And the way her body had remembered for her, and she'd found herself rotating her hips in the time-honored way, hopping into unaccustomed positions. Oh yes, she'd remembered thinking, I used to do this—as she'd kissed his chest, nursing on his vestigial nipples. . . .

Oh, dear, Jessie ordered herself, stop thinking of the vestigial nipples. . . . She had to descend to earth. . . . She reached into her pocket to hold the glove that he had lost, and she had found. What is love without a talisman? The old sheepskin glove kept the shape of his fingers, even the lines of his palm. She held it as, only last night, she had held his hand. She must remember to tell him that she had his glove; she had found it in her pocket, after she boarded the plane.

On this particular night, Butane Street appeared as desolate as a moonscape, lunar in its loneliness. The last people she had seen were two blocks past. Later, she would recall them also, as signs of the specific quality of this night. There had been three lone individuals—a drug dealer, incongruous for Christmas, peddling his pharmaceutical presents; a man exposing himself in a doorway; and a woman in a motorized wheelchair, buzzing past, a beatific smile on her face.

On another night, Jessie might have wondered how that woman could be happy, paralyzed, making her way alone, but tonight she thought she knew. On another night, she might have resented the drug peddler more, now she thought, It's terrible, but it must be anesthesia for people in pain. On another night, she might have been disgusted by the flasher; tonight, she felt sorry for him, waving his penis in the cold, tugging at himself for carnal consolation.

A great benevolence had descended upon Jessie; she was warmed and buoyed by her past weekend, the newness of being touched again. She had thought that might never happen. Especially now, since the past few years, and the series of harsh events, one of which had left its imprint on her body. Could it be so simple? That all she had needed was that touch? Could one other person make the entire difference? Between going forward, with an inner tremble, or rushing ahead, uplifted and glad, ready for whatever might happen next?

Tonight, she was facing a social challenge, but it didn't truly daunt her. If she looked at the logistics—that she had to prepare a party in less than an hour—she would have to admit defeat in advance. She was too happy to concentrate on details; her euphoria separated her even from herself. In her mind, she was back in Colorado. She was thinking not of what she had to do, but what she had just done. The kissing, the holding . . . she saw, in her mind's eye, his face, his chest—to which she had said a playful good-bye, ducking her head under his sweater as they sat in his parked car at the airport. She could still feel his skin, pick up the scent, and taste him on her tongue. She finally understood everything she'd ever read of magic spells and cloud nine.

Should she tell her friends about the weekend? Or, better to keep the secret, sweet and private, to herself? If she spoke the words aloud, would the spell disintegrate into the atmosphere, like the vapor rising from the gutter grate?

Stop thinking about this, she told herself. Get the apartment in order, cook the food, uncork the wine, light the candles. Her pace quickened, in step with her thoughts: get upstairs, turn on the oven, clear the worst of the debris. She recalled the mess upstairs— her laundry on the bed, all her research materials on the table and started to laugh.

I am doomed, she told herself, with an inner giggle. It was as if the gods had conspired. Not only had the weather not "cooperated"—it was now deteriorating. The ice storm that had delayed her return flight to New York by a day had now rejoined her here.

The wind picked up as she walked; the forecast was that snow would follow.

Jessie fought the river wind as she made her way on the long, final block west. The wind was so powerful it blew her one step back, for every two she took forward. A few times, she had to stop, to rebalance her shopping bags. Her hands gripped the sacks, heavy with Australian red wine, Pellegrino water, the five Cornish hens, and ten pounds of Yukon gold potatoes.

Oh why had she bought such heavy food? Why potatoes? Most of the women were dieting; they might get angry at the sight of the potatoes. They might identify with the potatoes. At the moment, Jessie herself felt not unlike a potato, bundled in her beige down coat, bulky and lumpy, her head sticking up like a knobby growth.

She had walked a good twelve blocks from Dean & DeLuca. Her boots had failed to be waterproof and now her feet felt like the potatoes too, only frozen. As she paused, one shopping bag slipped, and the bottom hit the slush on the sidewalk. The sodden paper gave way, and the hens slipped out, five goose-pimpled poultry corpses, falling into the gutter of Hudson Street. Jessie cursed as she tried to retrieve the hens. More groceries spilled into the street. The three so-called blood oranges that she had intended to serve macerated in cassis rolled toward a sewer opening. Oh, what had she been thinking to have a dinner party at her apartment? Why hadn't they all just chosen a restaurant? But that had seemed much too impersonal for this evening's occasion.

An hour earlier, she had hit the ground running. She'd dropped her suitcase off at the loft, then taken the airport cab straight to Dean & DeLuca to buy as many prepared foods as possible. Oh why had she gotten ambitious at the food counter? Why hadn't she just gone ahead and bought the meal, precooked?

As she crawled on the pavement, trying to retrieve all the food that had spilled, Jessie recalled her rationale. She wanted tonight to be different, so special . . . beyond catering, past takeout. She would cook every item herself, to ensure its perfection. That had seemed more festive somehow, more personal. It was just as easy to roast the hens as buy them already cooked and costing ten times as much. Those itsy-bitsy hens—it seemed as if the smaller they were, the more they cost.

I can do an apricot glaze, she had told herself, but she hadn't answered the unasked question: when? When would she have time? Then, of course, she didn't dare wait for delivery; she'd better get to roasting right away. She'd counted on getting a taxicab, forget the cost—it was a bad and also important night. Time was all that mattered. She'd stood at the curb, flailing for a cab, and of course, there had been none. So here she was at 5:30 P.M., with uncooked little chickens, going up to a semiclean apartment, with her five best friends expected in an hour.

It was impossible. They would understand of course—they were her friends. They had known one another for so long, seen one another's unretouched moments. This was the old Theresa House gang, her first friends in the city. They all "went back"; they'd seen each other naked, sick, crying, vomiting. But that didn't mean she should strive for such cinema verité tonight. This was supposed to be a festive occasion—it would be unpleasant to sit there, in the disorder.

As she bent over the pavement, picking up the cold little Cornish hens, Jessie mentally projected and could see the two weeks' worth of laundry piled on her bed. How could she clean up in time? All her research was strewn across the living room, the cat box was unchanged in the bathroom. . . . Her mind was reeling—what to do first? Set the table, roast the Cornish hens? If only she had time, how she'd love a hot shower. Jessie knew she'd be lucky if she got to pee, which she also had to do.

As she retrieved the fallen blood oranges, the phone rang in her purse. Jessie wasn't yet accustomed to the cell phone. She had ambivalent feelings about having one. Only a few weeks ago, she'd looked askance at the people walking, talking, down the street. She'd thought they looked like idiots, and now she was one of them. The beeps emitted, with electronic insistence, from deep within her handbag. For a moment, Jessie imagined her purse was talking to her, the voice of materialism, speaking up for itself. She struggled into a doorway and tried to answer, but she could hear only a high cackle, unintelligible against the howl of the wind.

Even though she knew it wasn't him—the man she had just begun to love—her heart had quickened, and she controlled her breathing as she spoke into the receiver. He had said he would phone her tonight, but later. She was sure he would keep his word—this man was so wonderful; he was creditable. It was still too early. "Eight o'clock" he had said. So this call had to be from someone else. It rang again, but now there was only a mechanized moan emitting from the receiver, as if the tiny cell phone had intersected some galactic disturbance high above her.

Jessie imagined the call was from one of her guests who had decided not to brave the elements tonight. Who would want to go out in this weather?

This was a stay-home night if ever there was one. Even Jessie thought of an evening alone in her big old easy chair, cuddled in a comforter, sipping hot soup, reading, patting the cat, reliving the private pleasures of her trip to Colorado. Maybe she should have called everyone from the airport, while there was still time.

But Jessie had gone to so much effort already. First, there had been the difficulty of choosing a date, on which they could all attend. Jessie had sorted through the details of all their calendars: six women, six schedules. Then, it had been almost impossible to convince Claire to accept a party in her honor. She had refused, saying, "It's too much bother." Jessie had to talk her into it, swearing not to call the party a "baby shower."

The truth was, they were all wondering about Claire; she had not seen any of them in three months. It was mysterious, not like Claire. She had dropped out of ballet class, their reading group, the subscription to the Manhattan Theatre Club. They had all invited her for dinner, a movie, anything, and she had avoided them all. This was odd, and Jessie wanted to see for herself. The party, the "it's-not-a-baby-shower-but-is" had to be tonight: they would never be able to agree on a new date, in time.

For a minute, she wished she'd never moved from Midtown; she wished she hadn't volunteered to be the hostess tonight. She fumbled in her purse, clawing through receipts, lipsticks, pencils, finally finding her keys at the bottom of her bag. The keys were industrial, hard and utilitarian, like the building, a former factory.

The name FRANKENHEIMER'S was still engraved above the door. The final irony, learned after she bought her loft, was that Jessie's own grandmother had labored in this very building in 1917, when it was still a millinery sweatshop. Almost a century ago, her grandmother had stood, possibly in Jessie's own loft, gluing feathers onto felt hats, for a dollar a week. Now, Jessie Girard, her granddaughter, had mortgaged herself for half a million dollars, to occupy the same space. How many feathers glued to how many brims? How many feathers to support oneself?

Jessie juggled the packages, dropped the cell phone in the slush, and suddenly became aware that a pile of what she had believed was rags had risen and was beckoning to her from the next doorway. He was a vagrant; she had seen him before—he wore a fur-lined flyer's cap, a peacoat, and open galoshes. He was begging, she guessed, although often he just muttered obscenities or screamed "It all sucks." Sometimes, though, he was oddly specific and muttered "They all wear the same perfume now."

Tonight he moved closer to her, and Jessie was startled to see that he was carrying a tote bag that was marked with a Ralph Lauren insignia: the miniature polo player, riding for the strike. Could this bum be a refugee from a Ralph Lauren lifestyle? That chilled Jessie more than the freezing temperature. No, surely not; he'd somehow come by the bag through illicit means. The Ralph Lauren bag appeared in rather good condition, two-toned, canvas and tan leather. The bum reached into the bag and leaned toward her. She could smell whiskey and his body odor, which was ripe and somehow fruity, like a spoiled banana. He breathed something in her ear, which she tried not to hear. She forced her door inward, and slid inside, before processing what he had said:

"Ecstasy."

"No thanks," she whispered.

Ecstasy. Shivering, glad to be indoors, Jessie rode the former freight elevator to the top floor, twelve, and stepped directly into her loft.

The loft was beautiful, what her friend Martha called "drop-dead beautiful" with its big views looking downtown to the south and out across the sequined stripe of the Hudson to the west. Jessie always wondered what Martha meant by "drop-dead beautiful"—that the place was so stunning, you could collapse in cardiac arrest? Or that the layout was so in-your-face gorgeous, that the less real estate–endowed would expire in envy? Martha touted fatal foyers and killer kitchens. Certainly, Jessie could agree, the stakes had risen in the city and a spire could cut through your heart.

Tonight, having left the mountainscape of the Rockies, craggy but somehow gentled by their snowcaps, Jessie returned to her urban vista with a shock. The high-rise offices loomed, hard-cut, sparkling giants of commerce—the edifices seemed to personify the business world. Were they always so glary? When Jessie was overworked or behind on the minimum payments on her credit cards, she suffered another sort of optical illusion—the city turned Cubist, its corners cut like daggers.

There was one office tower she could see downtown; her friend Lisbeth joked and called it the "Darth Vader"—the building was obsidian, and it did glare at her, challenging her to meet its aggression. Jessie had had day-mares of herself, sliding down its shear surface, fingernails clutching at glass, all the way down. The gutslide down glass. Jessie had not been born in the city; much as she had longed for it; within her was that stomach clutch of fear. New York was home, but she felt as if the welcome mat could be yanked at any moment.

Now, coming back after only a few days, Jessie was stunned by the way, in her absence, the loft seemed to have reverted to its former identity. It was as if the loft knew it was not a loft but a sweatshop: all that greeted her inside were the shadows, animate with a century of memory; the ghosts of cheap labor crouched in its corners.

She tripped over her soft-sided suitcase, jackknifed like a body. Jessie pitched forward into her 1,800 square feet of "raw space." A year ago, when she bought this "raw space," she'd relished the expression. "Raw"—it had seemed appetizing, a challenge, an architectural "raw" bar to sink her talented teeth into. She'd been happy to buy it "raw"—the only way she could afford it. "Rawness" had beckoned, an empty palette. She had not reckoned with how "raw" it would feel to live in an unfinished space, to try to work and survive in what had essentially been a construction site for the past eight months.

Tonight, returning after such a short trip, she felt, at first glance, that she'd lost what interior ground she had gained. This did not look, feel, or smell homey.

Jessie inhaled the scent of plaster, spackling. The instant she was behind her own door, the need to pee, which had been urgent before, became uncontrollable. The urge won out over her desire to check the phone answering machine, and the stack of unopened mail, shoved under her door. She crossed her legs and hopped in a near dance step toward the toilet that she herself had installed. As Jessie performed her odd jig she passed the cat, who lurched from the shadows.

At first Jessie thought the animal, desperate in its loneliness, was greeting her. The cat was one of those white cats, with blue eyes, that are born deaf. She had not heard Jessie enter; she must have responded to the vibration of her step and the cue of the light switch. As the animal weaved toward her, Jessie recognized that the cat was retching. The cat began to heave, a fur ball caught in its throat; her eyes rolled, staring up at Jessie as if to say "Help."

Oh, not now, Jessie thought. *Et tu,* Colette?

Jessie hopped into the bathroom she had built, without bothering to shut the substandard door that she had also installed. Inside the little gray bathroom, where the slate tiles had been set somewhat askew by her own hand, Jessie struggled to get her panties down in time, and crashed onto the half unhinged toilet seat. As she peed in this precarious position, she tilted forward on the askew seat and was brought into direct eye contact with a leaflet entitled "Buyer's Remorse" that rested on the floor, amongst other papers she had intended to stack for recycling.

I have buyer's remorse, all right, she admitted to herself. And she had something else that she'd read about in a woman's magazine on the plane—"hostess regret." "Hostess regret" was defined as a syndrome that strikes women an hour before guests arrive—the hostess regrets she ever planned a party. As Jessie sat there on a crooked little toilet seat, both feelings merged; "the buyer's remorse" and the "hostess regret." These twin emotions melded into the greater worry over her own fiery urgency, this burning she felt. . . .

Maybe she had more than a need to pee? Maybe she had contracted some exotic venereal disease from the man she'd gone to bed with back in Colorado? Venereal disease or just cystitis? Because she had known pleasure, did she now have to suffer?

No, she refused to suffer. So much sex. Cystitis, for sure. She recalled her honeymoon, twenty years before, when as a teenage girl, she'd returned home from the Caribbean with her innards on fire. So much sex then, too, but it had been the youthful, gymnastic intercourse she'd engaged in, with her husband, Hank.

Although she had no time to reminisce—she should clean and at least preheat the oven—Jessie could not help recalling the sensation of an overused vulva. Yes, so much sex then too . . . but repetitive, almost grueling intercourse. At nineteen, she had not been able to properly evaluate her honeymoon; Hank had been her "first." Now, many men and years later, Jessie did not want to regard that sex as "bad" or wasted effort, but she was even more puzzled in retrospect by the quality of those marital relations. While she had known they loved each other, that love had not been well expressed physically. Her ex-husband, Hank, could be tender in talk and intimate by mail, but when he entered her body, his spirit had seemed to depart. He had been entirely physical, avoided eye contact when engaged.

Her husband had been handsome, relentlessly virile, Jessie conceded as she sat, in slight discomfort, on her self-installed "throne," but she preferred what she had just experienced with a stranger to the emotionless exchange that had passed between her husband and herself for the twelve years of their marriage.

Intimacy, she supposed, wasn't acquired or learned—it was either absent or magically intrinsic: oh, in Colorado . . . the kindling in that man's eyes, desire and liking, a humor that had not impeded their passion (he had entered her while still trying to kick off one cowboy boot). Laughing, lusting . . . everything at once— alien and familiar.

Sex was mystery, Jessie admitted to herself. It didn't make sense. She and Hank had loved each other, stayed together . . . yet they had been less intimate than she had just been with a near-stranger.

She finished in the bathroom, tossed the "Buyer's Remorse" pamphlet in the wicker wastebasket. No time for regrets of any kind tonight. She'd better get on with it. . . . Clean or cook first?

Jessie had a method, the same one she applied to her work as a journalist. She evaluated the situation, tackled what was in front of her. Systematically, she solved the worst problems first . . . like triage at a battlefield. A dinner party was no different. She decided: a good hostess deals first with what would be most disgusting to guests.

The mess. Outside the bathroom door, she confronted the cat, Colette, who was now puking in great, back-arching spasms, spewing spirals of congealed regurgitated cat food and fur. This was a priority. Jessie grabbed a paper towel, and mopped up the cat's mess. Then she hauled out the vacuum cleaner and dragged it, roaring, around the 1,800 square feet. For the first time she rued her vast square footage. The vacuum began to backfire tubes of compacted grime that were a match for Colette's upchuckings.

And I wanted this to be elegant, Jessie thought. Now she'd be lucky if no one called the Health Department. She ran for her emergency weapons—the broom, dustpan, and a mammoth trash bag. Kneeling, she clawed at the vacuum bag by hand, stuffed the trash bag, picked up the worst of the lint, and dumped the kitty litter. She marveled at the calcified consistency of the cat turds. A stray cat turd rolled across the bathroom floor, and Jessie picked it up; she could feel a deep chill emanating from that cat turd, as if cat turds had a mysterious negative ability to retain frigid temperature. Oh, how was tonight going to be beautiful, festive with all this to handle . . . ?

She offered Colette a plate with pats of expensive unsalted creamery butter, said to be a remedy for fur balls and calcified cat turds. The cat licked, appeared cured, and collapsed in a heap before the unlit fireplace, on a throw rug. She began to purr, a near-snore of joy.

The scene could be salvaged. Jessie put the oven on high, to preheat, then looked around the room. Solve the most drastic problem first: clear the kitchen table, set the silverware. That would give an appearance of readiness, even if inaccurate. . . .

Jessie started to pick up the unsorted papers on the table and came eye to eye with a news picture, grainy black and white on thermal fax paper. Her hand stopped, and she stared down at his face. Him. The One. He was shown, his professional expression set—"Jesse Dark, civil liberties attorney, Native American rights activist, representing his tribe, descendents of the Anasazi in a defamation suit."

Had she inklings, all the weeks she had researched and studied these clips, that she would end up in a motel bed with him? That she would find herself, heels locked behind his neck, head thrown back, her throat emitting unrecognizable sounds of what she dimly called joy?

She tried to remember when she first felt the stirrings. Those preliminary days, across from him in court, she had noted his starched shirt, the string tie, the impossible fit of his jeans, the beaten heels of his cowboy boots. Yes, she'd secretly acknowledged he was one of the more attractive men she'd seen . . . but never would she have predicted that in another night, she would look up to the ceiling of a motel room and regard its stuccoed surface as . . . her glimpse of heaven.

No, she had had no idea. She had been taken unawares, thank God. Jessie had prided herself on her seriousness as a journalist. "He" had been a subject, not a potential object of affection. "He" glared back at her from her thermal fax image: "He" looked handsome, even in the grainy, poor reproduction, sulky and swarthy as his name suggested: Jesse Dark. Jessie giggled, transfixed: he looked so severe, who would have believed he was playful?

Somewhere in this pile of clutter, Jessie had a videotape that showed her male namesake (and possible soul mate) addressing a crowd of protesters outside a cave. Within that cave his ancestors, of the Anasazi tribe, were accused of killing their ancient enemies, cooking and devouring their flesh and then—this was the worst accusation—defecating their digested remains on the campfire.

It was this detail—that the ashes had perfectly preserved the human feces—that had allowed for DNA testing now, so many centuries later—that had caught Jessie Girard's trained eye and triggered something in her too, something she could not understand. What a defining moment, how astounding that scientists could re-create the specific incident: a moment of ultimate rage, that had taken place over a thousand years ago. In a sense that ancient fire had been relit, and the sworn enemies, reengaged. It was the sort of story Jessie loved. She had known she had to cover the demonstration, she had to interview the man who led it . . .

There was a book in it. And now, she felt, God help her, that she had to hear from that man again, that she had to touch him. . . .

Jessie paused in her preparations. She knew she had to put away all these papers, tapes, files, but the subject drew her and now, of course, she knew the man in the photograph. . . . Knew him? His DNA floated within her. Her thighs still ached from being held down by his hands, in those unaccustomed positions. She could, if she concentrated, recall the exact pressure of his tongue and teeth on her nub of flesh.

We went a little crazy, she recalled, happy. They had in fact, crossed some boundary in each other and come out howling on the other side. Although she would never have dared tell him—he was a cannibal, all right, she had thought, but only in the best sense.

No sexual reverie, she forbid herself. Jessie forced herself to resume tidying: she threw the extra items—her work, the newspapers, assorted junk of all description—on a bedsheet, bagged the whole mess, and threw it in the closet. Not a tip from Martha Stewart or a Hint from Heloise, but this hid a multitude of sins. She reserved the snapshots of Jesse Dark, of course. She couldn't throw him in the closet. She tucked the pictures in the utility drawer near the stove. Maybe she would show her friends, later, if it seemed appropriate.

No time now for recalled orgasmic joy . . . she had to roast the hens . . . glaze them . . . what had she been thinking?

Jessie could cook; she knew what to do. *Zing, zing, zing,* she washed and rubbed down the goose-pimpled little hens. *Zing, zing, zing,* she forced softened butter under their skins. . . . *Zing, zing, zing,* she rubbed them down with more butter, apricot jam, and ginger. Then she splayed out their legs; set them, in this mass undignified squat, into the hot oven . . . and turned the knob higher to broil. This high-heat method was the wild way to roast poultry; she could burn them into charred husks if she didn't pay attention.

Now, if she could prepare an hors d'oeuvre, she would stand a chance. Jessie opened her purse and extracted a jar so precious, she had hand-held it on the flight back to New York from Colorado. A jar of genuine green chili.

She could not resist. As she opened the sealed glass jar, Jessie spooned up a taste. It was a quick fix, for she had tasted green chili for the first time three nights before, in Colorado, during the dinner. That was the night she finally got up the nerve to invite Jesse Dark back to her motel room, and rewrite her own personal history with a series of fevered firsts—first time she ever slept with a "source" (not proud of that, but it paled beside her pleasure), first time she had a spontaneous orgasm on penetration, first time she shut her eyes and made a conscious decision not to control the event taking place. First time she did not edit her response but spoke without regard to the consequences of what she was feeling. First time she exposed her wounded body.

Remembering this, Jessie was propelled back to that moment, so unanticipated. How had she dared so much, so soon, with this stranger? Years of cautious sexual tiptoeing had been her style . . . walking tightropes of indecision. Maybe she would, no, she wouldn't. Being discreet in bed, even when almost screaming. Everything but the truth. She could not believe she had used the word *love*. Should she have bitten her kiss-bruised lip? Would that word *love* drive him away, or bring him to her? Jessie smiled as she spooned out the green chili into a dish. It was the perfect condiment to what had occurred: hot velvet.

Yes, he would call when he said. He was different . . . he was not afraid.

She scrubbed the potatoes and threw them in to roast, nestled amongst twiglets of rosemary, studded with garlic slivers, dressed in olive oil. Jessie was getting hungry now.

Mentally, she was back in the tiny Tex-Mex place in Coyoteville, Colorado, reliving that night's historic pleasures. . . . What a relief it had been to have a man seize the initiative.

When Jessie had approached him for a quote at the press conference, he had seemed polite but wary, his black eyes flicking over her face, appraising her. She remembered how hard she had tried not to seem like an idiot. She had stressed her Ph.D. in anthropology, emphasized her studies of tribal custom (omitting that her interest stemmed from becoming aroused, as a thirteen-year-old, reading of politically incorrect "Indian" capture in the western romance *Ramona*).

She had submitted, for his approval she supposed, her prize-winning book on the Jackson Whites—*Natives of the Ramapo Mountains.* How happy she'd been then, to perceive acceptance in his unanticipated dinner invitation—to the green chili place up the road. She had accompanied him in a daze of joy, trying to make conversation, her blood racing, a hormonal riptide already making her a little woozy.

As soon as they had sat down at a table, Jesse Dark had asked her why she cared whether the Anasazi were cannibals or not? She had thought for a while, sipping a potent drink over the salted lip of a heavy tumbler (in retrospect that serious margarita could take partial credit for her relaxation of principle, not to mate with anyone with whom she had any professional involvement) before answering.

"It was in the exact detailing of the scientific data," she had told him, "the accident of the ashes being the perfect preservative, the re-creation of that moment of rage that occurred over a thousand years ago. . . . That interested me."

He had looked at her then, with a hint of a smile. He had very chapped lips, and they seemed to crack at his unaccustomed expression. Later, he'd confessed he made up his mind, to get her to bed. "I knew you were angry, that you were hiding everything. If that moment obsessed you—you interested me."

They had talked until the café closed. They'd been oblivious until the waiter wiped down their table and turned up the lights. Jessie had been so pleased. For all these years, she'd sat down to dinner with dozens of different men only to ask herself the same question: could it be him? Only to hear her inner voice respond, No, not him, not this one.

Then suddenly, she didn't even have to ask: she had looked across the candle that guttered to its conclusion between them and said yes.

It was almost funny how attracted they were to each other. That this had not been the usual case of one wanting more than the other. What she'd seen in Jesse's dark eyes was a mirror. At one point in their conversation, his face had melted, gone suddenly soft, and his gaze turned downward, shy. Then, he had looked up at her—oh she wished she could have photographed that expression—so helpless, as if he could not say what he wanted. She'd adored him for that lost moment, when he seemed so hapless, not the tough guy who had held the national press at bay, but a sweeter fellow than she would ever have predicted from these news clips on her kitchen table. A sweet fellow looking to her, with unspoken hope.

Should she tell her friends what happened next? Should she show them his picture? Hold a screening of his news video? She was so tempted, but would it be safe to let this secret escape?

Maybe it was best kept safe, inside her. Sexual secrets could evaporate if you aired them in group conversation. Yet she wanted them to know: he had helped her more than she could have dreamed . . . it had not just been the usual. She promised herself not to relate the details. She would just imply she had "met" someone.

Jessie lit the candles on the kitchen table, set out six of her best china plates, and six linen napkins that had, thank God, come back from the Chinese laundry. For an instant, she thought about removing one of the place settings: Martha had said she could not stay. Some instinct instructed Jessie to leave that sixth place—opposite where Claire would sit, as guest of honor, at the head of the table.

The evening was taking potential shape. If she could just manage that hot shower and prepare a few more hors d'oeuvres, all would at least appear under control. Maybe she would tell them just a little. . . .

Jessie went and stood before the dressing mirror in her bathroom. She looked into her own eyes as she stripped for a quick shower. She expected to meet her familiar self, the person she'd been when last she stood here, only days ago . . . as if another version of Jessie Girard had, like the cat, waited for her to come home.

The woman whose fluctuant hazel eyes stared back at her did not much resemble the person reflected in the motel mirror in Colorado. Within her irises, something had turned, kaleidoscope-like, and tightened the focus with new-gained knowledge and, admit it, confidence. For God bless this man, this stranger, who looked forbidding from a distance in court, God bless him in close quarters . . . for whatever else, he had given her, he had given her his desire, unaffected by seeing her scar.

Jessie dared let her hand fall to her side. Now she looked at what she had avoided confronting all this past year: her own naked body. How reluctant she had been for the past eleven months, to show her body to anyone . . . even herself.

Now she stood on her own bath mat, a bit gritty with plaster dust, and remembered the moonlit walk in Coyoteville. The sky, cluttered with stars . . . electric, active in the heavens. The saloon doors were swinging open and shut, admitting and discharging men on joyous winter benders. There had been a true Yahoo! in the cold night air, and Jessie had been swept along with it.

She was dying to confide the details to her friends—how he'd paused with her, in the deserted doorway of a closed gun shop. He'd edged her against the locked door. The way he moved her, made her go backward; excited her past reason.

And there was another delicious detail—oh maybe it would be all right to tell her friends. She hadn't been dressed warmly enough, and he had been wearing an old oversize shearling coat. Suddenly, he had opened his coat and enveloped her in it, pulling her against his body.

She'd felt the heat of him, even through his jeans, then that twitch that signaled he wanted her. And she remembered thinking, Oh God, this is going to happen, just as his lips closed over hers, and his tongue invaded her mouth, and a corresponding thrust, trapped in those jeans, prodded against her belly.

He'd kissed her so hard. She had thought, for a few moments, This style of kissing is not for me. It's too aggressive—the tongue so deep, so fast, the harshness of his unshaved cheek, the unexpected hardness even of his lips. Like leather. And then, she'd been forced to acknowledge that he brought about an instant response; her thighs went wet, she was pasted together. It had been funny, embarrassing to respond that fast. Their conversation stalled, and they had torn into each other, all discussion of cannibalism abandoned.

When they reached her motel, they had been speechless in their agreement. She had fumbled for her key; he had used it to open her door. They fell into the room, not bothering to flip the light switch; just as well, that worked a singing fluorescent bar over the bureau. The drapes were open, and the moonlight had spilled into the room, illuminating what they would do with one another.

She had stood before him, naked as if on that moon. He was the first to see her since her surgery. She had paused for a second, silly in her insecurity, in which she wanted to cry out a disclaimer: "I had a beautiful body." Show him something like a "before" picture, so he would know who she really was . . . not this thirty-nine-year-old woman, who'd been through quite a bit, the most traumatic of which was obvious in the still-red slash across the left side of her chest.

She had wanted to issue a traveler's advisory before they undressed, but she had not found any words. So there she had stood, feeling truly naked for the first time in her life. Before the surgery, her body had been fine; she'd been nude before men, but psychically, she had been dressed. For an instant, she recalled what it had been like the last time she made love, how she'd thrown off her clothes and jumped onto the mattress. She'd felt the springs under her heels as she bounced, her hair swinging. And the man had said, "Do you know how beautiful you are?" And she'd laughed and said, "Yes."

No such self-assurance only three nights ago, with Jesse Dark, in that Colorado motel, no such bounce. She'd forced herself to hold still, be silent. She had so feared that she would see pity in his eyes. She remembered thinking, being really naked was showing yourself, flaws and all, and hoping somehow it would still be all right.

His eyes had questioned her, and then she'd whispered the truth. Her surgery, and the reason for it, had not been so drastic as it appeared. What she had was a warning of the disease, rather than the disease itself, what is aptly called a precursor. The prognosis was excellent, only the treatment had been severe.

Jessie had suffered as much from the "cure" as the condition, until now, until him. Whatever else he would do or not do in her future, Jesse Dark had already done what no doctor could—he had "kissed her better."

Now, safe at home in her own bathroom mirror, Jessie risked looking. She saw what Jesse Dark had seen by moonlight. Jessie did not appear so much mutilated as altered. On one side, the right, her breast was as before, full but still upright, rose tipped. On the left, the surface had shape but no detail, like the molded bosom on a naked store mannequin. Jessie was reminded of the "dollar dolls" she'd owned as a child, how the plastic breasts were suggested, without nipples; form instead of substance. She could not say the worst words, *cancer* or *mastectomy*. She hated those words, cancer the crab, taking its first bites of her, a literal nibble. And *mastectomy* reminded her of *masticate*—the crab chewing on the most delicate meat.

"I had an operation" was all she could say.

Did it hurt? He had wanted to know. "Not really," she'd answered him; the nerves had been cut too. All she felt now was a sense of constriction; it was unfortunate that it was directly over her heart.

Later, she told him the story, how the surgeon had even offered to "pick it out," but when Jessie had viewed her own films, she had acknowledged the true picture. Speck after speck in her left breast, specks that collected into constellations. . . . One could "pick out" that blasted star debris, that the doctors labeled "microcalcifica-tions," as easily as one could capture a cloud.

So the true breast itself was gone, and with it, for a year, her own sensation. Until now, until Jesse. He had whispered, "It doesn't matter." Would that hold true?

She had not confided in any of the other women, even to

Lisbeth, to whom she was closest in the group. All year, she'd hugged this secret to herself. No news was good news. No conversation meant that maybe it had not happened. Jessie had been too frightened to express fear. If she told people, it would seem more ominous. She would receive flowers in the hospital, there would be that buzz when she emerged. She had overheard so many whispered surgical horror stories at parties: "Oh, did you hear? She had. . . ."

No, not for her. No flowers, cards, or whispers. She had maintained "business as usual," even with a plastic "drain" under her shirt. She went to editorial meetings, bandaged under her blouse, and no one "knew." So maybe she could convince herself it was not true. She was too scared for conversation; her own mother had died of the more serious version. Who needed to say, "Now maybe it's me?"

Was it now safe to confide this history to her friends along with the happy hoped-for ending? No, Jessie decided. Why start a flurry of delayed reaction, overconcern? Why worry her friends and give voice to feelings she did not want to express?

She had denied herself the release of confession, choosing instead the consolations of privacy. And she would maintain that silence tonight. Tonight was for Claire, tonight was for celebration, for happiness. If she told any tales at all, it might be of her romance. She wanted to brag—"I did it. He loved me." He loved me, imperfect, as I am. Kissing a scar turns it to silk, restores sensation. I am healed.

Jessie smiled as she stepped under the hot shower. She wasn't thinking someone could arrive any minute, before she was ready. She was back in that motel room in Coyoteville, with that man who had surprised her with his sweetness. She was still marveling that a man with lips like leather could be kind.

She closed her eyes, feeling the water course over her skin, remembering how he'd touched and kissed her everywhere . . . how they had rushed the first time, to fit together, to erase what differences appeared, but the next several times, they had lingered. It had been easy then, to forget what had worried her; Jessie had forgotten everything, including who she was. And then it had been nice to remember, because he'd turned to her in the dawn and said, "Come here, I want to hold you."

Now, would he keep his promise? To call. Tonight. Eight o'clock. His time or hers? She wished she could be sure. It must have been "her" time. She tried to remember if he had been that specific. What exactly had he whispered in her ear—"My time is your time"?

Or would he disappear now, as men were wont to do? Would he vanish, lost in that psychic equivalent of the Bermuda Triangle, the postcoital divide? Or would he remain, a part of her, for now, forever? She turned off the water, toweled dry, and felt again that internal burning. Sexually transmitted disease or just cystitis? Pleasure or pain?

There was no time to dwell on what might be an unfortunate aftermath: Jessie threw on a bathrobe, then raced over to the stove. She pulled the Cornish hens from the oven; thank God, they had not burned. The glaze had worked: they shone, golden, brown, with flecks of apricot. The potatoes had not quite cooked through, and for a second, she considered finishing them in the microwave. She had the same contempt for her microwave that she had for her cell phone: more molecules moving around in the name of instant gratification. A necessary evil perhaps, but to be avoided when possible.

She put the potatoes back in the regular oven, to brown in the Cornish hen juices. With luck, they would finish roasting before anyone arrived. Jessie looked around—it was almost respectable. She ran to get a dress, then on impulse, pulled the sweater she had worn when she met Jesse Dark from her suitcase. Perhaps it held part of the magic spell. The sweater was white wool, and becoming with her long dark hair. She drew on brown leggings, her comfortable old house shoes, and felt she was almost ready.

She set the green chili, circled by a frill of poised blue tortilla chips, on the counter near the table. For decoration, she added a bouquet of tulips, semifrozen from her long walk to the loft, and placed the flowers, on the nod, in the center of the table. Then she positioned the wine bottles, two to start, on the counter. As she worked, she could detect the cooking aromas, the plumes of garlic- and onion-scented steam.

Now, the pièce de résistance: her gift for Claire and the baby. Jessie dragged out the carved wooden cradle that she had been saving for so long. The cradle was antique, perhaps 150 years old, handmade of course, with beautiful red-patterned woven straps. The cradle had originated in Lapland; it was designed to hang, like a hammock.

Claire will love it, she knew. No frilly pink ruffles, no acrylic fuzz. This was authentic and exotic: perfect for Claire. Jessie had bought it at an auction, thinking that maybe someday she might have her own baby. She felt a twinge as she propped her card "To Claire" on top of the cradle.

But no, she chided herself. Claire should have the cradle. Jessie stood back, for a moment, to admire the smooth wooden shape, rounded almost like an antique dough bowl. What fun it would be to see a baby in this, and how profound, that it had held babies for over a century. Jessie loved items imbued with history, and so did Claire—it was one of the interests they shared.

Jessie felt suddenly happy: she was doing this for Claire. She ran through her final hostess frenzy: setting out the wineglasses, lighting more candles, a fire in the grate.

The temperature—from the lights, the fire, the candles, and the stove—began to rise, driving away the chill that had crept into the corners of the vast and until recently "raw" space. The half-frozen yellow tulips seemed to revive and open in response. The loft began to glow, exuding a more golden hue that pushed back the shadows and banished the factory's past.

Jessie popped the cork on a bottle of the Shiraz "Aussie Red," and let it and herself breathe. She turned on the CD player—Rampal; Claire would appreciate the flute. Jessie herself enjoyed the first notes as they rose toward the loft's high ceiling. She might yet carry this off. She laughed as she took a preliminary sip of wine. It was amazing what you could do in an hour, if you had to. . . . Maybe one more hors d'oeuvre and she could consider herself ready.

She was washing a grape tomato, and preparing to stuff it with cheese, when the downstairs buzzer shrilled. She ran to the intercom and called, "Who is it?"

"It's me."

"Come on up," Jessie said, and pressed the button. She heard the freight elevator groan, lurch, and ascend again. Then the elevator shuddered to a halt beside her, and opened to yield her first guest.

Chapter Two

In which Sue Carol leaves her husband, goes astray in the subway, and buys a baby gift.

"Please Stand Clear of the Moving Platform"

Sue Carol didn't know if she was on the East Side or the West Side; she knew only that she was heading downtown. She had cried so hard, her tear ducts had dried up, and she'd taken out one of her contact lenses. She had pocketed the lens, in a tissue. Now, the lens was dried out and looked like a fingernail. She could not put that back in her eye.

So she swayed, clutching the subway car strap, trying to keep her luggage around her legs in a radius of security. Sue Carol was at a disadvantage and she knew it; she was squinting and blinking; she could see out of only one eye. She peered out of the "good" eye, scrutinizing the other passengers. Only three days ago the most recent subway attack on a woman had taken place, also on the BMT. ("Be Empty," she thought. Sue Carol could not help free-associating all over the place; it was that kind of night.)

The girl, who had been pushed, died. Her name was almost the same as her own: Sue Ellen. It had been hard not to identify with pictures of the dead Sue Ellen. She could have been Sue Carol, seventeen years ago, the week she moved to New York. The identical strawberry blond bangs, clear light eyes, smattering of freckles and

33

upturned nose. Even Sue Ellen's parents had looked like her own—the mother was a graying blonde, a bit fat, stuffed into polyester pants and wearing a flowered overblouse; the dad was lean, a golf cap on his bald head, his lips clamped on a pipe. They had sounded just like her own mom and dad, too, bemoaning that they had allowed their little girl to move to the city, from their "holler" in Slocum, Kentucky.

"This would not have happened in Slocum," Sue Ellen's mom had said. "She should never have left. We told her that the city was dangerous. She was so friendly; she had a smile for everybody, our Sue Ellen."

Now "our Sue Ellen" was paste, a mash of blood and bone, presumably shipped back to Slocum in a box, like the victim of an out-of-state war. Maybe the girls were like soldiers—not drafted, but volunteering for active duty, going off to seek their fortunes, find adventure in cities so different from their own hometowns.

It was not only Sue Ellen who was a statistic. It seemed as if the past year had an unusually high casualty rate. There had been the girl hit in the face with the brick; the other one, the brunette, who was slashed with a box cutter. What spooked Sue Carol was the uniformly fresh and beautiful appearance of the dead or injured girls—the succession of smiling yearbook photos had become a catalog of doomed wholesomeness and optimistic beauty. Were they typecast as victims? Did bright eyes and a big smile sentence you to extinction in the city?

Sue Carol had also been alarmed by the niceness of the neighborhoods where they were attacked. She had been able to distance herself somewhat from only one of the news stories—the murder of the social worker who was killed on a dark street in Brooklyn, after visiting a homeless shelter. She, Sue Carol, would not have walked on that particular street—at night, near the Brooklyn Botanical Garden, in

earshot of the random gunshots and screams of the city birds who survived in their synthetic jungle. No, Sue Carol would never have been
there, out alone at night. But the crimes that took place in "broad
daylight," as it was always expressed, on the busy avenue by
Bloomingdale's or crossing Thirty-third Street? Yes, she could have
been there. And the subway, of course, she could have been Sue Ellen,
standing at the edge of the platform, eager to catch sight of the train.
That could have been her, Sue Carol, shoved from behind.

The bystanders had said the man did not just push the girl;
he'd taken a running dive, to shove her with such force she tumbled in front of the oncoming train. The killer was recently
released from a mental hospital—he had been not bad-looking, not
one of the obvious, febrile-eyed, filth-encrusted vagrants from
whom you would know to keep your distance. No, he had been
pale and wearing a good leather jacket, and still, he had tackled a
beautiful young girl and watched her fall to the tracks.

The rumble of the train jarred Sue Carol. She was riding this
racketing rail to nowhere tonight—she was late for the party. She
had no idea, not a clue, where she was, or where she was headed.
The train screeched, stopped sharp; Sue Carol almost toppled onto
a tattooed boy, who had been swinging from the strap beside hers.
His eyes met hers; she saw herself reflected in his shades and the
tilt of interest in his body: she looked good; she looked good to
him. Instinctively, she moved her leg, nudging her shopping bags
and suitcases, trying to kick them closer, into the hemmed safety
circle of her winter coat.

She couldn't afford to lose anything else tonight. Sue Carol had
with her all that was precious: the family album, her wedding
book, her Stanislavsky *Building a Character,* a collection of love letters from Bob and the boys who had preceded him. Sue Carol had
stuffed her half of the files into an old Bonwit bag; she hoped it

wouldn't rip. She had taken everything of vital importance: her résumés, her photos, her reviews. She had packed them fast, trying not to stop to even glance at her eight-by-ten head shots.

It rattled her bones to see herself, looking so young, younger than she was really, and so pretty—just as fresh as Sue Ellen. And she didn't dare to pause to read that sheaf of love letters, yellowing already, written on cheap paper, written in the good old days before E-mail, cyber and phone sex robbed you of the record that, once, someone had cared. She should have married any one of those boys who wrote the letters; they were better than Bob, if not as good-looking. So she carried the correspondence, the literal baggage of her romantic past, as she fled the present, riding the subway toward an unknown future. Already half an hour late for Jessie's party, too late to buy a baby gift for the guest of honor, Claire.

Well, she could stop somewhere in SoHo if she ever got there; she could buy a present from an outdoor stand on Canal; they might have Chinese baby dresses, something cute, or she could offer herself and her excuses. It was better to show up late than not at all; she'd accepted, *rsvp*ed two weeks before—besides, she had nowhere to go tonight; maybe she could stay with Jessie.

Jessie had the space; she probably wouldn't mind. They'd been good as roommates long ago, when they first came to the city; they'd shared a suite at Theresa House, a residence for respectable young women with limited funds but unlimited nerve and desire. For a moment, Sue Carol had a mental flash of herself and Jessie as they had been, girls fresh from college, all of them living there, happy because they had so much hope (more than hope, they'd had expectation).

There had been the six of them then—Jessie, Sue Carol, Martha, Lisbeth and Claire. And tonight, they would all be together, again. In that instant, she saw a mental Instamatic—the six of them as young girls—Martha had been the oldest, twenty-five. Now she was the first to hit forty. Forty. That was worse than "turning thirty." Could it be? It seemed a second ago, they had been at Theresa House, all of them so young, new-minted to find their way in the city. None of them had yet given up; that was something, although they had met with disparate degrees of success.

Sue Carol thought again of the girls who got injured; the one who had been hit in the head with a brick. She had been sent away for therapy, somewhere in the South, but regular news bulletins indicated that she could not wait to come back to New York. And the girl slashed by the box cutter, she too had not turned on the city, even with thirty-nine stitches in her cheek. She had remained, by last account. The most seriously injured young woman, the one pounded onto the pavement by the mental patient with a hunk of cement, had recently announced her desire to return to the city, as soon as possible.

In her mind, Sue Carol could hear the Liza Minnelli rendition of "New York, New York."

"If you can make it here, you can make it anywhere, New York, New York!" But what if you couldn't make it here? Sue Carol wondered. Did that mean you couldn't make it *anywhere?* Or . . . you probably would do better wherever it was you came from . . . but hadn't wanted to stay?

Sue Carol had made it here: two years ago, she was featured in *Rainbows and Stars;* she was a "New Face" less than a decade ago, and she had got an equity card the week she hit the city. The problem with her success was that it melted like ice on a summer sidewalk. Fame was the big Indian giver—whatever Sue Carol had been granted in the way of celebrity had been almost instantly snatched back.

Last month, she had started waitressing again, at one of New York's newest, trendiest eateries, Vert, where everything that was served was green. Not just green to look at—but "green" in that it was organic and no cruelty had gone into the preparation of the food. There were actual debates in the kitchen, as to what shellfish might have souls.

What rubbed Sue Carol's nose in the vinaigrette (and it was getting real vinaigrette tonight) was that Vert was frequented by the rich and famous, by upcoming actors such as she had expected to be. And she was taking their orders.

Oh, some nights she had fun at the restaurant; she took it on like a part, like she was just playing the waitress. And friends of hers would drop in, and she could talk with them, on a break. So she wasn't really a waitress, she was something of a hybrid, a cross between a waitress and an actress, a professional *wactress*.

People in the business knew who she was, surely they did. And who knew, maybe some chance at the restaurant could turn into the part of a lifetime. Things like that happened in New York all the time. Mary Steenburgen had met Jack Nicholson when she was waitressing.

So there was a reason to stay. That's why even a head bashing didn't get a girl to quit the city. It was still the place of all possibility, the Capital City of chance.

It was wonderful, how anything could happen to you in a day, a night. Wasn't it? You should never give up. Tomorrow could be your big break—not the brick on your head or the concrete in your face, but the miraculous bonanza. And then the whole shebang was yours: you did your best work, with the best in your profession, and love was heaped upon you, in all its most interesting incarnations.

Oh, yes, Sue Carol, she told herself, you just hang on, hang on for another day. You can give up tomorrow, but not today.

That was a little character motivation she gave herself: don't give up now . . . give up later, when you are really through. And use everything, even pain, to enrich your art.

Even now, she recalled the lessons of Stanislavsky, Strasberg: "sense memory." What was she feeling? How was her body expressing pain? Remember the postures, the expression.

Before leaving the apartment, she had studied her reflection in the mirror: how green her eyes looked when the rims were reddened. She noted the runny nose, the listing of her body to the left, the slump of her shoulder, the depression even of her large and usually perked-up breasts.

Remember for "building a character." And what about her slowness? Her confusion? Dropping her keys? The holes in her shopping bag? The way her hands shook as she sorted the photos: she had felt like a thief in her own home, looting the shelves for what she might need, rifling through the shared past, to separate what was rightfully hers.

Remember this, she ordered herself. That weird buzz to her blood, the accelerated synapses in her brain, but also the crossing circuits: had she left the stove on? Yes, she had made that final kettle for tea, now it must be burned, welded to the electric stove top. Maybe she should turn around, take the subway back to Ninety-sixth Street, just run upstairs, turn off the burner? Replace the battery in the smoke alarm; she knew that was a goner. It had been tweeting for weeks.

Mentally, Sue Carol retraveled this route, to the huge, soot-stained building that was famous on the Upper West Side, for its great gloomy facade and the notable tenants who still lived within its stout walls. The Albatrope was a prewar fortress, with an enclosed but dying garden, a castle, peopled by semicelebrities. The cavernous apartments and fairly good address had attracted people in the arts for decades; the residents seemed to achieve fame, but not the ultimate acclaim. They were Oscar nominees, but not winners; actors who played second banana on successful series. Great character actresses but not movie stars. Was the building cursed, or blessed? Sometimes Sue Carol wondered if the New York fortress controlled their destinies, dooming them to middling careers, in which they forever teetered on the ledge of expectation. She had joked and called the building the Albatross, because even its stabilized rent had been a burden when both of them were between gigs.

In her mind, she could almost see herself running across the courtyard to B section, past the defunct fountain and the pigeons splattering the facade, their droppings an impressionistic mural, in shades of gray and black and white. She envisioned herself running back into the shadowed hall, riding the unmanned creaking elevator up to eleven, reentering 11H.

Would Bob be there? He had fled, saying she was insane; that he had to escape from her. Oh, he twisted things. Her throat ached from how she had screamed and wept; they had fought in a fevered trance, with more authenticity than they had at their best onstage. There was nothing like real life, Sue Carol reflected, nothing nearly as awful. She sniffled; they had met as scene partners in acting class. They had chosen each other. Fifteen years ago. Fifteen years wasted. Now, he was sleeping with other women, without regard even for being discovered, and maybe 11H was an inferno, flaming from her last gesture of comfort: the kettle set on for tea.

She imagined the yellow kitchen incinerating, her gauze curtains torched, the flames licking down the old-styled corridor to the big, dark bedroom, where they had lain together for so long. Sue Carol pictured the second bedroom, the potential nursery, that Bob used as his "office." She pictured the lovely rooms black-ened, charred: not just a broken home now, a burned one.

Maybe even the etiquette of violent, unexpected divorce decreed that you returned home, to turn off the flame? Or maybe she should call Bob on his cell phone, as she had sworn she would never do again, after finding this damning evidence, just to alert him to the potential charring of his now bachelor digs?

A squat man, with double and triple earrings, and a ring through one nostril, nudged her, seeming by accident as he lost his footing at the next quick stop. She moved away from the feel of him; he stank from cologne. Was he interested in her or her shoul-der bag? Sue Carol tried to hold the bag closer to her body. She'd had one snatched last year, and that was all she needed tonight, the night she finally, finally left him, left Bob, her husband of umpteen years. No, there was no turning back, for any reason: she was gone. The kettle could melt, the rooms smoke. . . . It was no longer her problem.

I have done it, she congratulated herself. I have really done it. I have left him. There is some crap even I won't take. She should thank him, really, for misbehaving so conclusively—the doubt about him had resolved at 3 A.M. At last. All her suspicions justi-fied. She had him, had him dead to rights. It was conclusive. He was not worth being married to anymore; he was a liar about everything. No longer was it a vague mistrust: she had him, she had the goods.

She tucked the little plastic sandwich bag in her pocket, where it rested beside the tissue with the contact lens. Good, it was bet-ter knowing, than worrying it to death. This way, she knew it was over. She had to end the marriage. It was clear, wasn't it?

Her forehead felt hot—not from fever, but rage, and the lack of sleep. Well, this was good. It was the right time to get divorced, if she had to get divorced, which she did, or she could just shoot herself. Or, she thought, I could sign on for one of those living-dead deals, when the husband does any cruel thing he pleases, and you pretend you don't know, but it corrodes your heart until, one day, you die or just get fat, and sit and watch TV.

Her mom had gone that way, filling the contours of her easy chair. Dad did things. Sue Carol had suspected for years. His late nights, his odd, contained manner. There was an explanation. He was still a handsome man, "gettin' away with it" as they said in Kentucky. "Gettin' away with it."

"Excuse me, miss," said the multi-pierced man, after he bumped into her rear end, as if by accident. Sue Carol made a sound of forgiveness, excusal. Moved her rear, so it faced away from him. She'd felt his interest, the prod of his prick, the sonofabitch. What was it with men, anyway? Were they animals? Just triggered by contact, any contact with a female? She knew all the expressions down home. In Butcher Hollow, Kentucky, men were not held in high esteem:

"He'd screw a snake if you held its head down" was a common expression. Her own mother, filling the chair, had played cards with other women also ample, who swelled into their seats as they dealt their hand.

"Yup, crazy ole men," her mom would say, "they'd all screw anything that would lie down or just bend over."

"All of them," agreed Greta, Mom's best friend, who said of her faithless husband, Vern—"All he knows is he's got a long thing, and she's a hole to put it in." "She" was "the slut in town," whoever that might be, the woman who tended bar at the Rock House, or the lady chiropractor who did more than crack backs, or just the "good ole girls" who liked to drink at the Butcher Hollow Inn.

Another frequent exchange between her mom, Sally, and Greta, was "Some nights, don't you just want to bite it off?"

The women munched crullers, or fried dough, as they talked—Sue Carol had no trouble imagining the two of them, some night, biting "it" off, a twist of flesh, not much different from the crullers. What was funny was that neither woman seemed to hate her husband. They had too much contempt to hate them. It was beneath them. Besides, they had each other, their sandwiches, the crullers, and the deck of cards. They had TV too, which they viewed together, enjoying the talk show chorus of more heavy discontents mouthing disdain and regret.

Whenever Sue Carol went home for the holidays, she was aware that the TV was never silenced, that the querulous voices of the "real life" contestants in the life misery competition shows were always there, singing backup to Sally and Greta's lament. Oh, yeah, some nights they just did want to bite it off.

But when Sue Carol's dad, Don, or Greta's husband, Vern, came into the warm kitchen, they were greeted with hot coffee and sandwiches oozing gravies. Desire was ultimately replaced by digestion altogether, and they would all spend their nights trading antacids. The marriages had turned to meals, ongoing, into infinity, until clogged arteries would kill them all.

Sue Carol had never regretted leaving Butcher Hollow. If the truth were told (and it had to be, at least to oneself, thought Sue Carol): she hated going home. She and Bob had to share the ruffled single bed of her childhood, compressed into a past that no longer appealed to her. Her room was maintained as a shrine, with the pink and fuchsia color scheme she had favored in high school. The tiny chamber now served as a museum to her defunct interests: cheerleading banners, Barbie dolls.

On those Christmases and Thanksgivings when they had to

stay there, Sue Carol had held on tight to Bob, almost wrestling with him to keep in the confined space of her girlhood bed. She could not wait to get back, to New York, her adopted city, to The Albatrope and 11H on West End Avenue. That oversize stabilized apartment—they'd been lucky to get 11H on West End, at Ninety-sixth Street, in the good old days when you might still luck out and get a cavernous two bedroom. The apartment was a bit dark, but it was spacious, high above the city, with its back to the river, and its face toward Central Park. That was as close to country as Sue Carol had cared to be, in all these past fifteen years.

The spires of the city were the landscape she loved; Central Park was enough of a forest, and the theater, especially the Actors Studio where she was now finally a member, was her church.

Theater had become everything to Sue Carol; she needed no other place of worship. She had started frivolously—because of her prettiness she was so often picked at audition. But in the past several years, her interest had deepened and every serious work of drama absorbed her. She had studied with Sanford Meisner disciples; read every word of Stanislavsky:

"There is nothing higher in life than Art."

It had gone beyond "getting the part"; she was intent now on understanding the way in which theater could open the heart, orchestrate the audience's feelings. In a way, Sue Carol was as much a convert as the Hare Krishnas, who had swayed, afluttering in peach robes and jingling tambourines on her street corner. Acting could instruct you on the other arts as well; lifting the veils on human subconscious, better, for her money, than analysis (which she had also tried).

If her cult was theater, her costume was black. Sue Carol seldom wore colors anymore, and only plain garb that would not distract from her movements or expression. She no longer secretly giggled at exercises that decreed that she stand, paralyzed, as a lamppost. Reason might say some of it was silly; but it was better than the shopping channel, fried dough, and MTV.

So on this night in question, for the dramatic role of her life, Sue Carol was costumed in a black turtleneck (to hide the softening of her jawline, the double crease in her neck, as age-identifying as the rings in a tree), black woolen pants, black cowgirl boots, good ones, from a handmade place in Kentucky, Joe Shine's. Over it all, she had slung an old mouton coat, with capacious pockets, that comforted her with its animal sleekness but weighed on her already burdened shoulders.

She had thought, for about two minutes, about just packing it in, and running home to Butcher Hollow. Giving it all up to squeeze back into the little-girl room, the ruffled bed, to be with her mom and Greta, who would comfort her and say, "There could be a prettier girl than you, Sue Carol, but we don't know who." She'd be nursed back to mental health on home drip coffee and those crullers, maybe swell to fill her own chair and be one of those easygoing old girls, who "help out" at home, not even truly sad not to have a life.

Oh, yes, Sue Carol thought, sometimes, existence is easier. Regret can take the form of flab; sorrow may be distracted by soap opera. You could catch up on a lifetime's worth of reading, or just do nothing at all. "Counting flowers on the wall, it don't bother me at all," a song half-remembered, her mother's favorite when Sue Carol was a child. Now Sue Carol conjured up the ruffled skirts on the bed, the Barbies, the high school banners, pinned on cork, and decided against it. Her mom could keep a museum of her youth, if she liked, but Sue Carol need not inhabit it, as a lifework's wax exhibit of her former self.

She loved her folks but not in a way that required spending

time with them. It was enough to forfeit the holidays, serving that life sentence, while living on a kind of parole, condemned to check in regularly to that little vinyl-sided "Dutch" colonial, being stuffed like the turkey into that little old room of hers.

The vinyl had been a new addition since Sue Carol moved away. The siding functioned as a plastic skin to keep the paint from peeling, but Sue Carol didn't like it—it made her old home look false to her, like a woman in thick makeup. Besides, the vinyl sealed the moisture in and the house felt damp. They'd traded exterior peeling for interior mold. Whenever she went home, Sue Carol helped wipe down the walls with a mix of bleach and cleanser. The smell, of mildew and the chemicals used to combat it, seemed to overpower the old scent of home, the aroma of a cooking stew, frying crullers.

How would it feel to come home bawling after a divorce? As she hung from the subway handle, Sue Carol couldn't hold back a grudged concession: maybe the bias of the women back home was the straight talk after all? Maybe when you got right down to it, men were "other," they were alien, another species, and all they did know was that they had "a long thing and you had a hole to put it in." How else to explain that presidents, politicians, doctors, lawyers, writers, professors—ignorant or educated—when they got to a point, after some years with a woman, she was no longer new enough, and they had to go somewhere else, put their pecker to someone else, to feel, what? Alive again or just turned on, potent? Oh, yes, some nights, maybe you had no choice, maybe you did just want "to bite it off."

Sue Carol almost laughed aloud, steadying herself again against the subway car pole. Her mom and Greta had come into their own, some years ago, when the news reported the story of the young wife who did just that—bit it off. And the "damn man" as they had expressed it, "had it sewn back on. Went on and posed for *Playboy,* had more other women."

"Nothing, nothing," Greta said, laughing, "will ever stop 'em once they start screwing around."

And so now Bob, her beloved husband of fifteen years, had joined that fraternity of faithlessness. Well, she, Sue Carol would have none of it—no forgiveness, no crullers, no life of spite TV. She was different, even if Bob was not.

She was smart, she was talented, she was good-looking, no question of that. She had always attracted any man she wanted; pushed them away, in fact. She was slim but big busted. Back home, they had said, "she was built," had a "body that wouldn't quit." And she could sing. If she had occasional doubts about her acting, she had none about her voice. She sounded as good as Dolly, with maybe some of the soul of Loretta. She was a high true soprano, and she would sing herself out of trouble, as she had a dozen times in her youth. She had sung herself out of the Dutch Colonial, sung herself out of Kentucky. Sung herself into marriage with a handsome, killer handsome actor, who came from old money (not that his widowed mother, whom Sue Carol dubbed the Spider Queen, gave him any of it), but still it was there, way back, in the background.

Sue Carol loathed Bob's mother, that Scorpio bitch, with the specific hatred a woman could harbor for her mother-in-law, the woman who had wrecked the boy who grew up to be her husband.

The Spider Queen was alternately flirtatious ("Oh, come give Mommy a big, big kiss") and withholding ("Get away from me, can't you see I have a migraine?"). So there was Bob, grown up confused about women, having to make hateful love to more and more of them, it seemed, to clear up his confusion, to achieve what? Some version of the Spider Queen, who would never shove him off her lap? She was horrible to them both about the money. She had inherited millions but carried only a tiny shiny black lizard purse (the size of a pack of tissues), as if to illustrate what she said—"I just don't have access to it, honey. You'll do better to earn it on your own." The daughter, Daphne, Bob's sister, had been institutionalized; when she wasn't in the bin, she went to Bloomingdale's or Bergdorf's and charged up hundreds of thousands of dollars of purchases on her card; all of which her mother had returned. Daphne then was returned too, to Silver Hill, and some new medication. The money made that whole family nuts, Sue Carol reflected, but it was better than not having it.

Sue Carol had always figured that dough was in the vault, and someday Bob, and his sister, would get to cash in on some of it. Having come from money was different than coming from none. Bob seemed to be less frightened, like he had an invisible air bag, should he crash.

The money.

Well, now there'd be a divorce, and should she or should she not go after some of that money? She'd been a good wife for fifteen years, so why not? And what about the apartment? After a discreet interval, shouldn't she get 11H? (*H* as in *Hell,* as she was always telling the Thai restaurant deliverymen when she ordered their takeout pad Thai noodles). Why should Bob's misbehavior entitle him to a two-bedroom rent-stabilized apartment with a distant view of the park and a backside slice of the river? Walk-in closets, and a kitchen she'd redone herself, in pickled pine? What about her copper pots, her Brazilian palm tree, the sofa she'd recovered with an old crazy quilt from home? Wasn't she, as the wronged one, entitled to more? Maybe even alimony?

Sue Carol straightened, gripping the pole, trying to see out her good eye. No goddamnit she would not take a cent. He was a dog, and she didn't want a dog's money. She would show him, she would show him she could succeed on her own. And he could keep the apartment; he'd sullied it for her, he could have it as his bachelor lair. She was thirty-six but she looked twenty-six, so let's start thinking like twenty-six. It was not too late: she could still become what she was meant to be . . . and on her own steam.

She looked down at her feet, at the Bonwit bag and the assorted totes that held all her worldly goods and history. She felt like her favorite character in all of dramatic literature. Blanche DuBois.

"I have always been dependent on the kindness of strangers."

Hadn't a man helped her with her bags over the turnstile? Wasn't there someone somewhere in the city that would help her land the next job, another lucky low-rent apartment? Yes, if she worked hard and believed, it would all come to pass.

Well, this was great, Sue Carol thought as the train roared into Fourteenth Street.

The car lurched; she felt the fat man press her again. "Excuse me, *miss . . . ,*" he stressed.

Sue Carol was glad she'd taken off her wedding band, a coil of entwined gold ropes, not un-snakelike in their twisted joining. *Miss.* She must look single already. Or maybe she just looked younger. People always said she looked younger than she was. Only last week, she'd gotten a callback to play a fifteen-year-old at a play at the WPA. Two weeks ago, a man in line at the bank, had said, "This *girl* was here first."

Girl. Even knowing at thirty-six that she was proud to call herself a woman, and be taken as such, Sue Carol had felt a flush and received the word as an unasked-for compliment. *Girl. Girl* meant she had more chances, that the years were not wasted but could still be erased. Just forget the last decade, she ordered herself, you're starting over.

Her mind must have wandered, that explained it, because she had meant to get off at Fourteenth Street, but the doors opened and closed before Sue Carol could gather up all her stuff. She was distracted by the fat guy, her own thoughts, her one-eyed vision.

Shoot, she had missed her stop, or a stop. Where the hell was Butane Street anyway? What was the right subway, the real stop? Sue Carol took a deep breath and prepared to ask the fat man for directions. Someone would know how to get there. She was going to get there, no question; she might be late, but she was going to make it.

I'm a comin', she mentally beamed her thought. Don't you girls worry about me, I'm a comin'. A comin', to help Claire. And party. And if she said one word about what Bob had done, what she had finally discovered about this stranger who had shared her bed for fifteen years, she would kill herself, 'cause tonight was for Claire, it had to be. So she was not even going to say one word, not one, about Bob. The exact facts, appalling and shocking as they might be, must not be related.

The evidence, even though she carried it on her person, preserved for all time, lest she ever forget his callous behavior, must not be produced and shown to her friends. 'Cause that would cast a pall over the party, for everyone. She just hoped they wouldn't be able to tell that she had been crying all day, that she had, in fact, possibly damaged her left eye. If any of her friends patted her shoulder or said a kind word, she would go all to pieces. She could take kindness from strangers, but not from her friends. That was too close to the bone; she would lose control, tell them the entire sordid story, and show them the damned proof in the plastic bag.

She did not want to cry, to break down in front of them. This was the part of her life; she had to play herself, and in complete control. She prayed she could fool them, that no one would diagnose her red eyes, raw throat, and what she feared was a heightened manner. Remember your training, she ordered herself, and forced a smile.

The train pulled into the final station. The conductor's voice issued a statement, impossible to hear over the metallic scream of the brakes and the static of the PA system, which she comprehended, as if on replay, as she stepped onto what he warned was "a moving platform." Brooklyn Bridge. Sue Carol was at Brooklyn Bridge. Oh, Lord, how would she ever find her way back to NoHo, to Butane Street, wherever it was?

Undaunted, Sue Carol picked up her parcels and headed for the steps. She was going to backtrack, a bit, uptown. I'm a comin', she mentally beamed her thoughts to her friends. I'm a comin'. . . ."

Forty-three minutes later, Sue Carol stood before Jessie's building. She had wandered the streets, lost but undeterred. She had not passed a store that was open that offered any kind of a baby gift. So she had resorted to the Korean deli, the last outpost of light and commerce, before the tundra leading to Jessie's street. There, she had wracked her brain as to what to buy for Claire. There was nothing, nothing that resembled a baby shower present. She could buy flowers but that didn't seem appropriate. She made an impulse purchase, not knowing how it might go over—then ran the remaining five blocks. She didn't want to be later than she was. . . . Surely, it wasn't too late.

The run, through the cold night, brought her breath up in sharp stabs through her lungs; Sue Carol began to gasp, felt a stitch in her left side. Her right foot seemed to buckle, and the ankle revealed an old weakness. Remember this, she instructed herself, just as her acting instructor would have wished, remember these exact symptoms. . . . These are the symptoms of heartbreak, loss, confusion, and despair, but in favoring my left foot, I am demonstrating my character's determination to prevail, to get where she is going. . . . And goddamned, I will. I have.

Chapter Three

In which Nina Moskowitz bakes a chocolate soufflé cake,
wonders whether it is safe to leave her mother tonight,
and surprises herself with an unlikely lover.

"Desire at the End of the Line"

Nina had not had solid food in two weeks. If her mother were still able to be her mother, Mira Moskowitz would have said something. Girls were too thin these days; it was unhealthy. Nina had big bones; she should have some meat on them, instead of starving herself down to a size eight when she had the bones of a twelve. Nina could not agree; her life was dedicated to becoming less of what nature had decreed: zaftig.

As Nina prepared to go out for the evening, she set out the prescription bottles and a detailed sheet of instructions that she updated daily in her laptop computer. The instructions were for two shifts of aides who would cover her mother's care tonight so that Nina could attend the party for Claire. On the counter were the detailed instructions to the aides, and a guideline sheet left by a hospice worker: "The Seven Signs of Approaching Death."

Nina did not dwell on what the printed sheet decreed: "Your loved one might 'pick' at the covers, refuse food, see the specters of deceased relatives. . . ." Instead, she went on preparing her mother's favorite meal of all time, kosher corned beef, with boiled potatoes and apple strudel. She had already set a flourless chocolate cake in to bake, her offering to the party in honor of Claire.

Nina was proceeding as if she could attend the party, although she had spent the last hour worrying whether it all right to leave her mother tonight. Much as she had tried to avoid reading "The Seven Signs of Approaching Death," she could not help fearing that she had recognized one this afternoon. Nina was adept at substituting action, especially culinary, for indecision. She would wait to make her decision when the other "caregivers," as they were now called, arrived. She would get another opinion, then Nina would know whether or not to go downtown. Until then, she would bake and try not to dwell on her mother's condition or the sexual tangent she herself had taken earlier in the day. . . .

As she cooked, Nina nursed on her own specially prepared drink from the diet center. She had been sipping the custom diet milk shakes for two weeks. She disliked their taste. Under the frothy sweetness was an unpleasant flavor that Nina suspected was ground bone meal, the touted "amino" acids that were to devour her own excess flesh. But the results were apparent: her waist, which had been obscured, now reappeared. Nina thought even her cheeks looked a bit deflated, rather than in their usual state, as if she were storing nuts for the winter. Nina had what her mother called "a Russian type of beauty," she was a *krasavetska,* or at least she would have been in Russia if she'd lived a century earlier, when girls with shivery bosoms, wide hips, and dimpling derrieres were prized instead of despised. She had a true Russian face—owing apparent genetic history to a tartar rape a few generations past. Nina's black eyes slanted, disappeared altogether when she laughed, and her flesh had a tone more Asian than Caucasian. Her perpetually tanned skin appeared shaded, as if by a subcutaneous current of maroon blood.

Damn that blood, she thought as she shredded cabbage for a homemade slaw to accompany the corned beef. Her thermostat ran high and hot. Ever since she was thirteen years old, when she'd first brought herself, by accident, to an unexpected crystalline series of spasms that she later learned to identify as orgasm, in this very apartment, Nina had been aware that her sexual nature was strong. Was it too strong was the question? It seemed to Nina that she was always in love or lust, hungering for some man, imagining him, then "knowing" him in the biblical sense, forever wondering if her libido was passion or pathology. And now, she had moved back into this apartment, this world of being her mother's child. And it appeared from her actions this afternoon, that Nina had also returned to adolescent passion, with its precarious hold on control. How could this happen to her, now, at thirty-eight, when she would have assumed she knew "better?"

The clues were all over the apartment. Nina had found the most important documentation the night she returned—a pink leatherette diary that she had left, locked, all these years, in her childhood desk, which was now for the most part overtaken by her mother's sewing "notions." But there it remained: the sex diary she'd written all through junior high and then high school. Actually, the pink leatherette journal was a "no-sex" diary, as it recorded her moral struggle with herself. Time and again, encounters with neighborhood boys ended in a stalemate (how apropos, the term). No matter how mores changed, it always seemed possible for a girl to lose respect, and Nina never did want to appear "too easy." There was a girl, Linda Gluck, who lived in the same building and was the subject of graffiti in the incinerator room. "Linda Gluck . . . rhymes with. . . ." Nina read that every time she threw out her mother's garbage. There, amidst the belching flame and the stench of burning trash, Nina had inhaled the message— she never wanted to see her own name scrawled on the wall.

When, five months before, Nina Moskowitz had done the

unimaginable—moved back in with her mother—she had also begun, almost immediately, to keep the diary again. She had lived away from "home," if you could call the twenty-one-story high-rise apartment, in the originally socialist-inspired Confederated Hill Project "home" (and she could) for almost twenty years. Of course, Nina was holding on to her own apartment, in Manhattan, on West Seventy-seventh Street and Riverside Drive. It was unthinkable to give up a good apartment in Manhattan, and she expected to return to it, after her mother died. But for the present, it was easier to live at her mother's apartment in the Confederated Project.

Mira Moskowitz would not live much longer; and it was out of the question that she live alone. That decision had been clear since last summer, the morning Mira toasted Pop-Tarts and set the kitchen curtains on fire and didn't notice. Rather than respond to the insistent shriek of the smoke alarm, she had wandered to her bedroom and shut the door. The neighbor had smelled smoke and called the super; the super called Nina.

What began as mere forgetfulness soon escalated into a fatal decline. Mira Moskowitz was found wandering on Mosholu Parkway, a major thoroughfare, in a pink peignoir and fluffy slippers. Mira Moskowitz was diagnosed as having hardening of the arteries and congestive heart failure. The word *dementia* was mentioned. The choices had been: admit her to a nursing home; take her to Nina's own apartment; or move into 21L, Building A, for the duration.

There had been one week, at the beginning, when Nina tried taking care of her mother at her own apartment on Seventy-seventh Street, but the arrangement had not been successful for either her mother or Nina. Nina had felt secretly relieved that her mother had preferred to go back up to the Confederated Project. The sight of the hospital bed, nearly filling her own living room, where Nina had enjoyed more than a few interludes on the rug, was somehow more alarming than temporarily moving back to the Bronx. Her little brownstone floor-through had been designed as a stage set for romance—palm trees, a chaise, cushy pillows beside the fireplace, thick Persian rugs. Redecorated for death, the hospital bed, commode, walker, all the accessories of age and infirmity, had spooked her, spooked her more than taking that long subway ride north, back in time, back to the past she had escaped.

Poor Mira. Carried into Seventy-seventh Street by attendants, she had looked confused in the pretty setting. In her spangled knit cap, and the pink peignoir, she seemed to know she didn't "go" with Nina's seraglio decor. Her mind, already vague, had wandered, and she kept asking Nina: "What hotel is this?" At one point, she imagined she was back in Odessa. With the charm that older patients sometimes have, she sang a little jingle, over and over: "Odessa is a messa." At midnight, she wandered, clanking the walker, bumping into walls. On the second night, she cried, like a child, and wanted to go home, back to Russia, where she hadn't lived since her childhood. Nina couldn't take her all the way back to Odessa, but the Confederated Project would do. Nina had a good sense of what her mother needed; the familiar setting, even though she had dementia, would comfort her. There were times when the familiar was all that mattered; convenience and charm were meaningless in a situation like this. Her mother needed her own apartment, her own slant of light, the clutter of sixty years of crochet work, the hum of her own refrigerator.

Nina had packed several suitcases, her computer, and rode the Ambulette with Mira, back to the north Bronx, where the end of the line was literal: Woodlawn Cemetery. She returned to the white brick "forbidden city," the projects, where she had spent her childhood. The projects had been built to house union workers— they were high-rise and middle class. The towers had risen like pueblos, flush to a cliff that overlooked the river and the roaring highway below. The complex was composed of four towers, and they reacted in an almost organic way to the thunder of the expressway; the windows trembled against traffic, the glass cataracted with soot. Almost everything and everyone inside was approaching eighty. Nina was engulfed, in an instant, into its hallway scent of incineration, chicken soup, cooked cabbage, and floor polish. And so her childhood resumed, a childhood, this time, burdened with responsibility—to care for Mira, arrange the shifts of practical nurses, and, in the last weeks, orchestrate visits of the hospice team, a social worker, two nurses, and several new aides. As Nina's responsibility deepened, her inner self seemed to grow more childlike: she occupied her old room, slept in a frilled canopy bed that she had begged for when she was ten, that now at thirty-eight struck her as ludicrous, designed for a dwarf. When Nina sat at her "old" desk, her knees jammed into the drawer. She felt like a giant, Alice in the wrong Wonderland, towering over every object, too big to escape through an ordinary door.

The smallness of the room and furnishings probably added motivation to her diet, although Nina didn't need much incentive. She was a chronic dieter, had been dieting for a decade. She'd tried the all-carbohydrate diet, the no-carbohydrate diet, the cabbage soup diet, the all-fruit diet, liquid diets, high-fiber diets, combination diets. Late at night, watching the insomniac ads for fitness, she'd ordered herbal potions to help reduce. In a manic moment, she'd ordered Weight Loss Soap, "watch your fat go down the drain."

For all this dieting, let it be noted, Nina Moskowitz was not fat. She weighed exactly 149 pounds (without shoes), and she stood five feet eight, also without shoes. Yet by the day's standards she was made to feel chunky, as squat as the old babushka Mrs. Belenkov, who sometimes helped with her mother.

Here, in Riverdale and the north Bronx, Nina could feel almost svelte: the farther downtown she traveled the shorter and heavier she seemed by comparison. In her own neighborhood, the Upper West Side, Nina considered herself borderline; down in SoHo, she felt she should be pushing a grocery cart. Whenever she visited Jessie or Lisbeth, the "Downtown friends," Nina always found herself walking behind some gazellelike twenty-year-old who displayed an unnatural distance between her thighs. Didn't they know thighs were supposed to rub together? Where did these girls originate? They seemed like aliens—tall, thin, but with improbably large breasts that needed no support. They pointed forward, nosing into the nightlife of the city.

Nina had a bosom, but in the Bronx, it was referred to as a "bust." She was busty. And her breasts were a literal drag. From the time they sprouted, they had caused problems. First the breasts came in too early, and irregular. For the initial phase of her "development," the right breast was larger than the left. Then the breasts equalized and became C cups that drew more attention in elementary school than Nina would have liked. Boys chased her, stuck out a hand to squeeze her breast, then darted away. When she walked, her loose-leaf binder pressed to her chest, they called out remarks, regarding "tits" and "boobs." As if that had not been distressing enough, the breasts soon gave in to gravity and sagged, their weight pulling on her bra straps. Within a few years, Nina had grooves worn into her shoulders, indentations where the bra straps were tugged by the weight of their burden.

Nina had toyed with the idea of breast reduction surgery but abandoned it. Every year there were a certain number of breast men who came courting: she did not want to lose this following. These men loved breasts; they were not critical of their condition. They nuzzled into the plenitude of the twin pillows of flesh, kissing, nursing, licking, touching. Nina could tell the breasts were important in her ongoing love life, so she resigned herself to the weight of them.

She did crave trimmer hips and the advertised "thin thighs in thirty-six hours." Diet and exercise were always on her mind. Her obsession had become her occupation—her salon, Nails by Nina, had expanded, in the late 1990s, and outgrew its identity. The nail salon became Venus Di Milo Day Spa in Riverdale, where north Bronx beauties would tone and hone, be steamed and wrapped, and emerge as less than they were when they entered. Business was good: Nina lived literally off the fat of the land. Even now, in her absence, the spa was "booked." Nina had trained her staff well—they could replace her.

But she still wanted to "lose." The one technique or pathology she had resisted was bulimia. No matter what she regretted eating, Nina never considered retching it back—if she ate it, it was hers for keeps. She was interested, however, in the surgical tales of stomachs being cut and resewn into the size of change purses. She liked the ads that depicted women standing in their former pant legs.

As her size decreased, Nina's mind also seemed to contract, her attention span limited to magazines and tabloid TV. The books in her old bedroom, at the Confederated Hill Project, were left over from her childhood—Nancy Drew, the Hardy Boys, *Anne of Green Gables, Little House on the Prairie.* Every night, she curled up, her old stuffed teddy bear at her side, and read part of the *Little House* series and was both alarmed and comforted by rediscovering her joy in these stories.

Mira, whose sight was fading as fast as her mind, seemed happy to be back in 21L, Building A. It was hard to believe that the impersonal design of the two-bedroom apartment, with its windowless bathroom and aisle kitchen, could inspire nostalgia. Mira had kept house here, alone for twenty years, and it was crammed with her mementos, bits of Russia stored near Riverdale: antimacassars on the old easy chairs, a sofa with needlepoint pillows, the "popcorn" quilts she had sewn all her life. Wherever you looked, there was handiwork—doilies, pillows, lamp skirts. Anything that could be dressed in a crocheted silk was wearing a ruffle, including Mira Moskowitz, herself.

Mira was a small woman, with a plump bosom (probably the genetic instigation for Nina's large breasts genes). Her face, too, recalled Russia; her eyes slanted, but her skin was fair, her lips heart shaped. When she was younger, Mira looked very much like the dolls she dressed. She had a slight tic that made her shake her head and purse her lips as if, like a more modern doll, she was animated by concealed batteries. Her manner seemed motorized, with only a few sentences in her "program," and the central sentence being the single word *fergessen.* For the rest of her retained "vocabulary," Mira Moskowitz could still spout the series of ritual endearments at bedtime and mealtime. But so far as new information or comment, more and more she fell back on her standby remark: *fergessen.* Forgotten.

It had started routinely enough, this *fergessen.* She had *fergessen* where she put her glasses, the keys, the grocery list, her medicines. Then she had *fergessen* her address, and now, even her name. She seemed to remember Nina's name, which Nina accepted as the ultimate compliment. Mira Moskowitz's love for her only child was the last thing her mother could forget. Mira Moskowitz might be confused, but she greeted her daughter each morning with the verbal stream of affection—"Ouchinka, touchinka, Mammala, ommala"—that gained in warmth what the words lacked in coherence.

Every day they had a ritual exchange of names. In the morning, Nina would run in with the tray, always the same breakfast—a poached egg, whole wheat toast with apricot jam, orange juice, and decaffeinated coffee—and she would say, "Mammal-le?" and Mira would reply, "Nina-le, ouchinka, touchinka." At night, she would say, in Russian, "Pasha, pasha, pasha pussy . . . sleep, Mammala," and her mother would say, "No, you, Nina-le. Ouchinka."

Nina was already dreading the silence that would replace this exchange when Mira died, as the hospice evaluation team predicted, in less than six weeks. She was grateful, however, for the mercies of *fergessen*—her mother had forgotten the difficult death of Nina's father, Saul, some years before from bone cancer; she'd forgotten the sad history of her grandparents, she had *fergessen* the Holocaust. What remained were her happy memories, her songs, her nonsense rhymes, and her appetite. If there was such a thing as a happy death (and they were not yet there), it appeared that Mira Moskowitz might achieve it. All day, as the sun streamed into 21L, and her parakeet, Chipper, cheeped, Mira Moskowitz sang and enjoyed the visitors, not realizing they were paid to help her die.

"Hospice means hospitable, doesn't it?" Mira said one day in a rare moment of near lucidity. "It's so you have great company." Mira Moskowitz charmed her caregivers, as they were known in the booklets, and sang ditties almost nonstop. Nina missed her more cogent mother but thanked God for the blessings of selective memories. With any luck, her mother might ascend to heaven from the Confederated Project without feeling pain.

The duration of the hospice period, in which a person is given "palliative" (only pain-relieving care), was expected to be six months. Most patients lived less time. Mira Moskowitz had "qualified," been diagnosed as "terminal" five months before.

She's going to beat the system, Nina had thought, not quite ready to accept what the doctors and nurses said. Qualifying for hospice had been a break of sorts; less paperwork to acquire practical nurses, the regular visits of an R.N. guaranteed, all the equipment delivered, within an hour, free of charge, for what was predicted would be a short duration.

In the past weeks, the hospice nurse had given Nina the literature: "Seven Signs of Approaching Death." Nina looked at the words, but could not concentrate on their meaning. "The dying patient will cease to eat and drink, the urine will become darker, the dying person might 'pick' at their bedcovers. They might see specters of their dead loved ones." Nina studied the page but could not absorb the information; she did better with *Little House in the Big Woods.* She read the Laura Ingalls Wilder book as a bedtime story to her mother, a reversal of the way the tale had been related in this very room, some thirty years before. . . .

No, her mother would beat the system; it was a joke on hospice. Even one of the aides, noting Mira's pink cheeks one day and the way she devoured the poached egg and toast, said, "Hey, we're going to have to disqualify your mother from hospice if this keeps up. . . ."

Nina had been happy to hear that, her own sense of things was that Mira Moskowitz was not ready to die. Nina asked the aide not to discuss her mother in the third person while still in her presence. She had already requested that she not watch game shows such as *Wheel of Fortune.* Whatever happened to Mira at the end, Nina wanted to protect her dignity. Maybe she was wrong, but it was what she felt.

"She understands, you know," Nina told the Jamaican woman, whose name was Flo. Flo's ebony face did not register resistance. But she said, "Her time is not here yet but she doesn't understand me. I have worked with them for twenty years. I know the signs."

"Them." Nina had flinched: Mira Moskowitz was one of "them," the dying, another species, the way Flo pronounced it. "Don't say 'them,'" Nina asked Flo, who she could see did not comprehend her. Once, Nina wondered: did Flo realize that she, Flo, too, would die someday? Or did Flo imagine that her career as caretaker gave her immunity? That she would always be on the other side of the bed, not in it, not one of "them"?

Flo herself was rather a beauty, with startling white teeth and pink gums. She always brought her own food, and was usually balancing a plastic container of jerk chicken or vegetables with rice on her lap as she watched Mira, for the "seven signs of approaching death." Nina had found Flo the most reliable of the aides; she was on time; she was efficient. She could carry Mira, lift her without effort, something Nina herself had strained her back doing. Mira was small but she had more "meat" as she herself would have put it, on her bones. She weighed a good 160, and it had been weeks since she had the strength to assist during "transfers" or when cleaned.

Nina did not want to register it, but at the back of her brain, where unpleasant facts were tabulated, she had noted that her mother's decline had accelerated. In the past weeks, Mira had ceased to be "ambulatory," was using the wheelchair for the first time, and now had to wear the absorbent diapers all the time, not just at night.

Nina herself had resisted, for Mira, on her behalf, the addition of the diapers. She knew her mother would have hated it, if she was cognizant. But the hospice team had insisted, and the truth was, the necessity of keeping her mother clean demanded the switch to the aptly named Depends. For the preceding weeks, Nina had been assisting her mother in the fiction that she was continent. She hadn't wanted to hurt her feelings by offering her the disposable diapers. As a result, Nina had been overwhelmed by the laundry, doing sometimes as many as five wash loads a day, in the basement of the Confederated Project. She had been willing to maintain the illusion that her mother could still wear normal underwear; it had been worth the work, she thought, not to concede defeat in that area.

The hospice had helped Nina to become resigned. Once her mother could not stand on her own, they had no choice. They had to keep the bedding and her mother clean. Nina often wondered what had happened in the millennia before such things as disposable diapers. The answer might explain the centuries of human misery. It would seem impossible to survive with any grace without them. There were now stacks of the paper diapers, with their neat blue seams, like capillaries, running through the white gauze surface. When wet, the diapers acquired an odd density, as if filled with gelatin—in fact they worked on the same principle as the dessert, transforming fluid into a gel. When the diapers could absorb no more, the blue thread turned yellow, and you knew to change the diaper.

You could do more for someone you loved than you ever dreamed, Nina thought, routine now in her motions, as she checked her mother and wiped her clean. The old woman looked up at her, blinking, and began to sing, "Baby your mother, the way she babied you. . . ."

Nina laughed, but the little ditty, a song Mira was repeating more and more often, made her daughter uncomfortable. "Are you warm enough, Mama-le?" she asked. This evening, her mother felt a bit cool, to tell the truth, and Nina wondered about it: wasn't that one of the seven signs of oncoming death, that she had tried not to read about in detail? And what about her eyes tonight? Her mother's eyes looked different, as if a fog had crept into the irises, ringing the brown centers with frost.

In a weird way, her mother, always a pretty woman, had never been more comely. Her fine-pored white skin had acquired a marbleized shine; the flesh itself looked smoother, gleaming. There was something about the particular color and texture that recalled statuary, pietàs, the Madonna. . . . Was her mother becoming less animate, more object? Nina forced herself to listen to Mira's breathing; she had been warned that if she heard a "gurgle," the infamous death rattle, then that was another signal the end was near.

Her mother's breathing seemed even, and Nina spoon-fed her some cherry Jell-O, that stained Mira's lips and gave her face, for a few minutes, an odd glamour. "Baby your mother," Mira sang, "the way she babied you. . . ." She asked for a song in return, and Nina, who had a fair voice, sang from memory, *Rushinka mit mandlin,* raisins and almonds."

As she sang, Nina imitated the inflections that she had picked up from Mira. *Rushinka mid mandlin . . . ,"* raisins and almonds, a sweet treat. . . . She tried to imitate her own mother's softness, the tenderness of describing the childhood dessert. How long ago was it that Mira had sung to her? Longer ago than could be measured in time. The very emotion inherent in the song, the sweetness of those raisins and almonds, seemed passé, long gone, antiquated. It was as if unabashed love had long gone out of style, quaint as the antimacassars and the woman who had crocheted them.

Nina felt suddenly that she might cry, and she did not want her mother to see. She got up and walked to the kitchenette and washed out the dishes. The aide would be here in five minutes. It would take Nina an hour to get all the way downtown to Jessie's. She had better get herself ready. She sniffed the kitchen air, inhaled a heady aroma. She had forgotten (was she going into *fergessen* also?) that she had set the flour-less chocolate cake in to bake, almost thirty minutes before. This was her social contribution to tonight's party: Nina had offered to bring the dessert.

She checked the oven, and it was good she did: the chocolate cake was brown and puffed high above the bake tin. Nina reached for one of Mira's many pot holders (crocheted of course) and removed the cake, careful not to handle it with any suddenness, lest it collapse. She took instant pride in it—the cake looked beautiful, the surface high, with just the right number of fissures and bubbles. It had risen evenly and not collapsed.

The more she dieted, the more involved with food Nina had become. She didn't violate her diet by eating. She absorbed her appetite by cooking for others. This cake was only the latest in an elaborate series of sacher tortes and prune pastries that she had pulled from the oven. For several hours a day, she cooked, preparing every delicacy Mira had ever fancied—homey browned cholents that simmered overnight, chicken soups from scratch, scented with dill, kreplach dumplings, tender to the bite. She grated carrots for her mother's favorite side dish, the so-called *tsimmes*. Nina had served the shredded salad to her mother for lunch, anticipating the old woman's delight and hoped for yet another ritual joke: "What are you doing, making such a *tsimmes?* *Tsimmes* meaning "a fuss" as well as the style of grating.

But Mira had been silent, only nodding that mechanical nod. She waved her hand—as if to say, "away." The silence and weakness had scared Nina. Was this another sign—the failure to eat? It was on the list. She had begged her mother, "Please, just take a taste."

They had had so many jokes, even in the first months of the now diagnosed decline. Her mother would laugh and giggle, "A taste, a taste," and then eat more than anyone expected. But not now, not today. Nina wondered now if she should risk going to the party for Claire. What if her mother died while she was out?

Nina decided not to leave for Jessie's until she had seen her mother eat at least a bit of her dinner. She had made her a corned beef, an old favorite, and its pungent, garlicky pickled aroma perfumed the small apartment, projecting memories of hearty meals. Corned beef and cabbage, with boiled potatoes, and apple strudel for dessert.

"What could be better?" Mira had often said; she was a great boiler of corned beef herself, spurning the "low-fat, low-sodium" for the real thing. "The whole point is, it has to be juicy."

Nina looked at the corned beef she had prepared: it was pink and juicy. She felt her own mouth water. She was tired of those diet shakes, but she liked the effect. Only this morning, she had slipped into a pair of pants that she had been unable to zip up last week. She had stood, jumping, the jeans caught around her legs— and omigod, those had been the size fourteen jeans, not the twelves. Now, the jeans went on, snug, but she could wear them. She was getting there, getting thinner, and as usual, there was nothing Nina wanted so much as to see less of herself.

She would not eat the chocolate cake, it was for the other women. Nina would be content to inhale it. She would take pleasure in watching her friends enjoy the airy dessert (not a speck of flour. The secret was egg whites, lots of them). Ever since she had started this last regime, eating had become a spectator sport: she was serving up marvelous meals to the practical nurses, the hospice volunteers, the social workers, the entire Mira Moskowitz team. They sat down at Mira's Formica-trimmed dinette set, which Nina had camouflaged with an elaborate cutwork tablecloth, and ate the surprise epicurean treats with dazed joy.

For Mira's few visitors, Nina did the same—offering beverages in crystal stemware, succulent stews, a cassoulet. As the weather grew colder and her mother frailer, Nina's cooking took on a heartiness that harkened back to her peasant origins. She even baked black bread, recalling Mira's yearning for the dark dense pumpernickel of her childhood.

With these feasts, the atmosphere in 21L had taken on a near-festive feeling, and Nina was glad for that. Mira, unable to recognize anyone but her own daughter, whom she sometimes mistook for her mother, was thoroughly enjoying her final days.

"Make a party," she chortled, "and everyone will come."

It was only at night, alone in her tiny ruffled room, that Nina felt the oppression of oncoming death. She had to sleep with a baby monitor, an electric walkie-talkie system that hung suspended in Mira's room, and on her own bedpost, so that she could hear if her mother called out in distress. Mira's breathing was even, but the sound of her respiration, piped into Nina's ear, made the link with her mother all too powerful. This was the aural umbilical cord, reversed. Her mother's breath seemed to synchronize with her own. Nina sat up, gasping, one night. Was she going to die when her mother died? It seemed possible.

That night, a curious thing happened that boomeranged Nina farther back into time, to her adolescence in this bedroom. Unable to sleep, she had opened that diary she had kept hidden for so long in the locked compartment of her girlhood desk. She began to read her blue handwriting with as much curiosity and prurient interest as if she were reading the private, unexpurgated thoughts of a stranger, the sixteen-year-old girl she had been.

She had to use a tiny key to unlock the pink leatherette journal. Once opened, the diary read: "The Penalty for Reading This Is Death. I am not joking, Nina Moskowitz."

As Nina reread and tried to decode her diary, she was alarmed by a sense of recognition. With Mira's breathing projected into the room, Nina read on, with growing dismay, of a crush that had consumed her twenty years ago—the boy had the eponymous name of Gordon Gold. He was atypically blond for the neighborhood, the only boy who looked at all like a Nordic god in the Confederated Project. He lived in B Tower, across from her own, and Nina had observed him as he lifted weights in his window, displaying a golden fuzzed body in peak condition. She hadn't used binoculars or anything: She hadn't wanted to see him clinically, or closer—the image of the blond boy rising rhythmically up and down, framed in his window, was at just the right aesthetic distance.

The diary recorded Nina's desire for him, how much she had wanted to touch his golden chest. It was not written in the diary, but as she read, Nina now recalled the boy and a summer night when, in a moment of sexual lunacy, she had stood in her own window and lifted her shortie pajama top. Later, she had consoled herself that the lights in her room had been out—he could not possibly have seen what had made her heart pound to reveal: that white flash of her breasts, exposed to him and the Cross Bronx Expressway beyond.

Yet, who knew what erotic ions inhabited the air between the two white brick towers? The diary recorded that the very next day, when she did, by chance, encounter Gordon Gold crossing the quadrangle of clipped lawn between the towers, his eyes met hers; he flushed and looked away. Later, he did approach her; he had just bought a sports car, he said, and he would take her to the beach.

To the sixteen-year-old Nina, this had been an invitation as exotic as a flight to the Riviera. Within hours, a scarf tied over her hair, a discreet two-piece, modified bikini bathing suit under her shift dress, she was sitting beside Gordon Gold in his red MG. Top down, radio blaring, they zoomed across a series of highways and a causeway to the listless section of bay that was known as Orchard Beach. Here the urban sea, defeated by its journey high into city limits, lapped at the many thousands of bathers, most of whom only waded into the suspicious water. The scene recalled Baghdad—there were sections where Nina could see only flesh colors, no water at all. As she edged in beside Gordon Gold, they seemed to be joining mankind in a tangible way, like Hindus bathing in the Ganges. In the diary, she had written—"Gordon led me into a sea of humanity."

Later, he had parked his car at a drive-in that was the automotive equivalent of Orchard Beach—a traffic jam, stalled before the screen. In the car, he began to kiss and fondle her; she felt the scratch of incompletely removed sand in her panties. He opened his own pants and put her hand on him. She had giggled; he was so firm; he'd felt like a flesh extension of his car, the human stick shift. Then he'd rolled onto her, and she'd realized, as his hand tugged down her bathing suit bottom, that he was intent on entering her, notwithstanding her virginity and the grit from the beach.

She had been kissing him back, scientifically, as she thought of it—to see if she responded. The kissing had remained clinical; she was too aware of his teeth and tongue. There was something dental, not passionate, in this, but as his hand touched her, more began to happen. She felt the liquid center of herself, and cried out as his fingers, first one, then the second, penetrated her . . . and began to mimic the motion that his penis would soon begin.

She had been stunned, but the gesture wasn't wasted. She heard a distant whimper—her own. Gordon Gold was proceeding at his own pace, which was fast. If she didn't stop him, what remained of her hymen would be torn, and he would have his way. He was parting her open, she was moistening; they were well on their way to the real thing when Nina forced herself to pull back and seize his hand. The movie on the screen was at odds with their own action: it was a political drama, with jurors and a judge. It helped clear Nina's mind long enough to remember the graffiti on the incinerator wall, and dull Linda Gluck, with her dazed expression, attributed to giving boys "what they wanted."

They wrestled for a few minutes; it wasn't easy to dissuade a seventeen-year-old boy, blinded by hormonal need to thrust. But she had stopped him. They drove home in silence. When he dropped her off at Tower A, he had not opened the car door for her. (A sign of disrespect, she noted. What would he have done, if she had acceded?)

She marched upstairs, rode the elevator to 21L, undressed, and stood in her window. It was not lost upon her that the next morning, a venetian blind was installed on Gordon Gold's window. The slats were always slanted down, for maximum opacity. Whatever Gordon Gold did after that, she could not know. The blinds looked dusty, shut. Across the quadrangle, Nina had been left alone with her desire and resentment, which never did rule out love.

The next pages recorded Nina's struggle with herself—the coded descriptions of what she wanted to do but denied herself. Nina could not decipher her scrawled code for "G.G. tried to M.N.O.M. but I only did S.K." The ongoing monologue regarding her possible "nymphomania" was legible. There were the dates that she succumbed to self-satisfaction: "January 9, fell down on pile of laundry in the bedroom, could not stop myself." She had read titillating literature, to confirm what she suspected: she was one of the hot-eyed, warm-blooded "nymphos" who were "born with this knowledge." They would be recognized by similarly inclined males, and doomed to lives of sexual excess.

Now thirty-eight, with some forty-three men (she would not deign to describe them as "lovers," to her sexual credit), Nina could laugh at the diary. Thank goodness, no one would call you a nymphomaniac today. That was the difference, Nina reflected. It was understood that a woman could have a sexual drive, as high or higher than a man's. That was natural. What had been unnatural was the condemning "diagnoses" of early psychosexual texts. Now she was entitled to have as many men, as much sex, as she wanted. That this freedom was awarded during an epidemic of sexually transmitted diseases was the chaser, the bitters after a beer.

Now Nina wished she had made love with Gordon Gold. Who knew what course her life might have taken? Instead she'd writhed in solitary ecstatic agonies for another six years. She should have felt free to enjoy herself. Well, it was late, but not too late, perhaps the eleventh hour, but the clock had not yet struck twelve.

She recognized her most recent sexual escapade (and you could call it that) in the patterns established with Gordon Gold almost twenty years ago. For the past three months, she'd been observing a man, quite handsome, who did his laundry in the basement under Tower A. Of course, taking care of Mira, Nina had been in the laundry room all the time, so the odds of running into the surprisingly attractive and apparently available man were high.

And she had to admit—they had "recognized" each other from minute one. . . . He was as highly sexed as she was—perhaps they sniffed pheromones, or just caught a quickening of interest in each other's gaze, as they stacked the fresh towels on the laundry room table. Whatever, Nina had felt the familiar sluice gates open, when he looked at her. He was, as they had said in the old days, cute. He was not especially tall, but his fitness was expressed in his posture, the bounce of his step. She was reminded of an animal, a lithe predator. He had golden skin, and his brown hair was flecked with gold, as if he had spent time in the sun. He seemed remarkably exotic for someone living in the Confederated Hill Project, and Nina deduced from his duffel bags that he was something of a traveler, and perhaps this was just a cheap way to keep a toehold in New York.

She slyly eyed his clothes and noted he wore natural cotton boxer briefs, a good sign. He seemed not to have any traditional garments; or perhaps those went to a dry cleaner. He was washing only T-shirts, jeans, the boxer shorts, socks, and some loose-fitting gauzy white shirts and tie-waisted pants. He wore a necklace that bore what appeared to be an ankh, the Egyptian symbol of life.

They had chatted, self-consciously, another conversation running under their remarks. She was right: he was a traveler; he gave seminars in yoga bodywork. He had inherited the apartment, 24P, from his grandmother. Nina could hear almost nothing he said; his eyes were pale blue; his gaze direct. His voice was low, deep and soft; he rolled his *r*s, almost a burr. "Arrrrrre you going to be around for a while?" he asked.

He invited her up to his apartment for an herbal tea. He was clear in his intention—"I had a dream of you," he said as he folded what appeared to be his grandmother's old fitted sheets (they were worn polyester, with sprung elastic corners). "It was a vision. . . ."

She had blushed. "Really?" she'd asked.

"Oh, yeah," he said. "Only I wasn't asleep."

The laundry room had become quiet then, save for an agitated wash cycle going on in the front machine.

"I also teach Tantric sex," he said, holding her gaze. "You know what that is." He left no room for rejection; if she went up to 24P, it would be for more than tea. He told her that he had a "vision" of their union, and asked her to wear all white . . . natural fibers . . . and to fast first.

He turned out to be one of those Celestial Seasonings guys. New Age. Nina might not have yielded to him had she not been in the exact situation she was in—but desire is the opposite of death, as Tennessee Williams said.

She ran through the rosary of why-nots: venereal disease, instant regret (fifteen minutes later, two people lying there with their underpants twisted around their ankles, wondering what on earth had been so irresistible?), potential insanity in the relation-ship (potential? He seemed a bit crazy in the first moment of eye contact, with that intense staring business). When he said his name, Nina had become a bit giddy: "Jerk?" she repeated. " Your name is Jerk?"

His name turned out to be an exotic form of "jerk"—Zhirac. Nina knew that could not be his real name; she suspected it was actually Jerry, that he was one of those Jewish Zen Buddhists who redefine themselves in an Eastern tradition.

Nina knew all of this, knew Zhirac was probably not ulti-mately going to be of significance to her, but as his blue eyes bored into her, she heard a psychic message: Tantric sex. Worse things could happen to her. Ten years before, she had a lover who was also a pseudo yoga fellow, and he had brought her much pleasure.

So she decided to be amenable when their conversation quickly escalated to how and when they would be alone together. There was nothing coy in Nina anymore; she knew she would have sexual rela-tions with him; that was what they both wanted and needed; they were both stranded in Tower A, a citadel of geriatric lifestyle; the warnings were everywhere: life is short. You will grow old and die.

So she was not displeased when he confided that he had been practicing celibacy but felt he had "reached the end of its useful-ness for his spiritual growth." She had no idea why a "vision" occurred to her at this second: but she very clearly saw his penis, potentially looking like a carrot.

As long as it still works, Nina thought as she agreed to visit his apartment, wearing only white, nonsynthetic fibers. He was going to fast too, he told her, to be in a higher state to experience their "union."

Her laughing at him, secretly, did nothing to diminish her desire. He was a fool, but a fool with a golden statuette body. She could almost sniff the *Kama Sutra* oil on him. She knew there would be sitar music and bedding on the floor. She was not inex-perienced with this sort of man; she'd logged in sea miles on waterbeds. They would have fun, if she could look past his sense of himself as a serious practitioner of erotic arts. She wondered if he had a good "lingam" or if it would turn out to be like the carrot she envisioned, too narrow and pointy for her pleasure.

She was confident of her "yoni." The other fake Eastern sex disciple had praised her "yoni" and maintained himself in her for an unbelievably long time, so long she feared for his health. As he sustained himself into a second hour (no kidding) Nina had finally gasped, and after a third orgasm had sent its final flutter through her and she was ready for something else (a drink? a snack?), she'd said, "You can breathe normally now," and the other fellow had sighed, and it was as if all the air had gone out of him; she'd felt his penis deflate like one of those long balloons.

She expected Zhirac would be much the same. How could she blame herself for keeping the assignation? It was so goofy, she had to go. She had spent so many nights by then, lying there, listening to the baby monitor, feeling her own life ebb with her mother's. Anyone would have gone, she told herself.

How could she have anticipated what would actually occur? You couldn't. Sex was filled with surprises, some of them unpleasant. Just don't think about it, Nina ordered herself, and for God's sake, don't ever tell anyone what happened. She issued herself an ultimatum: do not report to your friends on this ultimate degradation.

Now, getting ready to go to Jessie's for the party, she vowed to put Zhirac (Jerk) out of her mind. As soon as Flo appeared with her Jamaican takeout bag in hand, Nina excused herself to shower.

Instantly, inside the turquoise tile bathroom, that was decked with her mother's hand-wash items, and all the rubber gear and gloves, dishes for her teeth, the entire assortment of depressing accessories, Nina crouched, and plucked out her diaphragm. It had been six hours, she computed; she could empty Zhirac's love juices down the drain without risking a delayed impregnation. Working quickly, with a slight sense of revulsion, Nina rinsed out the diaphragm, powdered it with cornstarch, and set it back in its compact for a better day.

She stood under the shower for a longer time than usual, letting the hot water renew her sense of herself. She used a soap which she had brought from her own apartment, that smelled of sandalwood. She washed her hair with her mother's old generic shampoo, and that turned out to be a mistake.

Nina had been dyeing her hair for several years now; she tried not to let the roots grow out. She suspected she was almost entirely gray, and she didn't want to prove it. Instead, she had her hair treated with subtle, imported near-natural dyes that restored its deep, mahogany color. But when she emerged from the shower and blow-dried her hair, she saw that her mother's shampoo had been too harsh, that it had not only stripped much of the dye, leaving an unfortunate white stripe near her hairline, but it had also somehow chemically interacted to turn her hair a rather weird rust color. Her hair had oxidized.

Oh, well, there was no time to do anything about it tonight. Nina was rushed as it was. She had to set up the dinner tray. (She did not have faith that Flo would make the meal look as attractive as she would. Flo would use paper plates, which would be sodden, and Nina wanted her mother to dine off her best Czechoslovakian china.)

For another instant, Nina considered canceling, remaining here with Mira. There might not be too many more nights. But then she thought of Jessie, of Claire, of all her friends. It had been too long since she'd seen any of them; she'd been exiled to the Confederated Hill Project for seven months. She needed, as they say, to "get out." The long days and nights of attending to her mother seemed endless, but they would end. It was just that Nina needed a reprieve, and the incident with Zhirac had not been what she wanted; she needed her friends tonight as much as Claire would need her.

She had bought the baby gift weeks ago, a beautiful baby doll that simulated natural functions. It was anatomically correct. Nina knew it was an odd gift, but she thought Claire would love it; she could practice doing what Nina knew Claire had never done in her life: putting on a diaper, bathing a baby. Of all of them, Claire Molinaro had been the least likely to have a child.

Nina had paused while placing the doll in its tissued gift box. It did feel lifelike; she recalled the dolls of her childhood, then quickly set it into the box. She might still have a child; it was getting easier every day. They had freeze-dried zygotes, you could implant your own egg in someone else. . . . She shouldn't go down the road of thinking she might never have a baby. She had wrapped some personal presents for Claire also, a nursing bra (Claire would never think of that, and it was going to be so important). And a lovely nightgown, so that Claire could look pretty when she was in the hospital. She was going to a hospital, wasn't she? You never knew with Claire; Claire lived in her own world; she was not part of any system. Nina had worried about her for the entire time they'd known each other. All of them, the group that had met at Theresa House, wondered and worried about Claire—that was why tonight was important. Nina had to go.

She had just set the corned beef on its platter, on the adjustable bed tray, and given Flo the instructions, when Nina imagined she detected a change in her mother's breathing. As if there was a whisper of something more. . . . No, she thought, not now. Not tonight.

She asked Flo, who said, "No, you're worrying yourself, go on, you can leave. I'll take good care of her."

Will you? Nina wondered. That was one of the most unnerving aspects to this final illness—Nina had to put her trust in almost total strangers. Just then, the doorbell of 21L chimed. Nina opened it, and there, babushka in place, was Basha Belenkov, her mother's former cleaning woman, and "landswoman," a native also of that Odessa of long ago. Basha was wearing a fur coat and a net scarf with spangles such as Mira loved. Her hat and coat were sprinkled with snow. "The storm is getting worse," she said. "I thought I would sit with Mira."

Nina kissed the old woman's crumpled cheek, where so many wrinkles crisscrossed it looked as if she had pressed her face against mesh. Basha could not read or write; she was a true almost aboriginal emissary from the past. When she worked for her mother, Mira had given her instructions by cutting out photos of the goods she needed at the nearby Confederated Co-op Store. Basha bought by picture. The woman was short, wide, and wearing serious fur-lined boots. She seemed as if she had marched over from the shtetl to protect her friend and employer.

Nina had never been so glad to see anyone. She had nothing to worry about if Basha stood guard. The woman was fierce in her protection of her mother.

"I was a little afraid to leave," Nina confessed, "but it's an important night."

Basha looked in on Mira, who was not touching the corned beef but dozing, her lips pursed. Basha listened, intent on her breathing. Her eyes met Nina's. "Go," she said, "your mother is not leaving us tonight."

Instructing them to call her if anything "changed," Nina agreed to go. She kissed her mother, who smiled when Nina said "Mammala," and managed one "Ouchinka." Nina still worried about the woman's now fogged gaze, the hesitation only she, Nina, could sense in her breathing. She held her mother's hand in the guise of affection, and took her pulse as she had trained herself to do. It was sixty. That was pretty good.

"Ouchinka," Mira said, "Ouchinka, touchinka." The "Touchinka" convinced her—it was probably all right to leave. Nina felt that awful indecision again—what if, in spite of Basha standing guard, like a bulldog against death, her mother did die, or went into her final coma while she was gone? Could she live with such pain?

She held her mother's hand, it was so cool, the skin so thin. . . . Mira would never have left her, Nina, if she was the one who was dying, Nina thought, but maybe that was the difference between mothers and daughters. A mother would be rooted to that room. A mother would never leave. But a daughter had to go . . . and her mother would have wanted her to keep the appointment with her friends. That was another difference; she knew her mother would not have asked her to make what she called "a sacrifice."

Nina kissed her mother's cheek. Even if she, Nina, had a baby someday, her mother would never know now. Maybe Nina would never have a child, and her mother would not know that either. Maybe taking care of her own mother was as close to the feeling of motherhood as she would ever experience. . . . Maybe she should stay?

Something, not a conscious decision, forced Nina to leave the room, the apartment, the building. Her steps quickened, the farther she walked. Just be here, when I come home, she prayed, and pressed the down arrow for the elevator.

And so Nina found herself outside the Confederate Project while the snow swirled around the Towers, wrapping them as in a gauze winding sheet. A beautiful lavender light seemed to accompany the snow, and Nina felt a bit lighter as she walked, brisk, in her own fur-lined watertight boots, to the bus stop. She was in luck: an express to Manhattan bore down, its headlights beaming golden through the lace of falling snow. Nina, holding her presents and the boxed chocolate soufflé cake in a waterproof plastic shopping bag, hopped on board and headed downtown.

Chapter Four

In which Martha closes on a penthouse triplex,
is examined by a fertility doctor, and takes a limousine to NoHo.

Reproductive Value

Far uptown, Martha was looking at the oncoming storm from the window of penthouse 43. At that height, the storm appeared as a small black knot to the north. Martha noted it, but she was more taken with the vista of New York that was spread out below. A toy city, a board game of spires and artificial-appearing green squares of roof gardens. From this height, even the rivers appeared stationary; silver ribbons wound round the island of Manhattan.

Martha's view pleased her; but she preferred it by night, when the sparkle disguised Astoria to the east, an unpleasant reminder of where she had started her life. She liked looking north, where she was headed, even though the light was colder than the southern exposure in the double living room. To the north, rose even higher, more desirable buildings than the one she occupied. Only this morning, she had sold a triplex penthouse—thirty rooms, imagine it. Most people did not know what worlds existed above the city streets, what money could buy.

On East Sixty-fourth Street there was a woman who kept a Thoroughbred horse in her garden, behind her town house. On

Fifth Avenue, there was a man, eccentric as hell, who maintained a mansion for his thirteen Chihuahuas. Martha would kill for that listing, but so far the man refused to sell. He didn't live there himself, just the Chihuahuas, and their keeper. Oh, well, she would continue to cultivate the owner, a small bald man, who had a Chihuahua quality himself, by sending the little steaks from Omaha. Maybe someday . . .

Martha had worked hard to get the listing on today's sale, the triplex penthouse; she'd courted the sellers for two years, even though they were nasty cheapskates who served—could you believe it?—TV dinners to guests. They had thrown a dinner party and set out a single bottle of wine for six people. The main course had been cut-up frankfurters and processed rice.

Just thinking about that cheap bad dinner made Martha whip out her Palm Pilot and note: *Bring own wine to Jessie's party.* She reminded herself—there was some Veuve Cliquot in the temperature-controlled wine closet in her kitchen. She could take the champagne along as a hostess gift; that way she would know there would be something decent to drink. She didn't want to risk an allergy headache on that rotgut the other women drank to celebrate. She would propose a toast to Claire (of course Claire couldn't drink it, being pregnant). Martha made another note in the Palm Pilot: "nonalcoholic sparkling grape juice for Claire." This way, Claire could drink something too, for the toast, but not endanger her developing fetus. Martha had read an article about fetal alcohol syndrome, that liquor could cause all sorts of defects, including hairy babies.

Martha had thought of everything. In her goody bag, she had packed treats or items of interest for all her friends. Thank the god of Allah, she had been able to micromanage her schedule to squeeze in the shower for Claire, after all. If only Jessie were as well organized, it would never have come up. . . . How could she plan Claire's party on December 21? Everyone knew that was a terrible conflict for Martha. Donald's birthday. His final birthday as a bachelor. Her splurgy dinner was one of the major, circled events on her calendar before the wedding next summer. Martha had mentioned it godzillion times. You would think someone would have remembered. Maybe she should buy them all Palm Pilots for their birthdays. . . . Martha noted it, with a question mark. That was splurgy, but it would simplify their lives, and then they could synchronize their schedules better with hers, so that near disasters like tonight could be avoided. Yes, that's what she would do—she had all their birthdays in her file; she could buy five, at a discount. Martha had left the closing this morning with beaucoup dollaros, mucho zeroes. She could afford it. Yes, it would give her pleasure to see her friends light up at her surprise.

Yet Martha's joy was muted. Yes, she had sold the triplex penthouse as an exclusive listing, but she would have preferred to buy it. When Martha returned to penthouse 43, her own apartment had seemed a bit crunched; as if its ten rooms could have been tucked into the foyer of the triplex. She tried to tell herself, she hadn't really liked the verticality of the triplex, which had belonged to a film director and his newscaster wife, but the truth was Martha had coveted the cathedral ceilings, the balconies. Martha told herself it was too Gothic, with the casement windows; that her own wide plate glass windows were more open to the views, but she knew those diamond panes were priceless, the waviness of the old glass, a plus. People would pay more for prewar; they liked the quality of the past workmanship. Eighty years ago, you could hire Italian craftsmen. Now, you couldn't even find people to blow glass, cut stone, the way they used to. . . . Immigrants were better then, she reflected.

Looking out those old windows had given her a view as if through water; the flaws in the window, rippling, creating wrinkles where there were none. It had left a crease in her perception that she had found the ultimate abode, with the maximum "drop-dead view." In her secret heart, she had preferred the other property, wanted to live there instead of here, in her formerly beloved Ph43.

Now, as she readied herself to go out, Martha comforted herself by recalling that the bathrooms of the eighteen-million-dollar triplex had been inferior to her own. Funny about the old apartments; no matter how expensive, they tended to have crannies of neglect—an original 1924 kitchen, with an old gas stove on little feet—or toilets, such as the triplex's—eight of them, all narrow, with chain flushes. The tiles had been atrocious; not even the black-and-white classic domino patterns but hideous flamingo pinks and putrid turquoise, carryovers from a nouveau riche reign in the 1950s. The new buyers would have to gut the eight bathrooms, and even then, the design of the pipes would never permit the kind of powder-cum-dressing room, bidet and bath suite that Martha now occupied as she completed her toilette.

Her bathroom suite was twenty-by-eighteen, with charming alcoves for the vanity sink, and an entire wing for extra heavy terry bathrobes and her stock of monogrammed Egyptian towels. It had cost mucho dollaros but was worth every centime. So many zeroes, for so silent a flush.

Larger bathrooms were the trend, she reflected; it was such a selling point. And they did not get larger than hers. The sinks were genuine marble, the fittings, gold plate. Her mirrors were Venetian glass, and as the lighting fixture, she had a French chandelier that maybe came from Versailles. Martha had found Andre, an antique and antiquities dealer, who got her things, the less questions asked, for enough dollaros. He had not provided a provenance for the chandelier but showed her a picture in a history book, where it was hanging, guess where.

"Let's just say the empress of Austria liked it too," he had told Martha. And so now it was the centerpiece of her toilet. The room was white and gold, and its windows (three) offered her the best views of the city.

It was good that her bathroom was so beautiful, because Martha was spending a great deal of time in it. She eyed the temperature and ovulation charts taped to the Venetian mirror. There, in red, was the graph of her attempts, in the past two years, to conceive: a red line, going off to nowhere.

That was why today was important, more than important—it was crucial. After a year of trying, she had secured an appointment with Dr. Francis Hitzig, the most sought-after fertility specialist in the world. How could the girls have planned the shower for Claire for tonight?

Was this some astrological red-letter day? Martha did not entirely believe in such things, but a client had recommended an astrologer, and Martha had gone along and had her chart done, for the hell of it, and to cement relations with this woman, who was the widowed heiress to a hair dye fortune and wouldn't buy an apartment unless it was in the stars, so to speak. Martha's chart had been a doozy, costing beaucoup cash, but probably coincidentally picking up some interesting details: that she was a Capricorn, a goat, who would paw the earth, and find her mountaintop, that sort of thing. The chart had also noted six days on which not to make decisions. Today, December 21, was one of them. Her moon was in Saturn or something.

Today had to be the most difficult day on her calendar: not only was it her Donald's birthday, not even just an ordinary birthday, it was his fortieth, a marker, one of the "big" birthdays, but she finally had gotten the toughest gynecological date in the city, the appointment with Dr. Hitzig. Martha was his "5:15," an add-on to his scheduled day (the only way she could get in; she wouldn't even contemplate canceling). So tonight was the night of nights. It would be a challenge to hit her marks . . . uptown near Mt. Sinai, for Hitzig, way downtown for Jessie, then back up to Union Square, where she had a reservation for eleven months at the city's newest hot spot, Vert.

Why had Jessie insisted on holding the party at her loft, even though it was way downtown and totally inconvenient? On any other night, Martha would have suggested having it up at her own place, Ph43. Not only was Ph43 more spectacular, it was accessible, in a civilized section of the city, and she could have had it catered, and they would have relaxed like human beings, instead of running around like crazy people during the pre-Christmas insanity that had seized the city. And now, on top of that, "the storm of the century" was predicted.

Martha, standing naked before the bathroom full-length mirror, felt a sudden sensation in her chest, like a knock. She knew it was not a true panic. She had a minor physical condition that caused symptoms similar to anxiety—mitral valve prolapse. Her heart valve could malfunction in an eensy teensy way, causing some stop and start of oxygen that had the exact effect of being suddenly scared.

Calm down, she ordered herself. This will go like clockwork. It was a good day, so far: the closing had been smooth, with the oddity of some extra costs popping up . . . well, that happened. She had smoothed it over; her commission was in the millions, why not eat a couple of thousand in "miscellaneous" charges? Martha had been happy to do it and had left everyone smiling. The buyers, a pair of venture capitalists, would sleep tonight in the tower of the triplex, living happily for the foreseeable future, which might be a few months (properties were flipping fast these days), in their cathedral bedroom high above Central Park South, with its glorious "drop-dead *now*" view of the park.

Martha could kick herself for having that orange juice at the closing—the damned juice had brought on the near panic attack. Carbohydrates, sweets—especially fruit juice—spiked her metabolism; bad for her heart. In her euphoria over the day's events, she had forgotten and sipped some fresh-squeezed. Big mistake. Martha remembered the last time that she drank juice and ate a goddamned sticky bun, because an idiot seller insisted, and Martha had to be carted out of a bank in an ambulance. The allergic reaction had intersected with her natural hypoglycemia to cause symptoms of terror: sweaty palms, knocking heart, the capacity to faint. Once, she had hit a marble floor, hard, landing on her face.

Martha inhaled, exhaled, tried to slow down her heartbeat. She had to make a good impression on Dr. Hitzig, she just had to. . . . She had a strong feeling he was her last chance to have a baby. And she must have a baby.

She didn't resent Claire; she was glad Claire would not end up alone, after all. But it was she, Martha, who was equipped to bring a child into the world, not Claire, whose idiosyncratic lifestyle seemed a poor risk. And Claire had gotten pregnant, apparently without trying, in some lunatic romance she was supposed to tell them about tonight.

Martha made a vow to herself, not to judge. We're all different, she reminded herself, what is inexcusable behavior for me, might be condoned in someone like Claire. Martha did not know the details, but she could imagine, knowing Claire. Or maybe Martha could not imagine; Claire was the one person who always surprised her.

Martha promised herself, too, not to make the other women feel lesser. She knew enough to hide her gifts. Last week, she had been voted Realtor of the Year, but she better not mention that, or maybe she could, but downplay her accomplishment. She didn't want to rub their collective noses in the obvious fact—that she had more. It was human nature to envy. . . .

She would try, too, to hide her disapproval of the general reck-lessness of at least three of her very best friends—running around the city and the world as if they were still in their twenties, ignor-ing the obvious: they were running out of time, if they wanted to secure some contentment for the remainder of their lives.

There were certain verities, Martha thought, lying back on her bath mat and propping a shaving mirror between her knees, so she could get a sneak preview of what Dr. Francis Hitzig would see. You had to create a successful career, get married, or at least live with someone with a legal agreement about your assets (she and Donald had the "pre-nup," and a *pre*-pre-nup"), and have chil-dren.

Martha stared at the curved mirror image of her hesitant cervix, knowing someday it would probably have to be stapled shut, as her sister's had been. (Fertility problems ran in her family, but so did the solutions. That was why there had been so many Sloanes [for-merly Sarkises; the family had Anglicized the name, en masse, in 1982]).

Martha thanked her lucky stars again for bringing her such a perfect partner. She could not imagine a man more like herself than Donald Van Vranken III. She loved that he was "the third," forget that the first two were mentally compromised dodo poos, with only inherited bucks. Donald was handsome enough (you didn't want them *too* handsome, like Sue Carol's husband, then they cheated), and he came from money. Mucho, maxo, dollaros. She had glimpsed his assets at the pre-nup signing and lost count of his zeroes.

She strained for a second to listen, to hear if Donald was moving around in the apartment. He worked in a room to the rear of Ph43, as a day trader, facing the East River. She didn't understand exactly how he made his money; but she didn't need to. They went to wonderful restaurants together, getting into places that had a year wait for reservations. And the maître d's all recognized her, knew her by name. Maître d's needed apartments, too, Martha reflected. Everyone did. Or they needed an apartment for their son, their daughter. And Martha could help.

Yes, she and Donald Van Vranken III were peas in the pod, clones, despite their different backgrounds. They had identical taste, in everything from movies to bathroom fixtures. More significantly, he agreed totally with The Plan—not to formalize the relationship until it was assured there would be progeny, children. Otherwise, why risk the legal mess? He understood—his first wife had torn strips from him. The first wife was in the garment business, and Donald had joked that she had taken his suits for her next husband. Lucky, *they* had not reproduced, Martha reflected, or it would have been much worse. This was ideal: she would be the mother of his only children. No conflicts later. And they must have children. Everyone had to have children. Otherwise, your life would take on a downward spiral, ending in a lonely death. You would have no one to buy toys for, there would be little point to Christmas, and of course no one left to inherit when you died. She breathed in, out: her heart seemed to quiet, her pulse steady.

Martha feared for her friends, she did. She should not lecture them—they all tended toward depression, which she, Martha, did not. If her heart pounded, and her palms sweat, there was a medical explanation, and a medical cure. She had so many conditions fixed already: her nose, her saddlebags, her immediate causes for the infertility.

Although she could not discern in the mirror she held between her thighs, the surgical corrections that had already taken place, Martha knew the adjustments were there, in the pink apparently healthy crevice: her tubes had been opened, the damage from the IUD repaired. Martha could kick herself now for that damned IUD. She had always mistrusted it, hanging like an internal crucifix in her cervix. Martha had preferred things she could insert herself, such as the diaphragm. She had often used the diaphragm in conjunction with the IUD. But she had been afraid that the IUD would rip the diaphragm. Oh, well, it was all out now. The scar tissue had been removed, too, and she was, as she appeared—in the pink of health—other than the teensy heart thing, so Dr. Francis Hitzig would be able to help her, wouldn't he?

Now, would she pass muster? She held Donald's shaving mirror between her knees with some effort—she had prepared for Dr. Hitzig the way she would a lover. She had bathed, rubbed cream over her skin, removed all superfluous hair that had remained after electrolysis, and was now previewing her most private parts and trying to be objective about them.

Martha did not smile back at the reflection. This was serious: she wanted to make a nice impression. This afternoon she had undergone a bikini wax, administered by a Romanian woman at the subterranean spa below the Four Seasons Hotel on Fifty-seventh Street. Dr. Hitzig had to accept her; he had to like what he saw.

Dr. Francis Hitzig was the best fertility doctor in the world. "I can make any woman pregnant," he boasted. He was one of the first to take fifty-year-old patients. At forty, Martha Sloane would be one of the younger women to go to his office on Park Avenue.

But would she qualify? Dr. Francis Hitzig had a long waiting list; Martha had used her influence to get the appointment. She had sold an apartment to one of his patients, a socialite with a double uterus. Martha had given the double uterus woman first look at "something truly unique, one of a kind, tucked into Turtle Bay; a maisonette," and in return, that woman had used her influence to assist Martha on this latest and last leg of her long journey toward motherhood.

Martha Garbabedian Sloane (formerly Sarkis) had been to four doctors, three clinics. She had spent mucho dollaros, so much uncovered by health insurance. She had taken Clomid, been shot up with progesterone, injected herself with Lupron. She had been Zifted, Gifted, IVF was routine. You name it, she had tried it— mucus management, antibiotic systemic treatments, simple relaxation, standing on her head after intercourse.

Intercourse was now passé. Just as well, she reflected, the odds were better without sex. As she prepared to leave her apartment, Martha paused to admire not just the view outside, but also the vista inside. Martha had decorated it herself, with a little help from a famous designer for whom she'd found a funny little *pied-a-terre* "but on a knockout street."

Real estate was the key to everything in this city, and Martha had been playing the game long enough to know how to work the Monopoly board so that she always won. Everybody in New York wanted a nice place to live, and Martha controlled the sales of the best. She had secured for herself this entire top floor, of the Carthaginian, a tower of brass and glass that had risen on East Sixty-ninth Street. It would be nice to reach Park Avenue or even

Fifth, across from the museum, where Jackie used to live, but this would do nicely for now.

Martha was the star Realtor for Shipman-Harding, the company that owned thirty-five "prime" buildings in Manhattan. They were building more towers; they'd be done already if only those people in the neighborhoods would stop complaining about the towers shutting out the light on their streets, and casting shadows over the little old prewar town houses. Those people would have to give up, just as the old folks who lived at "The Cottages," that anachronism on Third and Seventy-seventh Street, had given up. You had to go higher now, use the air space. The sky was the literal limit. If you didn't like to live in a shadow, you should move to the forty-third floor.

Ph43 had not just the ten rooms and (this was her favorite part) a "wraparound, jump-off-for-joy" terrace. Ph43 had an atrium greenhouse dining room, and an indoor screening room. Martha was living, she thought, like a movie star. She finally had money, lots of it—her salary was seven figures; she even had expense money given to her, in crispy hundred-dollar bills—she almost loved these dollaros, her hundreds, more than her millions. The hundreds were so cool and minty green, folded sharp enough to cut, in her Kate Spade purse.

So, she had money—she was also finally blond—her colorist was an incredible genius. Even Martha had forgotten her natural color, God knows what it was now. She had become thin; liposuctioned down to a size six. Her nose, which had ruined her childhood, casting its version of a shadow across her prospects (her father had been Lebanese and it was his nose, that of an Arab rug merchant) that distorted her otherwise quite pretty face, was fixed. Her nose job was not cheap—she did not end up with one of those little piggy jobs, with the upturned, look-see nostrils, that pinched look. No, her nose was a success now; it was "appropriate," subtly thinned, the Lebanese hump removed. The nose was a triumph, an aquiline success, just elongated enough to be mistaken for real.

She had paid for the nose by getting the plastic surgeon "in" on the park side of a new building going up on Central Park West. In exchange for her nose job, he had gotten "the killer kitchen" of all time, everything Sub-Zero, Miele appliances, a walk-in freezer. The plastic surgeon was a carnivore; he loved aged meat. Now he had a goddamn herd of Black Angus "beyond primo" steaks, hanging from hooks in his own home. He was an incredible cosmetic surgeon; he had sculpted his wife and daughters, who had inherited his own nose, which he, in some defiant gesture, had declined to fix on himself. Well, I guess you couldn't operate on your own nose, Martha mused. But he had removed her father's nose from her face, thank you so much. . . .

Her father, Emir Sarkis Sloane, had also bestowed upon Martha his body hair—genetic shadows on her upper lip, arms, even her thighs and belly. But laser electrolysis had taken care of it all, save the "sensitive zone" near her labia. And she hadn't had to pay a centime: Martha had installed the electrolysis office in a primo space, at the foot of her own beloved Carthaginian. Every time she walked outside, she passed the ground-floor office, where all her superfluous hairs had been shocked or laser-ed off, to leave her smooth and silken. Now as she lay looking in the thigh-held mirror, Martha could rejoice in the cleared overgrowth that had once marred this view. Whoever invented laser electrolysis should get the Nobel Prize, she thought, there was only so far she could have gone with that forest she'd been given. It had taken 211 sessions to clear out. . . . Waxing kept up with the last line of hirsute defense—where the flesh had been too tender to use electrolysis. Now, all was done, perfect.

Martha sighed, set down the mirror, and stood to don her white silk lace panty and bra set. She looked back now at the full-length mirror (the other mirror had been a bit demoralizing. At the final glance, Martha had winced at her puckered nether face. It did not look as optimistic as she felt). Now, she slipped into some taupe panty hose, the Missoni suit, the beige; she had learned not to wear bright colors. She looked best in beige, brown, and of course, black. Then she put on her Prada wedgies, impractical but pretty. She liked the line they gave her legs, diminishing a slightly thick ankle. She left the bedroom suite and went to her coat closet, which was as temperature controlled as her wine cupboard—so that the furs would not disintegrate, the hides dry out. She pulled on her favorite coat, the sable, and contemplated herself in the full-length mirror that hung on the closet door.

She looked sensational, the coat was "to die for," but would those antifur crazies be out, this time of year? The city was full of granola heads, "nuts and flakes." It was a bit better than it had been before this mayor, when the antifur nuts had walked naked on Fifth Avenue or had themselves displayed in cages. As if they didn't have leather soles on their shoes, like everybody else. She had wanted to yell back at them, What was the difference? But maybe the sable would be more trouble than it was worth tonight; her friends might get jealous. She was just too fortunate. Maybe she could find something just as attractive that would not be so "in your face"? As she rooted through the closet, Martha wished the mayor still gave out keys to the city. When she was a kid, growing up in Astoria, mayors were always handing out keys to the city. She had wanted one then, she wanted it now.

Ah, ha. Her hand paused on the shoulder of the shahtoosh shawl-coat. How soft, how enticing. . . . shahtoosh was the most gossamer wool in the world, and she had paid mucho dollaros, two thousand, for the shawl, and had it incorporated into a coat, made from two more shawls. All told, she had paid $6,000 just for the rare fabric—and another two hundred to have that little Italian dressmaker in Queens stitch them together into a free-flowing coat that reached to the ground. The coat was glamorous, Martha thought, glamorous enough to wear to the restaurant later, but not so ostentatious as to be an affront to her friends, or an incitement to riot, on Fifth Avenue.

She put on the shahtoosh cape; it swung from her shoulders. The rare Asian antelope wool matched her golden highlit beige hair. She was tall, made even taller than her natural five nine height by the wedgies. She looked like she could take care of things.

As Martha prepared to go over to Mt. Sinai, some thirty blocks uptown, just over the border of the Gold Coast, as it was known, too near Spanish Harlem to stay chic, she took a last look around Ph43, and counted her many blessings. The forty-two-foot sunken living room was made for entertaining. From the living room, she had airplane-high sight lines, clear to the green impressionistic blur of Central Park, beyond the high geometric shapes of Fifth Avenue, out across the rivers to the no-man's-lands of New Jersey. She could see the world from where she was.

Everything in her apartment reflected her new status—the mirrored walls, the windows, even the brass furniture. Everything was so nice and shiny. In the kitchen, hung the French copper, scrubbed pink and gleaming. The cook, Selma, from Brazil, would be making tapas for tomorrow night, when Martha would entertain Donald's family. Tonight was his actual birthday, however, and she'd had a reservation for eleven months at Vert, which had replaced Daniel as "the place."

Her hope was that, at the dinner, she could surprise Donald

with the news that Dr. Francis Hitzig had accepted her as a patient. That was as good a guarantee as you could get in New York of becoming a mommy. Dr. Hitzig had impregnated several sixty-year-olds. He never failed.

But, as Dr. Francis Hitzig had explained, there was the damned "protocol." He could not accept everyone. He picked winners; she could tell, just as she did. You could spot a dog property; you could tell a dog client. You had to pick winners—then you were one.

Before leaving Ph43, Martha tiptoed in her improbably pitched Prada wedgies to the suite she had dubbed "the baby's room." It was perhaps premature, but she had decorated it for a boy. The wallpaper was cute, giraffes in the bedroom, toy trains in the playroom, and little rocking horses in the service hall where the nanny would sleep. It was perfect and it was ready. Martha intended to have a baby in twelve months.

Her formulas had always worked in the past. She'd given herself three years to make it as a Realtor in New York; she'd achieved her vice presidency of Shipman-Harding in just two. Then she'd given herself a year to find a husband, and she'd met Donald Van Vranken on Martha's Vineyard, and recognized him as "hers." His eyes, green like old money, his sunburned fair skin, his wealthy alcoholic parents, the psychotic brothers . . . it was just what she expected. They had a house on the ocean side of Vineyard Haven, with frontage. A great gray-shingled affair. She'd gotten one of her "prime property" shivers when she went to the Van Vranken compound for the first time: it was called Windaways. It crossed her mind that Donald was the only nonalcoholic in his family; the others might all die of cirrhosis, and she might inherit the estate one day. Until then, the brothers divided it as a time share among themselves, and she could count on it for the last two weeks of August, which were the most crucial to be out of town.

So the timetable now had to apply to having a baby, and she'd figured it out that it took four years to have a baby—one year to seek out the perfect partner (Donald, done, check that off). Another year to see if you could stand living with him (done, and she could stand living with him—he scratched his behind, passed a bit of gas, burped without saying "excuse me," had long silent sessions, left the toilet seat lid up, but otherwise he was perfect). He was exactly the height she liked, six foot one; that made her look smaller, and he was burly without being fat (made her look sleek, next to him). His hair was the same color as hers, so they matched. One night, last summer, she had caught a reflection of her and Donald at a party at Tavern on the Green, and she had thought, They look like a couple I'd like to meet. *We are the people I used to see through the window, I am inside now.*

So Martha Sarkis Sloane was who she had always wanted to be, and the timetable was on schedule. There was the baby to come— the year of "trying" was nearly finished. Next year had to be pay-day. Dr. Francis Hitzig would have her pregnant in a cycle or two—that was his track record, all winners. In an ideal world, which she almost inhabited, Martha would be "just" pregnant at her June wedding.

Martha closed the door to the baby suite and buzzed for the maid, Monica, a girl of pained sweetness who was an illegal immigrant from the Philippines. Martha gestured to the huge stack of baby gifts, wrapped and ready to go. Martha had gone overboard at Bergdorf's and the Wicker Garden. She had bought the entire layette and then some. And why not? She had the money; she'd never been cheap. Claire would be lost without her, on this pregnancy; who knows—maybe Martha would have to cover her for the birth. Claire was not in the real world. She lived in a studio, for God's sake. In a nothing building on nowheresville street, near but not even in, one of the worst neighborhoods of the city, the aptly named Hell's Kitchen.

"Get these down to the car," Martha instructed Monica. "I'll have the driver wait while I see the doctor, then I'll have to go straight down to NoHo, if I'm going to be able to stop by the party and still get to the restaurant in time to meet Donald."

Monica nodded and disappeared out the service door with all the wrapped packages. Oh, Martha could just kill Jessie and the others for picking tonight—three nights before Christmas; Donald's birthday, and her doctor's appointment! Had they been listening to her at all? How could they have chosen tonight of all nights?

Oh, well, she would manage. If traffic were not too bad; she could avoid the shopping drag at Fifth between Rockefeller Center and Bergdorf's. Martha would be able to get downtown to the utter wasteland where Jessie had decided to throw away her money on that hopeless dump, which would never resell, and still be at East Fifteenth Street, at Vert, on time. She just could not believe the inconsideration—of all nights of the year.

Moments later, she was sitting back, relaxed in the Town Car, making a deal on her new bodiless cell phone. (How sweet to have just the speaker, now her hands were free.) She addressed the driver, Matt, "Take Park up to Ninety-eighth Street and wait." She hoped Dr. Francis Hitzig ran his office on time. If he did, tonight should go like clockwork.

An hour later, Martha paced, talking into her phone—she could not sit any longer next to these aging forty- and fifty-year-old pregnant women—trying to fill the wasted time with more calls to clients. Dr. Francis Hitzig did not run his office on time: but the walls were papered with thank-you notes from women who had conceived. Many snapshots were thumbtacked to the wall.

Martha noted, not entirely to her delight, that many of the photographs showed twins, even several sets of triplets. The babies looked a bit "shmushed" she thought, maybe their heads had been pressed together in the womb; they had a slightly melted-down look, as if reflected on metal. But the babies all wore elaborate outfits, many had knit caps that she could identify as coming from Chocolat et Tartine or Bonpointe. Mucho dollaros, nothing cheapo, here. The clothes were cute, even if the babies weren't especially.

"Oh, please," Martha prayed, walking back and forth before the display corkboard, "just admit me to your goddamned protocol." She already knew the carriage she would buy; not one of these collapsible umbrella things—a deluxe English pram, with all the fittings. With that lovely, padded upholstered interior, and the tiny little pillow. Shopping for Claire had thrown fuel on the fire: Martha could hardly wait to buy more for her own baby.

At last, she was ushered into the examining room. Dr. Francis Hitzig, a handsome man, smooth-shaven, with cropped blond hair, was surprisingly young—he looked almost like a medical student. She knew he would talk to her about her history, the abortions she had in college (they proved her fertility but had done some damage), the endometriosis, the tipped womb, the surgeries on her tubes, the failed inseminations.

Instead, to her shock, soon after he entered her with a cold speculum and saw the most medically traversed cervix in the city, Dr. Francis Hitzig said, "I can take you, but not with your eggs, it will have to be a donor."

Not her eggs. Martha felt her blood roil. She was only thirty-nine and a half. What was he talking about? If they were not Martha's own eggs, it was not her genes, not really her baby. A sperm donor, yes, that was doable. Donald's sperm might be the problem anyway; they'd had to have occyte, shaving down her eggshells so that his weak (weak, half of them were dead) sperm could penetrate her hard eggs. Martha and Donald had already considered mixing donor sperm with Martha's ovum in the dish. But an egg donor? An egg donor?????

Upset, she almost yelled, as she sometimes did at Donald or Monica or Matt. Get with the program. Do you have ears? I said I wanted a baby. I meant *my* baby.

Her crotch ached where she had been probed. She hadn't gone through all this to carry another woman's (an alleged college student, hah) baby. As she sat up, her heels still in the stirrups of the examining table, Martha could not restrain her professional tone: "*That,* Dr. Hitzig, is a deal breaker."

Chapter Five

In which Lisbeth resists the seduction of sleep,
battles her landlord, and has a surprise encounter in the subway.

Sleeping Beauty on Seventeenth Street

On Seventeenth Street, snug in the back room that had been the original parlor of the brownstone, Lisbeth lay cocooned in comforters. She contemplated the partial view from her window, the dark blue sky, a match for the Art Deco cobalt glass-topped furniture with which she had "done" much of the apartment.

She was lying in bed, negotiating with herself on the pros and cons of getting up, or retreating into her dream. If she did not make the decision soon, it would be a fait accompli. She had to leave in a few minutes, or she would miss the party for Claire. The problem was that if she got up, she might forget the dream she had been having, and was even now tempted to retrieve. If she slid deeper into unconsciousness, it might be possible to resume the underwater love scene . . . or at least refresh her memory of the exact quality of the deep-sea encounter she had been having with an apparently faceless man who might, in the end, turn out to be significant.

Lisbeth Mackenzie had taken a dive into sleep at approximately 4 P.M. She had collapsed, as if knocked out by an unseen assailant. Her head had jerked a few times, and she'd fallen prone onto her bed. Afternoon sleeps were not new to Lisbeth, but the intensity of this particular descent into her unconscious had been so rapid that, as she tried to surface, she felt like a diver with the bends.

Lisbeth kept a notebook on her bedside table—she had been chronicling her dreams for the past year. She was afraid that this dream might be lost, if she didn't you know, *nail* it, right now. And this was the most important dream in a long time. She sensed this was a life-changing dream that would give her new insight into what she really needed to know to survive. It was a shame, she thought, as she lay there in limbo, that she should have such a conflict on a date that had been circled on her calendar for weeks: *party for Claire.* She had even marked the date with an exclamation point. *Party for Claire!*

For a moment she flirted with the idea of picking up the phone and giving her excuses. What could she say?—"An important dream is taking place, I don't dare leave my bed?" No, that wouldn't be acceptable. She had to go to the party. Claire would need her friends now. That had to take precedence.

Get up, she willed herself. But something, or was it some*one,* stopped her, had been stopping her all afternoon. Now, the negotiation with herself was approaching the point of no return. If she did not leave by 6 P.M., she would miss the party for Claire. There was also something, she vaguely recalled, through the haze of sensation akin to but not quite fatigue, something she had to do . . . something she had to mail . . . a deadline, of some kind . . . it was crucial. A few times she'd bolted half upright, in bed, and felt her heart pounding, the tattoo of truth: *You'll miss it. . . . Get up now, or you will miss it.*

She assembled her pillows as a near-human form, and hugged them. Her favorite pillow, the smallest and softest of a group of three, was filled with the highest quality goose feather down. Lisbeth had paid almost a hundred dollars for this pillow, but it was worth it. The little pillow settled under her cheek, cupped her chin, providing cushion and a whisper of support. Adding to its charm, was the Victorian pillowcase, also purchased long ago. The pillowcase was the finest quality linen, embossed and embroidered, white silk on the white linen, white-on-white; it was her favorite for the feel and also for its scripted legend: *Buon Reposo.*

The small pillowcase happened to have the highest thread count Lisbeth had encountered—380—which was what the pharaohs slept on; most often that cotton was imported, hand-loomed from Egypt. Lisbeth knew about thread counts—anything under 200 wasn't worth your effort to sleep upon it. Even 200 could be rough. How did people survive on polyester sheets? Did polyester even have a thread count, or was it a plasticity level?

She comforted herself and, on rare occasions, cried on this hand-trimmed pillowcase, and that thread count helped. If you were to suffer, she thought, suffer and dream, you should be ushered into the shadows of that dreamscape to which she fled as if to a destination, with a few amenities.

People in the business kidded Lisbeth about looking "younger" than thirty-six. Perhaps she *was* younger; if she factored in her nap habit, she had been awake for only twenty-six. In the years when she had worked as a model, bed rest had been a prerequisite—her literal "beauty" sleep. Now, unconsciousness had become consolation, her escape.

What were dreams? she wondered. Tricks of the mind, wishes, memories? Pieces of a puzzle one could never hope to solve? Or more mysteriously, recall of a forgotten past? Premonitions of a time to come?

Lisbeth had studied physics, astronomy. She wondered, endlessly, about the universe, galaxies, the dimensions of time and space. All moments existed somewhere, she knew—they floated in some unsubstantive form, out there, in the great beyond, the starry blackness. Light traveled, carrying with it the images of lives long gone. Every moment existed, somewhere, in space, in an infinite Milky Way of memories.

Only this afternoon, she had read in her Sunday *Times* about the neutrinos, those particles that so long had been assumed to lack mass. Now scientists had discovered that the neutrinos *had* mass, and that meant that there would someday be a cumulative effect; that the universe would stop expanding and collapse upon itself.

No one had ever been able to describe or even project what lay beyond the universe, beyond the beyond. It was toward this border, which Lisbeth saw as cobalt blue, too, like the glass-top Deco dresser beside her bed, that her mind wandered in its midnight explorations. Sometimes, in her dreams, she came too close to some solar brilliance and recoiled, pupils burnt—were there sunspots this season? Sunspots were supposed to change everything, in ways you could not fathom, here on Earth, even on Seventeenth Street, where it seemed everything had gone a bit crazy and you wondered whether or not you should get up and get dressed.

How could a place, such as she had "visited" in this afternoon's long dips in and out of dreaming, how could that seacoast not exist, somewhere? It must exist. She had seen too much detail— the white sand, the azure waters, ruffling white with a gentle tide—to doubt its credibility. She felt sure that place was real— but was it some beach she had seen years ago? Or her recollection of a picture, a film? The dream seemed to have more reality than her actual day, which she conceded was uncertain, like the weather outside her window.

Her fuzzed recollection of sitting at a jetty, the sea spray in her face, the man on a rock outcropping, the way they met, silent and for one purpose—all eemed an ancient memory. They had entered the ocean, bobbed together in that azure-turning-toward-turquoise sea. The man had not looked exactly like Steven Voicu—he had no face after all—but somehow he had evoked Steven. Was he Steven, incognito in her unconscious? That would be of a piece with the romance; that Steven Voicu would appear to her, under-cover, an emissary from the past she wished to recover. Or was this an omen, that he waited for her? That he was, in fact, approaching her in the near future? She resisted whispering his name.

Lisbeth blinked, bidding herself to reenter the world of her bed-room. She must get up, she must shower, she must dress. From where she lay in bed, she could see the stack of wrapped presents, for Claire, for the baby, set on a chaise lounge by the fireplace. It was late; she should be dressed by now. She could not miss the party.

But that unseen force, strong and seductive as the man's arms in her dream, pulled her back amongst the down pillows, the bur-row of the comforter, the deep ease of her futon set high on the reg-ular mattress. She slept raised up, like an Egyptian princess on her sarcophagus. Around her supine form, as in the land of the pharaohs, were the objects to escort her on her journey to the netherworld: an FM radio with CD player, tuned low to a jazz sta-tion, Lady Day intoning appropriately, "Why am I blue?"; a stack of novels, anchored by an old copy of *Oblomov;* her ashtray, with a single incinerated cylinder of what had been her final Gauloise, turned to an intact ash the previous evening; a matching blue bot-tle of Saratoga water; a half-empty wineglass. Lisbeth looked at the bedside table, where the Art Deco clock, set into more cobalt glass, seemed too paralyzed to tell time; it struck Lisbeth that even the clock had entered into a conspiracy this evening, to erase the bor-der between day and night.

Stay in bed a little longer, her inner voice encouraged, *you can still get there in time.* It's not polite to be *exactly* prompt. Fifteen minutes more of this softness, this warmth, one more moment of this dream. Maybe she could have it both ways; gain the significance of the dream and still emerge on time. Lisbeth wiggled undercover, carving out a deeper niche for herself. *In a minute,* she promised, she would wake up and brew an espresso from the little machine that squatted on her kitchen counter.

From where Lisbeth lay, she could see the slice of her view onto Seventeenth Street, and tonight this view included the street light, with its anti-crime phosphorous glow, and the skeleton of the maple tree that, in spring, summer, and fall, served as her exterior curtain. In season, the tree provided its chartreuse lace of leaves and continual inspiration for the artwork that was supplanting modeling as her true career. In June, the tree cast this room into a green gloom, but Lisbeth didn't resent even the loss of sunshine. The filtered light was just as beautiful, and she had tried to capture it on canvas, along with the fluctuant patterns of the leaves upon her walls. Her *Tree Series* were her most successful studies; they had almost all sold. Even the largest, *May Morning,* which stood, unframed, by the mantel, was "spoken for." A gallery in Luxembourg.

All year long, Lisbeth lived under the influence of that tree, the sole survivor of what had been a promenade of trees on her street. Now, only sickling replacement saplings stood before the other town houses, wearing what appeared to be braces and white plastic tree bandages. Lisbeth knew nothing of trees, other than that she loved the tree outside her window, more than *loved.* . . . She owed her emotions to it, and her career—and it was so convenient, as she seldom left her apartment. The tree was her view, her life's work, her most consistent love.

Now, on this bitter winter night, the tree was as nude as she. It seemed distressed without its leaves, black limbs thrown skyward to the winter night, as if supplicating . . . from heaven—what? More snow? Spring?

Winter itself pressed against the window glass. Lisbeth had fought her landlord against installing Thermopane—she had argued for the town house's historic past, the integrity of its beauty. He, Feiler, fought back, citing heat loss.

Feiler accused her of costing him. She had to open her windows when she painted—the fumes. So the cold came into 2A, and the old radiators rattled and coughed, dragging up the exhaust from the aged furnace that belched and grunted in the basement.

Heat loss, yes, that was what she was feeling this weekend. And the argument over the window—Lisbeth's refusal to permit "renovation" was just the tip of the extended battle over this apartment. The war for 2A had been going on for a decade. Feiler loathed his "rent control" tenants. Lisbeth had "inherited" 2A from her parents; she had every right to remain for what was, in today's market, the ludicrously low rental of $777.34 per month.

On her bedside desk, a stack of legal letters, all bearing their green-and-white cummerbunds of "certified mail," gave evidence to the endless onslaught on her tenancy. Only last night she'd brooded over the latest attack—an effort to "deregulate" 2A on the grounds of "luxury decontrol." Lisbeth knew, in her vague way, all the specifics. Her lifestyle might be nebulous—some days, she might not change out of her vintage scarlet silk kimono and do little but smoke her imported cigarettes and drink espresso—but she had excellent survival skills. She was in touch with the nuances of the DHCR (Division of Housing Rents and Community Renewal) and their office of rent administration. Lisbeth knew she was within her rights—she would have to earn more than $175, 000 a year, for two years in a row, to lose the protection of the rent board. And while she had, in a good year, earned that much, she had never done so, two years in a row. She might earn $175,000 one year, and $7,000 the next. As a part-time model and near full-time painter, Lisbeth was a "sole proprietor." She could deduct the costs of her canvases, stretching, framing, the price of oil paint itself, which had skyrocketed, an artists' version of the fuel crisis.

She had a business manager, a bald bachelor who she knew was secretly in love with her and had helped her to incorporate herself. Lisbeth was confident that she could not really be ousted, as long as he did her books, and she filed her legal responses on time. The bald bachelor, Murray, required some maneuvering—she would flirt but she wouldn't, you know, really give in to him. So that demanded mental energy, too. Some days she awoke, as she had this afternoon (to say morning would have been untrue; her regular wake-up time on weekends was 1:45 P.M. "sharp"), and thought, The hell with 2A, let Feiler and Feiler have it. The landlord's methods had become more harassing and Byzantine. Maybe she should just give up?

But even in her cottony, half-conscious flirtation with defeat, Lisbeth knew she had to remain. She was a prisoner of the city; this was her cell, and it was a beautiful cell. A floor-through like 2A, even with its defects, would fetch $4,500 per month on the open market. Which was why, in the past months, the war had escalated, and Lisbeth had spent so much of her time at the copy center and the post office, certifying her responses, documenting that they were "timely." Defending 2A was becoming a profession—no wonder she felt reluctant to rise from her cushioned bed and face the gray day. Tomorrow morning was another due date: if she failed to register the postmark today, tomorrow she would have to take the subway to Jamaica, Queens, to the fortress of the DHCR.

She envisioned the DHCR as a blackened arsenal of feudal internal warfare, wherein tenants, landlords, and thick-tongued, cross-eyed clerks argued over tenants' rights forever. Lisbeth feared that she would suffer a spiritual setback if she were to actually go to Jamaica, Queens, to this place called Gertz Plaza (even the name threatened an ordeal) and see that office. Lisbeth might never be allowed to leave Gertz Plaza. It would be a Bastille of Rent Control, where they locked you up and threw away your hard-cut Medeco key. Her beloved 2A would compress into a cube of contested space, a statistic among the millions. She might lose.

Which meant that, tonight, on her way to NoHo, she should stop at Pennsylvania Station's main post office, the one that never closed, and mail her certified response, return receipt requested. "I have *not* earned $175,000 in two consecutive years." Hah, it was funny—if she had earned that much, she might be able to afford another apartment.

But the bond with 2A went deeper than tenancy. It was not just an apartment, it was more than shelter, it was the shell on a snail; it was her second, armored skin that separated her from all manner of harm. In 2A, she felt encapsulated in her comforters, her music, her history, even her exhalations of smoke. It was her natural habitat.

Lisbeth lay back, violating her own and probably city fire laws that prohibited smoking in bed, by lighting another Gauloises with a wooden match from the downstairs bistro, Le Chat Blanc. She inhaled and sighed. Then she caught her breath—there was an instant echo from behind her headboard. A second sigh. *Awwwgh.* She concentrated—the next noises were muffled, but Lisbeth thought she could hear a slight scratching sound, like a mouse, from the wall behind her head. This was the latest weapon, employed by Feiler and Feiler: the old man Feiler had installed his fat (and Lisbeth believed) defective son in what had been a utility closet wedged into a hall space behind her bedroom. The effect was that this aging boy—Ferdie—lived in a box behind her bedroom. There was a statute that a landlord could seize an apartment for his own family use. Lisbeth guessed that Ferdie was the foot soldier in this strategic plan of attack, should luxury decontrol fail to evict her.

Once in awhile, she glimpsed Ferdie Feiler himself wedged in the hall, holding pizza boxes as he moved sideways toward his narrow door. It seemed to Lisbeth that the "boy"—he must be thirty, but his basketball sweatshirt and deliberately drooped jeans, to reveal the pink, pimpled half-moons of his upper buttocks, which matched his face in an unfortunate way, made him seem a perpetual and unpleasant adolescent. Yes, sometimes she saw Ferdie Feiler, but not often—usually, she only *heard* him, which made her perceive his presence behind her wall as that of an actual creep.

Now, Lisbeth held her breath, yet thought she detected an exhalation through the wall. This was punctuated by a mechanical spasm in the radiator, a knock and shudder as the furnace coughed up more heat. A low hiss of escaping steam sounded near her footboard, where it had already warped a section of parquet. There was no insulation, and she could hear Ferdie Feiler breathe and worse. He led a life of expulsions of air and (she imagined) phlegm.

No wonder she dove down, down, down to her dreams. There was nowhere else to hide. Her problem pressed against the wall, stopped just short of her pillowed head. *Buon Reposo.*

Lisbeth had been fighting sleep all day. Fighting and intermittently surrendering. She wondered if this was depression? A specific depression of the down comforter, a literal "downer" she could call it. The sensation was so long running and sometimes sensual, she could mistake it for pleasure. Perhaps this was a benign form of malaise that brought near-euphoria as she snuggled into her warm and safer place, where even the bedding offered assurance; Lisbeth felt embraced and loved as she slept. *No, she was not depressed.* She had descended, as if in a diving bell, and was perhaps risking a rapture of the deep, but she was not depressed.

She had always had an excellent relationship with her bedding.

Lisbeth had never been a child who had to be ordered to bed; she had been eager to go. She had grown up right here. This parlor floor had been her parents' before it had passed, by the laws of rent control, to her, as their surviving child. Looking around the bedroom, Lisbeth appreciated that this had been her mother and father's when she was small; she'd slept in the living room, in a niche, where, for a time, they had draped a fringed curtain for her "privacy," which of course had been nonexistent. But maybe she had not required privacy then. Her parents, both performers, singers, had entertained a lot, till late at night. Lisbeth had lain in the little bed, behind the curtain, and trained herself to fall asleep no matter what revelry was taking place. It had not been an unhappy childhood; she had felt safe. Even now, the sound of music, tinkling ice, not-very-distant voices, the radio or television, did not distract her from descending toward a good, true dream.

Now she recalled a gesture from her infancy: she raised her hands, as if in surrender against the two back pillows she plumped behind her head for added support. She allowed her hands, palms up, to slide back down the large pillows, so that the backs of her fingernails registered the chill of the percale. The sensation was somehow anesthetizing, drawing Lisbeth back in time to her nursery nights, when comfort could be imbibed from a rubber-tipped warm nipple. Her mouth remembered the sensation of suction, propelling the hot milk into herself, the repetitive lip action that lulled her toward a digestive trance. As a child, she had sometimes twisted the corner of her pillowcase, and sucked the starch from it, nursing hard, as if the linen itself could give succor. When tired or upset, Lisbeth still fingered her pillowcase ends, or worked the strands of her own long hair. When happy, she smacked her lips into sleep.

And now, one of her best friends was having a baby. There would be an actual infant. Conceived at the eleventh hour, God knows how. How odd, that Claire should be the first. Lisbeth recognized that it was essential that she go; she wanted to go . . . it had been too long since she had seen or even spoken with Claire. An odd distance had come between them during Lisbeth's last affair, as if the intimacy with a man had supplanted the friendship in some odd, unspoken way. In the past she and Claire had enjoyed long drowsy bedtime telephone talks, smoking and drinking in their respective apartments, linked by cable across Manhattan.

The chats stopped as soon as Steven Voicu began to sleep with her and stayed late. There had never been a conscious decision between the women not to talk; it just became awkward. You couldn't yak on the phone while lying beside someone. Maybe those long phone conversations had filled a vacuum or . . . maybe you could speak intimately with only one individual at a time. A distance that had never been there, widened into a chasm between Lisbeth and Claire.

Now, Lisbeth was eager to close that chasm; the man was gone, the breech, or whatever it was, could be healed—if Claire wanted to heal it, that is. Maybe there was nothing to heal, maybe it was all Lisbeth's imagination. Claire traveled, but she usually stayed more in touch, all those postcards from Mideastern mosques and Balinese temples. What had Claire been doing since her return to New York? Why didn't she return phone messages? Why had she disappeared, only to turn up, in an advanced state of pregnancy?

Get up, Lisbeth ordered herself. *Hot shower, hot coffee. Go.* But almost as if her pillows had become animate, this "bed partner" plumped by her own hand into something resembling Steven Voicu, the last man she had loved here, the last man, perhaps, ever . . . this pillow impersonating Steven Voicu, seduced her into staying, *just a minute more. . . .*

It was amazing, really, the way she had adapted to his absence this time. Never agonizing, or giving in to the respective heats of hate and love, Lisbeth had found the solution. It had taken her awhile, but the accommodation had been most successful. Far from being in pain, or in danger of loneliness, Lisbeth had discovered a secret ecstasy.

Tonight was almost the exact anniversary of Steven Voicu's departure. She did not want to call it his desertion or her abandonment. Steven was nicer than that; he would not have left unless he felt he had no other choice. And he had loved her, she had been certain of that. But she had also known, from the start, that his love was the love of weakness, that he had no courage to save himself, and so he would not, in the end, rescue her. She would have to do that, and she had.

A year. In January. Her mind, mercurial in some ways, functioned like a computerized calendar. Only ten more days. The exact anniversary. The affair, and she had to call it that, had gone on, with stops and starts, for two years. She had resisted it, at first. She didn't approve of making love to married men, and she regarded the wedding band on Steven's left hand as something similar to the alarm on merchandise that would summon instant arrest, if you walked off with what was not yours.

She could almost see the tag HUSBAND on the back of his collar: he wore expensive, soft cotton De Pina shirts (he knew linen, too, or his wife did). He had the look of a husband, even when she hadn't known he was married. He seemed a bit too cared for, well nourished, not like the crumpled newly divorced men she knew, who came at her, looking like they'd been hurled from a spin cycle, set to the wrong speed and temperature.

Don't start on Steven Voicu, she ordered herself. He, or the bedding, would seduce her again, and there would go the night. She had bought and wrapped her presents; she was going to this party. Lisbeth eyed last night's bottle of Merlot; left open to breathe, it exhaled its day-after acid scent. She thought of taking a gulp, decided against it. She would wait for the wine at the party, when it could be considered social, celebratory. Unbidden, the image of the frosted vodka bottle, stored in the freezer, appeared to her; it was special vodka, golden vodka, distilled by peasants in Romania. Steven had given it to her last Christmas, a souvenir of his ancestral village in the Carpathian Mountains. Liquid fire and ice; distilled joy.

Drink me, the bottle invited, as magical as Alice in Wonderland's, but Lisbeth's bottle could communicate through a frost-free GE refrigerator. How could they say vodka was "a colorless, odorless liquor"? Lisbeth knew well the distinctions, the faint aqua or gilded tint; the taste and scent of the temperature itself, sweetened by spiritual ferment? She thought about just sniffing it.

No, save it for when he comes back, she ordered herself. She conjured him then, with the secret trick that she had confessed to no one—and Steven Voicu reappeared in her apartment, looking handsome and elusive as ever.

She could see him if she concentrated on a space that he had once occupied. It was not that she actually *saw* him—it wasn't like *Ghost* or those old films on *American Movie Classics,* in which a phantom wandered around as a faint carbon of his former self while some characters could see him, but most people could not. Lisbeth knew Steven wasn't truly there. It was just that she could conjure him . . .

She could see him, sitting in her armchair by the fireplace, or stepping from her shower, a towel at his waist. He was white, like a ghost, but that was his actual complexion—Steven Voicu was so blond as to appear almost as a film negative of himself. He had the whitest blond hair, the palest lashes. His eyes threatened to fade from blue to white-violet.

Lisbeth did not have to close her eyes to imagine him: she summoned him with all her strength and saw him, full size, in the doorway where he had first kissed her. The doorway had a Moorish arch, an architectural feature, and it was within this arch that he had kissed her, at first socially, then sexually, his tongue providing the punctuation that ended their polite association and began the connection that soon meant so much to her.

Until that night, Lisbeth had known him in a tangential way; they had odd, coincidental acquaintances in common. She had once taken his course in photography at the New School. They had met at large parties; sometimes they frequented the same restaurants. For years, she knew he lived in the neighborhood, just a few blocks north. And she knew he was married, to a playwright famous for her nervous disposition. His wife was often away at regional productions; when in town, she stayed home, planning the next play, or mourning the last one's reception. She was said to be fragile, and there seemed to be some understanding that circled Steven Voicu like the smoke from the same French cigarettes that Lisbeth enjoyed, that if he left his wife, she might break down or even die. He wore his mild unhappiness like a masculine cologne. He had seemed resigned. The times Lisbeth ran into him, they always celebrated oddly joyous greetings, hugging, laughing, as if in these moments of reunion with a near stranger, she was also greeting her hopes, her dream of a man. Before they really knew each other, they seemed more familiar than they had a right to be.

He had started a habit of having long, lazy lunches downstairs at a particular outdoor table, at the bistro in her building, Le Chat Blanc. Lisbeth began to look for his white blond head as he bent over some foreign language journal. One day, he snapped her picture as she appeared. To her surprise, she did not hold up her arm, defensively, but smiled. The next day, he gave her the print, which he had deliberately overexposed, so that she looked as ghostly as he did. He had tilted his head in the European way (although he had left Romania twenty years ago as a boy) and indicated she should join him for an espresso.

They had sat and decried the influx of franchise coffee places in the city; they liked it personal, they agreed. An individual café. They had laughed about the flood of latte that had engulfed their neighborhood, even the outsize nature of the cups. It was the urban equivalent of the human head–sized Danish that had taken over roadside diners.

Lisbeth had laughed so easily with him; it had been natural to invite him up to see her place, her paintings, to set his portrait of her in a place of honor on her mantel. As soon as he had entered the sanctity of 2A, he had pressed her to him. He had been wearing his old raincoat, and she had surprised herself by reaching up and undoing his buttons. . . . She had not even recognized her voice, greeting him, calling his name as she drew him onto her. It was as if all their accidental meetings had led to this ultimate, purposeful joining of their true selves.

That day had set the pattern for their affair, even for its aftermath. Steven Voicu remained the Steven Voicu of that night, forever. When she "saw" him now in her apartment, he was costumed as he had been on the first day, and she always began by reliving how she had undressed him, removing the raincoat with the epaulets, then loosening his belt. They had fallen together onto her unmade bed, into the deep profusion of comforters. He had laughed as he had pitched her books and magazines, making way for them. Steven Voicu had a way of entering her, remaining stationary, then raising her up to him, so they rocked to and fro, looking each other in the eye, for what seemed like eternity.

And now he was gone. Even though he still lived in the neighborhood, somehow he no longer ran into her by accident; or took his coffee at the downstairs bistro. Was he avoiding her? Or had the kind fate that led them to crash into each other on so many occasions now abandoned them to separate lives? She looked for him everywhere, saw him nowhere except in her mind's eye, in her own bedroom. He looked unbelievably handsome in his ghostly way, but his image wavered, as if even the memory of him, in its exactness, would now disappear.

It was not his fault, Lisbeth told herself as she rose, leaving the warmth of her comforters and the essence of Steven somewhere in the heaped pillows. His fault had been his virtue: kindness, weakness, an unwillingness to hurt either her or his wife; therefore, of course, he had puzzled and wounded them both with his vacillations.

He had been married since he was twenty-four; that was the kind of man/boy he was. He and his wife had no children, but they had a dog, Cleo, a spaniel, to whom they were attached. Whenever Steve had mentioned Cleo, his voice had softened, and Lisbeth knew he loved that dog too much to leave her. Maybe, in the end, the dog had won him. He often walked the dog near her apartment, and Lisbeth had suggested that he bring her along on their assignations. But Steven's face had puckered with torn loyalties, as if it was wrong to involve the dog in his infidelity. So she had not gotten to see Cleo, only a picture of her, with Steven, in Central Park.

Now she conjured him as she had last seen him, pulling on a

heavy sweater, then the raincoat, looking at her, with his sweet but weak smile. Could physiognomy be destiny? Lisbeth wondered, recalling Steven's smallish, almost receding chin, the way his lower lip drew in, retreating naturally from mouthing commitments? Even kissing him had a technical hesitancy; it took awhile to grip onto his lips. His penis had had a correspondingly tentative entry at times, yet then it could rest, contentedly, as if it had, in fact, decided to remain with her.

Lisbeth could now recall the exact expression in his eyes, the look and light of love, shadowed near the pupils with, what, regret? Had he known then, that last night, that he was leaving, never to return? Was his exit premeditated? She studied his image, his ghost self, and thought: no. *He didn't know.* He appeared to her in his innocence; it was fortunate that such moments didn't disintegrate, Lisbeth thought, that this second of reality, which offered her solace, still existed in some solar system.

She sensed that the faceless man in her dream had been Steven Voicu; but she could not be sure. As she had concentrated on recalling his image, she also recaptured the gaze of that formerly faceless man: his eyes. They looked like his eyes. . . . *Was it an omen, then? That he might return? That he did, in fact, remain in some form in her bed?*

You couldn't take back nights of love; they had happened. Lisbeth walked toward the arch where he had first held her, kissed her. She touched the wall.

Lisbeth stood naked, white, thin, her bones jutting at her clavicle and pelvis. Her hair hung, long and fine, near as blond as Steven Voicu's: she felt almost dressed by her long hair, like her favorite heroines of the old fairy stories: Lady Godiva, or Rapunzel. Oh, yes . . . *Rapunzel, Rapunzel, let down your hair.*

The wind permeated the old glass of the bay window. Lisbeth

shivered and drew on a sweater and her underpants. There was no time to shower; it was too chilly anyway. She picked up a bottle of cologne and gave herself a strong spritz under the arms. She'd showered last night; that would have to do.

Quickly, she went to the tiny, old-styled black-and-white checkered tile bathroom (no improvements or Feiler and Feiler would up the rent), and did a swift but expert makeup. Sometimes, Lisbeth herself was startled at the improvement she could achieve with a few simple tools: a lip brush, brow pencil, and blusher. Her bones were good; they were too good. Her face, before the cosmetics were applied, struck her as skull-like, the white knobby forehead, the taut skin pulled over her cheeks. Her absolute lack of color—everywhere—not a hint of pink in her face, or even her lips. She was white and shades of gray; a charcoal etching, as she saw it, that, each day, she painted into vibrant life. As a model, she had worked with the best makeup artists in the business, and artists they were: Lisbeth had learned to contour, shade, highlight, blend. Within seconds, she saw the masterpiece: her face. She knew that she looked as everyone had always said—*beautiful*.

She slipped on her favorite skirt, the floor-length gray cashmere from a French designer but purchased by Lisbeth at Arthritis Thrift. It matched her sweater, a perfect accident.

Lisbeth gathered up her gifts, set them in a shopping bag from the store whose name both amused and annoyed her—Bed, Bath and Beyond—and pulled on a gray faux fur coat, and a matching gray cashmere cap. She picked up her gloves, and slid on her boots. They were fine boots, gray leather, smooth as butter. She sensed she would ruin them tonight, if it snowed again. . . . But she liked the way the boots fit; they had just a bit of height; they tilted her forward, gave her a sense of more support, yet kept her grounded.

She tucked the rental documents, citing her lack of luxury income, into her oversize purse that held more makeup, her keys and wallet, and left 2A. Out in the hall, Ferdie Feiler appeared as if cued. Had he listened to her getting ready? He grunted and wedged himself into the two-person elevator. She was now aware of his body itself, not even the wall to separate them.

"I think I'll take the stairs," she excused herself, leaving him, his sides almost touching the mahogany walls of the narrow elevator. He grunted again and didn't press the button. Lisbeth ran down the staircase, imagining Ferdie Feiler remaining like a sausage in the casing, in the elevator until she would return.

He looked even bigger than when she'd last seen him, and she wondered if Ferdie Feiler would continue to swell, to surreal proportion, and ultimately be one of those obesity shut-ins who have to be blowtorched from their rooms for medical aid. She shuddered; better get to Pennsylvania Station, the main post office, the only one open every single day, twenty-four hours a day, so she could post her documents and not further jeopardize 2A. She didn't want to lose on a technicality. Sixty days, she had to reply, and tomorrow was the sixtieth day. Oh, why did she always procrastinate? Her life was like that. She always just caught the train, paid the bill before shutoff, filed her taxes at midnight, had root canal before the tooth required extraction, even basal cells scraped from her nose before they could become squamous cells. Lisbeth Mackenzie was, forever, being saved, and saving herself . . . in the nick of time.

As she walked out onto Seventeenth Street, "her" tree shivered in the wind; it bent forward so far Lisbeth feared it might snap. . . . Maybe she should skip the post office, hope to wake up early in the morning, take the train to Queens. But what if there was another snowstorm coming? She'd better mail the damned documents tonight. People lost their apartments if they didn't mail on time. It wasn't fair, but that was the way it was. There had been a story about this in the *New York Times*.

Anyway, she wasn't quite sure the next day was "good"; how did they count the days? Business or calendar days? One missed day could cost her 2A . . . better not risk the delay. Mail tonight, play it safe; there would still be time to get to the party.

Lisbeth walked toward the Fourteenth Street subway station, annoyed at herself that she had not gone out earlier—now she would have to go uptown before going downtown again, to Jessie's place. A single snowflake fell and melted on her nose.

Lisbeth saw the flake descend; it was large, crystalline, lacy. As if this single snowflake had set off a light cue, the night sky deepened, gray to magenta, turned opalescent, lightened to violet, the backdrop color for snow. Lisbeth could not help but remember: it had been snowing when he left. Steven had said that he just needed to go home and get his books, his important papers, his clothes, so that when he came back to her, to Lisbeth, to 2A, to the bed and the comforters and the fire that sparked in her marble rent-controlled hearth, he would not ever have to leave again . . . in the true sense of leaving.

Of course, he had not come back. He didn't call. He didn't have to. She knew. She knew he had not been hit by a taxi, or had a heart attack. He had started to tell his wife, and his wife's sadness had stopped him. So he had become paralyzed, between the woman he was married to and used to love and her, Lisbeth, who was waiting. She understood. She felt his love palpable as the wind. He didn't have to explain; they had always known.

Okay, so he was gone. Almost a year. She had made what she regarded as the adjustment. She was not unhappy; she was not depressed. When the phone rang, she no longer expected to hear his voice. On the street, she no longer looked for him, in his familiar raincoat.

She lived now with her own version of him, the phantom Steven Voicu of memory, his light waves or molecules, that the laws of time and space had taught her were indeed in the atmosphere, in 2A. Their past inhabited her apartment; he existed with her, in a parallel universe, alongside her consciousness. What difference could mere physical presence make?

How well she had slept today; how strongly she had felt his presence. He had been there, with her, in the bed, somewhere to the right. She could smile at him, if she felt like. When she slept, her pillow became his chest. Everything in the bedroom had embodied Steven. If she leaned against the wall, the wall could become Steven; the plaster was cool, like his skin. Everything could become Steven . . . her jeans, even the sofa. Last night, she'd fallen into the sofa and into his lap. They had laughed and talked, told stories of where they'd been and what they'd done. They were always together now in 2A; it was working out perfectly. . . .

She walked swiftly to the subway and boarded the F train, uptown.

Lisbeth felt fine, really, so one can only imagine the spike in her spirit when she actually saw him: way down, far at the end of her subway car. It was really him. She would know him anywhere, his near–white blond hair, that raincoat, with the epaulets. There was a hole in one pocket where she used to place her hand—she could feel his thigh. Now she recognized him as the faceless man of her dream. He did not look like him so much physically, as he was of his spiritual essence. His eyes. As she saw that he, in that exact instant, recognized her, his pupils widened until they opened into a vortex, drawing her into his consciousness and the tunnel beyond. In that moment, she thought, involuntarily, of those neutrinos, all the particles that made up the atmosphere around them. She recalled the definition of a black hole—the place where gravity becomes overwhelming and sucks everything inward, where the universe reverses itself into the torrent of the unknown. As if that was not enough to establish the connectedness of all matter. As if she needed one more sign: there it was. At the very instant that the train and Lisbeth's perception of the man, with his pinwheeling pupils, sped toward the ultimate revelation, she saw clearly, pasted to the station wall, an advertisement for a cobalt blue bottle of an exceptional vodka. *My God, there was nothing to fear; everything fit.*

The train roared to a stop and the doors snapped open, then shut. She waved her arm to signal him, but in the crush of exiting passengers, somehow he vanished, and she missed her stop, Pennsylvania Station.

Lisbeth stood still, gripping the center pole as the subway car hurtled uptown, taking her farther and farther from where she was supposed to go and the man she most loved. She heard something, a primitive sound that came unbidden from her. . . . She didn't recognize her own voice for a minute, then, on the delay, she did— and Lisbeth knew, from the rawness in her throat, that she was calling his name.

Chapter Six

In which Nina and Jessie prepare the hors d'oeuvres, drink Aussie Red, spill secrets, and instigate the Martha conspiracy.

Crudités—a Duet

There is optimism to an arrival. Jessie's spirits rose with the music, with the leaping flames in the hearth behind her, with the cooking aromas steaming upon the stove. The freight elevator groaned to a halt, and the doors parted to reveal Nina.

Inside, the loft was aglow: Nina, entering, saw the candles lit, the fire crackling. She inhaled the combined scents of roasting potatoes, garlic and rosemary. The cooking smells, subtle only a moment before, wafted toward her on a warm draft. Nina experienced her hunger, the new tautness of her own tummy, as a form of exhilaration.

For Jessie, Nina herself arrived in a fragrant gust. Buoyed on the breeze of L'Air du Temps and a hint of sugarless mint gum, Nina marched in, stamping her fur-lined boots, and rattling her bracelets. Nina was also perfumed by frost, the scent of snow, as she offered her chilled cheek for a kiss.

There is also intimacy to a first arrival: Jessie and Nina were alone in the loft until the next guest would arrive. Their hug was heartfelt, exuberant. They cried out simultaneously: "You look beautiful!" then "No, you do."

Hugging her fresh-from-the-cold friend, Jessie felt herself ignite in the first true anticipation of the evening. She ignored the fact that she always felt this way, that as a rule, she preferred hors d'oeuvres to the main course, arrivals to extended stays. . . .

In the rush and gush of greeting, she felt an overwhelming happiness in seeing Nina. Jessie was so glad to see the other woman's smile, a smile that extended to Nina's dark eyes that crinkled near-shut in the Russian style. Nina, beaming, appeared all full red lips and high, Slavic cheekbones. With a flash of gum over her square, polished white teeth. An involuntary cry of "Yay!" seemed to come from both of them at that exact moment.

How wonderful that Nina had been the first to arrive—she was the least "pressure" by far; the one to whom Jessie most wanted to confide about the new love affair, and the one most likely to help cut crudités.

"You look terrific," they said in unison. They could be more physical, more specific and intimate, because there were no witnesses.

They commented, first on each other. "Your hair," cried Jessie. "Your hair was never red."

"It oxidized," Nina said, and they both laughed. They could tell the truth to each other, if they had time before the others got there. Jessie almost reached for the utility drawer, where, stored among spatulas, was the fax bearing the grainy impression of Jesse Dark. She was near-dying to share this image with her friend and scream like a schoolgirl: "Isn't he handsome."

"Something's different," Nina said, looking at Jessie. "Something's happened." She stood back and eyed her friend. Jessie had turned pink. There was no other word for it. Her cheeks were pink, her forehead was pink. And she was getting pinker by the second. She was carrying herself differently, too: her posture had improved, her waist looked nipped in, her hips somehow rounder.

"Something's happened," Nina diagnosed. "Something good."

Jessie, backlit by her candles, the lamps, the fire in the hearth, looked for a moment almost as she had as a little girl. Her dark hair, that usually hung straight, was curling into damp wisps around her face, picking up energy from the steam over the stove. She was wearing her magic white sweater, and the fuzzy white angora wool did convey somehow the romance that had happened to her while wearing it, almost as if her lover had left an invisible handprint. She appeared altered, a woman who had been caressed.

Jessie almost burst right out with it, that she had "met" some-one (an understatement). But something made Jessie hold back as Nina pulled off her heavy black woolen coat with the fake fur col-lar, and revealed herself, in tight jeans and a fitted sweater. Nina invited her to comment on the obvious: she had achieved the ulti-mate, physically—she had lost weight.

"You're . . . skinny." Jessie cried. "You look great."

"I must," Nina said. "Men are approaching me on the street. . . ." She lowered her voice a notch to sexual-secret fre-quency: *"Nine* of them."

She mentioned the man in the alley. "He said 'fifty dollars to . . .'" She laughed. "Isn't that a little low? Do I look like a whore? A *cheap* whore?"

Nina felt an immediate urge to do what she had sworn not to—to confide in Jessie, to relate the sordid details of this afternoon's encounter with the Jerk. To tell Jessie the worst, and so exorcise the demon. Nina wondered: did they have time?

Jessie, as the hostess, felt an instant liability. There were two problematic men on her street, possibly in her entry: the flasher, and the drug dealer. She felt the radius of her responsibility with a keen pain, like the onset of heartburn. If someone was seriously bothered, it would somehow be her fault.

Jessie often was reminded of that poor woman, long ago, who was "just the girlfriend of the girlfriend" and died in the car crash with the painter Jackson Pollack. Jessie herself had been driven on the road where the girlfriend had died, an accident of friendship and fate. Jessie had been shown the exact spot where that tragedy had occurred. The woman had died there, a fatality to happenstance, alcohol, and being the right friend at the wrong place. Because she had acceded to her own girlfriend's invitation: "Come. Come with me. It will be fun."

If a woman were attacked in her building or even just on her way to the party, Jessie would feel, not exactly to blame, but socially implicated . . . an accessory to destiny.

So what about the man in her alley? Was he flashing or selling? She wanted to know, although she was not predisposed to know which man would be considered "worse" as her guests walked the gauntlet of Butane Street. Please don't let anyone be raped, robbed, ripped off, or in any way seriously affected by coming here tonight, she prayed.

So, was he the man selling Ecstasy or the one exposing himself?

Nina burst out with her deepest laugh, and Nina was a laugher, belly-style. You could see her tonsils when she laughed. "The one with the little pink weenie . . . it seemed digital."

Jessie said she knew whom she meant. "I felt sorry for him, you know, so desperate, exposing himself—in every sense—in the cold, but I wish he'd expose himself somewhere else."

Nina made a face. "He almost made me drop the cake, and that would have been a tragedy. It's a flour-less chocolate cake. Don't let me eat any of it. It's for all of you."

Jessie accepted the package and sneaked a peek at the cake: it was so fresh-baked, she could smell the chocolate, the eggs, even . . . she suspected a fondant center. She thanked Nina. "You were the only one who offered to bake."

Nina explained that she could not eat, not solid food, until next Thursday, that she was on the Dr. Duvall Quickloss Diet. After next Thursday, she could have a chicken breast without the skin, but until then, only the shakes and packets of "secret energizing fat burner." She held up a packet from the reducing center that was labeled. "I get another one tomorrow. I don't truly eat anymore, not real food. I'll just mix this with some distilled water if you have some."

"Oh come on." Jessie indicated the set table, the steaming stove, the canapés she had not quite completed assembling. "You have to eat," she told her. "I have roasted five Cornish hens . . . it looks like a Cornish hen mass murder in there." She gestured to the kitchen area, where the hens, glazed, sat in readiness, miniature drumsticks, poking. Because they were alone together, Jessie felt comfortable in confessing she was hours behind in her party preparation, that she was jettisoning the idea of extra courses, but she had also, by a miracle, cooked a more than passable dinner. She ended with urging her friend, "You must have something."

"It's okay," Nina said. "I still take pleasure in watching others eat. It's become a spectator sport for me."

Nina seeing Jessie so aglow suspected the explanation was an affair, and now, she decided that she could tell Jessie about the Jerk. Nina went to the kitchen counter and automatically began to cut up crudités. She had helped Jessie before, and she knew what to do.

As she worked, slicing open the little red grape tomatoes, Nina kept up a stream of compliments: the loft looked beautiful—how did Jessie do it? The decorations were lovely, the antique bassinet, a find.

They also performed a somber refrain regarding Mira Moskowitz's condition. "How is your mother?"

"The same."

"The same," she had said, and that meant "still dying," a signal Jessie understood: her friend had come here to forget about terminal illness for a few hours; tonight was about the new life, and the old days.

Nina was thinking almost the same thing—what a relief it was to be here. She felt her dread of her mother's upcoming death recede, as if she had entered a sanctuary for the night. Here, the drama of her own life could be kept outside, far, far to the north up in the Confederated Project, which was already swathed in snow. Disease, death, old age . . . the specters remained up there, wrapped in their white winding sheets of snow, frozen in exile in the Siberian Bronx, while Nina enjoyed a furlough with friends downtown.

Here, life would once more be about friends, their lovers, triumphs or letdowns at work. . . . There was food to be enjoyed (if only as an observer) and wine, which she was allowed to drink. Nina was feeling the beginnings of euphoria even before she lifted her glass, which Jessie was already filling.

"It's just the Aussie Red, but it tastes like Old French," Jessie said, filling the crystal glass. They both laughed; they were not many years past the really cheap stuff; they had often bought only by price, drinking "$5.95 counter special" wines that lifted their spirits only briefly. A few years ago, they had decided anything under nine dollars had a backlash and caused hangovers, headaches, or simply rescinded its optimism too soon, in an acid reflux response.

The six friends did not drink white wine, save for champagne, which did not count because it was so superior. They had a running gag that there was no such thing as fine white wine, that the stuff was delivered, secretly, from tankers, like the ones that carted gasoline, and was pumped by night into labeled bottles to serve only at receptions.

"Bad white" was the generic beverage offered at business conventions, when white wine migraines could be attributed to the revulsion and tension, caused by staying in brand-name, bleak-but-comfortable hotels, with people you wouldn't speak to, unless required.

Ever since they had started making more money, the women had been drinking Aussie Red, because it was a buy, and tasted as mellow as a fine French vintage Cabernet. Jessie had bought three bottles of their favorite for tonight; a Shiraz, from a vineyard they knew by label: Rosemary Estates.

The Rosemary Estates tasted full but not heavy, and it imparted a pleasant buzz that improved everyone's perspective. The "robust" flavor complemented highly seasoned food such as Jessie would serve. Held up in a goblet, this wine had a clear ruby red hue that was pleasing to the eye, and a grapey "bouquet." It went down easily, and each woman could drink at least two glasses with her dinner and not worry about any ill effects. In case they drank more than that, Jessie kept in reserve her House Rotgut, a jug of something lethally cheap, the Chilean and upstate New York "blend," El Conquistador, that would "stretch" the evening, should the women consume more than she anticipated.

"So?" they each said.

"So," they each answered.

They both burst out, near screaming in the hysteria of their synchronicity. "You too?" Jessie asked.

They had always been telepathic when it came to pleasures or pain they might have experienced when apart. Jessie suspected because she had just had sexual ecstasies after a long hiatus, that Nina had done the same.

"You're in love," Nina accused.

Jessie turned pinker. No wonder the color was the commercial shade of femininity. From bassinet, to baby clothes, through Barbie to this thirty-nine-year-old blush, there was something to be said for turning pink.

"No, *you* . . ." Jessie deferred, refilling a glass of the Aussie Red for herself and taking a deep breath. Some instinct held her tongue, even as she rolled the potential confession on it. Maybe she should hold it back, or at least wait until after eight o' clock, when he would call. Maybe, in some mysterious connection between her and this now intimate stranger, her premature revelation of him could sever the link.

Let him call, Jessie decided, then maybe I will tell all. . . .

"No, *you*," she insisted. Nina turned slightly, raising her knife blade before cutting the next tomato. "Hey, do you want me to make my croutons?" she said, with what struck Jessie as a diversionary move. Did Nina have some hesitation, too?

"Thanks, but it's too late for croutons," Jessie said. "Everyone will be here any minute . . ."

"Tell me what to do . . . I want to help . . . I could make a pasta course?"

"A pasta course? I have the potatoes."

They laughed—they both loved carbohydrates; it didn't offend them in any serious way. Nina, in her less weight-fearing days, had made a pasta-topped pizza. And served it with garlic bread.

"Crudités or place cards? Take your choice."

"Place cards? That's kind of formal." Jessie felt her inner thermostat drop. They had to address the Martha issue, and fast, before the others arrived.

"Listen," she said, dropping her voice, in the paranoia of talking about a friend. As soon as she spoke, Jessie somehow imagined

Martha would overhear her. She often had a sense that Martha knew when she didn't pick up when she heard her voice on the answering machine. Jessie regarded Martha as all-powerful, wired: it was not inconceivable that her transmitters could pick up conversation blocks away. Jessie looked, suspicious, at her own phone, a bland white box positioned on the kitchen area wall. It had a speaker connection; its perforated mouth even reminded her of Martha, always open, receptive, picking up details, blaring secrets.

"I had to invite Martha. . . ."

"She would have been hurt," Nina agreed.

Jessie watched Nina root through the drawers for a sharper blade; Jessie knew her knives were inferior; she did not have good sharp knives. All her friends complained when they cut or chopped here. She cursed herself, when she sawed the flesh from chicken breast bones, and made a ragged mess of them. Jessie watched as Nina considered a huge butcher blade, a collection of cheap steak knives, and a cleaver. To peel a cucumber, Nina settled on a serrated steak knife instead of the proper paring tool. "Martha will ruin everything," she said.

Jessie revealed the plan then: "Martha is coming but she can't stay." She felt a bit of shame as she went on, but she knew the plan was sound, the only way that they could hope for a happy outcome tonight. She confessed that she had deliberately chosen the night when she knew Martha had a conflict, which was that she was taking Donald out for his birthday.

"So," she summed up, "Martha is coming, but she can't stay. . . ." The details amused them—that Martha had a reservation for eleven months. She would have to leave here by 7:30 P.M. or she would lose the reservation. . . . So, if Claire was late, as she almost always was, they might miss each other entirely.

Nina conceded it was brilliant social strategy; inspired. She looked over at the glazed Cornish hens and counted them: five. Jessie had not even bought a hen for Martha. Nina felt a bit of actual drool start in her mouth—the hens gave off an aroma she could almost taste. Jessie still had bought one extra hen; Nina would not be eating hers, and of course, Martha could not stay. "You," said Nina, "are an amazing hostess."

Hostess, Jessie thought, reflecting that the word *hostess* was one noun that had not made the gender neutralization. No one would refer to a woman as his or her "host" for the evening. She also recalled that the word *host* shared its linguistic origins with the word *hostile.* Was there something there? Some bitter seed in the hors d'oeuvres? A touch of poison in the pistou?

The two women moved closer, as if they could somehow be overheard in the vast space of the loft. Their heads bent together, their dyed brown hair picking up faint violet highlights under the industrial light fixture as they chopped crudités and plotted.

Jessie conceded the plan was clever, and ultimately compassionate. They had not slighted Martha by excluding her, which would have been a declaration of war. But they would not risk what they all secretly referred to as the Martha Effect.

"The bluff . . ." Jessie revealed the place cards, with the names written in her best script, with a gold gel pen: *Claire, Lisbeth, Sue Carol, Nina, Jessie,* and *Martha.*

They had a great giggle, placing the *Martha* card on the table in the most prominent spot, so that if Martha glanced at the table, she would not be even the least suspicious. . . . Nina surveyed the set table, with Jessie. They both took large gulps of the Aussie Red; they were feeling the effect now, and this buoyancy resulted in a mistake they would pay for later.

"Since she can't stay, let's fake the hand, and put Claire's card next to hers."

Even the joke made them pause. "Too risky," Nina said. "Even if Martha sits down for a minute, she's a loose cannon; she could say anything to Claire."

"I feel guilty," Jessie confessed. "I feel guilty talking about Martha."

Together, in the drone of friends who know they can never sever the ties with another friend, the two women said, in ritual despair: "She's basically a good person."

Jessie, as a writer, knew she liked to edit out adverbs; they got in the way, they undermined. *Basically.* Was Martha *basically* a good person? If so, why could she be so deadly? "She's basically a good person," Nina repeated, without any conviction.

She moved her own name card as far from Martha's as possible, then returned to the butcher block. Nina began to saw away at the cucumber, taking off too much of the pale green flesh as she tried to remove the skin with the steak knife.

Jessie's sense of Nina, conditioned from their two decades of friendship, was that not all the news was good. She looked at Nina a bit more closely as Nina stood, under the industrial light fixture, near the sink. Jessie could see now that her friend's hair really was oxidized, and the telltale white stripe at the part indicated a lapsed effort to conceal the gray. While Nina looked attractive as ever (she was always called "attractive" not "pretty," or "beautiful") Jessie noted that Nina was wearing more blusher and a darker lipstick than usual, as if she had some need to apply more vibrant color. Jessie thought she detected pallor beneath her base makeup, and chalky highlighter under her friend's eyes. Why? To possibly disguise some smudges of what . . . insomnia, anxiety? Or was she sick?

Jessie chastised herself; she felt too critical, noting her friend's flaws. Such scrutiny was a professional habit, observing people, describing them. Looking for the Achilles heel, even when you didn't want to find it.

She was glad to see that Nina had slimmed down—not just for the improvement in her friend's appearance and for the touted "health reasons" that didn't truly concern either of them, but because she knew when Nina was overwhelmed, she ate. She was not one who "wasted away" under stress—she thickened. Grief and despair, perversely, took the form of fat. When Nina's father had died several years before, Nina had slabbed on forty pounds, thickening so much that she had given away all her "thin" girl outfits, and resignedly gone on to shop at a Madison Avenue store for "larger sizes" with the misguided name of The Forgotten Woman.

So the thinness, for Nina, was good, however it was achieved. But Jessie observed that her friend still showed a slightly distracted manner, and her voice went high as she rattled on about the baby gifts, the shower that they weren't supposed to call a baby shower.

"God," Nina was saying, "I haven't been to a baby shower since I lived in the Bronx." They had a lot of them there, Nina went on, dicing onions, that was what the Bronx was for. The boroughs were for having babies. That was one reason Nina had moved out of the Bronx, and risked her luck, by moving at twenty, into the Quaker residence Theresa House. Theresa House had been for girls who did not want to rush into marriage and motherhood. Theresa House, as stated in its charter, was for "young women seeking to accomplish in careers in the city, and would benefit from the protection of an official residence for respectable women." Nina had checked in by default: at twenty, Nina had not found a "steady," and she headed for Manhattan as a sanctuary where it was considered desirable to remain single. No wonder she had loved her new friends there, upon meeting; no wonder the friendships endured.

The girls Nina had gone to school with had children so long ago; their children were no longer children. There had been a girl in her high school class who had been pregnant at fifteen. Her water had broken in social studies. The "kids" didn't even bother with birth control then; those were the days when teenagers just denied sex took place. Cynthia Greenspan. She had named her baby after John Travolta. So he must be John Travolta Greenspan. John Travolta Greenspan might be . . . Nina computed . . . twenty-one.

"So?" Jessie said. "Something happened? Come on, sit down . . . I can do the rest."

Nina demurred. "No, no, no—I look thinner standing up."

And Jessie felt prompted to ask, "Are you okay?"

"You want the truth or something we can both live with?" Nina shot back.

Jessie stopped what she was doing then, setting the name cards for Lisbeth and Sue Carol.

"Nina."

Her friend recognized the tone. Nina was a call for truth.

"Come on," Jessie said, "if there's something you want to tell me, tell me quick . . . before the others get here."

Nina took a breath and another swallow of the Aussie red wine: in vino veritas. Why not relieve herself of the burden of what had occurred only seven hours before up in 24P with Zhirac, hereafter known in her personal mythology and history only as the Jerk. Or was it too disgusting to report?

"Well," she began. "You know that guy in my mother's building? He's a Zen Buddhist but he's Jewish? He invited me in for . . . herbal tea. . . ."

Jessie nodded. "One of the Celestial Seasonings guys." Celestial Seasonings was a sexual shorthand among the friends: tea typed a man. He would be most likely "food sensitive," probably vegetarian, but he might use soft drugs; most often he would know yoga and Eastern sexual practices. He might or might not be skinny, but he would most certainly be on the ambisexual, more female-oriented side of the chart. The beer, booze, wine, and even coffee drinkers were harder, more macho. But the Celestial Seasonings men, like the tea, could be good for you—light, healthy, with a natural sweetness. Jessie herself had enjoyed a holistic night with a man in the East Village who drank only Morning Thunder.

"Red Zinger," Nina amplified. It poured out of her then, how she'd been interested in the Jerk because of the circumstances, that for a while she had even thought he might be genuinely spiritual, a potential gentle, sexual friend.

Nina paused. She didn't know how much to relate, or how much time she had on the clock before someone else arrived: it was after six-thirty, the others should be here. Now Nina wanted to get it out of her system, but she wanted to share this confidence alone with Jessie. Jessie would understand, she would be discreet. Jessie also, from the look of her, had just been similarly engaged.

She didn't think Jessie would judge her, but would Jessie privately think she was crazy to have gone up there to 24P? Would she be repulsed from the get-go by the details, the frankness of the "invitation," the lack of social frills? Jessie had always struck her as more circumspect.

But Jessie was leaning forward, pink again, and Nina guessed she would not disapprove, so she risked telling her the part about fasting first, then going up to his apartment wearing the white, nonsynthetic fibers. Then Nina paused, wondering how to describe the exact quality of having sexual relations with Zhirac

Macklis (for that was the name on his door). She stared at a carrot, before slicing it—the carrot was an organic one, young, with a bend and fine roots that emanated like hairs from its orange shaft. Should she mention the weird sexual organ?

"What happened then?" Jessie wanted to know.

Nina began to describe how Zhirac had greeted her, wearing what looked like a huge white diaper (just what she wanted to see). It wasn't a Depends, fortunately; it was some Indian wrap garment. . . .

"Well, he was wearing what looked like a white diaper and as soon as he shut the door—" Nina was saying, when the buzzer from downstairs shrilled.

Damn. Nina and Jessie looked at each other. There was no more time for a private talk. It would have to wait until they could find a few minutes more to be alone together.

"Who is it?" Jessie asked into the metal mesh mouth of the faulty intercom. She didn't know why she bothered; the sound quality was so poor, that it could be someone saying "Jack the Ripper" and she would admit him.

From downstairs, on Butane Street, came a reply so wispy, the women who waited upstairs could not quite decipher it. It was the smallest voice in the world, whispering, "Me."

Chapter Seven

In which Lisbeth is denied a smoke by a startling distraction. . . .
Loyalties shift, and a phone call worries the group.

Chapter Seven

Trio

Lisbeth walked the blocks downtown in stunned delight. She crossed at the intersections, unobservant of the red lights. It was a miracle she was not hit by the many skidding, occupied taxis that had taken over the thoroughfares like so many out-of-season bumblebees. At a street corner, buffeted by the strong wind, she paused to celebrate the moment and, on impulse, bought a bouquet of flowers from a vendor, who had sealed himself in behind a clear plastic curtain. Lisbeth picked white lilies, for the hostess, Jessie.

She had seen him, seen Steve. The intersection of dream and reality had vaulted her to a new plane. In one instant, her entire inner life had to realign—Steven, the real Steve, was and was not the Steve of her mind, her bed, her imagining. He was thinner, shorter, older, for starters. His eyes had that haunted, hollow look. Was it the vortex of the universe, or had he possibly taken something? No, Lisbeth rejected the idea of drugs.

But Steven, the real Steve, had looked at her, and his eyes had been the eyes of all her imaginings, of imaginings that had predated her knowing him. He was of her soul, for all eternity. The molecules had moved in the air between them; there was no mistaking the laws of physics, which had clarified for all time her belief system and expectations.

Lisbeth almost tripped on a manhole cover, from which a wisp of steam spiraled skyward. Her heart hammered, her face felt hot. She had been somehow embarrassed, too, to see him—as if she had surprised him on purpose, caught him in the act of going on with life. She had felt oddly exposed, as if she'd also been caught making love, alone. Which, of course, she had been doing.

But this was a sign, if ever there was one. It was 180 proof: Lisbeth could hardly wait to tell her friends. Proof. She was not out of her mind, not deluded. . . . Proof . . . this went so far beyond her and Steven Voicu, she wondered if she should not write to a scientific journal, or E-mail a site for the paranormal.

There was order in the universe, a vortex that had spun him near her, would bring him even closer, she sensed, on the next orbit. Lisbeth was so distracted as she reached the entry to Jessie's building that she didn't notice Old Howard, for that was his name, waving his phallus at her, a phallus that had a movable foreskin.

The aging exhibitionist had to signal with it, not so much tugging himself to pleasure as to get Lisbeth's attention. His mouth opened and he grunted something, too. Still, she did not acknowledge him.

The entire purpose was that she watch, that someone see . . . there was no release until then. He could have stayed home, in his own rented room, if he didn't need a woman to watch.

Lisbeth stopped in her tracks, the baby shower gifts dangling in their glossed shopping bags. She had planned to have a final cigarette before going upstairs; that was the only way she could smoke these days. Otherwise, people either forbid or warned her about her smoking. Now, of course, she knew she could inhale at will: everything was fate, anyway. If you were going to die, you would. If not, you wouldn't. She was intent on extracting the narrow white tube of the cigarette and her cobalt blue lighter.

She wanted to duck into the partial shelter of the entry and light up her Gauloises in commemoration of this night. It was at this moment that she saw the space already occupied with Old Howard, in full flail of his engorged flesh.

Huh? she wanted to say. What's this? She was also annoyed: she would not be able to light up and have her covert puffs. Oh why did her little habit have to be sidelined because of his? She knew she should react, scream or curse him, but in her state of mind, she felt primarily curious.

Oh, sex could be so mechanical, she observed, this repetitious yanking toward what. . . .

"Now why on earth are you doing that?" she asked. "Isn't it too cold? What *are* you thinking?"

Old Howard looked at Lisbeth. She could see that no one had ever addressed him like this.

"It's no good, you know," she advised him, generous since her reunion with Steve. "It just makes you more alone afterward."

Whether her words or the chill had effect, she did not know. The man dropped his penis, a useless item, and slumped back into the shadows of the doorway, closing his coat, like a curtain. He looked offended, as if she had broken some flasher/flashee etiquette, in which she was not allowed to speak to him in this fashion.

Lisbeth sailed past him, buzzed, and was admitted. She could hardly wait to tell the others, about Steve Voicu. She had seen him, she had actually seen him. She did not consider telling Jessie about the flasher—it would seem a bit rude, a criticism of her vestry, like noticing dog feces.

"Steve," she cried as the elevator doors parted and she stepped into the loft. "I just saw Steve." Even she heard her voice rise a bit too high, as if she had some squeeze on her windpipe. She could barely aspirate as she said "Steve." His name came out of her as a gasp.

Jessie and Nina were there; they exchanged a glance. Lisbeth knew, at once, that she should not have said anything, especially in front of Nina.

"I thought Steve was finito," Nina greeted her.

Finito. Lisbeth was offended.

No, she explained, they were just going through a transition. She handed Jessie the bouquet of lilies, so white and bridal (and why not?) This shower was as close to a bridal event as Claire would ever have. Lisbeth set her presents down on the coffee table. The glossy shopping bag held two wrapped gifts—a lace night-gown for Claire, and a matching christening dress for the baby.

She slid out of her coat and looked around for the wine. There it was, open and breathing, the Shiraz, red as rubies. Lisbeth loved the Aussie Red, but would it be rude to request vodka first?

Jessie was the perfect hostess; she seemed to read Lisbeth's mind and opened her own freezer. "I know what you like," she said, and handed her a frosted glass, then poured from a frozen vodka bottle with a red Russian label. It was not quite the same as the vodka Lisbeth stored at her own home, but she was grateful to Jessie.

When a third woman enters a room, it is clear which two women are the closer friends. Triangles always come to a point. And so from the moment that Lisbeth entered, Nina edged side-ways to the countertop-bar. Lisbeth was aware of Nina, conducting a diatribe against Steven; she referred to him as "that shit."

Jessie salvaged the moment by saying, "I think when they are attractive, they deserve to be called something else."

"Thank you." Lisbeth swallowed the vodka, and the synapses surged through her brain, sending more good news, fanning out tributaries of forgiveness. She could overlook Nina's remarks. Nina could get very angry with men. What had happened to set her off? It struck Lisbeth that Nina looked drawn, her makeup somewhat warlike, the brows too penciled, her lipstick applied inaccurately to her mouth, missing the edge by a smidgen. Her mascara had also smudged, "raccooning" her eyes. To Lisbeth, Nina looked distorted, her face out of focus.

Nina moved away from the other two women. There can only be two best friends, and she knew the minute Lisbeth appeared that the original alliance, forged back in Theresa House, would reassert itself between Jessie and Lisbeth. There can be only two *best* friends, after all . . . so Nina stepped aside. She knew her place: she was the runner-up.

As Jessie and Lisbeth exchanged their greetings and hugged, Nina felt a bit less loved, sidelined. She moved to the kitchen counter that Jessie had set as an impromptu bar, and refilled her own goblet of the Aussie Red. She drank more deeply, thinking, Jessie likes Lisbeth better.

If the truth be told (and it must tonight), Nina preferred Lisbeth to herself, too. Lisbeth was arresting; she looked more beautiful than ever tonight, if ghostly, with her blond fine hair hanging, dressed all in pearly gray. She had a dramatic aura, without striving for it, as Sue Carol would. And Lisbeth was so thin.

Maybe thinness was the single most important factor for lovability in the world. Nina saw evidence of this everywhere: men tolerating insanity, greed, stupidity, cruelty, infidelity from women, just because those women were thin. She knew it was socially incorrect to say so, but she had seen the proof. Thin women got away with a lot. And the skinny women looked more comfortable, agile at their underweight—no squeezed zippers, popped buttons, confining jeans such as Nina had on, and were even now pinching her oversensitized crotch. On the thin ones, everything fit. Lisbeth's size three long skirt hung loose, soft—she could move around without anything jiggling.

Of course, Lisbeth was also nice. She was gentle, delicate. Even Nina wanted to protect Lisbeth, pick her up as she would a bony, beautiful wounded bird. Nina felt like a giant standing near her: and to think, in Theresa House, they had borrowed each other's clothes. Now Lisbeth could fit in her pant leg.

Nina knew she was not supposed to touch solid food until Thursday, when the Dr. Duvall Diet Plan would allow her that chicken breast with the skin removed, but suddenly she found herself contemplating a grape tomato, tiny but ripe and engorged with Gorgonzola. Nina did not even like Gorgonzola—it reminded her of what she wanted to forget—what could happen to the veins on her legs, but she felt an almost irresistible urge to eat some. You would think observing Lisbeth's emaciation would instill more willpower in Nina, but, instead, the other woman's thinness made Nina feel hopeless. She would never be that thin. So why not snack? A nosh—a nibble. Nina had a weird taste in her mouth from dieting, an almost metallic bitterness. She wondered if that meant she was in a higher state of fat burning, if that bitterness was in fact a good sign.

Instead of noshing, though, she heard herself begin to nag Lisbeth. "Come on," she said, "you have to eat. . . ." The allegiance that had been between Lisbeth and Jessie weakened, as Nina enlisted Jessie to look at how emaciated their friend was, and to make her eat something.

"I eat," Lisbeth defended herself.

"What?" Nina asked.

"Triscuits," she answered.

Lisbeth wished again for her cigarette; they were going to start on that "anorexia" business, force-feed her like one of those geese who are fattened for pâté. Actually, Lisbeth ate; she ate a lot, really. Sometimes, she ate pure fat. She put butter on everything, even the Triscuits. She ate candy, too, chocolates, truffles. She was not anorexic. She had a wild metabolism. Sometimes, she did forget to eat. But she made up for it, fixing herself fettuccine in cream sauce at 2 A.M. or spooning through a whole pint of french vanilla. She even bought more fattening ice creams and cheeses, on purpose. She had found a new brand of ice cream that featured hunks of pure fat cookie dough, studded in the mix. She herself was concerned about the twin sag of her tiny buttocks. Lisbeth knew another model, Anouka, who had lost her ass entirely, and had silicone implants put fore and aft, with cleavage on top and to the rear.

"I never thought I'd say this," Nina said.

Then don't, Lisbeth warned her, mentally.

"But you're too thin for *Vogue*."

"No one is too thin for *Vogue*," Jessie interjected, a defense.

"But their thinness has some oomph. They're always leaping around, extending their legs on boulders . . . looking striated on beaches."

"I haven't been in *Vogue* in a year," Lisbeth snapped. "It's mostly *JAMA* now. *Journal of the American Medical Association*."

Jessie and Nina looked so horrified, Lisbeth couldn't resist adding: "I'm a Prozac model." She clowned, letting herself go limp, her long hair veiling her face. "When life's simplest problems become unmanageable, give her Prozac. . . ."

They all laughed then; she was kidding.

"No, I'm not," Lisbeth insisted. "The medical companies really pay for ad work. I'm working my way up to Thorazine. I flew through a cloud on Zoloft."

She ended with a sentiment they all appreciated: "It helps pay the rent."

This allowed the women to segue into what Jessie always regarded as "the business segment," when they congratulated each other on how well they were doing in their respective professions. It was a ritual; the flash of their shields. Nina remarked that her spa, Venus Di Milo, had expanded, taking over the Dunkin Donuts next to it. Her professional district, Riverdale and lower Westchester, the Pelhams and New Rochelle, was divided into junk food parlors or weight-loss centers. One hand fed the other, as they say.

"The business runs itself," she said, "I barely have to be there."

They both complimented Jessie on the docudrama that had been filmed of her latest book, *The Jackson Whites of the Ramapo Mountains*. The book had been retitled *Mountain Men . . .* and blurbed, *"a wilderness one half hour from New York City."*

"It didn't get that high a rating," she demurred. "But I was able to buy the tiles for the bathroom."

This turned the conversation to a second staple: the apartment situation. The two women then oohed and aaahed over the changes in the loft.

"You've really made it homey," they said, almost in unison.

They stared at the attractive features: the fireplace, the soft peach silk shade that Jessie had hung over an industrial light fixture.

"You've made it yours," Nina complimented.

"The lights are pretty," echoed Lisbeth.

Jessie wasn't sure: "I have so far to go."

There was a moment of silence, in which Jessie sensed the other two women missed her old apartment, the cramped one bedroom, 4B. It had been cozy, and convenient. Her two old slipcovered sofas had been edged catty-corner to each other, fostering a compulsory closeness; the women had loved to fall into this arrangement, like baseball players in the dugout.

Now, Jessie noted, her friends seemed be standing, warming themselves near the heat of the oven, and the fireplace that sparked and crackled at their backs. Jessie glanced over at the shadows, wondering if the others felt the chill that emanated from the dark corners of the loft. She shivered, and took another sip of her wine.

"When my ship comes in," she said, "I want to buy one of your tree paintings for that wall."

Lisbeth immediately offered her a painting.

"No, no. That's your livelihood." Jessie knew Lisbeth's earnings now stemmed more from the oil paintings of the tree, than from her modeling jobs, which did seem to be phasing out. . . . Jessie didn't really grasp Lisbeth's finances. The other woman always wore subtle but costly clothes, but she often carried only a few dollars in her purse, and she murmured of painful credit card debt. She rolled her big eyes and whispered "too much revolving credit." So far as Jessie understood, Lisbeth had been paying one Visa card with another, making the minimum payments as the permanent balance mounted.

"I want to give you the painting." Lisbeth insisted.

"I can't accept it as a gift. . . . Let me buy it."

Jessie and Lisbeth did this all the time: they fought off each other's generosity. They traded "no, I couldn'ts" and "please, I want you tos."

"For God's sake, Jessie, take the picture," Nina said. "You could use something on that empty wall."

They all stared at the blank wall: it did loom vast and naked, one section had not been completely replastered, and a herringbone pattern of raw wood was exposed, the rib cage of the loft. Across from this abraded wall, were the long windows. Beyond them, the cityscape loomed.

What heat loss she must have, Lisbeth thought.

She would like to paint the view someday, although she found it somewhat hostile. Those high-rises lit at night, like vertical bar codes. High-rise, high priced.

"They're turning lights down now," Jessie remarked. "The energy business." She went on, how she would love to do an exposé of the Darth Vader buildings—what power gluttons they were, and how their sealed windows would make it impossible to adapt, should the rolling blackouts reach the East Coast.

"Please, no social consciousness tonight," Nina begged. "It's a baby shower, for crissake. No rolling blackouts." On another night, they might have debated the various national and international crises, someone might even have offered a petition to stop stripping the rain forest. Certainly, they would have criticized the president, the mayor, and worried aloud about the economy. But tonight was different, this was a party to celebrate a personal first: Claire, the first to become a mother.

They had spent all fall arguing politics and expounding on issues. Lisbeth often spoke for conservancies, and Martha accosted them for contributions to her favorite charities. But tonight was personal, and all evening, their conversations would reflect that, lingering over the aspects that contributed to tonight's purpose. Right now, they were focused on two events: the women were anticipating Claire's arrival and dreading Martha's. They were in some suspense as to who would arrive first. Nina and Jessie had not even needed to debrief Lisbeth regarding Martha.

"I know she had to be invited," Lisbeth said when she noted the place cards and moved hers farther from Martha's. Lisbeth set her card at Claire's end of the table. She could hardly wait to see Claire. She wondered if her friend's pregnancy foretold her own: wouldn't it be lovely? A baby with Steve. She could hardly wait to tell her about the subway sighting, the confirmation of Steve and their certain place in eternity. Claire would understand.

"Can I smoke before Claire gets here?" Lisbeth asked.

They both glared at her. "Are you crazy?"

Oh, Jesus, Lisbeth thought, I'm going to end up on that roof fire escape. She'd climbed up there last time, saying she needed air, when all she wanted was a smoke. She remembered the occasion not unfondly; that moment alone in a drizzle, chain-smoking three Gauloises, to fortify herself for the smokeless zone downstairs. Oh, how she could taste that rough tobacco on her tongue, it was like inhaling France. . . .

"*Claire* smokes." Lisbeth said, to no one in particular, in defense.

"Once a year." Nina shot back.

"I'm sure not *now*," Jessie added. "I'm just so relieved that she's coming."

This brought unanimity to the group: they began to speak all at once, how strange it was that Claire had vanished. That no one had seen her in months, that she seldom even returned phone calls, that she was evasive on the subject of the man, the baby, everything. Lisbeth added a tidbit, as all, except Nina, munched the crudités, in their nervousness. Suspense took the form of nibbling now.

"Claire said she would tell us everything, that she was saving it for 'in person,' " Lisbeth said.

"I promised not to call the shower a shower," Jessie said solemnly. "But of course, she is going to need everything. . . ." She pointed to the cradle, which was already partially filled with wrapped gifts. She picked up the one thing that wasn't wrapped— a soft, cuddlesome toy lamb, and worked the key on its stomach. It immediately uttered a piteous "baah" and began bleating a mechanical *"Baah, baah black sheep, have you any . . . ?"*

"Omigod." They all looked at one another. The repetitive, recorded ditty alarmed them: *This is real. Claire . . . is having a baby.* They agreed it was odd, that she was the least likely candidate.

"Do you think we'll all have babies now?" Lisbeth asked.

"No," Jessie and Nina answered.

They grilled Jessie on what *exactly* Claire had told her, when she did finally accept the idea of the party.

"She was very vague," Jessie admitted. "I couldn't get a thing out of her. All she said was—"I'm grotesquely fat.""

"Oh, she won't be fat either," Nina said.

"Even if she is, she'll get her figure back after the baby," Lisbeth contributed.

"I haven't gotten my figure back, and I haven't even had a baby," Nina said. "I can't get my figure back after a meal."

The phone rang. Nina and Lisbeth instinctively reached for their cell phones like guns. Jessie almost injured herself, leaping toward her wall phone, which was the one that was ringing. *It might be* him. He had said "eight o'clock," but maybe he couldn't wait. . . . Oh, God, she could not get strung out, waiting for him to call tonight. She was so far beyond that. He was out there, in Colorado, not only far away in terms of distance, but now inhabiting that twilight zone of postsexual involvement, the infamous postcoital divide, into which many men vanished forever.

I'm beyond this, so far beyond this, Jessie told herself, taking a breath as she answered. She banged her knee against the refrigerator, in her haste to "beat" the answering machine.

She heard a gritty roar through the receiver: not Colorado, the bowels of the BMT. She could even hear an inchoate call to "stand clear of the moving platforms."

Straining to decipher what was being said, Jessie could barely make out Sue Carol's voice. The woman sounded as if she was trying not to cry. There were awful pauses, and she kept repeating, "I don't know where I am. . . ."

"You're fine, you'll get here, you're in control," Jessie advised. She hunched over the phone receiver, concentrating on what Sue Carol was saying. And giving her directions. The other two women, sensing drama, edged closer, saying, "What? What is it?" Nina adding, "Something's wrong?"

"Just take the next downtown train. . . . You will be fine. You are not far. You sound better."

No sooner did Jessie set the phone down, than she felt she had to report to the other two women. "She sounds awful."

"She's divorcing Bob," Lisbeth guessed.

"Again," Nina said.

Chapter Eight

*In which Martha is drawn back to Theresa House,
thinks she spots Claire . . . and is molested
by the flasher.*

The Limo Lane: "Please Yield . . ."

Martha, riding in the Town Car, a Lincoln with butternut leather upholstery, cursed the traffic that had come to a near halt ahead of her on Fifth Avenue. A dead stop would have been preferable; this was maddening, the way the driver, Matt, had to ride the brake. Martha lurched forward, an inch or two at a time. She would have gotten out and goddamn walked if she weren't wearing those Prada pitched wedgies, and she didn't have to go so far downtown. Again, she cursed Jessie for insisting on having the party at her place.

Now, there was a real chance that Martha would not be able to go to the party at all, if she was going to keep the restaurant date with Donald. This could mean that Martha had a car loaded with baby gifts, a goody bag for her friends, and it might all have to be delivered without her personal touch. So there would be no satisfaction in all these purchases, no little kick at how well they would be received.

Martha looked at her Cartier watch, the one Donald had given her as a preengagement gift, and noted the time: 6:07. She made an executive decision regarding the baby shower. If the gridlock didn't unlock, and she was not past Fourteenth Street by 6:35, she would scrap the baby shower and head straight for Vert. Even during this maddening delay, Martha micromanaged her time; she had made and received seventeen cell phone calls and was half-heartedly watching the news on a wristwatch-size television set. She had already poured herself a drink of liquor she never touched: Donald's Cutty Sark. She rattled her ice.

Now, she had an irresistible craving for a cigarette. Although she had expressly forbidden Matt, her driver, to smoke, as they sat there for the second full quarter-hour in gridlock approaching Eighty-sixth Street, Martha rolled down the power partition that separated them and asked if she could "bum one." Only to get the bad news with the packet of Nicorette gum he handed her over the divider.

"Sorry, ma'am," he said, eyeing her only in the rearview mirror. "I quit on account of you told me. . . ."

He spoke with a brogue; Matt was fresh over from Sligo, Ireland. He had thick tousled blond hair and a freckly complexion. He was a good-looking guy, except he lacked teeth. As Martha studied the young man's face in the mirror, she could not help staring at what appeared to be the black remains of a tooth, more a toothlet, a narrow living toothpick where an incisor should have been.

She popped open her Palm Pilot and noted to make an appointment for Matt McElroy, the driver, with her dentist, that genius of cosmetic dentistry, Dr. David Smilow.

Martha sighed: she could see the future in her driver's gap-toothed grin. She would pay to have the boy's teeth fixed, and he would leave her. She could feel her life's philosophy well up, as bitter as the bitten aspirin on her tongue. She was getting a tension headache. That was what always happened; she did right and was punished for it. But no amount of betrayal would stop her from doing right again the next time, Martha vowed—this was her role in life: to keep trying to do good. She would not let the ingratitude of her recipients stop her. She was bigger than that. Her mother had given her a lovely cross-stitch sampler: A GOOD DEED NEVER GOES UNPUNISHED. Martha treasured it.

"Thank you, Matt," she said, mentally forecasting the day he would give his notice. He was a cute boy; those blue eyes, flecked with flurries of white. All he really needed was teeth. She would fix his teeth and he would become a movie star. "I'll take the nicotine gum. . . ."

She chewed it hard—it wasn't a cigarette, but she had quit three years ago . . . this would have to do. 6:27. She was pissed. The traffic had moved perhaps four feet in ten minutes. A cacophony of car and taxi horns blasted her Lincoln, before and aft. She struggled to hear the news, a weather girl proclaiming that "the storm of the century" was expected to hit New York City sometime tonight. "If you don't have to go out, don't" was the single audible sentence of her broadcast.

Merveilleux, marveloso, Martha thought. She chewed the gum rapidly, extracting some chemical juice from it so quickly, that what remained in her moving mouth was a wad of something utterly tasteless, the consistency of caulking.

A mistake, Martha thought, spitting it out and stuffing the wad in the empty, clean ashtray. Now that awful taste would probably sabotage her dinner with Donald. Vert was said to offer the subtlest flavors in the city—the restaurant should be good, for a prix fixe of two hundred dollaros per person, and that was for "the tasting menu." With wines, her dinner with Donald would cost five or six hundred dollars. It was amazing what had happened to restaurant prices. They were more like rents, just keep adding the zeroes. Only last weekend, Martha had entertained clients, and experienced the five-figure meal. *Nouvelle,* no less. Something for MOMA on your plate—a minimalist itsy-bitsy fleck of a sea urchin on a rare leaf, drizzled with a stippling of low-fat sauce. Pretty as a picture and the same price.

Sometimes Martha considered investing in art instead of going to dinner. It was an idea. Or, instead of going to a French restaurant, you could fly to France, and eat there. She knew the *prix* was too high, but she was still looking forward to Vert. Only the very rich and very famous could even gain entry. The maître d' rejected Pulitzer Prize winners.

Everyone in the city was talking about it, and trying to get a good table. It did sound fun. The food and decor were "green"— *vert.* That was clever, right there. And green as in the color and "no cruelty" also, so everything you ate had died without pain. Experts had studied it, and now they knew how to kill a lobster so he did not feel the scald.

Martha asked Matt to turn up the AC in the car. It was frigid outside, but in the stalled car, the temperature had risen, and Martha was breaking out in a sweat under her shahtoosh cape. That was all she needed tonight: a stain.

The cool blasts were instant: Martha inhaled, exhaled, relaxed her body. The headache clamped on her head, as a vise, seemed to relax, although her left eyeball still felt as if it might roll out of the socket and onto her cheek. Her heart pounded a bit: the sugar in the Scotch, maybe some in the gum. What was she thinking tonight? Was she losing control? She panicked that this might not be an ordinary panic attack, but something more alarming.

She considered calling Francine, her therapist. Francine would give her "the fifty-minute hour" on the phone. For three hundred dollars. Or Martha could call her mother, Athena Lucille Sarkis Sloane, for free.

Donor eggs . . . How dare he, how dare Dr. Hitzig make her wait for that goddamned appointment, so that she could conceive and finally have a child, and then tell her she would have to take donor eggs? Donor, my ass, no donor eggs, she thought. From a college girl. I bet. What college was that? "Bimbo, U." And how many dollaros, how much lire, how many zeroes for the egg of a donor who would no doubt turn out to be white trash?

So now what? She had been so primed to give Donald the good news: "Sweetie, not to worry. Dr. Hitzig took my case, and Dr. Hitzig never misses. . . ." She had the speech prepared, to deliver over the first sip of Veuve Cliquot. *(Oh, no, she had forgotten to pack that chilled extra bottle, now, if she ever got to Jessie's, she'd have to drink what they all had. And the sparkling nonalcoholic grape juice for Claire. She'd forgotten that, too. This was not like her. She was losing control. She had to get hold of herself . . . quick.)*

She was losing it. She, Martha Stephanie Garbabedian Sarkis Sloane, who never forgot anything, was having lapses. Was it Alzheimer's? Or just a normal panic attack? The blood sugar thing hitting her brain pan, in a new and awful way? She checked the Palm Pilot and put in a call to her nutritionist. The problem could be yeast.

Hitzig had made her feel ready for the Dumpster. What had he called her—*"an aging prima gravida"?* Only she didn't even qualify, to get *gravida.* Oh, this was not her day, her night. Maybe that moon in Saturn had input. She was not supposed to do anything of importance on this date, and now look. Martha didn't believe in that astrology nonsense, unless the chart was completed by someone who knew what they were doing, but she sensed there was some awful order in the universe at work tonight.

Maybe she should ditch the baby shower, give up the idea, stay cool and collected, go straight to Vert, and be there when Donald arrived? Think of something else to celebrate.

She punched in her speed dial. "Mommy," she said. "The doctor said my eggs are old."

Thank God Athena Lucille Sarkis Sloane answered on the first ring. Martha took comfort in imagining her mother, comfortable in her private suite at the Hacienda in Hartsdale, an "assisted living community in exclusive Westchester." She heard a rattle, as her mother must have set down some mah-jongg tiles, or perhaps a prescription bottle, the twin totems of her lifestyle at the Hacienda in Hartsdale.

One of the wonderful things that Martha had been able to accomplish with her new seven-figure income was to get her mother situated. Actually, she had moved both her parents into the assisted living facility, but her father had died the day he arrived. A DOA in the lemon-and-avocado Duce and Duchessa Suite. He would never use the golf clubs she had bought him, to celebrate the move.

Martha flinched, recalling Emir Sarkis Sloane. She had a momentary vision of her father, with that prognathism and the low hairline that he had bequeathed to her, which she'd had to electrolysize off. On him, the hirsuteness had somehow enhanced his brutal good looks. Her father had had a black single eyebrow that knit in a perpetual scowl. His eyes had burned, black fire, with what? Anger? Lust?

Emir had roared through his life; it was no coincidence his idol was Zorba the Greek. Emir had been a self-made man who triumphed over everything that had been an obstacle to his desires. He sold rugs to support himself and the family, in addition to three mistresses and God knows how many casual women and near prostitutes. Daddy had kept women stored all over Queens, in high-rises.

Martha and he had fought, as near equals, when she was gradu-
ated from business college. He had wanted her to work for him.
She had wanted to go in business for herself. They had shrieked
and thrown shoes at each other in the office when he cut off her
allowance. She had moved out, taking the room in Theresa House,
a refugee from patriarchy.

Her mother only ever said one thing about Daddy: "Show him
respect."

Show him respect. Martha had shown him respect. She had not
given him obedience, but as she grew wealthy, he forgave her.
Perhaps he even respected her, for being so like him—self-made.
In his final years, she had been the dutiful daughter; her single failure was not to have reproduced. Her sister, Debbie, had borne a
daughter. There was still no grandson, no little Emir, no dark scion
to the rug fortune. Martha had yet to deliver that longed-for
grandson, but she had, in the end, shown Daddy respect, visiting
him as the years passed, suffering his tirades in silence.

Oddly, it had been his death that drew her back into her
father's life. At his death, Martha had to handle her father's affairs.
She discovered the most major mistresses, all in carpeted one bed-
rooms, with fur vaults. They, the mistresses, had luxury apartments, with excellent square footage but inferior views: they all
looked to the industrial east.

Martha didn't know if her mother knew, or not. How strange
his end had been—a stroke that took very little but his voice and
the strength on the left side of his body. How Emir had dragged
himself around that last year, completing business as usual. His
eyes had spoken for him: raging. *Do what I say. Don't talk back.*

Then, the day he moved into the Hacienda at Hartsdale, the
second and fatal stroke had been immediate. Martha had respected
his end: she knew on some level, Emir Sarkis had willed it. When

his real life, of business deals and mistresses, gambling trips, fine food and wine, was over . . . it was over.

For Mommy it had been different. Even while her husband lived, after the girls had grown, the high points of her week had been the bingo and mah-jongg games with girlfriends. Occasional dinners with the same girlfriends, Gladys and Edna, when Emir was away. Now, it was as if he was away—forever. Her girlfriends, other widows in their sixties and seventies, were, despite their coifed blue hair, still her soul mates from school. These women, Gladys and Edna especially, filled her mother's day.

Each of her parents had made their own adjustment—Emir's had been to die; her mother's had been to play bingo and enjoy lectures. An easy out, for both.

"Mommy," Martha said. "The doctor says my eggs are no good."

"He's wrong," Athena Lucille Sarkis Sloane said without hesitation. "See another doctor. There's a woman here whose daughter is forty-seven and having twins. They mix it up in the glass. I know you, you'll find a way. . . . There is no reason your sister, Debbie, has a baby and you won't. I was forty-one when you were born, before tricks, and look at me."

"How are you, Mommy?" Martha remembered to ask. "How's your leg?" Her mother suffered from something called "a milk leg." Martha didn't quite understand it, but it had something to do with her stress when she had been pregnant; that the extra weight burden had flipped the wrong switch in her leg vein valves and she puffed up. Forever.

"Okay when I sit," Mommy answered.

They chatted another minute, said their "I love you, sweeties," and Martha relaxed against the cushioned backseat. Mommy always made her feel better. Martha could find a solution; now she was confident. Of course, she checked her Palm Pilot—the little gadgets were like electronic masturbation, and you could come twenty times a day.

There, sure enough, was a significant listing, under "Infertile Friends": *Helen Fishbein.* An acquaintance. Martha had gotten Helen Fishbein a deal on an adjoining neighbor's apartment, enabling Helen to break through the wall and have a twelve-room apartment, river side, on the Drive. As Helen Fishbein had lived twenty years in hope of "breaking through" somehow, somewhere, she would be grateful to Martha.

The image of Helen—blond, nose bobbed, perky in running shoes—rose up before Martha as a vision of possibility. Helen, famous for a very successful face-lift, had also, just last January, had her own eggs implanted in a surrogate.

There was more than one way to skin a zygote. Now this Helen Fishbein looked eighteen and was running around the Hamptons with a set of twins, who had her coloring and intelligence but had been carried to term in the womb of a Guatemalan cleaning woman, for an outrageous sum of money. How many million pesos? Past counting. But Helen Fishbein's own eggs incubated in the Guatemalan.

Thank God. Martha calmed herself, recalling this bit of promising information. There are still good solutions out there, if you research and micromanage the process. Martha wondered if the same Guatemalan woman might be available, and if she continued to clean while impregnated? No, the cleaning would probably not be a good idea. The pregnant woman should not inhale Fantastik.

As if in tune with her new ebullience, traffic eased, and Matt McElroy zigzagged between other limos, and hit a straightaway, catching every green light. He flashed his black smile at her in the mirror.

Oh baby, Martha mentally addressed the boy. Am I going to get you teeth.

She was so happy now; her generosity was overflowing. Martha made a mental note to give more to charity. Not that she didn't "tithe." She donated more than 10 percent of her annual income to charities. Martha gave endlessly, whenever, wherever she was asked, not that anyone appreciated it enough, or even arranged to photograph her at the benefits.

She gave *mucho* more dollaros than many women who were pictured at receptions in the Metro Section every week. She did not know what you had to do, really. Name a disease, she was into it. Martha gave to multiple sclerosis. She gave for all kinds of cancer. She gave big-time to arthritis, because she feared it. And to stroke research, because of Daddy. She was supporting one of those little orphans in Africa, with the belly. She did more than her share. Even the shawl she wore, the cuddlesome shahtoosh, had been picked up at Memorial Sloan Kettering for a cause. Tumors of the something or other.

6:29 and the traffic was moving: she instructed Matt to escape the shopping crawl on Fifth and dart through the park tunnel on Sixty-fifth Street, if it wasn't clogged.

The passage was clear; Martha sighed, taking in the partial view of the Children's Zoo, the spire of a mini castle. The blue plaster whale of her own youth, and Noah's ark, were taken down long ago. She didn't miss them; this was better.

The West Side was a stroke of genius. Now, they could scoot down to NoHo in no time—she might make the party for Claire after all. Inspiration struck as she punched at her cell phone. She could call Claire, see if she had not left her apartment, if you could call it that, it was really a room. If Claire was still there, Martha could offer her a ride. Now they were only minutes from where Claire lived; it was on her way.

Martha punched in the number as the car nosed toward Fifty-sixth Street. Martha listened as the phone rang. She could picture Claire's room. 312. In Theresa House. Claire was the last holdout, the only member of the original group to remain in the women's residence. Martha recalled her room—it faced front, to the traffic on Ninth. It had been right next to her own room, 314, which had a better view.

As they coasted down Ninth, she peeked down the side street, West Fifty-sixth, and saw, to her shock, that scaffolding had been erected in front of Theresa House.

"Turn in there," she ordered Matt. "I have to see. . . ."

She could almost not believe her eyes: the top of Theresa House had been removed. The upper six stories had been decapitated. The bottom three floors remained, but as a platform for the construction of a jutting pink brick tower, that even as she watched was being enhanced with some sort of glassed-in tower atrium. It looked a bit like the thing Donald Trump had erected on East Sixty-eighth Street, where the old Foundling Home had stood for so long. It had the same phallic energy, the identical glowing tip.

Martha had Matt stop the car. She stepped out onto her old block. Martha stared up at the facade under construction and punched in Claire's number. She had a sense that the phone connection would be better, while standing on the pavement right outside the building.

For some reason, as Martha read the billboard attached to the scaffolding, she heard Donald Trump's voice in her ear, talking about exchanging women, after one of his many divorces—"The flesh of a woman of thirty-five is not the flesh of a woman of twenty-five. . . ."

And now, this flesh-colored tower attached to the base of what had been a Quaker residence for women alone in the city. The billboard depicted an artist's rendering of what would be the final edifice: Theresa Towers, a condominium "fine residential apartments with windowed kitchens" and "concierge services." The name of the developer did not appear, so it must not be Trump. Martha scanned the print, detected only impersonal initials—K.A.C.A. Corporation.

As she stared at the idealized mural on the billboard, of couples strolling into the enhanced image of the flesh-colored tower, passing a few chartreuse trees in bloom that did not yet exist on the street, Martha had to admire the enterprise. It was similar to what had occurred uptown at The Cottages. A small portion of the original structure had been retained, probably because of the architectural detail of the lobby and entry, or to satisfy local activists that the landmark building, while not official, had some lasting merit to the soul of the neighborhood.

Martha looked up, grateful, the brick beheading had stopped at hers and Claire's old floor: 312 and 314 were still there. Her own corner window was still there, with the double exposure, and Claire's with the single view, now obscured by what appeared to be an exotic curtain that evoked rural Japan, the blue and white of a simple kimono. Yes, that was still Claire's room, clearly. There was a huge avocado plant still visible. They had all eaten the guacamole ten years ago, from which that pit had been supplied. She could see tendrils of Claire's jungle, a profusion of green, pressed to the windowpane. Martha speed-dialed Claire, again on the cell.

Martha imagined Claire's old black rotary phone that sat on a desk beside her bed. The phone was shrilling. It sounded insistent, even to Martha. *Come on, Claire, answer.*

A machine picked up. Martha could hear music playing. For a long time. *What is this? A new overture?* Then, at last, Claire's recorded voice, captured in all its maddening fluctuations, on the tape: "I don't think I am here, but maybe I am, in what sense? Leave a message, if you care to . . . I may or may not call you back." Then, unexpectedly: "Love ya."

Martha waited, then spoke after a chiming series of beeps. "It's me, sweetie. . . . I just thought I could give you a lift down to Jessie's, but. . . ." Martha was surprised that her own voice faltered. She sounded not herself, even to herself.

"I guess you have left." She stood there, for a moment, so stunned and disappointed not to be able to scoop up Claire. She was not one to reminisce, but unbidden, she had a memory of standing right here, fifteen years ago, calling up to Claire.

Claire had been her first friend here: Martha met her as she, Martha, was moving her suitcases into the room next door. In her spirit of rebellion against Emir, she had almost fallen into Claire's room, when the other girl invited her in for "a drink of something against the rules."

Now, on the pavement, Martha felt rooted to another moment, fifteen years before, when she had stood right here on this very spot, calling up to Claire—they were going to a party. "Come down, hurry. . . ." They were going down to the Village, to the party, then an after-hours club to hear Sue Carol sing.

Martha shook her head—that was a long time ago, along with the nights they had all worn bathrobes and fluffy house slippers and sat around, watching old movies on the rec room TV. Martha got back in the limo and instructed Matt to drive on, down to NoHo.

Her headache, which had been receding, came banging back, clamping on like the helmet worn by a Viking maiden. Brunhilde.

She leaned back, held an ice cube from the Scotch to her brow. So what to tell Donald? That they would have to segue from inseminations and IVFs, to surrogacy? What a "present" for his fortieth birthday.

She squeezed her eyes shut against the pain, as if you could pull a venetian blind on the brain. She was worried about tonight, not just the restaurant, but after. . . . They should have sex when they got back to Ph43, it was his birthday, after all. This new information would not help with what was becoming a problem. . . .

Don't think about Donald's poor penis, Martha ordered herself. You've had enough for one day. She had been considering giving him what men liked a lot, a b.j. (With a blue ribbon on it?) for his birthday to help him with his itsy-bitsy problem down there, that weird pleat that had come into his penis. He was folding, like an accordion, in midthrust. She could do it, if she put her mind to it, to prove her love.

Martha opened her eyes, and good thing, too—or she would have missed Claire. There she was—right outside the limo, running, gawky in her pregnancy, along Ninth Avenue. She looked different, but it was Claire, all right: Martha would recognize that unkempt hair anywhere . . . and there it was, spilling out over the baseball jacket . . . that long, curling red hair, now suddenly frizzled with gray. Martha rolled down the window and screamed, "Claire."

Claire turned around, her face blanching, as she stared at the black-windowed limo. Did she even see her? Martha wondered. She screamed her name again. Oh Claire looked just terrible: she had gained an enormous amount of weight; she was grotesquely fat. How could she wear what was some high school kid's outfit? She was absurd in hot pink spandex leggings and high-top sneakers. And her face . . . it was bloated almost beyond recognition, her neck all ropey and striated. If she hadn't been so obviously swollen in pregnancy, you would have said this woman was too old to carry a child.

"Claire," Martha yelled, giving the scream full ballast from her lungs.

"Claire."

Claire, if that was Claire, turned away and hopped on the Ninth Avenue bus. Martha gave in to her migraine then, willed herself to lie quiet, concentrate on the red darkness of her closed lids, and hoped that she could recover in time to enjoy the party and somehow get through the dinner with Donald and whatever might follow. She turned off her phone, sighed, and actually seemed to have some spasmodic descent into a minisleep.

She jerked awake when Matt pulled the car up to 16 Butane Street, Jessie's building.

"Wait for me," Martha told Matt. "I may not stay long."

He offered to carry the bulky packages up to the loft, but Martha considered this and said no. "I don't like the street. Stay with the car. I can handle it."

And so, burdened now by a large box and four shopping bags, the handles of which cut into her palms, Martha entered what had been Frankenheimer's factory, and paused in the vestibule to buzz Jessie. She didn't even have time to appraise the renovation that was occurring in the vestry, where the original marble was being restored, because she was assailed by the sight of a man in the final throes of his self-inflicted ecstasies.

He was an older man, grizzled and gray, in a great military sort of coat, that was open. His hand was working, hard, the bit of flesh, that, to Martha's chagrin, had something she had spent the previous evening trying to achieve on her fiancé: a full erection.

His gaze, which had been turned upward in the idiocy of impending release, swiveled in their reddened sockets to meet Martha's eyes, as she took in this finale and heard the agonized yelps of his conclusion.

On the intercom, upstairs, her friends heard only some static that they did not realize was Martha, yelping.

Chapter Nine

In which Martha arrives and a most dire warning is issued,
only to be ignored.

Quartet

Why was it, they often wondered, that Martha had such a deadly effect? Why did she always leave them feeling diminished? Why did they dread her so, and yet never make the break? The women were speculating on just this subject when Jessie heard the buzzer, and the strange sounds emanating from the foyer downstairs.

"Let me in," Martha roared. "There's a problem down here."

That sounds like Martha, Jessie guessed, depressing the admittance buzzer. Damn. It was only 7:06. Martha would almost certainly intersect with Claire. Even on Claire's relaxed timetable, she would be getting here any minute.

As the women heard the elevator cables groan and they knew Martha was ascending, they made a few quick predictions: "She'll attack me first," Nina said.

"No, she'll comment on my weight loss," Lisbeth volunteered.

"She'll tell me to sell the loft," Jessie guessed.

"Then she'll give us all horrible presents."

Jessie knew Martha well enough to fear her gifts. When Jessie bought the loft, Martha had given her some depressing texts on women's financial insecurity. Of course, Martha had been annoyed—that Jessie had not "gone through her" to buy, that she had bought a place on her own, out of the Martha Uptown orbit.

In another arena, Jessie also credited Martha for her own fears of venereal disease. In recent years, ever since her own engagement, Martha had become obsessed with venereal disease. She actually mailed them all clippings featuring each new outbreak: "One in Four People Have Herpes Now!" "Do You Know Chlamydia Is the Fastest Growing Infection in the Hemisphere?"

She had alerted her friends to new strains of antibiotic-resistant syphilis and was an early advocate of testing for sexually transmitted hepatitis. Martha was always saying if she hadn't gotten her broker's license, she would have become a doctor: it was clear what her specialty would have been: STDs. She always fired off those initials as a verbal SAC missile: "You girls"—she always called them "girls"—"better keep your eyes peeled for STDs." She E-mailed them bulletins and left phone messages when a new television special, regarding sexual plagues, would be broadcast.

"What makes Martha so devastating, is she *is* pretty well informed," Nina was saying as the freight elevator yawned open to reveal Martha, marooned inside. The other women gaped as they viewed this tableau vivant—Martha, surrounded by shopping bags and mammoth cartons with handles. Martha was draped in a gossamer shawl-like cape, and had obviously had her hair and makeup "done." She looked lovely, perfectly groomed, but she was standing on one foot, like a crane, and her eyes were bright with alarm.

She hopped on one Prada wedgie, into the center of the loft. She held the other foot aloft.

"A wino pissed on my shoe," she announced. "Right downstairs." Then she fired off directives: "Get me a paper towel. I don't want to touch it. . . . Does anyone know? Does piss tarnish brass? Get these gifts . . . would you?"

Martha took a second to appraise the others, fired off a group compliment. "You girls look great. None of you look your age. Isn't this going to be terrific?"

Nightmare, thought Jessie, staring at the mountain of presents, the hopping Martha. Her own voice sounded tinny as she offered the roll of paper toweling and asked, "What have you got in all those packages?"

Even for Martha, the woman had outdone herself: there were giant shopping bags, the two massive cartons, assorted smaller presents that seemed about to tumble out of the bags that were so overweighted, they were now ripping.

"Whatever you all bought will be extra," Martha said, with the first of her broad smiles, displaying mucho dollaros' worth of cosmetic dentistry. "I bought the whole layette."

Jessie, Nina, and Lisbeth stared at her, aghast. She misunderstood their expression, and said, "Why not? I've got the money. I've never been cheap."

As the others stood speechless, Martha wiped down the Prada shoe. She snapped open her Kate Spade purse and produced a tiny aerosol of disinfectant and blasted the designer footwear. Jessie was familiar with the little spray can: she knew Martha would use it on her phone, too, and on any surfaces she touched in the bathroom or kitchen. She was always on the alert for microbes.

"Are you sure it's piss?" Lisbeth asked in her most intellectual tone. "I saw a man down there a few minutes ago, but he was not pissing. . . ."

"Old Howard." Jessie spoke the name in defeated recognition. That old Jack-Off was at it again, in her entry. Oh, God, why tonight?

"Old Howard," Martha repeated. "You mean you know him?" She issued an aside, which Jessie accepted as she had so many of Martha's *Consumer Reports* bulletins from the shopping front. "Don't buy these bargain brands of paper towels, they are less absorbent. Buy Bounty. I'll send you some—you have room to store the jumbo twenty-eight-roll packs. Don't say no; it will make me happy."

Jessie stood, numbed and paralyzed already, in the actual presence of Martha. How could she have ever thought this woman could be contained, even for a few minutes? She was mythic, like Beowulf.

"It will make me happy" was the preface to all the generous gestures that had undermined all of their self-confidence for almost two decades. It was the rationale, Jessie supposed, that allowed Martha to behave like this.

"Old Howard. You know him?" she was saying. "I just assumed he was just some disgusting old wino who wandered in to a warm place to piss."

"I think he ejaculated on your foot," Lisbeth whispered. She pronounced the verb *ejaculated* very precisely.

"Ugh," Martha said. "But I don't think so. I walked in; he had his back to me, and he was holding, you know, his thing, and he turned around and that's when he got me."

"Well, he does piss, too," Jessie considered. "Actually, he pisses in there on a regular basis. No one in the building seriously minds him. We think he may keep away the muggers and the burglars." She was aware that she was baiting Martha, but it was irresistible, like bearbaiting was alleged to be. The other two women, Lisbeth and Nina, laughed.

Just as the personal thermostat in the room had shifted when Nina and Lisbeth entered, and the loyalties adjusted, an even more profound change occurred with the addition of the fourth, Martha. Martha's entrance fused the loyalties of the other three women, and they stood, united, by the wine bar, against her. As they laughed, Martha flinched, and her inner voice noted, What's this? Are they starting to resent me because I have more . . . ?

Martha reminded herself to minimize her accomplishments. Why rub their noses in her success? There was nothing she could do about her obvious advantages, her clothes, her hair, but, out of consideration for the others, she told herself: don't mention the big sale this morning or the award for Realtor of the Year, or the upcoming honeymoon trip to Lake Como.

She would have popped open the Palm Pilot and jotted these reminders, but there was no way she could do that without the other women noticing. "Maybe wino piss is a great crime deterrent," Lisbeth was joking. "Maybe it could be bottled."

"Or put in aerosols," Nina said. She stood, planted, between Jessie and Lisbeth: the troika, now in action. How much could they bait Martha without her realizing what they were doing, and striking back, with bared fang and claw.

"Go ahead, laugh. You wouldn't think it was so funny if he pissed on your shoe." She frowned, eyeing the damp Prada. "This was new."

Martha wondered herself why she had revised the bum's action. On some lower level of consciousness, she knew he had, as Lisbeth said, ejaculated, but she could not allow herself to acknowledge it. Piss was bad enough. If she accepted the fact that he had ejaculated, she would have a dilemma. She would have to insist that the bum be tested for STDs, although, she comforted herself, it was unlikely she could be infected through high-quality shoe leather. Yes, piss was bad enough. It was all she could handle at the end of the day.

She ducked into the powder room and, leaving the door open so she could still converse, scrubbed her hands. "I can't stand other people's piss on me," she said. "It's bad enough going into ladies' rooms and finding all those splatters on the seat."

"Those are bad," Jessie conceded. "I always wonder—how do they get there? I never leave splatters."

"It's all the women who've been taught not to lower their asses to public surfaces. They're afraid of contamination. So they crouch over the seat," Nina had to interject.

"Ruining it for everybody else," said Lisbeth.

"If everybody would just sit down, it would be great," Nina said.

"Can we stop talking about urine?" Martha asked. "I need a drink. And, Jessie, I apologize. . . ."

They all looked hopeful—was she going to leave right away?

"I forgot to bring you some Veuve Cliquot. And I was going to buy the nonalcoholic sparkling fake grape champagne for Claire." Martha emerged from the bathroom and noted Lisbeth sipping her vodka. "And anyone else who might think it wise to refrain from drinking alcohol."

Jessie rushed toward her with a full glass of the Aussie Red, which Martha accepted, even as she qualified, "I hope this won't give me a migraine. I'm allergic to anything under twenty dollars a bottle."

"It was a value," Jessie defended. "It would have been twenty dollars, but it was on sale."

"It's a lovely wine," Nina said. "Very full-bodied."

Martha's eyes, subtly shaded in tones of a brown eyeliner known as Ash Auburn, bored into Nina. Her gaze flicked over the other woman, who, out of habit, shriveled, slumping to diminish her breasts. She knew a strike was coming, but she didn't know where Martha would hit.

"You're looking more fit," Martha told her.

"Thank you," Nina said. "You never change."

"Thank you, sweetie. Your hair's oxidized." She delivered the volley from the side, already turning toward Lisbeth, who had sunk down on the sofa and was also trying to become smaller.

"And you," she addressed Lisbeth, "you look so pretty sitting over there . . . so itsy-bitsy, like a miniature of your former self. Well"—she smiled the Martha smile—"I guess it's all the style."

Now me, Jessie thought.

Martha walked the border of the great raw space. "I see you did a lot of the work yourself. Good for you, for trying. When your next book sells, you can hire professionals to do things over. . . . You're so smart to keep the costs down now." She stood back, against the abraded wall, and appraised the entire loft. She squinted her professional gaze.

"You could get your money out," she said, after a pause. "How are you finding the neighborhood? Are you getting used to it? It still doesn't bother you? Coming in late at night . . . alone?"

Jessie had a premonition then, that this was the night when the Martha Effect would have to be dealt with, for all time. They had come close, last Christmas, when she had offended them all by giving them subscriptions to *Modern Maturity* ("I know you're not there yet, but it is so good to see what's coming up: you can plan financially for your retirement now") and gift certificates for makeovers at Georgette Klinger ("You'd be surprised what can be done. I can recommend a great liposuction-ist.").

If only, Jessie brooded, there was a central liposuction drain, and Martha could be slurped down it, at least for tonight. "I smell kitty." Martha was saying, then she sneezed. "Allergies!"

Martha turned to her. "Could you lock the cat away, just for a tiny bit, so I can breathe long enough to see Claire? You don't mind, do you?"

Jessie controlled her expression and hoisted the twenty-year-old cat, which uttered a plaintive mew, as if to say "What? What is this?" as she was dislodged from her pillow in front of the fireplace.

"Sorry," Jessie said, setting the cat in the bathroom and closing the door.

"It's all right," Martha said, misunderstanding the apology. "You know, Claire shouldn't go near her either . . . the toxoplasmosis."

Jessie could see Nina and Lisbeth huddled together now on the sofa, both drinking. Lisbeth was eating all the little stuffed tomatoes, without comprehension, in her nervousness.

"So?" Martha said. She loved to start sentences with "So?" It put everyone on the defensive right away.

"So!" Jessie said.

"So it doesn't bother you?"

"No," Jessie snapped. "It doesn't bother me. I love coming up here, late at night, alone."

"You're so brave." Martha moved to the long windows. "And the view is sensational. It's just the right aesthetic distance. You don't miss Uptown?"

"I love it here," Jessie lied. "I just spent a year fixing the place up."

"That's the ideal time to unload it." Martha's voice turned sweet, her lips pursed: "I'm so concerned about you." She glanced down at her shoe. "Look what goes on down there. The neighborhood's literally a toilet." She saw Jessie's face and amended, "Of course, you've made it charming. Your magic touch."

Martha resumed a favorite theme, the importance of selling fast, in a seller's market. "Everything is buyers and sellers, sweetie," she told Jessie, with an aside to the others. "It wouldn't hurt you girls to learn this, too. You have to sell while you still have your value. This is the top of the market, for you, Jessie. Sell before this slips. You have a wraparound mortgage, I could work with that." She summed up with her broadest smile: "A foreigner would buy this."

Jessie moved back to the oven; she could smell the potatoes, the garlic, and the rosemary. God, don't let them be incinerated. She grabbed a mit and yanked open the oven.

There was a God: the potatoes were just at the edge of becoming scorched. The garlic and oil sizzled and popped as she removed the pan and set it on the counter.

"Oh," recognized Martha, as she would the children of a friend. "The little golden Yukon fingerlings. Yum. Don't let me eat anything, I have to save myself for the restaurant."

Great, Jessie thought, an opening for her exit. "I know. . . . God, I would hate for you to be late. . . . There can be awful traffic, and it's impossible to get a cab. . . ."

"I brought a car and driver," Martha snapped. "I can't leave until I see Claire. So?" she resumed.

"So?"

"So wouldn't you really rather live in my neighborhood? Near me?" Her voice assumed a professional singsong. "I'm condo-ing a town house on Sixty-fifth between Madison and Park—"

"*Condo-ing* is not a verb," Jessie corrected her.

"It is now. I just condo-ed a thirty-five-story apartment tower with an indoor shopping palazzo and an underground gym and garage." Her voice softened. "Mondo condo." Martha could not completely keep the pride out of her tone as she added, "I sold a parking place for eighty thousand dollars."

"Is it pretty?" Lisbeth wanted to know.

Martha looked at her. Pretty? "It's a parking place," but she qualified, "it's attractive." Martha sipped her wine, addressed them all, in a professorial tone: "You know, more and more, in the questionable, borderline neighborhoods, driving 'in and under,' risking no street exposure, is going to be the way to go. That's where it is at, already, in most cities. See D.C."

Nina began to build steam. "Listen, Martha, I grew up in the Bronx. You don't 'deal' with the neighborhood by remote control. You work on social services, you—"

Jessie offered Nina the bowl of green chili.

"Try this. . . . I brought it home from Colorado." Please, God, she prayed, don't let this disintegrate into a fight. Just get Martha out, without fatal insult, and let the rest of us enjoy the party.

Where on earth was Claire? It crossed Jessie's mind that maybe the guest of honor was not going to attend. And Martha would never leave until Claire appeared. . . .

Martha continued the pitch for Mondo Condo. "Enclosed living. That's where it's at. Malls work. They just need to be bigger. You girls have to have some vision: I think someday Florida will be the first enclosed state. It would be smart, if you had to stay in a dicey area, to get yourself indoors, complet-mento."

"I can't believe a parking place is eighty thousand dollars," Lisbeth murmured.

"It will appreciate two hundred percent in two years," Martha predicted.

"If the city is still here in two years. Did you read the *Times*? About the neutrinos?" Lisbeth asked.

Oh, here we go, thought Jessie, munching a tortilla chip and scooping up some of the green chili. She ate now, too, without recognition, although the spicy chili sparked her recall of Jesse

Dark. She looked at the wall clock: 7:25. . . . In just a half hour, he would call. Wouldn't he?

Just thinking of Jesse Dark fortified her to deal with the evening's obvious social challenge. Jessie Girard relaxed a bit, ready to enjoy Martha's take on the neutrinos. Lisbeth had stood and was gesturing in the air:

"They are all around us in an invisible sea. . . ."

The others all followed her hand motions, as if they expected the neutrinos to appear. Martha had a look of concentration, similar to an expression of unself-conscious straining, as if constipated.

"Huh? Huh? I don't get it." She looked around. "Like microbes?"

Lisbeth broke the news to her gently: "Their presence means that someday the universe will stop expanding and collapse upon itself."

"Not Midtown. Or the Upper East Side. Even the Upper West Side will hold." She touched Lisbeth's arm. "Sweetie, I'll keep an eye out for you, too. I know your landlord, Feiler . . . he wants you out."

Lisbeth suddenly felt a little woozy, but another sip of the frozen vodka straightened her right out, and she ate the lemon rind. "I'll be fine in 2A," she said. Martha turned her attention to Jessie, who, for the life of her could not remember how to fix the salad dressing: more vinegar or less?

"And don't you worry, Jessie," Martha assured her. "When you say go, I can get you out of here. I have idiots coming over from Yemen who know nothing: they would love this location. And now that we know you're so handy, I can get you a fixer-upper closer to civilization."

Martha moved her largest carton, nudging it with her foot while she asked Jessie for a knife. "I need to cut this twine. I want to set up the crib—I bought her one, it's divine—don't tell her what I spent, it makes me happy—I want to erect this crib and fill it with my smaller gifts. It will make a better . . . display. I tried to think of everything—and I have."

Jessie gave her the knife Nina had used to hack at the vegetables. "I'm sure, amongst us, she'll be getting everything she needs . . . and that's the point of tonight, isn't it?"

"What she needs," said Martha, sawing at the twine, "is a husband."

Lisbeth had a talent for piping up with the most impossible rejoinders. "But she said she doesn't have room for one in her apartment."

Martha appeared not to hear her; she was intent on assembling a portable crib. She was sliding the wooden slats, shoving the walls into position. "I have to work fast. I can't stay. I have to leave almost immediately. Kick me out in five minutes. I mean it."

You had to admire how efficient Martha was: she had that crib erected, and it was now being filled with a group of smaller presents. "I don't know how you could have done this to me, Jessie. Tonight of all nights. The one night of the year that I can't stay. Donald's birthday. The big 4-O. What were you thinking? Do I hear myself talk? Have I said this what godzillion times. You know I want to be here for Claire, but I can't possibly stay. Kick me out in five minutes. Promise."

Nina, Lisbeth, and Jessie all said: "We will."

Jessie took a breath and decided to reclaim her role as the hostess. "Listen, Martha," she said, "we are going to be just a little traditional here tonight. I want Claire to open all the gifts, and we will pass them along in a circle."

"But mine is too large," Martha insisted. "Look. It's nicer this way."

Worried that Claire might arrive before Martha's departure,

they resumed the conspiratorial huddle. "She's going to make Claire feel awful," Jessie whispered. "What can we do?"

Martha lifted the crib, almost menacingly, in the air. "Oh, feel this frame. It's solid. It cost over three hundred dollars. Don't tell Claire—I don't want her to feel . . . indebted." She looked around at them; her eyes had that overbright look.

Nina, observing, thought, Martha looks berserk tonight, something awful is going to happen.

"Do any of you know?" Martha was demanding. "If Claire is covered?"

"Covered with what?" Lisbeth asked.

"Blue Cross. Blue Shield."

Jessie felt she had to intervene. "Martha, that's not our business. Please don't bring it up when you see Claire."

"Oh, fine," Martha said. "I'm supposed to watch while she gives birth at home on a flokati rug or an African bedspread. Is she planning to have any medical care? Wake up, ladies, if you love your friend. I fear the worst . . . I have a sense of these things, and ever since she did her disappearing act, I have had terrible concerns which were verified when I saw her on my way here."

"You saw Claire," Jessie almost screamed.

"She was unrecognizable," Martha reported. "I wasn't going to mention it; you'll see soon enough. I . . . I thought . . . she was a bag lady. She is completely disheveled, wearing a baseball jacket and unlaced high-tops. She's bloated beyond belief. . . . I hate to say this . . . she is . . . hagged out. Her face is all striated and her neck is ropey. . . . Quite frankly, she looks too old and out of control to be having a baby. She needs our help."

The women sat, stunned. "I'm sure if she was that unrecognizable, it wasn't Claire," Jessie said, finally. "Maybe it was someone who resembled her. . . ."

Martha insisted. "I screamed her name, and she jumped on a bus."

Jessie stood and looked nervously at the elevator door. Poor Claire. She couldn't walk into this.

"Listen," she said, "we really have to talk before she gets here. We all care about Claire. She's obviously . . . vulnerable. I think we should be . . . careful, careful of what we say to her. We don't want to strike the wrong notes."

At that moment, the buzzer sounded. "It's her," Martha cried, rushing to the buzzer. "I'm so relieved. I was afraid I'd miss her."

She pressed the admittance buzzer before Jessie could.

Downstairs, a woman leaned heavily on the button for GIRARD, 12A. She was a wild woman, all right, screeching to be heard—not just upstairs but in the vestibule, where Old Howard had made the mistake of resuming his efforts.

"Oh, you creep," yelled Sue Carol, trying to hang on to her various bags. "You just put that thing away."

She grabbed something from one of the totes and slammed him with it. She realized as Old Howard fell back against the wall, that she had hit him with "Our Wedding Book." Now, all her photos, a yellowing wedding invitation, some love letters, and her high school diploma fluttered to the vestry floor.

As if on cue, the admittance buzzer sounded, and Sue Carol gathered up her scattered belongings and shoved her way into the inner sanctum. "Now look what you made me do," she screamed. "Oh, men, crazy old men. Some nights, I do just want to bite it off."

Old Howard, running in his open, broken-backed galoshes, fled.

Chapter Ten

In which Sue Carol materializes, afire, as Medea on Butane Street, carrying evidence of indiscretion and an odd gift.

The Witching Hour

Sue Carol could have risen to the twelfth floor on the heat of her anger. She was levitating, she was so mad. Lord how she hated Bob for this. She had wandered, carting her life's most precious memorabilia, through the frozen city, risking frostbite and being mistaken for homeless (mistaken? she *was* homeless) all because he couldn't keep it zipped.

Even as she seethed, Sue Carol retained some of her training, enough to note her responses and symptoms. Her observations, her "third eye," would come in handy, if she got to play Medea.

Remember this, she told herself, the energy of anger, the super-human ability to move out, organize.

She squinted, trying to check her reflection in the metal elevator door. She couldn't see correctly with only the one contact lens. She looked fuzzy. Grief is confusion, she reminded herself. Not expressed in tears but in dropping things, and losing important items such as money, keys, contact lenses, and Metrocards. Loss is literal.

She did not even have her right glove now, and who knew what condition her fingers were in from gripping that damned Bonwit's bag with the love letters, résumés, and her wedding pictures?

Would she end up fingerless, grasping at her hopes with stumps? She sensed that what had separated her from the needy, the outcast, and the deformed was a membrane that had been punctured earlier in the day when she made her awful discovery. This is bedlam, she told herself, the end of the world as I know it.

But she was packing some solutions: she had bought some tiny blue pills from a man down the block—Ecstasy. She sure needed some. She had an old prescription bottle of dog Valium, for a dead pet. There was help in her hip pocket if she needed it.

Was this what she looked like now? That sloping face, the Mongoloid eyes? Sue Carol prayed this was the distortion of the metal elevator door. In any case, her image split, and she faced the group, whose faces sagged in disappointment as she entered.

"Well, hey thanks," Sue Carol greeted them. "You all look glad to see me."

"We thought you were Claire."

Claire. Lord, she was in a state: she'd almost forgotten the purpose of the party. Sue Carol dug into her bags and pulled out the little sack that she'd acquired at the Korean grocery. Squinting around the loft, she saw the crib, loaded with wrapped presents, and said, "I didn't really have time to buy a gift, so I stopped at the Korean place back there a few blocks, and bought"—she took a breath as she produced her purchases—"some incredible vegetables."

The group—Martha, Jessie, Nina, and Lisbeth—continued to stare at her without comprehension. Sue Carol displayed the tiny eggplant and miniature zucchinis.

"Well, they're all little *baby* vegetables. . . . Lucky I spotted them as I was running by. I thought, What darlin' little carrots and what a sweet tiny little eggplant, and there's even a little miniwatermelon. That's good for a baby shower, isn't it?"

"She's lost her mind," Nina whispered to Lisbeth.

Martha snorted. "You must have spent three ninety-nine."

Oh, God, Jessie realized, I'm the hostess. This is up to me.

"You brought yourself," she said, leading Sue Carol deeper inside the loft, taking her gloveless frigid left hand, "that's the main thing."

To her shock, Sue Carol glared at her. "Don't say a kind word to me. If you do, I will go all to pieces. I can take anything but kindness."

"You look beautiful," they all said.

"Do I?"

"Yes."

"Gorgeous," said Nina.

"Lovely," added Lisbeth.

"I don't know how you get away with it: you look great," Martha said.

"Oh," said Sue Carol. "You don't think I look old, sad, beaten down, and ugly?"

"No," they all said.

"You are all too kind, I have such good friends. And maybe I do look okay, if people keep telling me I do. I keep getting callbacks to play an ingenue."

"You look so young," Lisbeth complimented. "Really, you do."

"It's my height. My size. I'm not young, I'm just short. I have wrinkles. . . ."

"No," Nina said.

"Yes, I do. Three. I wear these bangs so my forehead wrinkles don't show. See."

Sue Carol raised up her bangs, and said: "Count 'em. Three!"

"You're being silly," Nina told her.

"Oh, yeah, well I'm wearing bangs to cover my forehead, and a turtleneck to hide my neck. So if I do get away with it, maybe it's 'cause there ain't that much a me showing."

She squinted. "I can't see out of my left eye," she explained.

"My contact lens dried out, and now I'm having a duct problem. I cried so hard, my duct just done dried out. Don't get me started why, but I may lose the sight of this eye because of you-all-know-who. . . . Do you believe it?"

"What's he done now?" Nina wanted to know.

"Nope," Sue Carol said, drawing upon her dignity. "I'm not even going to get started. That's over. It is history. I am gone." With her "good" eye, she scouted the loft. Where could she bunk?

"Jessie, you don't mind if I stay, just till I find a place? I cannot go back to that apartment after what happened. I never want to see it again. It is sullied, polluted, desecrated by the events that have taken place there tonight."

Jessie looked around the loft, too: there were no room dividers. Her bed was shoved in the corner. There was the couch, and that was it. She had space but no rooms.

Sue Carol seemed to sense her dilemma. "You don't have a spot for me? It's inconvenient? I can go somewhere else, I don't know where. I'll think of something, always do." Sue Carol reached to pick up her bags.

"No, no, of course, you'll stay," Jessie said, stopping her. "Take my bed. I'll sleep on the couch." *I'll never get any work done while you're here,* Jessie thought, *but I better do this.*

Sue Carol appeared to brighten; she lugged her bags over to the corner, and tossed them onto Jessie's bed.

"Now if I start to cry," she instructed, "you all just tell me to shut up and sit in the corner. If I spoil tonight, I'll hate myself forever. We are all going to have the best time. . . ."

"We are?" Nina said.

"I just have to see Claire, she's being so brave." Sue Carol's chin began to tremble.

"Bite your lower lip. Hard," Jessie instructed.

Sue Carol bit her lip, used her impediment training from the William Esper School. *The fight to control tears can be more moving onstage than the exhibition of complete release. The choked voice is the more effective tone. It is permissible to be inchoate, as long as the emotion is clear.*

Sue Carol wanted to wail; she wanted to bawl like a baby. She wanted her mother, but she didn't want to go home to Kentucky. She would never get out of there, if she did. She would end up in a BarcaLounger, her only forward momentum executed by the recliner controls. She thought of her mother, with the wet bar in her chair console. Of her dad, who now seldom rose save to relieve himself. *No,* she had to take this last stand in New York. She had to use the force of her pain, the vigor of her unbearable agony, to propel herself to a new level. She could release this energy in her audition on Monday. *Medea.*

This is the most emotion I have felt in a long time, Sue Carol acknowledged. I feel totally alive, in that I am in utter agony. I could jump from this window if I felt just an itsy bit worse. So now I understand suicide, she thought, to escape from one's self, to punish the wrongdoer. . . . To leap to one's rest.

Use this, she told herself. *Depression is rage turned inward.*

Jessie looked at the clock: 7:34.

"Martha," she said, "you made me promise. To kick you out in five minutes. If you don't leave now, you'll be late for your dinner."

"So?" Martha was asking Sue Carol.

"So?" Sue Carol was refusing to spill the beans.

"You've suffered some new degradation?" Martha guessed.

"Oh please," Nina said.

Jessie stared at the kitchen counter, at the five little glazed hens. She made a final prayer, even while suspecting it was doomed: *get Martha out of here, and then let Claire arrive . . . the evening could still be salvaged.*

"I can stay another minute," Martha threatened. "I can't leave without seeing Claire."

"You know Claire," Jessie said, "she runs very late. She was late before she got pregnant, now she's probably later."

Jessie knew she was babbling, but she was moving Martha toward the door, toward the coat hook, where her shahtoosh cape was hanging. . . . *Oh, God, just get her out of here,* Jessie vowed. *I'll do anything.*

"Claire's being so good, so strong . . . I could cry." Sue Carol was starting again.

Lisbeth said, "Martha, I think you could go. I have no sense of Claire coming anytime soon . . . I think I would feel her . . . presence."

"That's ridiculous," Martha said.

Jessie tried another tack: "Donald. He's turning forty. The big 4-O. You don't want him to sit alone at Vert. Waiting, wondering. . . ."

"I'll get there," Martha said, "after I see Claire . . . I just have to see her."

Martha was thinking, I'll be damned if I just spent three thousand dollaros on baby gear and I don't get to see her response. She had been looking forward to Claire's expression, her gratitude, all day.

Jessie managed to drape the cape over Martha's shoulders, and edge her closer to the door.

"Well, maybe I could come back after dessert," Martha was saying, giving in to the first signs of indecision. "I've had the reservation for eleven months. We confirmed twice today."

Oh, goody, she's leaving. Jessie exulted—too soon. The women had all gathered to say good-bye to Martha, when they heard the downstairs bell ring.

Chapter Eleven

In which Claire makes a shocking entrance that galvanizes the evening and offers up her own gifts and an unanticipated confession.

The Guest of Honor

The woman Martha saw on Ninth Avenue was not Claire
Molinaro: the heavy, graying redhead, in baseball jacket and
untied high-top sneakers, was a homeless woman, on her way to
the soup kitchen and bread line at St. Malachy's, the actors' church
a few blocks away. She was not even pregnant; she was just overweight.

At the exact moment that Martha thought she saw Claire,
Claire was lying in her bathtub in the sawed-off surviving section
of Theresa House. She could hear the phone ring, but not Martha's
voice on the machine. The water was running, and her music, an
old 78, Caruso, "La Donna Mobile" filled the room with opulent
sound.

Claire had lit nine candles in a circle around the deep claw-
footed tub. She had set her towels to warm on the exposed radiator.
She was splashing and soaking like a mermaid, a pregnant mermaid, who felt buoyed by the warm suds that did, in fact, take the
weight off.

She thought of her baby, deep within, floating also, hearing the
music, as they now said was possible, and she smiled. Claire was

playing her best recordings for this baby. She could almost see the baby, captured in a rainbow bubble, an internal version of the major suds that threatened to overflow the old tub's gleaming, porcelain flanks. As she always did, Claire blessed whoever built this bathtub; it was more than a tub—it was an environment. Seven feet long, three feet deep. They did not make them like this anymore.

But they did break them like this, Claire thought. The last week had been startling: the dismantling of the old Theresa House. So many tubs, identical to hers, thrown onto the street. It had been so crazy and stupid: they sold tubs, not nearly so nice, down near Jessie's place, in NoHo and SoHo, at shops with names like Urban Archeology. The tubs were worth thousands of dollars. But the hatchetmen had come, sledgehammered, busted them on the street. The workmen, mostly Croats, who had battled then fled the Serbs, now fought old plumbing in America. Far from their native land, they smashed with neutral expressions: they had seen and done, or experienced worse damage, Claire thought.

She could not help but notice, as someone who had long ago enjoyed a summer in Dubrovnik, that these workers seemed to have imported the darker conflicts of Bosnia to Ninth Avenue. On the sunnier side of memory, Claire could recall cafés, a strong Turkish coffee, served in demitasse, delicate plum pastries. Gypsy violins. That was the former Yugoslavia she had loved, cherished.

She reminded herself that that country, in every sense, no longer existed. She shut her eyes, floated. She remembered a vineyard, an arbor table set with wine, cheese, and fruit, more of the coffee, brewed for her. In that time, in that village, Croats and Serbs had seemed to be friends, lovers, relatives. Now, there had been murder on both sides, in that sun-dappled vineyard. Claire shuddered, in response to a new, resounding thud, as another tub was extracted from the old plaster walls where it had nestled, offering Theresa House residents comfort for over a hundred years. Claire could hear the men, yelling in their guttural dialect. They were not so far from her, maybe yards away, in a condemned bathroom.

Were these men employed to smash Theresa House, former members of death squads in Eastern Europe? Had they imported their revolution, on a small, inanimate scale, to her block, where the victims were now porcelain bath fixtures?

The violence evoked the same visual and sound effects: plaster dust rose, there were more grunts and cries. The men shouted at one another across the rubble. The effort of destruction was everywhere around Claire. The building shook, from vibration, as jackhammers broke up sections of the lobby and blasted out the wing that had once held the Theresa House communal dining room and a library.

A small "recreation" room had been spared, the place where Claire and her friends had gathered to play music, or watch old movies and concerts on the small color television, that had sat, looking alert, with its rabbit ear antennae perked.

The room remained, but the TV had been replaced with a wide, flat screen, and the rabbit ears were no longer needed. A satellite dish had sprouted from a subroof, in the alley. Now, as Claire lay in her tub, she could see the dish, an outsize metal tulip, through the bubbled glass of the bathroom window. She viewed the gray trumpet shape as a potentially fatal flower, open to microwaves and blocking what had once been a somewhat pleasing view of the inner courtyard garden of Theresa House. The satellite receiver pointed a gray piston toward the city sky. Inside Theresa House, television reception was now clear, delineated down to the nose hairs of newscasters, who seemed permanently on air, speaking in modulated tones of disasters occurring elsewhere. Claire worried that the satellite dish emitted potential radiation, but the management had assured her that, in fact, the dish worked as a giant shield. Within room 312 and the inner pod of her tub, Claire was probably safer than anyone in the city from random "rads."

She had calmed down about the dish, but as she lay submerged in her beloved tub, listening and actually feeling the reverberations of the shattering of the other 1900s bathtubs, Claire quivered underwater, sensing these shock waves as indoor tsunami. The future was coming, at an awful acceleration, and she could not quite foresee the ways in which she would be affected. She had tried to save the tubs, but no one had listened to her.

"Wait," she had cried, "I know someone who will take them." "They," the henchmen of renovation, did not even look up at her. The smashing went on, not just the tubs, but pedestal sinks, butler's pantry shelves, all artifacts of the more graceful time—when "things" were built to last, when objects were designed as art, when a bathtub could recall an entire culture, and a sink could support itself, graceful and fluted, an ode to an urn.

The replacement sinks were Formica-topped boxes, with plastic insets. The tubs were molded "units" in which the bathwater could never rise above low tide. In the small cheap new tubs, the bather would be stranded, half-exposed, a lobster washed to the shallows, beached on the wrong shore. Claire had watched, all week, as the new "units" were delivered to Theresa House. Just let them try to take my tub, Claire had thought. They'll see a revolution.

Claire allowed herself one more luxurious descent under the warm bubbles. She inhaled the mists, scented with bath oils she had bought in Greece, Italy, and Turkey, and a lavender essence that she had carried in her purse from Le Lavandou, France. Aromatherapy, with marvelous excess. Claire lived on the principle that "more" was "more"—she had poured every known infusion of herbs and flowers into this hot bath, and she believed that they all helped her relax.

Claire was relieved that the armies of architectural destruction had stopped short, just before her door, on the third floor. *Saved.* From the guillotine. At the final floor. Her tub spared, with her in it. . . . If they had come here, for her, she did not know what she would have done. Some things were essential for life. Music and a good tub. I would have fought for my tub, she told herself. Call for a SWAT team, but you will not take me from this tub.

Caruso reached his top note, the high C, and held it. Claire's heart rose with it, the emotion. She smiled. Heartbreak, elevated to art: what more could you ask? She could also hear the flat A, as somewhere above her, in Theresa House, another tub fell under the axe.

Life was change; today that change included wreckage, the dust of demolition—how it seeped in, even through her sealed windows: The dust had been in her room for weeks, sifting in a fine powder over all that Claire owned, over Claire herself . . . which necessitated taking even more and longer baths.

When the aria ended and Caruso reached his finale, Claire emerged, pinkened, from her long soak. Her fingertips had puckered. She must have been in the bath for hours. It was after six; she would be late for the party, but Claire smiled—her friends knew she would be late. They always told her the time was an hour earlier.

Claire Molinaro inhabited her personal time zone, not Eastern Standard but Claire's "International." Often, she synchronized seven hours ahead, as if her mind and spirit were still abroad, as she had so often been. In New York, this meant Claire was most alert at night, that she had become nocturnal, which suited her just fine.

Claire had always felt she walked somewhat against the grain; that she moved in an opposite direction. When people went to work, she went home; she'd often traded day for night, and night, with its glitter had won her soul. She had spent most of her "career" playing music in joints that closed at four, then hanging out some more with the other musicians. Eventually, she found her way back home, to Theresa House, the room with the tendrils of plants and the bird, with his head under his wing.

Maybe her favorite time was that dawn patrol back uptown. . . . Sometimes, she walked miles, the city almost to herself. Like a private dream, a sleepwalk on the sidewalks. . . . She would walk until New York woke up for her; when the porters appeared to wash the streets, and the scents of coffee and hot bagels perfumed the air. She loved then, to stop at her twenty-four-hour deli, she tried to hit it just as the day's new *Times* smacked down with a satisfying *thwack*. She never failed to revive, then, to face what might come, with something even more satisfying than hope—her anticipation of some surprise, combined with all that she had come to cherish as familiar.

So now, as dark descended, Claire's biorhythm ascended; she was revving up, becoming more alert, more eager for action. The candles, the warm tub, the bubbles, even the big rough towel on the radiator, recalled her Night of Nights, the night the women wanted to hear about . . . the night she had. . . . What should she call her condition? Claire didn't care for the expressions relating to pregnancy—"gotten knocked up," "impregnated," or, God forbid, "preggers," which is what they had called it in her hometown of Dullsville, Pa. (The town wasn't really called Dullsville; it was

Dooleyville, but in Claire's mind, her childhood joke stuck.) No, she could never say she had gotten "preggers." If she had to choose a word, she would pick "conceived," because that is what she had done, in her mind—"conceived." She had conceived a child and an idea.

How much should she confide? Should she tell all? Claire blew out the candles, which occupied glass jars of varying colors and dimensions. These candles had been witness to what happened here. They had illuminated the scene—the man's naked body and her own.

Claire patted herself dry, laughed, remembering her joy that night. The Night of Nights, oh, yes. She should tell them a little, share the pleasure. Claire shook her hair, disdaining a hair dryer. Let her hair air dry—it was too frigid a night to go out with wet hair. She could not afford to catch cold.

On her dresser was a still life of items that she no longer allowed herself—a tiny drawstring purse in which was hidden some very good grass, a pack of Turkish cigarettes, a decanter of Metaxa brandy, an individual drip espresso pot, and some mystery little green tablets, said to combat a cold, that a medical student in the Alps had given her. Claire could laugh, just remembering how she had gotten sick after posing naked, on skis, atop the Matterhorn. The pills had worked, but what was in them?

Contraindicated goods of all nations, Claire thought, looking at the collection with desire. Oh well, after the baby . . . the baby. It was hard to believe that in just several weeks, a real baby would arrive . . . would be here, in her room, 312.

Where on earth would she put it? The room was packed to the rafters. The baby fit in, as she was, inside Claire. They were like a set of those Russian nesting dolls. But soon, the baby would emerge. As if in anticipation, the baby kicked . . . a tattoo against

Claire's full belly. The baby would be like her, active, a wanderer, she thought. Like the man, too, the father. She smiled, remembering his backpack. He had been a portable person, too, carrying his essentials, traveling, as she used to, "light."

She rubbed her hair with the towel, heated by its contact with the old radiator. The warmth embraced her, and she remembered more. . . . She saw, for some reason, his skin, so browned by the sun, except, where it wasn't. . . . Would she dare tell her friends the insight she had experienced when she looked at him?

Go on now, she told herself, get down to NoHo. Don't disappoint everyone. Jessie would have gone to a lot of trouble. For a moment, as Claire rubbed her hair, and felt the heat of the towel suffuse her, she felt truly expectant: tonight, in some way, made the baby, the birth, more imminent. Wheels were turning, other than her own. She massaged some cocoa butter onto her stomach, so taut yet fluctuant, like the earth during a mild quake.

Claire wondered if she would have stretch marks; she supposed she would find out soon enough. On her travels, in the many nude spas she had visited in Europe and the Mideast, Claire had seen hundreds of naked women. She knew what happened to women's bodies. Some women bore babies and remained as they had been; other women had skin that shirred, like silk that had snagged. Those women were left with this scar tissue puckered, as if the expansion waists of their garments had permanently adapted to flesh. Claire had seen the slash marks of cesarean sections and even a double belly button, souvenir of surgery for an ectopic pregnancy. She had read the writing on the belly, buttocks, breasts, and thighs, in the blue or red script of burst capillaries that etched their legend of what a woman's body had borne. Some women seemed marked, ravaged by their pregnancies; others remained unaltered, smooth-skinned as girls into their own old age.

Claire wondered if it was an advantage to be fit, or not. She had been a runner, a swimmer, a cyclist, all her life—but perhaps the muscles had been so strong, a more destructive process had been required to accommodate the baby as the baby had grown.

Claire had experienced a symptom that she had never heard of—ligament pain, as the muscle strained. The pain was not severe; it was just unexpected. Her body was still containing the baby; maybe she would have been even bigger, more cumbersome, if she had not been so flat-bellied at the start.

Her travel alarm rang: she had set it so she would not forget. Better move along now, she ordered herself. Mentally, she plotted her course down to Jessie's place in NoHo. How should she go? By subway, bus, or bike? What would be quickest tonight? For some reason, her heart hammered, and Claire broke out in a light sweat. Maybe it was just the heat from the steamy bath; why should she be nervous tonight?

Calm down, she commanded. She would get there when she got there, and instinct and history told her, it would be just the right time. Claire left her beloved bathroom and went into the twenty-by-eighteen-foot chamber that she had, for so long, called home. The small space appeared larger than its dimensions, because of the twenty-foot-high ceiling, with its crown moldings. The single bay window was floor to ceiling, and it bowed creating an illusion of space. Claire thanked the gods, as she always did, for the great window, the cathedral ceiling, the solidity of the plaster.

Even under assault, 312 stood mostly intact, if a bit opaque from the fine grime. Claire took stock: how compact her belongings appeared. The only way to survive in this space had been to build shelves. Everything had to remain in its spot, or the result would be chaos—and even then, sometimes, it was chaos, she admitted. You didn't want to see this room, when she had to dress for a recital, in a hurry. If you looked too hard for a single sweater and couldn't find it, in five minutes the entire chamber looked as if it had been ransacked.

Claire's "life support" systems were miniaturized: the half-size refrigerator sported burners on top. There was a "dressing alcove" sink that she used to rinse her few dishes. A bookshelf held her Bavarian china, a bamboo steamer, and assorted new and cleaned chopsticks. On one wall, books rose to the ceiling, and on the other, her bicycle now hung from hooks. A small jungle of house-plants stood before the window, leaves unfurling, stems extending toward the sun. Her little canary, who had been an illegal immi-grant under the old Theresa House rules ("No Pets"), hung from a bamboo cage. His name was Joe Bird, and he sang whenever music played, water ran, or the street noise hit a certain decibel.

Claire loved little Joe Bird: he was a cheery little guy, a true feathered friend. Until her new adventure, taking care of the canary had been the closest Claire had come to motherhood. She hid him from the "authorities," the super of Theresa House, who had sometimes complained of unexplained chirping coming from her room before she installed her soundproofing panels. Claire bought Joe Bird "treat sticks" of honey and specialty seeds, yellow egg wafers called Birdie Biscuits. She had nursed him through pneumonia by mimicking that famous expert, the Birdman of Alcatraz, and covering his cage while keeping a lit lightbulb inside to warm him.

Joe Bird survived and competed with Pavarotti, Caruso, Cecelia Bartoli, whoever else was singing. Sometimes, he set his swing in motion and "danced" on his gravel-paper-covered floor, looking up and, Claire would swear to it, using the motion of his swing as a metronome. Not all musicians were human, she reminded herself, and the birds were there first. If she loved the baby half as much as she loved Joe Bird, they would be ecstatic in here, Claire thought, changing his feed and water dishes before preparing to leave.

Canaries were sensitive to cold but loved light, so Claire draped a sheet of clear plastic on the north-window side of Joe Bird's cage. He trilled, in response. Claire warbled back at him; they often performed duets. Then she looked around, knowing she would feel better if she left 312 somewhat straightened up. It seemed even more important than usual tonight, to have her life at least appear in some sort of "order."

Keeping house here was a kind of magic trick: the boxes in boxes; the towers of books—a place for everything, but often nothing in its place. Center stage were her bed and her musical instruments: the krummhorn and her bassoon. The instruments rested on supports, which made them appear almost animate, child-size coinhabitants of this room. Of course, the instruments moved only when she lifted them off their stands, to take them to rehearsal or a recital.

Where was she going to put the baby? The remaining floor space was almost entirely taken up with her bed, which was really just a futon, set upon a second futon, covered with bright silk and velvet pillows Claire had collected from her travels through Asia, Africa, and Europe. She had a souvenir pillow from almost every country she had visited—there were dozens. The bed was also draped with a duvet, and a "crazy quilt" her elderly neighbor, Mrs. Rice, had given her. The effect of the bed was quite lush and colorful. Like her tub, the double futon served beyond its function as an environment.

Between the bedding and the wall, there was only a narrow aisle of space, and into this interior passageway, Claire had squeezed a six-foot-high Victorian burled walnut armoire, to contain her clothes. The room had not come with a proper closet; originally 312 had been a public room—a library, or perhaps, Claire liked to imagine, a music salon. The Victorian armoire served to hold not only Claire's clothes but also even a small file cabinet, with her important papers. Tonight, the armoire was more crammed than ever, because only last Monday, during the onslaught of the final "renovation," Claire had discovered a stack of fabrics and papers, all her neighbor Mrs. Rice's belongings, in a Dumpster, in the hall.

That had been a shock: where was Mrs. Rice? She had not seen the tiny silver-curled little woman in several days. Had she, too, been "removed"? That occasionally happened, after the death of one of the elderly residents—the body was carried, in a black vinyl bag, out through the freight elevator and the service entrance to the alley, then out to an unmarked funeral wagon.

But no, thank goodness, Mrs. Rice had not suffered that fate: Claire had found out only yesterday that the old woman had been whisked off to subsidized housing in Brooklyn. But her move had been sudden, orchestrated by others, and Mrs. Rice had not been able to take a lifetime's accumulation of quilting, and stacks of sheet music. Claire had saved the fabrics, the music sheets, and planned to take them to Brooklyn as soon as she could visit Mrs. Rice.

That visit might have to wait now, until after the baby. The subway ride to Brooklyn loomed like a trip to Uranus. Claire could not wrap her mind around the logistics, the different subway lines, but she would get there, she knew she would.

Claire had this instinct to hide, until after the baby. Was it some throwback, evolutional mechanism? An animal urge? To protect the unborn? Or was it related to her odd sleep pattern? She had been resting during the daylight hours, going out most often after hours, to the all-night grocery around the corner, shopping for her food in the literal lunacy of the fluorescence of the midnight city. The other shoppers and clerks seemed to be participants of her somnambulant dream.

Why was she hiding? Claire hid even from the answer. There was something, a shadow, something she did not want to confront. Hiding, she felt safer, spared from more change, before she was ready.

Everything would be all right. It always had been before. She had a magic lucky star, Claire knew, she would be fine. . . .

Here, in 312, she lived in her own climate, the humidity of her bath, and this was the climate in which Claire could flourish. She composed, she dozed. She fixed snacks, she listened to music, and she took care of Joe Bird.

In the moist air, she, the bird, and her instruments were spared the rigors of dry heat and the weather; her indoor jungle, started from seeds so long ago, flourished, too, growing higher, higher, thicker and greener, reaching toward the light that streamed, sometimes too bright, through her one wide window.

The greenhouse effect; it was here, she was living it. But it was good. Sometimes, she could smell her potting soil, the plant food she poured into her store-bought earth, and she felt as if she were one with her avocados, bananas—the plants could qualify as near-trees, her vegetable offspring, growing, growing. As Claire surveyed her small domain, she was satisfied.

Within 312, all was still beautiful, more than beautiful—fecund, fertile, alive with music, sweet with scent. Somehow, the baby would fit here, too; they would cuddle together; people who loved each other didn't take up too much space. In other countries, whole families, groups, existed in smaller rooms than this. Everything would be all right, not to worry. . . . The bird trilled, agreeing. Birds were smart; they had proved that.

The baby would be here, there would be love. . . . Claire could suddenly almost sniff the scent of a baby. Was it only last May, that day on line at the fruit stand, when she had pressed her lips to one small head? That stranger's baby, offered to her, to hold, to kiss, by a woman who sensed what she was wanting. . . . Was that what made her feel ready later that night? The natural perfume of a baby; they said it was some genetic trick: to make you love them. Claire laughed. It worked. She had inhaled the scent of that baby, and soon she would hold her own. She held her baby inside, the best of her many secrets . . . ready to burst forth.

Claire pulled on her wool tights, with the funny pouch she was not yet accustomed to, and would not be getting accustomed to. Soon, she would wear her regular clothes again. Then she stepped into her sweatpants, for added warmth, tugged on the ski sweater she had picked up on one of her many trips to Iceland. This winter, everyone was wearing the wool knitted caps, with the folk pattern, but she had had hers for years. She tucked her long red hair up under the hat, added a muffler, and then an extra sweater. She slung her backpack over her shoulders; it was heavy with her bike lock, change purse, and a few surprise gifts she had included for Jessie.

Claire never wore a coat; coats weighed her down. She most often moved around the city on her bicycle, and coats were awkward on the bike.

The big question tonight was: did she dare risk riding the bike down to NoHo? She had acknowledged that her biking days were almost over, that she was getting more and more cumbersome. That this week, most likely, she would just have to say, it was going to be impossible, until after the birth.

But maybe one more ride? The final ride before the birth. She couldn't risk being off balance much longer, but she wanted to arrive downtown tonight flying her colors, so to speak, showing that she was still her old self, not grown conservative or stodgy. The bike would be easiest, cheapest, quickest . . . and she loved riding it. The old snow had been cleared, the streets were bare, an open road.

Claire had taken the bicycle out of the storage room when the Rape of Theresa House had begun. She knew the bike would disappear if she left it in that commotion. And this was a special bike—a Peugeot, a present from an old boyfriend.

Last week, some kids had stopped her on the street, and said, "Hey, where'd you get the antique bike?" and she'd laughed. Claire had thought of the Peugeot as her "new" bike, a recent innovation. She had felt, at that moment, like Rip van Winkle, waking up to some New World. Claire had only recently gotten a computer and risked venturing into cyberspace. So far, she liked cyberspace, and she had already made friends in twelve countries. Easier on her phone bill, too, which some months exceeded her income, despite the international billing plans. Claire tended to talk longer the farther away a friend was—there was some correlation. She was always yakking at length to someone in New Guinea or Egypt, and keeping it short with a friend on Twenty-eighth Street.

She walked the bike down the hall, sidestepping the dropcloths, the splattered plaster. Even though K.A.C.A. Corporation had allowed the bottom three floors to remain, they were not encouraging the old-time tenants to do so. The heavy-handed Croat renovation was in full sledgehammer, and two clarinetists and a painter had already moved out. Maybe she should get it over with and go to Florence or Budapest, or another city overseas where she had friends and fun.

Maybe New York was over, maybe the city was being destroyed, or at least altered past her recognition. Maybe this was no longer her city. She had been here for twenty years, fled to Fifty-sixth Street and Ninth Avenue at sixteen, run away from Dullsville, Pa., to come here. But had the city accelerated, passed her by or become an inhospitable, unaffordable place?

Maybe Claire should flee, have her baby in a country with a more mellow culture, and national health insurance, to boot. She had friends in Italy and Sweden, Israel and Greece. Claire knew she could get on a plane tonight: she was a frequent flyer with friends, even lovers, all over the world. She had, as they say, "miles."

Claire got on board the elevator, which also seemed to be somewhat victimized by the renovation, draped in splattered cloths. The elevator lurched to a halt a few inches above the landing. No wonder the old tenants were abandoning Theresa House. They might be let out, between floors, literally shafted by K.A.C.A. Corporation.

It would be a shame to lose her room, really it would be a shame to lose her tub, Claire thought as she guided the bike out through the lobby, which was in the process of being chopped in two. Space was too valuable, she reflected. The gracious lobby would now be compressed, most of its square footage given over to medical offices on the ground floor. She passed another shattered tub, lying on its side, near the freight elevator entrance.

Don't think of this tonight . . . there was a party, and that was all that she should concentrate on . . . having some fun with old friends. She was grateful she was carrying so well. She guided the bike through the entrance.

Outside the door, under the old tattered green canopy that still read THERESA HOUSE RESIDENCE FOR WOMEN, Claire swung onto her bike without much difficulty, paused just to adjust her balance (that was a bit trickier), then took off, pedaling hard, down Ninth Avenue.

The night air was so cold, it hit like an invisible wall. As Claire breathed in, she could feel winter enter her lungs . . . sharp, defining her air passages. The wind whipped at her face, pushed her backward, as if the weather would try to stop her. She felt her cheeks burn, the skin seemed to go dense and then numb.

She did not shiver—the warmth that seemed to emanate from the very center of her being, where the baby grew, radiated and reached her fingertips as they gripped the handlebars. She flipped the gears; her legs pumped the pedals. She began to move against the headwind.

Claire paused as she passed the fruit stand, the prophetically named Eden Market. She would not be having this baby at all had it not been for two separate occurrences that had occurred here, at her neighborhood fruit and flower market, on that single day, last May.

She hadn't even remembered that it was a holiday that May Sunday—it was Mother's Day. Her own mother was long gone; she had died when Claire was only two. Claire had only wisps of memory—the scent of powder, cologne, the brush of a woman's silken lips as she drifted down to sleep. If Claire had any associations at all with Mother's Day, as a holiday, they were unpleasant: her father had remarried immediately (an insulting four weeks after) and to a woman, Herda, who seemed to have spawned from some Germanic version of a Grimm's tale. Herda put the step in stepmother, all right. Claire suspected that her father had married her because he could not afford child care, and he worked in the steel mills all day. So Herda, who arrived as a housekeeper for a small salary, stayed as his wife, without pay. In the end, her father had paid dearly, and so had Claire.

Her father lived in a tense marriage that seemed doomed to last. He had sold his soul for "three square" and his shirts folded.

But he and Herda looked at each other with a hate that was so powerful, it competed with love. They could never separate.

Claire had avoided them both, for many years now. On that Mother's Day, she would not even have considered buying lilacs or candy for Herda. Herda was the reason Claire had left home. Claire could not tolerate her father's choice—it was as if he had killed even the memories of her own mother, who, Claire had been told, had been joyous, free, and beautiful. Like Claire, her mother Lila had been a musician (only more classical, in the confines of their lives, she had played the church organ). There were photographs of Lila—she had been a pale blonde, big boned, like Claire, with the same full mouth and wide blue eyes. How could she have been replaced by Herda, a troll who wore knotted stockings and orthopedic sandals?

Even in Dooleyville, Pa. (Dullsville to Claire), Herda had been infamous for her parsimony: Herda washed plastic plates, and did not understand recycling even as a concept. She saved every container she had ever purchased, rinsed and stacked in the kitchen, in perilous piles, begrimed.

More seriously, Herda had been cruel to Claire, cruel like a stepmother in those awful fairy tales. It was no exaggeration that she would have preferred that Claire had died, too. But Claire had been no willing victim. Claire gave back what she got—when Herda slapped and spanked her, Claire cleverly had tucked a book under her pants, and Herda slammed her own hand. The first time Claire put on high heels, Herda called her a tramp, and Claire made a point of stepping on her stepmother's open-toed sandals as she squeezed past her in the container-crammed kitchen.

At sixteen, Claire had run away and never looked back to Dullsville. So on that Mother's Day, only seven months ago, she had no thought of Herda, but she had been recalling her own mother, in the soft focus of childhood memory. Her mother had been good, she was almost sure of that. She remembered that flowery scent of her, the brush of her lips on her cheek. She recalled crying and crying, her mother rocking her to sleep. She had only one distinct memory of her mother but it was, as they say, "a beaut": she had been nursing her, and it apparently had been time to be weaned.

Claire had begged for one "last time" with her momma's "boobies" and her mother had hesitated, then laughed and said, "Oh why not? Yeah, sure." And so there it was, the taste of love, directly transmitted, lingering now, more than thirty-four years on the palette of pleasurable memory.

But on the Mother's Day in question, Claire had been resisting sentiments; she had even thought, Oh, Mother's Day, an excuse for an industry. Greeting cards and lilacs, single roses and chocolates—an industry invented to express love that should be there, unmarked by the calendar.

Then, on the line at the fruit and flower stand, her life changed: there had been a woman ahead of her on line. The woman was not exceptional, pretty in an ordinary way: a smallish woman, with straight brown hair, but she had been holding an extraordinary baby. The baby had looked at Claire. Claire could swear that the baby really did look at her, with utter and adult perception. She was wise, that baby: she stared at Claire with huge blue eyes, as if to ask some important question—*What? Why?*

Still, Claire would have just thought, nice baby, except for what had happened next. The mother had to juggle her purse, and packages, and she set the baby on the counter. It had been Claire who saw the baby start to slip, and she had acted, without thinking, pure reflex. Claire reached out and caught the baby before she could fall.

"Oh, God," the woman had said. *"Thank you . . ."*

She must have seen Claire's expression, for Claire had caught the baby and been captured herself. The scent of that baby's hair, the sweetness of her skin, the incredible density of her little being. The baby had a specific weight that was at once heavy and light within Claire's arms.

Later, Claire supposed it was that old maxim: *You don't know you are thirsty until you are given to drink.* Claire had breathed in that essence of baby and felt for the first time, the ache.

"Do you want to hold her for a minute?" the mother had asked.

Speechless, Claire had nodded. And she lived a lifetime in that minute, loved that baby, somehow truly fell in love with a stranger's baby, then kissed the downy soft head good-bye.

Did this incident with the baby have anything to do with what happened later? Was Claire under a spell later that night when she wandered back to the fruit stand?

Was the first baby a contemporary cupid? Maybe, Claire told herself. She pedaled harder, past the Eden Market. Who knew why things happened? Maybe it was all accidental. Her course had changed forever that night, and now, here she was, seven months later, on her way to a baby shower, even if her friends swore not to call it that.

Claire had resisted the idea of the party, but now that she was on her way, she could hardly wait. They would want to know everything. Claire savored the details, in anticipation of sharing the story of her romance.

She must have been smiling, because she passed a Latino man who called out to her, "Oh, *Mamacita!*" He loved her. Claire laughed, speeding past him.

It was strange what might lift your spirits . . . the lust of the Latino men in the neighborhood had been a sustaining and uplifting force. They pointed to her belly and smiled and made kissing noises. She knew some women might be offended; the men were so intimate with their eyes. She understood enough Spanish to translate: they wish they had been the one to . . .

"Yeah, yeah, yeah," she giggled, if she was pedaling by fast enough. "Love ya."

"Hey, beautiful." another man yelled.

It was impossible to tell if Claire really was beautiful. Everyone saw her as beautiful because she always seemed so happy. She did have a beautiful smile: her teeth were a tiny bit "buck," and she showed some gum, but her grin was good enough so that wherever she went, people commented on her smile.

"A million dollars for that smile," a man said when she turned the final corner onto Butane Street. He was just a bum, unkempt in an old military greatcoat and unfastened galoshes, but he smiled when he saw Claire.

She made a bright if incongruous sight on this winter night. She wore electric-colored sweatpants, several sweaters, a bright folkloric knit muffler, and a fuchsia bike helmet with a rearview mirror. Her red hair still flew behind her, escaping the helmet, and she was singing in Italian, as she pumped the pedals of her old mountain bike, *"La donna e mobile. . . ."*

The street was deserted save for a limousine, parked in front. The driver sat, dozing, his head slumped forward, but he kept the engine running, Claire supposed, for the heat. The street looked so empty, so safe, and the night was so cold, that Claire almost neglected to lock her bike. But she'd lived in New York for two decades, and by habit, she disengaged the front wheel and used a cable to secure the bike itself to a NO STANDING street sign.

The ride had invigorated her, but she paused to take another deep breath before entering the former Frankenheimer factory.

They would all be upstairs, waiting to see her. She had avoided everyone for so long, and she herself hid from the reasons why.

For an instant, she considered bolting, returning to Theresa House, her bird, the music, the status quo of the past six months. Sometimes, she thought, being pregnant seemed enough . . . as if she should just sit, and watch her belly grow, feel the heartbeat and the kicks, wait for the baby's entrance. She had felt oddly busy, while on the surface doing very little, or nothing at all.

But the night was deepening, the cold was sharper, biting through the sweaters when she had been in motion on the bike. Still, the headwind had exhilarated her—she had met the challenge to ride down here. She was used to carrying things, seventy-five-pound backpacks were her standard, so the baby didn't throw her much. Still, it probably was her last ride before the baby, she decided—her balance had been a bit tricky. But she had made it, that was the main thing.

Her biorhythm, which was now nocturnal, began to rise, and Claire could feel her cheeks flame: *Yeah, the night was young. I'm going to show 'em,* she thought, and went inside.

Upstairs, her friends waited. And waited. Claire arrived on International Claire Time: 7:35 P.M. She was over an hour late.

On the twelfth floor, Jessie was leading Martha to the door. She had picked up Martha's cape/coat, which she alone recognized as being made of the wool of an antelope that was on the endangered species list, the shahtoosh. She wondered if Martha knew the cape was illegal, that the importers had been fined and sent to prison. She debated whether to bring it up as she held out the coat so that Martha could slip her arms into it.

No, Jessie reasoned, tonight it was more important to get Martha out the door before Claire arrived. Or we will all be on the endangered list.

"But I want to see her!" Martha protested. "I'll stay just a minute more. . . ."

"Oh no," Jessie reminded her, "your reservation, Donald." There was a chorus from Nina, Lisbeth, and Sue Carol: "No, don't miss that dinner reservation."

"Donald," Jessie said, "his birthday. You can't let him sit in the restaurant . . . alone."

It almost worked. Martha was at the elevator, and Jessie had pushed the button, in every sense, when the buzzer sounded for the final time. Who could it be? There was only one person, it had to be, it was . . .

"Claire," they cried out in unison when she appeared, the elevator doors parting to reveal her there, pregnant but not so dramatically "showing," rather startlingly dressed in warm-ups and a knit cap, and holding her bicycle wheel. She pulled off her cap and let her fire red hair spill down to her shoulders. It was hard to say who was more lit than the other when Claire grinned, showing the gap between her front teeth as she looked at them, and they all cried out: "You look beautiful."

Chapter Twelve

In which the group is reunited and Claire spills the beans.

"You look beautiful."

"You look beautiful."

Yeah, yeah. She looked beautiful. Claire didn't think she was—beautiful. She had big feet; she was a bit broad-shouldered; and of course she had those slightly overdeveloped thighs and calves, from all her biking, hiking. She was a great strapping "girl" (at thirty-six, not really a girl but still girlish) with a big smile and a laugh to match. *Yeah, yeah: she was glad to see them.*

In fact, she was instantly stricken that she had stayed hidden for so long.

"I know, I know," she apologized en masse. "I've been bad—but I've been better. I should have called."

She moved quickly into the center of the loft, and they surrounded her. For an odd instant, Claire felt as she did when she traveled in the more exotic outbacks and remote islands—that she was so different from the natives, that she had become an object of intense curiosity. In New Guinea, the aboriginal people had reached out for her curling red hair and tried to rub off her freckles. Here, the women touched her stomach, trying to detect the baby, as if this was their introduction to the life inside her, as well

235

as their reunion with the old friend they now laughingly greeted as "Hey, Mama."

"So?" said Martha, demanding an explanation.

"I know, I know," Claire apologized. "I kept meaning to call. . . ."

"I left you seven messages," Martha said.

"I kept meaning to call, to call you all . . . but then I didn't, and then it seemed too much time had gone by."

The instant she had entered 12A, Claire was glad that she had come: the loft was warm, lit, and five smiling women greeted her, all near-screaming their delight. For a moment, time eclipsed, and they were all just twenty, hardly more than girls, and squealing like children.

She *was* sorry. Claire saw what the women had given, the preparation that Jessie had done: the heaped presents, the cradle. She appreciated the party atmosphere of the loft, the candles, the fire, the set table and steaming pots on the stove. The scents of roast Cornish hen, rosemary, garlic, onion, and potato perfumed the air. Claire inhaled it all: Oh, God, she was hungry. This was no ordinary hunger; this was biological force majeure.

The hunger hit as an irresistible impulse. It was the baby, of course, drawing nourishment, needing more. Claire had finally understood, in the past few months, all those tales of possession, of a little demon crouched, devouring someone from within. Only last night, she had sawed through an entire turkey breast, eating it in an automatic, uncontrolled way, bite after bite until it was gone. Then she had ordered Chinese takeout for two, for herself, and since no one was looking, licked the plate clean.

Now Claire swooped to the coffee table and scooped up a fistful of tortilla chips. "Forgive me: I'm rapacious. Starved. Stop me if you want any. . . ."

"It doesn't matter," Jessie said, accepting Claire's apologies for the group. "It's okay. It's all for you. Nothing matters but—you're here."

Claire, while munching and exclaiming over the green chili as a hot dip, also cried out over the gifts, their generosity, their forgiveness. She was humble: "All this for me?"

"It's from all of us," Martha said. "I bought the complete layette and the crib."

Oh, God, she's starting, Jessie realized. She refastened the shahtoosh cape on Martha's shoulders

"Great, you got to see Claire," she said, physically moving Martha now. "Just in time so you can get to the restaurant. It worked out perfectly." She looked over at Claire. "Martha has to leave, it's Donald's birthday: he's waiting at Vert."

She felt Martha balk on the very doorstep. "I just want to see her open my gifts . . . I'll stay another minute."

Shit, Jessie finally cursed, in her head. She had a strong premonition now. She didn't even want to acknowledge it to herself, but she could see a conversational collision, dead ahead, as clearly as she would have noted a ROAD CLOSED sign on the highway.

Meanwhile, Claire was digging in her backpack; and she pulled forth a package, wrapped in a plain brown paper bag.

"Jessie . . . this is for you, before I forget. I've been meaning to give you this for months. I hope you like it."

"I love it," Jessie said, producing the hunk of what appeared to be sandstone from the package. "What is it?"

Claire was busy apologizing to the others: "I have things for all of you; I just keep forgetting to give them to you."

Martha snatched the stone. "This looks like mortar." Nina asked if it was "rock cocaine." Sue Carol said could she have some, if it was?

"It's a piece of the Wailing Wall," Claire said. "I picked it up last year when I was in Israel."

They all stared at her.

"It fell off the Wailing Wall. It really was . . . just lying there, I wouldn't hack it off."

As if they had rehearsed this ritual a hundred times, the women moved their orbit to the sofas and added a few occasional chairs, so that they formed a circle, with Claire at the crown. She sat in the center of the larger of the two couches, and the others gathered around her.

Jessie, as hostess, felt a slight reprieve: the mood in the room was good. There was a general ebullience communicated by Claire; and of course, in the social arena, she was saved from disaster—her guest of honor had materialized.

Now, if only Martha would leave, they stood a chance for a celebratory evening. The food was fresh from the oven, sizzling hot, and she could serve as soon as Martha departed.

Martha, in fact, began to appear somewhat more manageable. She had not taken a seat, as the others had. She was demonstrating to Claire how to raise and lower the bars of the portable crib. In the roomful of six women, several conversations were crisscrossing. While Claire was nodding, in happy oblivion, at Martha's crib demonstration, she was also describing how the Wailing Wall had felt to Sue Carol and Lisbeth, who seemed especially interested.

"It feels a bit . . . soapy," Lisbeth said, rubbing the sacred stone.

"That," said Claire, "is from millions of people touching it. The whole wall feels faintly coated. I guess that's what happens when millions of hands touch something, it gets . . . soapy." They passed the stone, hand to hand.

"Can you feel all the concentrated prayer?"

Lisbeth said that she did. She seemed reluctant to let go.

Eventually, she passed the stone to Sue Carol, who said, "Maybe it'll give me luck."

Claire told them how the religious Jews offer their prayers and wishes, written on tiny scraps of paper; these messages are inserted in crevices in the wall.

"It's very sacred," she said. "Seeing them, stuffed everywhere. Some of the messages fall out . . . hundreds of them. They look like . . . spitballs."

"Did you leave one there?" Martha wanted to know.

"You bet," Claire said, with what struck Jessie as unusual intensity. But then Claire grinned, "Oh, I forget."

She rose and moved over to the crib, where Martha was pulling out more and more of the presents that she had packed inside. "More from me," Martha cried. Claire walked over; as Claire walked, Jessie noticed her friend reached back and touched her spine, as if her back might be feeling the weight of the baby. It was the first "pregnant" gesture Claire performed; and Martha noted it also.

"Should you be riding a bike?"

"It's easier than walking." Claire laughed.

Uh-oh, here it comes. Jessie almost squeezed her eyes shut; if only she could shut her ears, too. Martha was "starting". . . .

"I question the wisdom of riding a bike. Your center of gravity must be way off. Also, it is supposed to snow again. How will you get home?"

Claire ignored the last part of the question but pirouetted before Martha to answer the first.

Claire straightened. "I don't *have* a center of gravity. Maybe this"—she touched her belly (the second "pregnant" gesture of the evening)—"is correcting it. I'm faster against a headwind than I ever was before."

"What if you go into labor on the bicycle?" Martha asked.

Jessie pressed for the elevator. "Martha, you made me promise. *It's time.*"

But Claire was taunting Martha: she had her hands on her hips, and she was grinning her biggest grin and saying, "Well, it might be wonderful, Martha. I just happened to hear the most fantastic story of this woman racer out in Missouri or someplace, and she *did* go into labor—during a hurricane. Her husband was not around, so she just rode all the way to the hospital herself . . . fourteen miles through heavy rain, and when she got there, she had a fast, really easy delivery. And she left the hospital the next day."

"On the bike?" Lisbeth wanted to know.

"Oh, yeah." Claire threw a wink at the group gathered around the couch. Martha couldn't see her expression as she added, "She had a baby seat on the back. So you see, there is nothing to worry about."

Martha walked over to her, her mouth pursed. Jessie saw "the look" and recognized it—the criticism masked as concern. Oh, no, she thought, bombs away.

"That woman," Martha said, biting off the word, "had nothing to do with you. That woman was . . . *married.*"

The word *married* stayed in the air, like an odor.

"Donald," Jessie reminded Martha. The elevator reached the loft, the doors gaped in invitation. Martha made a quick nudge with her elbow. "Wait . . ."

Claire ignored her; she was clowning, strutting her stuff for the other women. "I never felt better. It clears up your skin . . . and look at this." She tugged her sweater to reveal—"*Cleavage.*"

She did a mock "dip" and came up crunching the last of the crudités.

"Aren't you nauseated in the morning?" Martha asked.

"I'm never up in the morning. I slept through the first three months."

"The first trimester," Martha said.

"Is that what it's called? I missed it then. The first trimester."

"When the brain is formed," Martha notified her.

"Oh, is that when it happens?"

Was Claire unnerved? She was devouring the hors d'oeuvres, popping grape tomatoes in her mouth rapid-fire, crunching through stalks of celery.

"Delicious," she declared. "Stop me. I'll eat the coffee table. I have no control. I'm so hungry all the time. I just can't stop myself. This afternoon, I bit into a chunk of Styrofoam."

"The demented appetite," Martha diagnosed.

"Please, Martha," Jessie begged. "Your dinner. Donald . . ."

"In a second . . ."

"Claire, have something to drink . . . sit down." Jessie, distracted, did not realize that she had set the trap.

"Oh, lovely, I'm dying for something. Goodie." Claire moved straight for the open, breathing bottle of Shiraz. "Rosemary Estates, our house wine," she said, pouring herself a full goblet.

"It was only twelve ninety-nine on sale," Nina commented, refilling her own glass. "But it tastes like fifty dollars, and it'll dull the pain."

"It'll destroy your DNA, that's what it will do." Martha moved toward the bar. For Jessie, it was like watching a bus accident. It seemed to take forever, but in actual time, it was over in a second. Martha reached for Claire's glass before she could sip.

"Oh, come on," Claire said, "a little red wine . . ."

Sue Carol added support. "Don't hurt, don't hurt a bit. Listen, my mama drank juleps all day when she was carrying and look at me."

Martha did look at Sue Carol. "Uh-huh," she said. Then turning to Claire, "Your chromosomes—"

"Are already wrecked."

Claire looped her arm around Jessie, who did not know what to do. They did arrest pregnant women who committed substance abuse didn't they? And now there were warnings on the subway, and even on some beers. "Hazardous to the unborn child." Yet, what about Europe, where everyone had wine with dinner, for all time? Were entire nations defective?

"What about Europe?" Jessie said, sounding weak, even to herself.

"*Look at them,*" Martha almost spat. "They could do better. Maybe wine is the explanation for everything. The world wars . . . their weird movies. I went to six countries last summer, and I saw a lot of subnormals. Just because a whole continent is careless is no excuse for you, Claire. You know better. Or at least, I thought you did."

There was a pause. Jessie could feel tension rip through Claire like electric current. A short. She knew Claire, for all her good humor, could also flare. Claire had her own anger, buried deep, volcanic during rare eruptions. If conditions became too combustible, Claire could blow.

"Martha," Claire said, being careful to enunciate, just like Martha herself, "thinks I am bad to have a baby without a husband."

"I didn't say that," Martha said. "Are you engaged?"

"No," Claire said with a laugh. "I'm pregnant, I don't want a husband. I don't have room for one in my apartment."

"But you're still seeing him?"

Jessie felt her hostess resolve strengthen. "Please, Martha, this is a party, not an inquisition."

"It's all right," Claire said.

Lisbeth said, "Oh, you promised. You promised you would tell us about him when we were all together."

Jessie loved Lisbeth, but at that moment she could have killed her.

"Don't even think about getting married," Sue Carol contributed. "Believe me, you are better off, darlin'."

"Come on, tell us about the guy," Nina invited.

"When I've had something to drink," Claire said. She was still smiling, but her tone was too level.

"How about some Pellegrino? I have two kinds of mineral water, sparkling or flat?" Jessie suggested without hope.

"No, I love red wine." Claire grabbed her glass by the stem and raised it to her lips. She grinned. "I'll just inhale it." She breathed in, gave a great mock sigh.

"There go the arms and legs," Claire said, sniffing.

Is she really going to drink? Jessie wondered.

Claire moved back to the couch, the coffee table. She scooped up more green chili with the tortilla chips. She set down the glass.

Yes, Jessie silently cheered. Just eat. She could see Martha, almost swaying in indecision. Martha could not bring herself to leave, while this drink issue was still undecided.

Claire plopped down on the sofa and started ripping open the presents. Jessie noted the first gift, the glossy white package from Lisbeth.

"Open mine first, I have to leave," Martha instructed.

Yes, open hers, so she will leave, Jessie mentally directed.

Claire had already lifted up the lace tatted baby dress. "Oh," they all cried. "It's exquisite."

Lisbeth edged closer, taking a seat beside Claire. "It is lovely, isn't it? I couldn't resist." Claire pulled out a bonnet that was also in the box.

She tied it on her own head, before Martha could say: "That's for the baby."

"It's nice on Claire," Lisbeth defended. "And the other night-gown is for you. I see you two, all in lace."

"I hope it's a girl," Claire said.

"You mean you don't know? Didn't you have an amnio?" Martha asked.

Claire didn't answer.

To fill the awkward moment, Nina jumped up and almost shoved her gift into Claire's hands. "It's from me, and my mother . . . you remember her."

Claire opened the box and lifted up the baby doll.

"It's anatomically correct," Nina said.

Jessie noticed that, as Lisbeth had, Nina colored, flushed with new emotion as she offered her gift; she gave Claire the gift, but she also waited for that moment of acceptance, to see joy in the other woman's eyes. Each friend wanted to present the right gift, you could see that, but there was also something more, some antic-ipation never felt before.

Claire's not just the first, Jessie thought. She may be the only one of us to have a baby.

She heard herself say, "The cradle is from *me*. It's over a hundred years old, from Lapland."

Claire ran her hand over the smooth wood and sighed, "Oh, Jessie. . . ."

"Interesting," Martha said. "Looks like something for the Smithsonian. Is it safety approved?" She began to tell tales of babies whose heads got trapped between the bars of outdated quaint cribs.

Claire set the little doll into the cradle. They all leaned over the ancient wooden baby bed and stared down at the naked little doll. It was a boy.

"When I say correct, I mean co-*rrect.*" Nina laughed.

Jessie was struck by how lifelike the baby appeared; she was also stunned how it felt to see the "baby" in the cradle she had bought so long ago, in her own hope of someday. . . . Oh, stop, she ordered herself.

"You know it's uncanny," Claire was saying, holding the doll up again. "This actually looks like the father."

"He was plastic, with blond acrylic hair?" Lisbeth asked.

"So?" Martha wanted to know.

"You did promise to tell us."

"Come on. . . ." Sue Carol invited. "Give us the sordid details."

"Where is he?" Martha asked.

"He went back to Athens," Claire answered.

"Athens?"

"Georgia," Sue Carol cried.

"Greece," Claire corrected her.

"Greece." Martha's pronunciation evoked rancid olive oil, suspect souvlaki.

Even Jessie, who did not usually pry, wanted to know. "Is he Greek?"

No, it turned out, he just worked there.

The women settled into a semicircle now. Sue Carol sat crosslegged on the floor; she was holding a small pillow from her own home, Jessie noted. Lisbeth sat beside Claire and Nina on her other side. Jessie perched on the edge of the couch. Martha stood, both hands on the back of Jessie's old easy chair: she still seemed poised to go. It was possible she would leave before an outright disaster, Jessie told herself, without conviction, if Martha could get enough information to satisfy her curiosity, or prejudgment, whatever it was. But Martha's eyes fastened onto Claire. Her expression was something Jessie had never seen before; Martha's face actually seemed to contort in envy and curiosity, then purse into pruney disapproval.

Claire, for her part, was now clearly enjoying herself. She indeed had the prescribed "glow"; her freckled face shone in the candlelight. There was pride in her voice when she said, "He's an architectural engineer."

"Really?" Even Martha sounded impressed. "I love architectural engineers. And that's a good sign. He must be educated, intelligent, and the general rule is the child will inherit the *higher* intelligence."

Oh shut up, Jessie thought. The others looked at Martha.

"Well, that's good, isn't it?" Martha said, wondering why they all stared at her. Then she said the line that they had loved to quote, way back, in the Theresa House days, when Sue Carol used to entertain them with dead-on Martha impersonations: "Did I *say* something?"

"Did I say something?" Martha was asking. They all giggled.

"You're late. You are going to miss your entire dinner with Donald," Jessie reminded her.

"I have to hear this, then I'll go," Martha said.

"He's restoring the Acropolis," Claire announced.

Jessie felt relief from a worry she had not acknowledged that she had.

"I love him already," she told Claire.

"That's a good one," Sue Carol said.

"Um," Lisbeth said, "an artist. Steve's an artist."

"They're all artists," Nina said. Instantly, she regretted how bitter she sounded. The Celestial Seasonings guy had left this tinny aftertaste, or was she in some metabolic overdrive, the longed-for but odd condition known as "ketosis"? The cooking aromas were driving her to salivation; no one can detect a cooking scent better than a dieter. Nina felt like a bloodhound. She could pick up a trace of chervil. The upcoming saga of sexual romance had whetted her appetite, too; her gut rumbled, in combined hunger and frustration.

Don't be toxic, Nina ordered herself, Claire's adventure appears to have ended happily.

"He restores antiquities," Claire continued. "He works for hours, days, weeks, even years sometimes, just to lift some delicate object out of the rubble."

"When will he be done?" Martha demanded.

"I don't think the Acropolis is ever *done,*" Jessie told her. "It's kind of ongoing, isn't it?"

"The Acropolis is forever," Lisbeth added in her dreamy way.

"He drags the job out," Martha pronounced. Then, the first direct hit:

"So? So he won't be back in time for the baby?"

Claire looked at her. "I don't know, Martha." She stared straight back at Martha and said in a very low, level voice, "I don't know if we should see each other again. It might not be the same. These things are pretty mysterious. We had a great night. . . ."

"Just *one?*" Martha sounded surprised, as if this was worse than even she had anticipated.

"Not just one. The one." Claire beamed. Should she go into detail? About the Night of Nights? She had never spoken this aloud, but she had relived it in her mind a thousand times, her best night, the Night of Nights, *oh yes.*

She teased them a bit, even while deciding to tell. "In the morning, we just kind of wanted to escape from each other. We had rug burns on our thighs. . . ."

"Rug burn?" Martha cried.

"From friction against the carpet," Nina translated.

Martha blinked; she was trying to imagine how on earth that happened.

"Sometimes, when you have been so close, you just have to flee."

"It was so intense." Lisbeth understood. "When the boundaries vanish, it seems dangerous, as if you could disappear."

Jessie thought, Oh, yes, you can disappear. She was thinking of Jesse Dark. She glanced at the kitchen stove: she could just read the clock. It was ten to eight. She felt as if all her internal organs realigned, tensing to hear the phone when it would ring.

"Hey," said Sue Carol, from her position on the floor. She was leaning back against the base of the sofa. She was drinking pretty steadily, Jessie noted. Sue Carol had taken one of the Shiraz bottles intended for the actual dinner and set it on the floor beside her. Jessie made a mental note: to watch if Sue Carol had too much. Sue Carol seemed to be refilling her glass every other minute. When Sue Carol drank too much, she could become, well, strange. On a more pragmatic level, Jessie wondered if Sue Carol keeps up her wine intake, will there be enough of the good wine to last through dinner?

"Hey, you're skipping the good parts," Sue Carol said.

"You were in love, weren't you? You wouldn't have the baby if you weren't in love?" Lisbeth asked.

Jessie looked at Lisbeth's glass and was both relieved and surprised to see that it still held the vodka. She was startled to see that Lisbeth had taken out her pack of Gauloises and blue cobalt lighter and rested them on the coffee table. She isn't going to smoke, is she?

"Was he worth the trouble?" Nina wanted to know.

The look on Claire's face was the answer—her face softened, right in front of them. Oh, yes, Jessie thought, you're in love. . . .

"I was in it, all right," Claire said, "that's why I decided to go ahead and have the baby. Who knows when I'll fall in love again? It could be years."

"And by then you'd be infertile," Martha said. She then gave her formula for conception: the Martha Plan—four years to have a baby, two to seek out the perfect partner, one year to see if you can stand him. . . .

They had all heard this before and laughed. The Martha Plan was so un-Claire-like. Whatever she was or was not, Claire was a creature of the moment; there was no Claire Plan. Or so they thought.

Claire was reliving the Night of Nights. Now, sitting here, in this room, lit by candles, while an increasing wind blew outside, and low music played, Claire leaned back and enjoyed the luxury of recollection.

She told the women how she'd spotted him, The Man, in her peripheral vision.

"He was somewhere to my right, near the tangelos," she began. "And you know, how you notice someone or you don't? How you make an instant decision? Yes or no?"

"Yes," Jessie said. She was thinking of the night in Colorado: *Oh, yes.*

"Yes, handsome, interesting, I thought, but I did not see a way to know him," Claire was saying. Then it was out of her hands, literally: he took the avocado she had been holding and said, "Here, let me get you a ripe one."

They had had a funny conversation then. "We talked about the difference between the fruit outside and the fruit inside. Like how do the fruit store owners make the decision?"

"They're trying to move the rotten fruit," Martha said.

"No, it wasn't rotten, only ripe."

"Hum, you buy that fruit . . . those cheap raspberries. They have fungus," Martha said.

Fungus. STD of fruit.

"His name was David," she told them. And he had spoken easily with her. She had, of course, liked the way he looked: his long, lean body, the gold beard, sea green eyes. She noticed his hands, large, with prominent blood vessels, tanned from outdoor work. He had wonderful eyes, she said . . . and that was most important.

"We just *knew*," Claire reported, "we knew, the second we looked into one another's eyes . . . knew we'd be together and it would be great."

"This is a man," Martha said. "You met at a fruit stand. You're not saying . . . ? You conceived a child with someone from the street?"

"It didn't happen on the street. We went up to my room," Claire said.

"But you met on the street?"

"She said the fruit store," Lisbeth defended.

Martha delivered another maxim: "Anything not at a party, through work, or through friends is 'on the street.'"

Claire argued, "What difference did it make where you met them? They're the same people they are at parties or at work."

"No, they are not," Martha said. "No matter what happens next, they are privately thinking, The corner of Fifty-sixth and Ninth, and then the contempt and abuse can start, because you were something he found . . . *on the street.*"

"You are going to miss your dinner, Martha," Jessie said, knowing this was now the eleventh hour.

"In a second," Martha said. "So you took this person from the street up to three twelve, and . . . ?"

"And made love to him, yes, and conceived this baby, yes," Claire confirmed.

"On the street," Martha kept saying. "On the street."

"Oh, you can meet good ones on the street," Nina snapped. "You met Donald on the beach, what's the difference? So there was sand."

"It was not the beach, it was the Vineyard. And we were introduced—we had the same dentist."

"You're in the clear," Sue Carol said, in a poisonous voice.

Uh-oh, Jessie realized, Sue Carol seemed to be deteriorating; even her "good" eye looked reddened, set in an inebriated squint. But Sue Carol could be dealt with: she would cry, pass out, or vanish to the bathroom to "self-medicate." She might even leave, run back to her own apartment, back to Bob. Sue Carol was a secondary problem to Jessie: Martha remained the main obstacle to a successful evening. She had to leave before she committed some irreparable harm.

Jessie almost dragged Martha by the shahtoosh cape back to the door.

"Listen, Martha, it's time for you to go anyway. But could you please not be so . . . so judgmental?"

Martha gave her the "concerned" expression. "Jessie, now *you* worry me. I don't know what you think of this, but I can't sit here silently and listen to another word about this Greek creep that she met on the street at the height of a sexual epidemic."

Jessie looked over to see if Claire heard. Thankfully, Claire seemed utterly transported and was going on about how the man told her which bananas to buy—the spotted brown ones not the green ones.

" 'They look bad,' " he told me, " 'but they taste good.' "

Jessie hissed in her lowest whisper to Martha, so that Claire could not hear: "Listen, he obviously wasn't in a risk group."

"They're all in a risk group. They're out there, dealing death with their . . . And now Viagra extends the time they can go around doing it."

"Why do you seem so *glad?*" Jessie whispered. "It's too late now, anyway."

"I'm not glad, I'm sad, sad to be proven right again. I was right all along. I always said it was unhygienic. That you have to have your men tested. I was right to shine high-intensity flashlights on men's genitals as early as 1984! Then I was only looking for herpes."

Nina seemed to overhear and want to partake in both conversations. "Hoping to find some . . . ," she murmured in Martha's direction.

Then Jessie *ssssh*ed her, rolling her eyes in Claire's direction. "Watch it, Martha. . . ."

"*I* should watch it?" she hissed back. "What about Claire?"

"Did he pay for the fruit?" Nina wanted to know.

Martha leaned forward, finally, a sensible question. "Did he pay for the fruit?" Martha repeated.

"I did," Claire said.

There was a silence as the information was absorbed.

"He bought some Hawaiian pineapple," Claire added.

"Big spender," said Martha.

Claire didn't appear to hear her. "It was just understood," she was saying, a catch in her voice, "that we were going to eat all the fruit together. He even got some yogurt, the sixteen-ounce size. And he said he was going to show me how he makes this really great fruit salad. . . . We just naturally started walking back to my apartment—it was as if we had known each other a long time. And when we got up to my room, he really loved my having the bed in the center of the room."

"Well, why the hell not?" Sue Carol asked.

"Not everyone has liked it there," Claire confided. "Then he mixed up the fruit salad." She paused, maddeningly, to munch tortilla chip crumbles. The hors d'oeuvres were gone. Claire pasted the bits to her fingers, licked the tips.

Nina moved closer to her, and Jessie could see that she was very involved in the account, almost as if her own life depended on it. What on earth had happened to Nina this afternoon? She was so unlike herself. Her face, in repose, sagged, sad in a way Jessie had never observed. Even her voice sounded wan. "Before you did anything?" she asked Claire.

"Yes, before we did anything," was the answer. According to Claire, this David said, "It's really better if it sits for fifteen minutes first. The juices flow."

"Oh, I like him," Lisbeth cried out. "Is it okay if I smoke?"

"No," Martha said.

Claire offered to sit downwind.

"No way," Martha said. "Secondhand smoke is more lethal."

"Then can I bum one?" Claire asked.

Martha almost screamed. She could still taste the nicotine gum in her mouth, which did nothing to sweeten her response. "Go on, finish the story," she said to Claire. "I have to go, but I need to hear the rest."

The other women had already started buzzing among themselves about how much they liked "him." The consensus so far was that he sounded "really good."

"At least he mixed the salad, that's something," Martha said.

Claire blushed: should she tell all? The memory was still fresh.

She was recalling David—how he explored the borders of her domain. Why did men prowl around your apartment first? "He really explored three twelve." She asked the others, "Why do men always do that? Open the doors? Poke around? It's almost like they are looking for something."

Sue Carol suddenly seemed more sober. "They are looking for signs of other men."

Later, Jessie would remember her remark as more telling than it had sounded. At that moment she, too, was caught up in reliving the drama that had occurred in Claire's studio/bedroom. Claire was radiant now, extolling everything about this man: how he had recognized her musical instruments—he had known what they were. "The first man who could identify a krummhorn."

Nina was anxious to cut to the chase. "When did you take off your clothes?"

Claire looked at her and blushed, her face so red her freckles seemed to blend into themselves, like a Seurat seen from a distance. She looked down at her curving lap. Her voice went even lower, to convey the sexual hush that followed.

She whispered, "He said, 'Let's take a bath together first.'"

"And what did you say?" Nina had to know.

"I said okay." Claire related something Jessie could appreciate, how, by luck, she had just cleaned the bathtub and had a special bottle of oil and some scented candles.

"That certainly was fortunate," Martha commented.

"Who went in first?" Sue Carol asked.

"He did."

"I'm trying to picture it: what was he wearing?"

Claire's voice was soft, low: the women leaned closer to hear her. "Jeans," she said. "A shirt. Plain white underpants. Gray socks. He had a really nice body underneath. He looked beautiful."

"Men aren't beautiful," Martha said.

"This one was. He has this great mouth—"

"God knows where that mouth has been," Martha interrupted. The others *shssh*ed her now.

". . . with the full lips," Claire was saying, "really good for kissing. . . ."

"I don't like them too full. It can get sloppy," Martha added.

"He didn't . . . get sloppy. Oh, kissing is a talent," Claire declared.

Jessie privately agreed, recalling Jesse Dark's hard kisses, how she had initially not preferred that style, then melted down in response. Yes, talent was involved.

"Well, Bob's are famous," Sue Carol confided.

"Donald's lips have a lovely, dry texture," Martha contributed.

"Did he have a big one?" Nina asked.

The others laughed, but they wanted to know, too. "There are other considerations than how long a man's member is," Martha said.

"Member?" Jessie said. "Sounds like it belongs to a club."

"It does," Sue Carol said.

Nina agreed. "But I wasn't thinking so much of length as width."

They then made a big to-do of *sssh*ing her. Claire smiled at Nina and said, "Just right."

Nina seemed satisfied. "Did he say you had a beautiful body?"

"He didn't comment. We just greeted each other like old friends."

"Who happened to meet in the bathtub," Martha interjected.

No one paid any attention to her now. They were under the spell of Claire's whispered account. Even Martha leaned forward as Claire said, "The candles were burning . . . we smoked a little grass . . . and the room turned iridescent, like the bubbles; we played with them, then we dried each other off. I have these big rough towels that feel so good, I heat them on top of the radiator."

Jessie was impressed. "I'm gaining fresh insight into your life, Claire."

"I'm going to kill myself," Lisbeth said.

"Go on," Nina invited.

"Yes, go on," Sue Carol urged. "Don't leave me hanging."

Claire flushed again, and to their surprise, stood up and walked to the window, to stare out at the cityscape.

"I can't look at you and tell you this," she said. Her voice dropped so low the women all tilted toward her in a tropism of sexual curiosity. Claire continued, "Oh, I don't know what happened next . . . it gets fuzzy. I guess he turned on my radio. And I remember saying, 'Would you like to dance?' And he said, in this really low voice . . . it was different from his usual one, 'Yes, I'd like to. . . .' "

Claire turned slightly toward them.

"We never did dance," she confessed. "I think we took maybe one step. And that was it. We just stood there. It was as if we could wait . . . to start. I don't know, it seemed . . . momentous but I think"—she gave the group her smile—"we could still laugh. My knees just went. I started to sink to the floor and then . . . he whispered it into my hair, so low, I couldn't understand a word except that he had asked a question. 'Do you like . . . something or other?' "

"And what did you say?" Nina asked.

"I said yes." She gave a soft laugh, remembering. "Apparently, I was ready to agree to anything. Maybe he just said, 'Do you like me?' " She shook her head. "Oh, I don't know. Anyway, I remember we were kissing, and I could feel the bristle on his upper lip . . .

and the feel of his cheek against mine. . . . And then, well, it seemed accidental. Sometimes it seemed as if we weren't moving at all . . . except for the tremble in our arms, and then the tremble was inside us too and. . . ."

Claire turned back to the window. "And then, well, we fell asleep on the floor and woke up later. It was very dark. I woke up first and watched him sleep. He must have somehow felt me watching—he opened his eyes right away."

Her voice dropped down so they could almost not hear as she finished. "And I'll never forget how he smiled."

The women stayed silent, as if they were physically absorbing the story. They didn't move until Claire tried to break the spell by laughing and cracking a joke. "Hey, don't quote me."

She had not meant to relate so much, was it a mistake? Would the memory disintegrate? Her eyes met Jessie's, but Jessie seemed tranced out, as if she had mentally gone somewhere far away. And she had—Jessie was back in Coyoteville, in the motel room, reliving her own moments of sexual suspense.

For every woman in the room, Claire's tale had provoked a response. Now they recalled those rare moments when men and women connect, truly. For some of the women, her account served to return them to permanent markers in their memory, beyond the best times, to that rare union that was something sacred. For those who did not have such a memory, another reaction set in, like gangrene.

How long the women would have remained in their separate reveries, under the influence of this account, we don't know because Martha's cell phone beeped. It was Donald. He was at the restaurant.

"Oh, God. You've got to go!" Jessie snapped back into the moment and led Martha closer toward the elevator. She pressed the button, again. Please God, Jessie prayed, let her get in this time.

"No, no," Martha was saying into the tiny phone.

"Listen, sweetie. You have to understand. I'm so so sorry . . . this is very important." She cupped her hand over the phone. "I can't talk, they're all around me. I'll tell you everything later. . . . It's absolutely essential that I"—she eyed the group—"*stay.*"

We're doomed, Jessie thought.

"Don't make this sacrifice," she said to Martha, although she knew it was hopeless. The others stood frozen, reacting to the realization that Martha would now be with them for the duration.

Jessie, seeing her friends' stricken faces, performed by hostess reflex. She lifted her glass and said, "A toast. A toast to Claire."

They all raised their wineglasses, including Claire. Jessie did not actually see Martha make her move—a running dive for the wine before Claire could sip. But she did see the result: the wine spilled, and a stain, as if from a fatal wound, spread across Martha's chest as Claire's glass splashed onto her. The toast proceeded in a moment of utter chaos; the words had already escaped their lips and had their own momentum:

"To Claire."

And at that exact moment Jessie thought to check the stove clock, and saw that it was five after eight. He had not, after all, called.

She felt her spirit, which had risen with Claire's account, plummet. How could she have been mistaken about this man? She had been so sure. . . . Damnit now, she was so beyond waiting for a man to call, it made her burn with rage. She wanted to break her new cell phone—kill the silent messenger.

She had forgotten what it felt like to fall in love; she had forgotten this, too; the sickening fall from safety, the crash after flying.

Jessie looked at Claire, envied her, envied her casual pride, her total independence. Claire Molinaro waits for no man to call. Claire was famous, in their circle, for saying she would have none of that waiting around for the cell phone to beep business. Claire Molinaro really did not wait: maybe she cared, but she did not brood. She was emotionally transient, she moved on.

I wish I could be more like Claire, thought Jessie, instead of being filled with self-loathing for doing what she was—waiting for both her cell phone *and* her kitchen wall phone to ring. She had given Jesse Dark both numbers and her E-mail, rawspace@earth-link.net. These days, there were too many ways for a man not to keep in touch. She felt the urge to check all of them . . . voice mail, message machine, and E-mail. *Oh, for the days of Emma Bovary, when you could get your bad news, or your "Dear Emma" on scrawled parchment, in an attractive wicker basket.*

What exactly had Jesse said? "Eight. . . . My time is your time"? Why did he have to put things so obliquely? Did that possibly translate into his calling at eight his time, which would be ten o'clock here in New York?

Jessie decided to indulge herself awhile longer, not to take the dive: he'll call at ten, she decided. His time is my time.

She chose to believe in Jesse Dark, and in love, for another two hours, anyway. *"L'chaim,"* she said, raising her glass to Claire. "To life."

"Skol," said Martha, through her glass, darkly.

Chapter Thirteen

Four courses: Sue Carol produces "the evidence"; Lisbeth goes up in smoke; Nina breaks her diet; Martha goes flambé.

Dinner Is Served

Jessie transferred the golden, crisped hens to a serving platter and garnished them with chervil. She set the roasted fingerling potatoes around the hens. I wonder if he left me an E-mail, she was thinking as she tossed the salad. Jesse Dark avengeanasazi.com.

While Martha was in the bathroom, rinsing her stained blouse with salt and club soda, the women talked about her briefly, "behind her back."

"Well, I called it," Nina said. "I knew Martha would never leave."

"She's a little tactless," Lisbeth whispered to Claire.

"Promise you won't let her upset you, no matter what she says?" Jessie said.

"I thrive on disapproval," Claire answered. "It reminds me of home."

"Seriously," said Jessie sotto voce. "If she gets more crazed, I will ask her to leave . . . *forever.*"

"Oh, you wouldn't ask Ivan the Terrible to leave. You're relentlessly polite," said Sue Carol.

"Oh, just watch me: I have a threshold, and she is at the brink.

One more truly terrible, hurtful remark and she is out of here." They heard the water run in the bathroom. *Martha.*

Then it hit Jessie, just as she burned her finger as she mistakenly touched the saucepan handle that rested too near the gas burner. "The hens," she cried out. "I only bought five."

"Martha can have mine," Nina said. "Ice water," she said, indicating Jessie's finger. Jessie plunged her finger into a glass of ice water, stunned at how successful the treatment was. At least she would not be permanently scarred by tonight's dinner party. "Thank you," she said to Nina.

"I'm almost a doctor," Nina remarked.

"I remember," Martha said, a bright new smile applied in mauve lipstick. She emerged from the bathroom. "I remember when you wanted to be a neurosurgeon."

"It was just an interest," Nina said. "I liked reading about the ancient Egyptians, how they drilled right into people's heads."

"Trepanning," Lisbeth said. "They called it trepanning. It let a lot of pressure off the ancient brain. The Egyptians had such marvelous ideas, the afterlife, the preparations . . . the decoration of the tombs. Isn't it fascinating that every culture had some version of the same belief system? The gods of the underworld, a journey to the next world. Doesn't it make you wonder?"

"Where is Egypt today?" Martha asked. "It's not happening for them. Even tourism is down. Since the tourists were beheaded by the whachamacallits at the pyramids—that was a deal breaker. Donald and I have now had to rule out so many places for our honeymoon. Afghanistan is over."

As she set out the hot platters, Jessie could hear Claire saying how it would be nice to see David again, but "these things were pretty mysterious. . . . If I don't see him again, that's fine, too. It was a great night! Which should produce a great baby."

"There's no correlation," Martha said, walking to take her seat at the head of the table. She was dabbing at her damp blouse. "So now I have a wet, salty stain."

The others had taken their places, as the cards indicated; Martha faced across the table to Claire. Jessie and Sue Carol sat on one side, with Lisbeth and Nina opposite them. The lines were drawn. The dull knives waited.

"Great sex makes great people," Claire declared. Jessie noticed Claire was the only one attracted to the potatoes. The others had set the fingerlings neatly to the side of the plates and were routinely forking up mesclun greens. They nibbled.

"No correlation," Martha repeated.

"There's no correlation?" Claire challenged. She stared straight across the table, and Jessie could see this would be no truce. They were gesturing with forks, dueling cutlery.

Claire waved her salad fork. "Most people are conceived in boredom, and *just look at them.*"

Her eyes locked with Martha's.

"Well, I'm *just saying. . . .*"

A titter ran round the table, passed along with the sourdough baguette that Jessie had neglected to warm in the oven, but which she had thoughtfully presliced, to avoid difficulty in cutting. She had set both salted and unsalted butter on the table, and a small bowl of the pan drippings, to use as a gravy. A new restaurant had opened downtown, where the French chef served pan drippings and crusts of bread. Drippings, Jessie thought, humble chic.

"I'm just saying," Martha continued, "that you shouldn't even conceive of conception unless you are really ready to have a child. You have to (a) own your apartment, (b) have a partner, (c) be able to afford live-in help, and (d) have great medical insurance in case the baby needs"—she searched for a medical condition—"ortho-donture."

"Claire has great teeth," Sue Carol said, gritting her own. Sue Carol had carried a second bottle over to the table and set it beside her glass. Jessie made a hostess note to get out the jug of rotgut red, El Conquistador, the Chilean bargain from an unknown vineyard outside Copake Falls, that was known to blend foreign and domestic wines into a cheap brew they sold at upstate New York "tastings." The great jug squatted under the kitchen cabinet, next to some industrial-strength solvents. Jessie predicted that she would need to stretch the Rosemary Estates. The bottles were already almost empty. Sue Carol, alone, had accounted for a major part of the consumption.

"We've never seen his teeth," Martha said.

"Oh, he had quite the overbite," Claire taunted her.

"That will cost you, in the long run," Martha predicted. "I don't understand why if you had to do this, you didn't at least go to a . . . a sperm bank, so that you could know something about the father."

"And who would you know better, Martha?" Claire asked. "Someone whose medical file you'd seen, or someone you'd made love to?"

"Well." Martha paused. "You would at least have some genetic information. What if this fruit store guy carries a gene for neurofi-bromatosis, or your child needs a bone marrow transplant someday and your marrow is not compatible? What do you do then? You have to be responsible, you have to be prepared . . . I just wonder how you can consider yourself ready, that's all."

The others glared at her.

"He's sounds like a lovely man," Lisbeth said. "He reminds me of Steve. I'll bet his genes are fine; you have a sense of someone's genes when you look into their eyes," Lisbeth said.

"Yes," Jessie said, "the eyes are everything." She was surprised at how sad she sounded. He *could* still call.

"And you really don't want more from him?" Nina asked Claire.

"I *have* more," Claire answered. She touched the rise of her belly. "And this is better for me. I never saw a marriage I envied."

Jessie remembered her own marriage, and not with longing. For an unbeknownst reason, a moment from her marriage to Hank resurfaced. She had been waiting for him, on a city street, at a pre-arranged spot. He had not been able to catch her attention until he honked the car horn at her. "Clean the wax out of your ears," he had said, when she finally saw him and hopped into the passenger seat.

Clean the wax out of your ears, she thought. Oh, yes, she had. Could you fall out of love as suddenly as you fell in? Could you fall into hate, instead? She'd resented her husband from that day forth, and it had seemed to her that his blue eyes, formerly so beautiful, had become closed to her. Her marriage, as she felt it to be a marriage, had ended in that minute. But she had hung around for a decade, unable to admit the fact. *Clean the wax out of your ears.*

"Sorry, Martha," Claire was saying, "I feel no particular urge to run down the aisle."

Claire *really* was independent; it wasn't an act, something she feigned to attract people. She didn't, it appeared, need anyone . . . really, Jessie thought.

"If a man doesn't call," Claire said, "I don't see him again," and laughed.

Jessie knew Claire's world was filled with men; if anyone she knew possessed pheromones, those secret sex attraction enzymes or whatever they were, that person was Claire. She couldn't go anywhere without men buzzing 'round. It was clearly her lack of need that drew them. And if they didn't come through for her, she seemed able to forget them and concentrate on the next man she met. She traveled emotionally with the same ease with which she had toured the world: Claire gave transience a good name. She traveled fast, light, and stayed only where she felt wanted and wished to be. Now, in the grip of a relapse of lovesickness, Jessie envied her.

No one can sit at a dinner table with more of an edge of appreciation than Nina Moskowitz did that night. Determined not to eat, she sniffed the air, her belly growling. Nina sat, eyeing the food, coveting even the condiments (she had been known to lick mustard off a spoon, or swipe a fingertip of ketchup off someone else's French fry platter). But tonight, although her stomach was audible and her olfactory sense as keen as a hound's, she resisted all temptation and ripped open her Dr. Duvall Diet System Powder, and poured it into her water glass. With a glum look, she used her fork to swirl the congealed gray dust into a gelatinous sludge of a drink that was supposed to leave her "satisfied." She could smell the butter. . . .

Martha tucked into the Cornish hen that had been intended for Nina and said, "Yum. Jessie—this is fabulous. You know you could have saved yourself a lot of time and effort: Dean and DeLuca sell these already roasted and glazed, but of course yours has that *je ne sais quoi,* and it was cheaper for you, wasn't it? Not so many dollaros, and you can skip a zero. You're such a cook. But why didn't you let me do this dinner at my place and have it catered? Then you could have enjoyed yourself."

Next, Martha looked across the table at Claire. "So you feel capable of raising a child totally on your own? Without any support? No husband or even boyfriend, to help out? All this, financed by playing the . . . krummhorn?"

"There's an interest in antique musical instruments," Lisbeth said.

"Well, they're not playing my song," Martha snapped.

Jessie spooned more sauce on her own hen: it was "yum." The food had worked out—if only they could get a gag order on Martha.

"Claire is a superb musician," Jessie said, defending her friend. "She's in demand. She won a Yaddo fellowship."

"That was lovely, when was that, in 1998?"

Claire said she always got a gig when she needed it.

"There are always those renaissance festivals," she said. "But I can't explain the miraculous quality of my salvation—when I *really, really* need money, the phone rings."

Martha bit into the miniature drumstick. It was as big as her pinkie.

"Delish," she pronounced. "But I must object."

Jessie decided to stop her before the main course was spoiled.

"Martha, take it easy. We're here to celebrate Claire's having a baby, not emphasize potential problems."

"Damn straight," Sue Carol agreed.

Jessie looked at her: Sue Carol's eyes were bloodshot, the right eye seemed about to close into a permanent squint. Sue Carol was not just in her cups: she was far gone. One blue eye was near shut; the other was rolling, like a panicked horse's. Sue Carol asked, "Do you have any wetting solution I can use?"

Jessie jumped up and ran to the bathroom and returned with the plastic squirt container of saline solution. Sue Carol began to fumble, pulling things out of her pockets. "I had that damned lens in here somewhere."

A small plastic Baggie slipped to the floor. Sue Carol picked it up and tucked it in the pocket of her snug jeans. Jessie saw the clear little bag and wondered, Was Sue Carol "doing" drugs again? Not that her friend had a real habit; but Sue Carol was the only one in the group who rewarded herself at the good times by doing a line of coke, or smoking a superior joint. Jessie wondered if Sue Carol, distraught, might now be finding comfort in something pharmaceutical? She sensed Sue Carol was approaching a crisis tonight, despite her repeated protestation that "this is the best thing that could have happened to me, leaving Bob: it was high time." How *high?*

Martha routinely remarked to Sue Carol, "So, you're drinking again? I thought you'd decided you couldn't handle it? I was so proud of you when you were considering at least Al-Anon, even though you were still saying the problem was Bob, I thought you were beginning to see, it was both of you. Remind me to send you a new book called *Codependency—The Love Crutch: When Your Lover Is Your Enemy.* You'll find it so helpful. You know it's not just the alcoholism, the cirrhosis, you have to think of your skin. Alcohol is aging."

"Oh please," Nina said.

"Thanks a bunch," Sue Carol said.

"She said things magically always work out," Lisbeth contributed. "And I know what she means. . . . It's all fate, it's already written."

"That was helpful, Lisbeth," Martha said. "So . . . I see you have your cigarettes with you. I thought you quit when I did. You haven't seen the latest studies?" Martha pursed her lips into that little moue of concern. "Oh, please, let me treat you to a patch. For Christmas. Smoking not only causes you-know-what; it creates wrinkles. It's like subjecting your face to a process similar to constant leather tanning. Do you want to look like Samuel Beckett?"

"Yes," Lisbeth said, reaching for her pack and the lighter.

"Martha," Jessie said, "this is a celebration, to celebrate the good things that have happened, Claire's baby—"

"Oh, this is a celebration?" Martha said. "This should be an intervention."

She leaned onto the table.

"Listen," she said to the group, "I did Claire's taxes, so I know. Her income is less than her phone bill."

"Hey, that's the life force," defended Sue Carol. She was standing, attempting to squirt wetting solution in her "bad" eye. Jessie went to her, whispered, "You need a mirror," and led Sue Carol over to the wall where an oval glass was hanging.

"Awwwghggh," Sue Carol screamed at her reflection. "That's me."

Jessie peered into the reflection. "You look better than that. This isn't the greatest mirror."

Sue Carol concentrated, trying to reinsert the lens into her eye. "No," she said, "my eye's so sore, I can't wear a lens anymore. So now I have to go through this blind in one eye."

"You'll be fine."

"I need more wine," Sue Carol said.

"We're almost out of the good stuff," Jessie whispered to her. "I was about to open that jug from under the sink."

"Ah yes, a fresh jug." Suddenly Sue Carol was happier, giddy, admittedly while still staring out at the group through one red eye. "Let us open the jug to breathe. . . ." She assumed a professional waitressing tone. "Would anyone else care for something from the bar?"

"Sit down, Sue Carol." Jessie saw that her friend was weaving slightly. "Sit down . . . I'll get it."

"No I want to. . . ."

"I'll have some more wine," Nina said.

"Let me check the wine cellar," Sue Carol offered, then fell to her knees and crawled to the kitchen sink cabinet. "Ah, yes, I see an excellent Chilean blended red, the world-famous 'Conquistador—The Chilean Grape That Conquered Columbia County.'"

She turned to address the entire group at the table. "You all ought to come eat at Vert. I work lunches Monday, Friday, Saturday, and Sunday. You should see me in my cute uniform—it's green too, rain forest green, a spandex dress designed by Versace. Versace is dead, but his sister hires someone, so the name is the same. I just look so cute in it. You really should see me, I do the job as if it were a part. It's fun for me that way. I have created an entire characterization of myself as a waitress. Here, may I offer you our new wine selection?"

"Oh, could it complement the one we just had?" Lisbeth asked.

"I don't know if it is the same year."

"Any year but this one," Nina said.

Jessie could not help but laugh. The women were clowning as they had, years ago, at Theresa House, when they feigned fancy dinner parties, serving chips and ginger ale. They had once carved a whole rye bread, pretending it was a turkey.

"Sommelier," Sue Carol said, kneeling before Jessie. "Sommelier. Does a jug wine have to be opened ahead of time, to breathe?"

"Oh, yes," Jessie assured her. "They are very heavy breathers. They need an extra hour."

"They pant," Nina contributed.

Sue Carol dragged the Conquistador jug onto the floor. "Does anyone want to sniff the screw-on cap?"

"It doesn't even have a cork?" Martha asked.

"Oh, sniff it," Nina said.

Sue Carol reached into her hip pocket and withdrew some more of her ammunition—a twisted little joint, the blue pills purchased on the street, and a prescription bottle from her veterinarian for the deceased Yorkie who had required Valium for his nervous indigestion.

"You're not mixing drugs and alcohol?" Martha said.

"Not yet," she answered. "And I'm feeling so good, I probably won't. I want to know just in case—what goes good with Valium?"

"Nothing goes good . . . *well* with Valium. Those combinations can kill." Martha seized the joint from Sue Carol. "I will not stand here and watch you endanger yourself."

"It was just a little insurance, Martha, so I could self-medicate. I have to be at my best now."

"I'll keep custody of this." Martha tucked the joint into her Kate Spade purse. Even as she did, Jessie heard a little warning gong: why didn't Martha toss it?

Meanwhile, Sue Carol had unscrewed the bottle of Conquistador, and was proffering it to Nina, who held up her glass. Nina sipped, made a face. El Conquistador did taste like a cross between vinegar and lighter fluid.

"I think it's gone off a bit," Nina said.

"Oh, dear . . . here." Sue Carol poured from the half-empty bottle of the Aussie Red she'd been keeping beside her own glass.

"Here . . . and forgive me, I drank up so much." Sue Carol slumped back into her seat. "Shit," she said, folding her arms on the table and placing her head down, like a punished schoolchild. "I can't keep nothing straight. This *is* like work."

Jessie moved to her side and rubbed her shoulders. "It doesn't matter, you're not working tonight."

Sue Carol began to rant then—she could remember all of Ophelia and none of the Specials of the Day.

"Shit," she said. "I always say it is 'encrusted tuna.' Encrusted all right. This shit's been going on for ten years—it could keep up. Do you know how old I am?"

"Thirty-six and a half," Martha said.

"I am a thirty-six-year-old waitress. . . ."

"You're an actress," Claire insisted.

"A wactress. A hybrid cross between a waitress and an actress . . . a professional wactress." Sue Carol corrected her. "And something tells me if I don't get a part soon, I'm just a plain old waitress whose real business is knowing the house dressing . . . green vinaigrette. Vert vinaigrette."

Martha said, "Just think, though, you are at least working at the newest, hottest spot in the city." Her expression changed a bit. "I'm supposed to be there tonight. How is the food really? As good as they say?"

"It's okay," Sue Carol said. "Too bad I'm not there to wait on you and Donald."

"You know, Martha," Jessie suggested, "you could still go, and join Donald for at least dessert."

"I told my driver to come back for me, at eleven," Martha said, her tone final. "I sent him out to get a little din-din. Donald will be fine. He understood. Really. Men are not sentimental about birthdays. We'll go back to Vert."

She beamed. "I already booked the upstairs dining room for the wedding supper."

Martha turned back to Sue Carol. "So you think he'll really get a great meal? His favorite thing in the world is shaved truffles in vodka sauce . . . over infant sea urchins on a shingle of polenta."

"I'm sure they will give it to him," Sue Carol said. She sniffled and wiped her nose with the dinner napkin. "Oh what's the use? It's all set now: the haves and the have-nots, the doers and shakers, and the waiters . . . And I'm a—"

"You are a wonderful performer," Claire told her.

"Yeah, what was the last thing I did? That revival of *Oklahoma* . . . it was so long ago, it's a coming back again, it's even retro."

Jessie noted that Sue Carol's southern accent, which sometimes vanished, had come back in force, smothering her words like gravy on biscuits. Along with the accent, came her "down home" attitude: she was slouching, squinting, and dropping her *g*s as she downed more and more of El Conquistador.

"You were so moving, you were exquisite: I held my breath when you sang. You were. . . ." Lisbeth paused so that the others could join her, and they did.

"Terrific," they all cried.

"Oh you were terrific to come see me," Sue Carol said, "but that was three years ago. At a dinner theater." She sniffled again. "I can't get away from food no matter what I do."

"Well, can't you count *that* as the highlight of your career and go on and have a baby?" Martha suggested.

"I can't do much, Martha," Sue Carol answered, "but I don't kid"—she pronounced it *keeed*—"myself. I'm not going to reproduce because I'm giving up on the rest of mah life."

She laughed, as acid as the wine she was drinking. "When I broke up with Bob this afternoon, I said, 'Well, at least I still have my career,' and ain't that the biggest joke? *What career?*"

"So now you have nothing," Martha said. Her tone was not mean but thoughtful, as if she was trying to comprehend.

"Would you like to see a menu?" Sue Carol said, jutting her jaw and biting her words off.

"Well," Martha said, realizing she was being attacked, "wasn't I the one who suggested you study computer programming?"

"Jesus, Martha," Jessie said. To herself, she said, I better get to the next course. She still had to macerate those damned blood oranges, and serve them in cassis. She bolted back to her workstation at the kitchen counter, and began to saw away at the orange rinds with one of her defective, dull knives.

"Sue Carol will get a great part," she said, to everyone. "I just feel it."

Sue Carol said, "It's all over for me, all over. . . ."

"Oh, no." Claire got up, went over to her, and dragged her friend back to the wall mirror. "Now look at yourself. Look at that face. Look at that hair. Gorgeous. Look at that body. Great." There was a chorus from the table: "You're wonderful, don't sell yourself short."

Sue Carol looked out, with her good eye, and bawled again. "Bob slept with someone else today."

"Is there evidence?" Martha asked immediately.

"Yes," Sue Carol said.

"I'm sure you're worrying over nothing. Come on, let's have these macerated blood oranges, I'm serving them in cassis. Everybody?"

Jessie began to clear the dinner plates, feeling a bit panicked herself as she viewed the skeletal remains of the tiny Cornish hens. Was there anything sadder, she thought, than the remains of a dinner? The salad plates had mesclun leaves pasted to them; her balsamic dressing was pooling like old brown blood.

The group was mesmerized by Sue Carol, who was transfixed herself, as she related her tale of infidelity to her mirror image and to her friends, reflected behind her. She blurted out "the main part" in one breathless summation: Bob had been "acting different, he was a bit strange." Then she built to the current catastrophe.

"Two weeks ago, somebody started calling our apartment, and hanging up when I answered. . . ."

"Maybe it was telemarketers," Martha mused.

"No," Sue Carol argued. "At the same time, Bob started working out with weights. He developed his abs."

"Fits," Nina said, in confirmation.

"I don't see why," Claire said. She tried to divert Sue Carol from the tale of adultery. She began a funny story of how, on her nocturnal schedule, she had begun to watch late-night fitness infomercials, and discovered, "Insomniacs of the city must be obsessed with 'abs, abs, abs!' That is what is happening at three A.M. And by four A.M., they are obsessed with 'glutes.' "

Sue Carol, undeterred, continued the saga of the "other woman." "She called again yesterday. . . ."

"How do you know it's the same one who hung up?" Jessie said, trying to diffuse this subject.

"It's the same kind of ring." Sue Carol mimicked a shrill, hysterical electronic phone buzz. "Besides, she only hung up the first few times. Now, she's getting bolder. She talks."

"What does she say?" Lisbeth wanted to know.

"She says, 'Is Bob there?' "

A dispute erupted among the women: Nina thought this was suspicious, the others insisted it could all be "innocent."

"Did she leave her name?"

"No, she just said 'a friend.' "

Nina snorted: *Guilty as sin.* She had other reasons to suspect Bob was having an affair, or affairs. She sat back, focused on the candle burning on the dinner table, took another swallow of wine, and debated confiding the incidents that began July Fourth a year and a half ago, when they had all rented a beach cottage up on Cape Cod, and Bob had playfully grabbed Nina, in the guise of steadying her in high surf.

He was an awfully desirable man, Nina reflected, and he was

direct. He had whispered in her ear how "sexy" he found her. From then on, at every social occasion, he had employed a silent vocabulary—whenever he touched her for any ordinary reason, he had exerted that subtle sexual pressure. Assisting her into her coat, resting his hand on hers as he pulled out her chair at the dinner party table . . . always, there was that extra second of physical contact that signaled desire. More than once, during a casual, husband-of-a-friend's kiss good night, she had felt pressure from his lips on hers. She'd known he wanted her. That was not so unusual. What had alarmed Nina was that she had wanted him, too.

We are like vampires, she thought, those of us who are more highly sexed. She was a bit sympathetic to Bob; she could see he was almost beyond control, that he could never stay in the confines of marriage, that he was not a domesticated animal.

It must be like being married to a panther, Nina thought. Bob was lithe, dark, heavily muscled, and he paced. There was a story, in this very neighborhood, of a woman, "outed" by a neighbor, who was caught living with a leopard. She had raised the leopard from a cub, and kept it in her loft. The animal had grown enormous and restless.

How could you live with a big wildcat or a man like Bob? Nina wondered, without expecting he would want to break out of the cage, and you might get hurt? But she could see how someone, especially Sue Carol, would want to . . . any woman would want him.

As a husband, he was a nightmare. As an actor, he was intriguing—because of his hooded eyes and swarthy complexion, he most often played somewhat appealing Mafioso. He was dark, with the shock of pale blue eyes, but it was definitely his deep voice, and his upper body development, that put him physically in the top percentile. Bob was "cast" as seductive but demented. His most well-known role had been in a cookie-cutter film that mimicked the *Godfather* movies: he had played "Nicko," a pathological seducer and hit man, whose famous send-off line was: "I'm sorry but I have to blow you away."

When he wasn't playing hoods, he performed Shakespeare in the park, doing mostly villain roles. His voice seemed to emanate from some virile source: he could really project. Onstage, he had a magnetic energy. Offstage, Bob had to run five miles a day to work off that energy, and still it seemed to be there, anyway. He was sensual, too; did a bit of drugs, drank, admitted going for shiatsu massages. He was on the road more than he stayed home.

Against her own will, Nina had imagined touching the fine hair on his muscled forearms . . . or running her hand along his developed thighs. At the beach, that summer, he had demonstrated pectoral and bicep twitching, and Nina had not been immune. When he twitched, she had twitched. Nina knew that the other friends regarded Bob as "a narcissistic, self-centered, slightly obnoxious hunk," but Nina could not hold all that against him.

As she thought of Bob, Nina was still monitoring Sue Carol's tale of distress. Lisbeth, as ever, was inquisitive without being, as they say, "judgmental," regarding the mystery woman who called. "How does she sound?"

"Sweet," Sue Carol answered, her voice poisonous.

Oh dear, Nina thought, *that could have been me on the other end of the line. . . .* The "other woman" was probably just some other single woman whom he'd met somewhere, and given his secret signals . . . and now that woman was seeking him, perhaps against her own moral code, but lonely and desirous, and he had touched her. Nina felt a bit sad and was suddenly attracted to the sourdough baguette that she had been resisting. . . . *What if she just bit into the crust?*

Nina had an involuntary memory, and a relapse of her own desire, recalling the inevitable night when Bob had "escorted" her to her door, and suddenly pressed himself against her. He had been thrusting, to gain entry, and Nina, stunned, had fallen back into the apartment. He had stalked her in her own narrow foyer and flattened her to the rug in two seconds. He'd tackled her, with his professional wrestling hold, and to her own shame, she'd felt her mouth and everything else open up under him, but she had somehow dredged up her principles: *No, no married men, no, never the husband of a friend.*

She had extricated herself from what she noted was an incredibly efficient hold: his hand had already infiltrated her panties, and she had been about a centimeter away from what Nina would admit was her point of no return. She had started to moan, even as she interjected her soft whispers of "no we can't, this is crazy," and evoked the name of her friend as a prophylactic, before he could engage an actual one on his errant member.

"Sue Carol!" she had cried out.

"Oh yeah," he had said, remembering he was married.

"I'm sorry," Nina had whispered, to keep the ending friendly, "but I have to blow you away."

He had left her laughing, which was what she wanted.

And so, that night (was it only a year ago? It had been a December night, cold as this one . . . yes, almost the exact anniversary) Nina had gotten a grip, as they say, and put Bob out of her apartment, like a tomcat. A tomcat, for whom she had affection. She had actually ruffled his hair before pushing him toward her building's tiny elevator: "Go on, scat. Go home."

Then thrown herself to the floor, her blood running, chugging mixed messages: she had not known whether to feel sorry or glad. Ever since that night, whenever she saw him, socially, she could almost taste him. Should she tell Sue Carol about Bob's behavior?

For an instant, Nina almost opened her mouth to confirm Sue Carol's account and strengthen her friend's resolve. But something made her bite her admittedly slightly guilty tongue. Sue Carol had found out about his infidelities; Nina did not need to embellish the case and add further hurt. There was an unwritten etiquette to adultery; Nina felt her correct course was to be silent, unless her account was absolutely necessary. If Sue Carol lost her resolve, perhaps Nina should relate the incidents of the undersea squeezes and the hand under her panties.

"Let's not get into this," Jessie was saying as Sue Carol ranted on about her "evidence." "You've left him, that's enough."

"He had the nerve to say I was crazy," Sue Carol yelled. "Am I crazy? You tell me. For years, I suspected, I could just smell it on him . . . but he would say, 'Oh, you are just so jealous, Sue Carol, get over it.' But he was cheating the entire time, I guess . . . but I could never get the goods on him until now . . . until today. And now I got him."

She dug deep in the pocket of her form-fitted jeans and withdrew the plastic Baggie Jessie had spied earlier in the evening and speculated contained some drug. Sue Carol held the clear plastic bag up to the lamplight.

"You tell me. You tell me if this is all in my head? If I am imagining this." She opened the Baggie and withdrew something. The women all leaned closer, to examine the evidence, which was virtually invisible to the naked eye at three feet.

"It's her hair," Sue Carol said, in a terrible, triumphant tone. "And I found it in our bed."

Sue Carol held the long hair (it must have been shoulder length) with distaste for the "creature," as she referred to her. This creature, who was so debased that she had come right into Sue

Carol's own apartment, into the sanctity of the marriage bed, to roll around with Bob while she, Sue Carol, worked for the conjugal cause down at Vert.

"I actually called him on his cell," Sue Carol related, "and said, 'Honey, should I work late or not? We could use the money, but I won't if you are getting lonesome.' Oh, I knew that horny bastard could not be on his own for ten extra minutes: I called it."

"Are you sure the hair couldn't have gotten there by some other means?" Lisbeth said. "Maybe it was a cleaning woman . . . ?"

"This hair was on my pillow. My pillow. And the slut had the gall to use my toothpaste, my toothbrush, my hairbrush, and I suspect even my perfume—it looks like it's way down in the bottle: I know it was full. Couldn't she have the class to carry her own little slut kit with her? She had to be intimate with me, take this from me, too." She sniffled. *"Je reviens."*

The women sat, nodding, considering. These were offenses beyond mere infidelity.

"And there's more," Sue Carol said. "Oh, this goes beyond any minimal standard for even horny male behavior. He knew . . . he knew . . ." Sue Carol started to weep. "How I been feeling lately, that I been at the edge of giving up. . . . This isn't like him cheating when he's on the road. I wouldn't like that, but I think I could even handle it—something anonymous, taking place in a . . . a Howard Johnson's. But not *this,* not *now,* not in my own bed while I am out being a waitress to support us, and thinking—what I have worked for all my life will never be. And on top of that, I know what I know, and he's been telling me that for years, I've been crazy." Her eyes—or, more technically, her eye, for the right eye was still out of the picture—suddenly got a hunted look. "I'm not crazy, am I?"

"Let me see the hair," Nina suggested.

Nina examined it, holding the long black strand to the light.

"Asian," she identified it. "Undyed, untreated, therefore most likely, young. Asian or American Indian. . . ."

"Indian. Tribal preference has reverted to 'Indian,'" Jessie corrected her. God, everything tonight drew her mind back to Jesse Dark.

"And you want to hear the worst part?" Sue Carol asked.

"Yes," Martha said, moving from her place at the head of the table to where Sue Carol stood with the hair.

Jessie tried to stop this. "Look," she invited. "These oranges are really macerated now. . . . Let's try some."

They ignored her; they were all possessed by the hair. Even Jessie could not help but glance at it.

"Well," said Sue Carol with grim relish, "when I called and said, 'Should I work late, or come home so he wouldn't be lonely?' he said, 'Oh, I have to work too, honey, so why don't *you* do the extra shift?'"

Sue Carol waited for the massive intake of breath, the communal gasp at this disgusting behavior. Nina thought, Boy, he is *bad*.

"When I got home, he was in bed, asleep. I had brought him a Baggie full of Alaskan king crab legs. He woke up. I guess he smelled them. I said, "Honey. Treats." And he was going for the crab leg when he kind of sat up in bed, and that's when I found it. The hair."

"And you brought him crab legs," Jessie said, setting down the platter of macerated blood oranges so she could hug Sue Carol. "Oh, you're so sweet. I love you." Lisbeth, Claire, joined the huddle. "Oh, we love you. . . ."

"Oh, I love you all. I hate him."

Nina could not hate—she could only recognize. "He's typical."

Martha lunged for the hair, seized it. She stood her ground, facing off Sue Carol.

"Listen," said Martha. "It's not too late. You never saw this hair."

"I already accused him."

"Take it back. You were mistaken. This is . . . nothing. All men are unfaithful. They're not like us. But it means less when they do it. It's just a diversion, like going to the fights. He might as well have gone to the Knicks game. It's the same thing."

Sue Carol tried to grab the hair. "Hey, let me have that hair—it's my property."

"I'll keep custody of the hair," Martha said to Sue Carol. "You listen to me. Thank God you told me before it was too late. You almost lost everything. You can still recoup. You do not acknowledge that this American Indian was in your bed. Let me tell you something . . . it could be construed as disgusting, but I feel this will help you."

Martha took a breath. She did not like to expose her parents' arrangements, but she could see that it would be helpful. "My father," she announced, "was unfaithful to my mother twice a week . . . always with chunky redheads."

She glanced over at Nina by habit. Nina flinched. Not only was she now a chunky redhead, she actually had had an encounter with Martha's father, Emir Sarkis Sloane. It had been at the party to celebrate Martha's engagement; somehow, Emir had managed to squeeze next to Nina in the restaurant passage to the rest rooms. Oh, damned these breasts, Nina had cursed. They had gotten her into a bit of trouble then—Emir had kissed her. It could not have been social—they were not saying good night, only making their way to the bathrooms, and she had felt the wet underside of his lower lip. He had held her lip in a half-bite, half-kiss then muttered, "I could take care of you."

"That's nice of you to offer," Nina had said (oh why had she felt that idiot need to be polite?), "but I can take care of myself."

Now, as she listened to Martha's account of how her father kept mistresses, Nina was given the luxury of envisioning the life she could have enjoyed as Emir's mistress—a pillowed existence in a high-rise in Queens. She, too, could have gazed off to the industrial east, performing acts of love that Martha's mother, Athena Lucille, would not.

"My mother did not mind," Martha was saying. "I think she was grateful to those other women. It's like Monica Lewinsky—Hillary should have sent her a thank-you note."

A roar of outrage rose up from the other women. Martha went on. "There have always been sexual systems: wives hold a place of honor, while other women may serve as . . . receptacles." Martha made an expression with her mouth, similar to when she had tasted a cheese she claimed was rancid. "It's been a mistake of our quote 'liberation,' that we now are expected to do these lower duties . . . offer these services, that frankly, should remain commercial." Martha smiled at her own analogy. "Like a sexual shoe shine."

So, how did her mother handle it? Martha wanted them to know that "every time my father acquired a new mistress, my mother bought herself a nice new dress." She smiled and paused for emphasis. "They were married for forty years . . . until he died." She took a sip of the El Conquistador. "She had an *incredible* wardrobe."

Jessie was shaking her head as she placed the platter of macerated blood oranges in cassis in front of Martha. "She had twelve fur coats," Martha emphasized. "They were both happy."

Privately, Martha was thinking—sexual etiquette had become too egalitarian, now even she was expected to service Donald, albeit only on special occasions such as tonight, his birthday, and she would have to do it, and do it out of love . . . but she was not looking forward to it. It was just as well she had skipped the dinner at Vert—she might risk upchucking a seven-hundred-dollar supper. Not that she found b.j.'s that repellent; it was just the damned gag reflex: how did Monica Lewinsky and the others do it? It was natural to retch when something jammed down your throat. Martha had made a note on her Palm Pilot: "Improve b.j. skills." She could study technique from Andre, her stylist, who was gay and probably knew some tricks.

Still, she would never object if Donald chose when he wanted that, to go to a professional, as he did when he needed his back cracked or his toenails pedicured.

Martha had evaluated Sue Carol's situation long ago: Bob was a womanizer, a substance abuser, and a bit of a star. Sue Carol was a thirty-six-and-a-half-year-old wactress: she should stay the course. Sue Carol would not improve her lot by leaving. Martha feared for her friend. She saw, as in a forecast: Sue Carol as a counter girl at some Greek diner downtown, returning home to a shabby studio or at best a high-flight walk-up one bedroom. Unless she could lock onto some alimony. Which Sue Carol was too feisty and pig-headed to do. So her friend stood to lose everything tonight . . . Martha wanted to help.

"Reconcile," she advised.

"Dump him," Nina advised. Bob had gone too far; she was sorry she had ruffled his hair now—this was despicable, below infidelity. His behavior was . . .

"Scabrous," Jessie pronounced. "It is not even the adultery, it is the total contempt for their marriage."

"I don't think he's with you spiritually . . . the bed business bothers me, your bed is sacred," Lisbeth contributed. Martha stood, shaking her head, holding up the long strand of hair.

"You never saw this hair," Martha instructed Sue Carol. She grabbed Lisbeth's cigarette lighter from the table, and before anyone could stop her, torched the hair. The smell of incinerated hair polluted the room.

"Hey, that hair was my property!" Sue Carol yelled.

"Forget him," Claire advised. "You'll meet someone you'll have more fun with."

"Yes, forget him," Jessie urged, "and have some macerated blood oranges in cassis." She set a plate and tried to lead Sue Carol back to her place at the table.

"Easy for you to say, you always meet men," Sue Carol said to her.

"Me?" Jessie said. "How often? Every three years."

"You had those two marine biologists," Sue Carol said.

Jessie stopped in her tracks. Michael and Paul. In her excitement over the new man in her life, she had almost forgotten his predecessors.

"Paul is in Antarctica, and Michael's in Micronesia," Jessie said. "I haven't seen either of them in three years."

"But they love you," Sue Carol accused.

Did they? They were nice men, Jessie reflected, but because of their similar occupations and their requirements to explore distant oceans, she almost never saw them. They had also, in some odd way, become synchronized—they seemed to visit New York rarely but on the same weekend, so they, in effect, canceled one another out. She told Sue Carol the truth.

"Most of the time, I'm alone."

"You don't mind?" Sue Carol asked.

"I love it," Jessie said. "I get more done."

"More what?"

"Work. You know, with men or without men, we make our own lives."

Sue Carol suddenly picked up her Bonwit bag and veered

toward the doors of the freight elevator. "Going down," she cried. "Uh-oh. Not for me. I can't live alone, I can't live without Bob. . . . Maybe I should just go back uptown and see how he's thinking."

"I wouldn't," Nina said.

"I could go home, forgive him, and then punish him," Sue Carol said, as if inspired.

"That's not a bad idea," Martha conceded. "Then tell him more medical horror stories. Does he know about venereal warts? Tell him . . . give him the statistics. It's a sexual sewer out there. One out of four has herpes, and now they know it can be spread even when it does not appear to be active. And almost one out of one has chlamydia. And don't forget AIDS, now they say the virus can live in saliva."

"That's terrible," Claire intervened.

Jessie stood between them, another plate of macerated oranges in cassis in her hands.

"Look," Sue Carol said as she pressed the elevator button for down.

"I been with Bob since we were kids" (*keeeds*). "Nobody's perfect. I don't know if I can even eat or sleep without him."

"Oh come on," Nina snapped. "He was always on the road."

"Yeah, but I knew he was coming back," Sue Carol said. "Even then, I could hardly sleep . . . we have a position: spoons. We sleep like nesting spoons; his back to my belly. I need him, I need him . . . I need to feel his heat, to hear his heart beat."

Jessie blocked the elevator. "We all like that," she said, "but there are times when it is better to be alone." Jessie said that, but something in Sue Carol's remark about the nesting spoons had evoked the long sleeps of her marriage; Hank might have been dull while awake, but he'd been satisfying, unconscious. His charm lay in his body temperature—he had been warm, not sweaty, and had a personal scent similar to vanilla.

Truly, Jessie had never slept so well as she had when she was married. She understood what Sue Carol was saying. There was a biorhythm to marriage, one that medical science had proved could prolong your life. That was what was so seductive—more than sex, it was the synchronization of two separate selves. She recalled how Sue Carol and Bob would lean against each other when they sat on her couch; they fell asleep curled up like cats. It took years to develop that degree of comfort. Even a wonderful affair, such as the one Jessie had just begun, did not offer such consolation yet. In fact, the excitements of a new lover did not encourage rest at all. The last two nights, she had lain awake in Jesse Dark's arms, falling asleep only in short takes, from exhaustion. She'd woken with a start, as she did in a "foreign" land.

Lisbeth walked over and touched Sue Carol's elbow. "Jessie's right. You develop your inner resources when you are alone." She smiled over at Jessie. "You know one night I came over here, without calling, and you know what Jessie was doing? Cooking bouillabaisse for herself."

"That is impressive," Martha said. "What do you do with all the fish heads?"

"I freeze them," Jessie said.

"That's great, but it ain't for me." Sue Carol picked up another of her shopping bags. The stacks of paper, photos, seemed to be about to spill from a ripping Saks sack. Jessie knew she could not let Sue Carol go out again, into the cold night, so clearly discombobulated.

"Look," she said, pressing the elevator button to close. "I never told you why I left Hank. . . ."

"He burped and didn't say 'excuse me,'" Lisbeth remembered.

Jessie laughed. She had forgotten that. But it was apropos. The burp of boredom, unrelenting matrimony, till malaise did them part.

"I was used to him," Jessie confided. "It was bearable. In a way, being married to Hank gave a focus to my discontent. I was vaguely unhappy, and when I looked over at him, I knew why." He once told me to 'clean the wax out of my ears,' so I finally listened to him."

"So it could have worked out," Martha cried. "Listen," she said to Sue Carol, "reconcile. Married is better." To Jessie she said, "Did you consider having kids with him?"

"His eyes were too close together," Jessie said as she put her hand out to retrieve Sue Carol's shopping bags. "Finally, I didn't even want to resent him anymore. I wanted to be more than some catalog of injustices, a record of hurts . . . of what he'd done, what I'd done."

"Catalog?" Sue Carol said. "Well, if you were a catalog, I'm the Sears of grievances. Oh, he's hit every base. He's good at this. He's the best."

Superlatives? Jessie thought. A person's speech pattern revealed everything; on some level, she thought, her friend was valuing Bob for the amount of pain he could inflict. It was her measure of him: he was the best.

"Superlatives?" she said aloud. "Sue Carol, you are too impressed."

"I guess." Sue Carol seemed to deflate, and Jessie led her over to the couches. "Here, we can have dessert at the coffee table," she suggested, "then open the rest of the gifts."

"I have more," Martha said.

"Oh, yeah," Sue Carol said, "and here." She handed Claire the bag from the Korean grocer. "This is from me. . . ."

The women sat down, resuming the semicircle of the gift ceremony. There was a stunned moment as Claire withdrew the miniature vegetables from the plastic sack.

"Oh," cried Claire, and Jessie held her breath. "Well, I love them. I'll make a spoonful of ratatouille."

"It was a dumb gift," Sue Carol acknowledged. "I was in a hurry. If I had time, I would have gone back to Kentucky, and come back with the family cradle. I wasn't thinking. . . ." She crumbled again, hunching on the sofa, gripping her knees into a fetal position.

"Oh why," she wailed, "is he sleeping with someone else?"

Maybe there was something wrong with her, she confessed to the others.

"You're perfect," they said.

"You ain't slept with me. He once told me"—Sue Carol seemed about to bite her kneecaps she was so distressed—"he once told me—other women are more passionate. They get so carried away, they actually *flip* him out of the bed."

"Oh they all say that," Martha dismissed.

Sue Carol looked at them all with her good eye, which was now almost as bloodshot as the bad eye: "Are you? Are you"—she pronounced it *yew*—"are you all flippers?"

The group looked at one another. Jessie made an attempt to put the musical lamb into circulation, crying out, "Oh, look at this darling little lamb, and it goes baah." But the women were leaning forward in concentration.

"Come on," Sue Carol begged. "We've known each other all these years, had all this wine and cheese, and heart-to-heart talks, none of us really knows what we're like when we're alone with them. Are you? Are you all flippers?"

The answers went counterclockwise with the lamb.

"I get the job done," said Martha. "I flip Donald . . . occasionally . . . to be polite."

"I never flipped Steve," Lisbeth said, musing. "I thought about it."

"Oh, sporadically," said Claire.

"Well, I never have," said Nina.

Jessie overhearing, as she carried over the rest of the presents, laughed and confessed, "I'm a flipper. Every time. I guess it's those long intermissions. I once tossed Paul against that wall."

The others stared at the great vacant wall, the one with the abraded section that needed to be replastered, or at least Sheetrocked. Jessie remembered the night; it was half in jest but she had tossed Paul at a moment of centrifugal passion. He was a small man, all muscle, and he had sprung like a rubber band. He had been her last lover, three years ago, until now, until Jesse.

Against her will, she looked at the stove clock; it was after nine o'clock. "My time is your time," he had said. He would call her at ten, she was sure of it—almost.

"Omigod, good Lord, then *it might be me.*" Sue Carol was wailing. "Bob may need . . . a more passionate partner. . . . This might be me. . . . Now, I don't know what to do." She tried to stand, as if to leave. She held her head. "Oh, now the room's spinning."

"Too much wine," Jessie diagnosed. "Can I make you coffee? Tea?"

"My blood is running, the walls are undulating. Oh, don't let me close my eyes. . . . If I close my eyes, there's no hope, I'll be sucked down into it."

Sue Carol could feel it now, the internal twister that was suctioning her brains into her cowgirl boots. Oh, good Lord, this business with Bob was actually killing her. She had to fight against it; it was an irresistible, destructive force. "I could play Medea," she cried out, and then, after swaying metronomically for what seemed like minutes, she toppled over.

Chapter Fourteen

In which Jessie becomes violent, Sue Carol contemplates the tile floor, and the party takes a turn. . . .

"Ask not for whom the cell phone tolls. . . ."

By ten to ten o'clock, Jessie's belly clenched; he had to call her; she could not be wrong. He had "kissed her better": professionally, he was a champion of truth, and a battler against injustice. He would not hurt her. Or if he had second thoughts in the postcoital divide and was going to disappoint her, he would be brave enough to say so. . . . She forced herself to attend to the matters at hand.

I am too old to watch the clock, for a man's call, she told herself, but "too old" to hit the wrong nerve.

Okay, she told herself, I am too accomplished, too smart, and have too sophisticated a perspective to wait for a man to call. She willed Jesse Dark, and the anticipated call, from her mind. She was the hostess, and she had to take care of her guests. That was the priority.

The party had hit turbulence when Sue Carol passed out. She had revived, with cold compresses, but had now disappeared into the bathroom for long periods of time, during which the others did not forget her but called out: "Are you okay in there?"

Was she okay in there?

Inside Jessie's bathroom, on her uneven tiles, Sue Carol lay, pressing her forehead to the gray ceramic.

You are building sense memories, she told herself. Remember this. . . . She could still smell the scorched hair, the acrid scent of her incinerated marriage. Fifteen years up in smoke.

Recall these symptoms, she emphasized to herself, the fevered interface just beneath your forehead skin, the saliva filling your mouth, the cool nausea snaking down to your gut. It would all be good for a part, someday, even if it was near unbearable tonight.

It was nice of Jessie to say that she could stay here; but Sue Carol had also noted Jessie's expression when she'd shown her the only bona fide bed. Sue Carol's presence would be distracting; it was not convenient. Although she knew she could remain here at the loft for the foreseeable future, Sue Carol felt a physical pull toward her own apartment uptown, toward Bob, toward the rumpled comfort of her own bed, the privacy of her own bathroom. That was the only home she really had, the only place she truly belonged. At this moment, familiarity mattered more than fidelity.

And now, that sanctum had been invaded by a strange woman, by Bob having sexual relations with her there. Polluted by a hair. How could she crawl back there, to the sullied bed? In her heart of hearts, Sue Carol suspected that Bob's latest transgression was deliberately "in her face"—so that she would do just what she had done: leave him. It was a coward's ticket out of marriage. He accomplished two objectives at one stroke—the adulterous liaison, and the end of a long marriage that had apparently begun to wear on him. Sue Carol knew that Bob was aware of the unspoken ground rules—she had her pride. Perhaps she'd chosen to ignore a great deal, but she could not ignore this. Back home in Kentucky, there was a saying among the circle of women there—her own mom, and Greta, and their card- and bingo-playing buddies: *a man doesn't leave you. He makes you leave him.*

Maybe it was true. Maybe having an affair in so blatant a way, desecrating the marriage bed, was his way of kicking Sue Carol out. In that case, maybe she should go back up there and confront the sonofabitch. . . . Or, more diabolically, pretend the entire incident had not occurred?

There were secrets in her marriage, why not one more? She almost retched, recalling the most serious. The baby. The baby who would have been thirteen years old now. "A Christmas baby," as he would have been known at home.

The abortion had not been her fault; it had been by default, as it were. The doctor, an idiot on West End, who marketed "sexual harmony" tapes, had failed to diagnose Sue Carol's sole pregnancy. The pregnancy had not been planned; it had defied the odds. She had conceived when medical lore said it was impossible—at the start of her menstrual cycle. That night Bob was flown out to test for the lead in a series, *Nicko,* a comedy about a lovable young Mafioso stud. He had said good-bye, sexually, bending her over the piano bench, taking her in deep thrusts that had apparently scored, so far as biology was concerned.

Two months later, her doctor was treating her for "amenorrhea," failure to menstruate. Treating her with drugs to "bring on" her period, treating her, incorrectly he had admitted later, when the home pregnancy test she waved at him proved her instinct right, and his "expert opinion" wrong.

Known "monster-producing" synthetic progesterone—that is what the quack had been injecting in her buttock, every week. Sue Carol had her choice: abortion or giving birth to what medical science decreed would probably be a hairball with teeth. She had almost opted for a malpractice suit, but when she went to pick up

Bob at the airport, he had been gray with dejection. His TV pilot had not been "picked up" in L.A.

He had regarded the failed series, *Nicko,* as his last, best chance. Privately, Sue Carol had agreed, although she had said, "Baby, it doesn't matter." It had: they had grieved, holding each other in their king-size marriage bed, mourning their separate losses.

Nobody's fault, she'd thought then, no series, no baby. Why tell him?

She hadn't. If she had not had that crappy doctor, she might have a child now; they would have a different marriage. Maybe being a father would have changed Bob, maybe. . . .

She remembered the cramping. Lying in a legal clinic behind Bloomingdale's, all the other women sniffling and going home with their boyfriends, or husbands. She had taken a cab, crosstown, alone.

Sue Carol stared at the gray and white tiles; she stared at Jessie's bathtub and shower stall; she stared at her friend's loofah and sponges, the small glass shelf holding her shampoos and a glass with an upright toothbrush, and everything struck her as alien. She could not envision herself waking up here the next day and perhaps the days after. . . . She wanted so much to go home.

Don't you dare crawl back in that hole, her inner voice instructed. You will be saying, Go on, do anything you like. I have no way out. She imagined her return to 11H, to the silent apartment, to the sickening embrace of what would be a life sentence of "anything goes, Bob." If Bob was home. She envisioned the alternative: herself, waiting for him, to show up—alone?

Was this going to evolve into one of those marriages in which the man is allowed to have another "partner"? No, sirreee. Sue Carol smiled at her reflection, for encouragement. The movement of the facial muscles can sometimes instigate the emotion; a smile can make you feel as if you had reason to smile.

Sue Carol spotted some field greens caught between her teeth; she removed the blackening shred of frisée. Grinned: if she could last this first night here, she could make it anywhere. One night away from home, and she might be free. If she could wake up tomorrow, to a new situation. . . .

She realized she had left her makeup bag outside, with her luggage. She wondered if Jessie would mind if she used her toothbrush, just this once? No, the germs. She rubbed the toothpaste onto her finger and rubbed her front teeth, swished some water from the sink, and decided, instead, just to borrow her friend's unwaxed floss. Sue Carol worked the tough thread to and fro, shocked and a bit thrilled by how much lettuce she removed. You could make a change, if you just tried, she told herself.

For insurance, so she would not backslide into regret and race for the BMT uptown, Sue Carol reached into her pocket and contemplated two pills, the dog Valium, and the mystery blue tablet purported to be Ecstasy. She decided on the known versus the unknown and washed down the Yorkie tranquilizer with a glass of water that tasted faintly of toothpaste. She braced herself to reenter the party and the roomful of women. This was her choice, tonight: could she stick with it?

Outside, in the living room of Jessie's loft, the roundelay of gifts continued, with much *ooh*ing and *aah*ing over fuzzy receiving blankets, tiny clothes, hand-knit booties (not hand-knit by the guests but by grandmothers who supplied a West Side boutique). There were "gag" gifts such as the nursing bra from Nina ("I bought it for myself by mistake") and "treat gifts," (the gift certificate for a massage, from Jessie). The gift circle was an ancient ceremony enacted, by instinct not memory, by the women present.

Going clockwise with the gifts were the revelations, as the women spoke with a candor that increased with the lateness of the hour. *In vino veritas:* they had all, except Claire, drunk quite a bit of wine. From the Aussie Red, they had achieved a mellow inebriation. Later they all wondered if the switch to the jug of El Conquistador had added to the rawness of the exchanges and confessions that followed. If there was truth *in vino,* perhaps a harsher wine elicited a harder truth.

Sue Carol emerged at last from the bathroom, singing, "Delta Dawn, what's that flower you have on? Could it be a faded rose from days gone by?" Martha glared at her. "Do you think that's appropriate?" she asked.

Sue Carol became silent and slipped back onto the couch, and accepted the cup of ginger tea that Jessie had brewed and offered. "Anti-nausea," she advised.

"I'll take some, too," said Claire, the first sign that she was affected by the accrual of gifts and confidences. For Claire, a retreat had begun, into some corner mezzanine of her mind. As the gifts and objects piled up, in the crib provided by Martha, her sense of the reality of the oncoming birth, the soon-to-be-present baby, began to assume a new and unsettling credibility. Somehow, Claire acknowledged to herself, she had not truly envisioned the reality or even the hardware of motherhood: and now, here was Martha Sarkis Sloane with her arsenal of gifts.

Martha's presents had long been a joke in their group. Martha ran what the others referred to as her "disaster" clipping service— she mailed alarming news items to all the women, whenever possible. The news was usually followed by an antidote—when Claire had gotten her favorite gig, to play her bassoon on a cruise ship in Bali, Martha had mailed her a list of intestinal parasites that she could absorb, and a bottle of worming medication. Even under ordinary circumstances, Martha had an uncanny knack for giving gifts that seemed to be disguised criticisms—diet books and weight-loss gadgets for Nina, cleansers and guides to financial planning for Jessie, texts on anorexia and cartons of truffles for Lisbeth, and an entire library on codependency for Sue Carol (whom she also "treated" to a course in acquiring a real estate broker license). To Claire, Martha had actually donated her preliposuction size ten designer business suits ("It will make a difference in your appearance, when you go in for a job"). This was a private joke Claire had shared with the others. They laughed when Claire had modeled the structured suits, "oni"s and "ini"s. Claire had never been seen in anything more tailored than her bicycle shorts or the veil-like East Indian skirts she wore for performance. It was a sight gag when she held up an Armani suit. "Business drag," she called it.

But tonight, Martha had outdone herself. Her gifts threatened the least appealing aspects of motherhood: even the materials—plastic and rubber—and the primary colors struck Claire as garish. She didn't want to take the crib home, or the Jolly Jumper, from which Martha predicted her baby "could swing in a doorway while still being confined."

Martha had included baby gates, a tiny potty, a feeding seat that would hook onto the dining table, a back carrier, and a strombrolla. The only items Claire genuinely liked were the clothes and receiving blankets; Claire nuzzled the soft cotton knits to her cheek and remembered comforts from her own infancy.

But such pleasure was short-lived as Martha presented what she called her "maternal library"—which included texts from which she began to read, in her loud, brassy voice:

"Painless childbirth—even natural childbirth isn't natural," she blared. "It must be learned." Martha panted, demonstrating the breathing, and offered (what a nightmare) to be Claire's Lamaze partner.

She went on to prepare Claire for the sight of "her newborn": "Your newborn will be no beauty," she read, "he will be covered with fine dark hair known as 'lanugo.' "

"Oh, please," Nina interjected. "My cousin had a baby, and it wasn't covered with lanugo."

"Everyone is covered with lanugo," Martha insisted.

As she read, Lisbeth began to toy with the Jolly Jumper, which Martha had strung from the loft's main ceiling beam. Lisbeth was slight enough to slip into the hanging seat, and as Martha droned on, Lisbeth began to swing, a somewhat vacant expression on her face.

Jessie noticed; could that beam support Lisbeth's weight? She decided that it could: the girl must not tip ninety pounds. As the hostess, Jessie also noticed Claire's increasing pallor, a damp sheen that had come to her complexion as Martha read on. . . . *Was Claire all right?* Jessie had a more serious intimation of disaster, as Claire stared down at the gift potty seat. Jessie could see this whole evening, which had already hit some highs and lows, going down what Sue Carol called "the shitter."

"Martha," Jessie interrupted. "I think you're getting a bit ahead—"

"She has to be prepared," Martha insisted. She jumped up and brought over a box, still in a drugstore shopping sack. "Look. Look what I got you."

Claire opened the bag and withdrew a medical-looking gadget with a rubber syringe and more fittings than Jessie could comprehend.

"What is it?" she asked.

"It's a breast pump," Martha cried out. "For when you're having problems lactating."

"I'm going to be lactating?" Claire asked.

"Oh, yes, but it may not be easy. I know women who have had to take lessons in breast-feeding, there are courses, and still"—Martha looked sad—"they failed." She squeezed the bulb on the breast pump with some energy. "Oh now I wonder if I should have gotten you the electric pump. They really drain you. You'll be pumping your milk, and storing the excess in the freezer."

Claire looked doubtful, and of course, Martha misunderstood: "Don't worry. If you can't produce, La Leche will rush some fresh-squeezed breast milk over to you." Then her brow knit in a frown of worry. "But whatever you do, don't pour the fresh hot milk onto your frozen milk . . . it will thaw it."

"I don't even have milk and now I have to worry about thawing?"

Jessie noticed Claire's expression; she was wide-eyed with alarm. Jessie had a premonition then, of what would happen later. . . .

"Let's not talk about lactation," Jessie said, desperate, trying to avoid the crash she knew was coming. "Why don't we serve that dessert before it's too late?" Unable to resist, as she walked to the refrigerator to get Nina's chocolate cake, Jessie noted the stove clock reached 10 P.M., sharp. As if on cue, her wall phone shrilled.

Thank God. Jesse Dark. Oh, I do love you, she thought, flinging herself at the wall. "Hello?" she answered, almost out of breath.

She concentrated for a moment, then said, "No. I am not interested. Please scratch me from your solicitations."

The others, listening, thought Jessie sounded unlike herself, almost rude.

"I don't want your card, and there should be a law against the interest rates you charge." Then, she softened. "I'm sorry, I know you're only a phone sales person, and you're just trying to make a living. But cut my name from your list, please."

Then she slammed down the phone to see the others staring at her.

"Well," she said, "it was Citibank. Offering a new card. It's usury, legal usury. My next book is an exposé on credit—*Death at the ATM* or *Killing Ourselves with Credit.* Why does the government allow this? I want the answers."

"You're not kidding," Lisbeth said, swinging harder in the Jolly Jumper. Jessie was vaguely aware that Lisbeth now had an unlit Gauloises clenched between her teeth. "Don't smoke," she cautioned her.

"It's not just lung cancer," Martha chimed in, "you should consider cancer of the tongue, lips—"

"I'm just sucking the filter," Lisbeth said in a small voice.

Jessie sagged back onto the sofa, beside Claire. "I was expecting someone else to call," she admitted. "No one you know," she added.

Jessie reached for El Conquistador, which whatever its defects, had the virtue of being bottomless. She poured herself another glass and swallowed. *So good-bye, Jesse Dark.* No more golden chest, vestigial nipples. No more good loving. No more laughs while lusting. No more lips of leather. . . . No more soulful stares. . . .

Okay, so be it. But the wound would not cauterize. She wanted to know why. Was it because she had said the word *love?* Was it to do with her wounded breast? How could he forget her so fast? Jessie felt an almost magnetized pull toward the cell phone she so disdained, which rested, like a little gun, on the coffee table.

She was not going to resist calling him; she could feel it. But she had her pride, too, so she got up, picked up the tiny black cell phone, and walked to her window, raised the frame, and tossed the phone out into the city night, to the blackness of Butane Street below. When in doubt, kill the messenger, even or maybe *especially* if the messenger is silent.

Her friends were staring, but only Martha dared speak: "What on earth was *that?* Didn't you just buy it? It looked like a good phone. Go down and get it. Return it. There must be a warranty."

A warranty. Wouldn't it be wonderful, if there were a warranty when you made love with a new man? That you could get your pride and your feelings back, within fifteen days. Jessie felt her face flush; the action had, perversely, heated her. She felt as she had one night, long ago, when she had slapped a man in a restaurant for calling her a "cockteaser."

Did contact with new men have to end in humiliation?

Remember the good part of the experience, Jessie was telling herself. That was three days of ecstatic sex, laughter, and closeness. They happened . . . they existed . . . no one can take them back. She looked over at Claire and envied her—not just the baby within her, but also her ease with herself and others. Claire could weave in and out of relations with men; she was graceful, herself, at leaving. She truly knew that more good times were ahead; she didn't cling.

Jessie knew her own weaknesses; her loss of confidence in the face of powerful desire. She was fine with the other men in her life; with the Michaels and Pauls, who were pleasant companions and lovers, but no more. But when a man truly moved her, she was helpless. She did not want to say good-bye. The damned wedding gown came out of her imaginary closet. Admit it, she thought, I have envisioned a wedding outdoors, on the mesa, life with him in a pueblo. Papoose.

Logically, she did not want that much from Jesse Dark. She wanted to see him again, make love some more. I wasn't done, with you, she mentally addressed him—a sign she was entering into one of those ongoing internal dialogues. But Jessie also knew that her flaw—the failure to abandon desire and hope—was also her strength. Later, she would remember, that even as she had thrown the cell phone, and officially declared herself off the waiting list, a nugget of faith had remained, indestructible, like the microchip that could determine so much of what a mechanism could accomplish.

Aloud, she said, "I have come to loathe the technology."

Nina, who had been subliminally aware of her chocolate soufflé cake all evening, bolted for the refrigerator. "Let me get the cake. I'll just help serve it." She could smell the semisweet chocolate as she wet a knife under the kitchen sink faucet. "We have to cut it with a wet knife. God help us, if we do it wrong . . . it could be tragic."

"I'll get the cake plates," Jessie said, moving toward the pantry shelves, ignoring the stacks of dirty dinner plates. "I'm sure this will be delicious."

"Everybody but me gets a piece," Nina announced. "It should be good. It is absolutely flour-less." Then Nina and Jessie distributed the cake plates. As Nina handed Claire a slice, Martha cautioned, "I don't know if Claire should. She could get sugar crazed or develop gestational diabetes."

"Oh, please," Nina said. "The secret is egg whites."

She gave Claire a cake fork. "Eat up, Mommy."

Before Claire could lift the forkful of cake to her mouth, Martha interjected, "It must have three thousand calories." Martha resumed her place on the second sofa. "You know, at the rate our metabolisms slow down, after thirty-five, we gain two pounds a year."

"So what?" Claire said. "Good men will love us as we are."

"What good men?" asked Nina. She had her eye on the remains of the cake; how well it had baked. The dark chocolate consistency was perfect—dry and crumbly on the surface, moist within. . . .

"So . . . ," Martha continued, setting her plate back on the coffee table. "When I'm seventy, I'll weigh one hundred and eighty pounds."

"You mean life is a long depression ending in overweight?" Jessie asked. She already regretted the cell phone tossing; she'd just have to buy another one. But it had felt good for a minute—action was stronger than inaction. Passivity was defeat. She had known she was going to have to act—and she did not want to humiliate herself by telephoning Jesse Dark. Her impulses had been triggered by the new cell phone, the need for instant gratification. She could resist an old-fashioned black wall phone. Maybe he would still call her, with a brilliant excuse. A few years back, there had been a news item about a woman who was expecting a call from a man she had just met and fallen in love with. When he didn't call on time, she had the police check his apartment. The man had been found dead of a massive coronary. That was a valid excuse. Anything less than force majeure was dreck. Jessie spent a moment imagining dire events beyond Jesse Dark's control, then tuned back into the couch conversation. She noted that no one had tasted the cake yet.

"Good men *will* love us as we are," Claire was saying. "Remember when I went to Juilliard? For some reason, I got so fat. I still met men. I think I met *more* men. It doesn't matter." Claire almost confided to the others about the men on the street, whistling and making kissing noises at her belly, but she didn't know if anyone would understand why she didn't mind them.

"Oh, no," Martha said, covering the cake with a piece of plastic wrap. "It's all over as far as new men when you're forty. New men don't want you then. That's why you have to have an old one of your own."

"If it's like that, I'd just as soon skip it," Jessie said. She wanted to taste the cake; it looked so light.

"Maybe you will . . . skip it," Martha said. "A lot of women give up on men. Even the great old sex symbols. Remember Brigitte Bardot?"

"Bebe," Lisbeth said. Bebe—nostalgia inherent in the nickname for Bardot, the long-ago, now-aged nymphet.

"Now she's living with thirty-five canaries," Martha informed them. "And of course, some women turn to other women. They force themselves, for political reasons. I don't get the physicality. Can you imagine?"

The others just looked at her.

"I mean, imagine satisfying another woman? It would be so . . . so difficult. Just imagine rotating your finger on some little nub of flesh no bigger than the average pencil eraser, for fifteen to thirty minutes? You'd have to be motivated."

"Passion justifies all actions," Claire said. "Sex is never justified except by desire. If you look at it clinically or coldly, none of the actions seem anything but redundant and unhygienic."

"Now you're talking," Martha gushed, imagining agreement. "Do you think anyone really likes oral sex?"

The others stared at her. "I mean *giving* it," she said. "I don't mind being on the receiving end. But try as I do, I just cannot buy that some women really love to give blow jobs."

"I only object to the word *job*," Jessie said. She was reminded at this moment that she had yielded to an irresistible impulse back in that motel bed in Coyoteville. She wasn't sure whether she had wanted to perform the specific act so much as she wanted a closer look at what she now recalled, with tragic longing, as a most noble and elegant male member, that had tasted faintly like shiitake mushroom. The silken crown, the deep cleft.

Yes, Jessie thought, Claire was right, desire justified everything, and anything. What had occurred had been languorous, tender . . . she would never have described it as what Martha called a "b.j." She had initiated it; he had been sitting in an armchair, before the fireplace in her room. She had been resting at his knee, her head against his thigh, when she had responded to a natural prompt. She would never have called what followed "a blow job."

"I dislike the nomenclature," she announced to the group. "Makes it sound like work."

"Isn't it?" Martha sounded angry.

"Well," Nina contributed, "I don't like it, if the man insists on it. I hate when they hold my head down."

Everyone looked at her in horror—not so much at what she described, but at the anger with which she had spoken of it. What on earth had happened to Nina?

"I defy someone not to gag, when they thrust," Martha said. "It's physically impossible not to."

No one was speaking to her at this point, but Martha couldn't comprehend. "Well, don't you think it's tedious?" When there was no response, she said, "A lot of women are already living alone with dogs."

"I like dogs," Lisbeth said.

"Well, good," Martha said, "but would you at least get a big dog? I have an aunt who makes entire outfits for a Chihuahua. Hats. Little coats. Even tiny boots."

"I bet they match her own outfits," Jessie said.

"Actually, they are a little more elaborate," Martha reported. "You know, I wish you'd gone to dinner with Donald and me last week. . . . We went to Le Cirque. You would have learned something."

"Oh, please," Nina said. "What?"

In spite of themselves, the other women listened attentively to Martha, who was clearly building a case.

"All right, I'll tell you," Martha said, as if she had needed convincing. "The couple at the next table. Nice looking. But a bit older. Maybe late forties. They had brought"—she held her breath for emphasis—"a stuffed animal with them. And, they ordered for it."

"A la carte?" Jessie asked. She flashed a look to Nina and Claire, who were also near laughing. Sue Carol seemed stupefied, and Lisbeth simply nodded.

"Go ahead, laugh," Martha said to Jessie, Claire, and Nina, who were beginning to convulse. "You don't think you could go that way? It sneaks up on you. After a certain point, there are no men, no sex. You just get rashes."

She sighed and set down her second piece of cake, barely touched. "So you end up wearing the funny hats, talking to yourself on escalators. Wearing too much rouge. Applying lipstick above your mouth."

Sue Carol flinched, returning to the conversation. She was seeing in her mind's eye a woman in her own neighborhood, who walked around in gold lamé, a gold lamé dress, gold lamé cape. The woman was made up, with a whitish face powder and overdrawn vermilion lips. Her hair was a frizzed corona of dyed blond over gray. She wandered the neighborhood like that, every single day, the ghost of sex symbols past. What was awful was that Sue Carol could see that the woman had once been a beauty.

"Eleanor Rigby," Sue Carol sang. " 'Her face in a jar by the door. . . . Oh, where do they all come from?' "

Jessie was sinking into her own sofa and into a depression among the pillows. She felt as if she'd lost someone, as if she'd lived an entire life in three days with that man in a motel room in

Colorado. Now, she almost regretted going to Colorado, becoming involved with the story of the cannibalistic Anasazi.

Before the trip, she had been content, hadn't she? She glanced over at her afghan, slung over the easy chair, her books piled on the end table next to her favorite coffee cup, the oversize blue and white French café au lait saucer. Before her trip, she had not known what she was missing, and now she did.

Jessie drifted, mentally, from the group, her mind wandering back to the night skies over Colorado. If only you could do something as trite as turn the clock back; she'd relive those nights, inhabit them. She saw him again, naked by moonlight. When he looked at her—hadn't something passed between them? Something unique? She remembered turning him over in bed, kissing his back, crying out at the bruiselike mark at the base of his spine: what was that?

"That's my Mongolian blue spot," he'd explained, laughing, "proof I am the genuine article."

When she checked back into the group, she could see Martha had made some segue and was displaying her earrings. "No one has said anything about my new earrings," she said in a fake little-girl voice.

"They're beautiful," everyone said, in a collective dispirited tone.

Martha went on, of course, about how Donald had given them to her, as a prewedding gift.

At the mention of the wedding, the other women exchanged sick glances. Martha's wedding was the sorest point in their lexicon. They were all dreading the wedding; she'd been planning it for years, even before she had met Donald. She had the dress, the menu, and the choices for flowers. This had been described to them all in what they regarded as insane detail—the petals would be white, tinged with violet, to match the tablecloths. Hydrangeas.

They had heard her plans before, but now Martha recited them like a mantra: "The wedding itself will be at the Fifth Avenue Presbyterian Church. The reception will be upstairs at Vert. . . . Then we have chartered the largest private vessel for hire in the world, the *Ataturk,* and we will sail across the Aegean, and finish our honeymoon on Crete."

As there was no response, Martha tried to engage them by including everyone "and of course, you'll all be in my wedding."

"Will we have to wear turquoise?" Nina asked. This was a reference to Sue Carol's wedding, at which they did wear turquoise, with dyed-to-match turquoise satin pumps.

"Ecru," Martha answered. Then she turned to Lisbeth and said, "And I want you to be my maid of honor."

Even Martha seemed to realize she had offended the others, so she added, "It's nothing personal. She's the most photogenic." And amended, "And of course, you'll all be in *some* of the pictures."

Lisbeth begged off. "No, anyone would be better."

Martha looked around at the women and assigned each a role in her wedding: "Jessie, I thought you could recite a little poem, about Donald and me. Our love. And Nina—of course, you can do my nails and makeup . . . and Claire, you'll bring your instruments?"

"I don't know . . . I may be too large, I may not be back in shape," Claire said, begging off.

"We can put you in a muumuu," Martha offered, "or you can stand behind a partition . . . if you're embarrassed by your appearance."

Then Martha got up and shook Sue Carol by the shoulder. "And you, sweetie, I want you to sing."

"'Delta Dawn,'" Sue Carol blared, "'what's that flower you have on?'"

"Not that," Martha snapped.

"Listen, Martha," Lisbeth said, still dangling in the Jolly Jumper. "I don't think I can come to the wedding."

"But it's months off," Martha said.

"I just don't want you to count on me," Lisbeth said. "As maid of honor. I've been feeling kind of woozy lately . . . I've felt so funny since Steve."

"I think Steve is not in the picture," Nina said.

"Oh no, no, *au contraire*," Lisbeth told them. "I told you I saw him on the subway tonight . . . and I know it was an omen, that we are getting closer. I don't think it was a coincidence that he appeared tonight, of all nights."

She swung closer, anchoring her feet to the floorboards. "You know," she confided, "we never talked about getting married."

"Because he was already?" Martha asked.

"It was only a technical marriage," Lisbeth said in defense. "But it was painful for him to extract himself. Steve is a very kind man; divorce is an unkind act unless both agree. No, we didn't talk about getting married, but we did talk about . . . having children . . . I made that christening dress for. . . ."

"Oh, God . . . take it back," Claire cried.

"No, I want you to have it," Lisbeth insisted. "I'll crochet another one when. . . ."

"So he is coming back?" Martha asked.

"Ssssh," Jessie warned her.

"Don't encourage this," Nina whispered to Martha. Nina knew she could withstand Martha's interrogations and criticisms; she wasn't certain Lisbeth could.

"Oh no," Lisbeth assured her. "It's fine. There's no reason for concern. We never broke up or anything like that. The last night we were together, it was the best."

"That's always a bad sign," Nina commented.

Jessie wondered: *Was it?* Most of her thoughts were still on Jesse Dark, her mind was reeling, her blood running. Try as she could, only half of her was here in this loft. But she became drawn to what Lisbeth was saying, as she could understand it. . . .

"It was snowing that night," Lisbeth remembered. "We lay on my bed, just watching the snow . . . there was a kind of violet light. We fell asleep on and off. And I had the most wonderful dreams. You won't believe this, but we were having the same dream, something about floating together in a turquoise sea, the sun on us. The dream went from his head to mine . . . these things happen when you are very close."

Jessie shut her eyes; she could feel what Lisbeth was saying. Yes, she had felt close, more than close; she had known some kind of communion with a man who had been essentially a stranger. But the difference between them was that now Jessie willed herself to snap out of the trance; to refuse to nourish the dream of love alone. She listened, unnerved, to Lisbeth's account.

Lisbeth had suffered for several weeks, walking around, she said, as if she were on Mars. But then, she had found her solution, the accommodation that was working so well: she had read his letters first, then listened to all the songs they had liked. And . . . she couldn't quite explain it—but she had started to feel better.

"Finally, I felt great," Lisbeth said. "It's as if he hasn't gone at all." She confided it all then—how his presence occupied her apartment, how everything could become Steve, the wall, and even the sofa.

"We're very happy," she concluded. "We never fight!"

"I don't get this," Martha said to the others. "She rubs herself against the wall?"

Claire took a sip of her now tepid ginger tea. Lisbeth's story had unnerved her. She had no phantom men back in 312, at Theresa House, but she lived with ghosts also—the soul of her nearly unknown mother, and the small life that inhabited her own body. These were two people to whom she addressed her thoughts, and those thoughts had lately become urgent enough to qualify as prayers.

"Don't think," she ordered herself. "Just be. There's a bit of time left."

"Listen," Nina was telling Lisbeth, "you have to cut down your reaction time. A year is too long. I've got my time down to an hour and five minutes. You have to snap out of it."

She's right, Jessie thought. Cut the reaction time, that's the answer.

"I've been left by millions of men," Nina told Lisbeth. "I've been rejected by men I didn't even want. But you see . . . I'm still here. And I'm fine about it, really."

Really? Jessie wondered.

"Absolutely," Nina reassured her. "Cut your losses, and you can even enjoy yourself. You know in a funny way, I fall in love every time. It's that lost, blind thing they do at the very end. . . . They seem so helpless. For a few seconds, they all belong to me. I feel like I can carry men in my arms forever, I feel like I should nurse them back to health."

She looked at the crumpled packages on the coffee table. "I wonder if that's why I bought that nursing bra . . . by mistake." Nina went over to Claire and sat down on the floor beside her. Claire set down her half-eaten piece of cake, and ruffled her friend's hair.

They had reached the hour when anything can and would be said. Restraints and constraints had been removed, and they were both fatigued and excited, unable to say anything but the truth.

"I have this dream," confessed Nina. "Oh this is really dumb—
that I'm breast-feeding grown men—long lines of them. We seem
to be in a kind of barracks. Well, it's military. I think a naval hospital. . . ."

"I once dreamt I was a cook on a submarine," said Lisbeth, con-
firming the universality of such subconscious impulses.

Claire wanted to know, "Do you have this dream often?"

"About once a week," Nina said. "Then I go out with one, and
that seems to cure me. They don't want my solace. The second I
start to offer them something, they start for the door, pulling their
pants up as they go. . . . Is there any sound as loud as a zipper on its
way up?"

"No," said Sue Carol.

"They slide down silently enough," Nina continued, "but what
a racket on the return trip."

As the women sipped El Conquistador and considered what
Nina had said, they began to become aware of the sound of
hurtling garbage can lids, the clatter of tin cans, and the city wind.
It was as if the forces of nature had turned up the volume. Jessie
shivered, watching her large plate glass window: it seemed to
bend, or was this another optical illusion?

Nina went back over to Lisbeth, who dangled, like a mari-
onette, in the Jolly Jumper.

"When I was younger," Nina told her, "it used to bother me,
the way it's bothering you. But now I find, I can even take a kind
of nourishment from it." Absently, without thinking, she uncovered the cake plate and began to fork up errant chocolate crumbs.
She gave the Jolly Jumper a little push, and Lisbeth swung
slightly, like a child in a swing.

"Now," said Nina, "I just smack them on the tushy and say 'so
long.' I guess I like my babies six feet tall. Ah, they don't mean me

any harm: they're just gone. In a way, they make me feel strong."

"You are strong," Claire said. Lisbeth and Sue Carol agreed. "You are strong," they said.

Jessie stared: Nina seemed unaware that she was now taking automatic bites of the cake, one right after the other, as she spoke with her mouth full: "Oh, why does something always have to spoil it? Some flat remark, a too hasty exit? Like this afternoon . . . I got over it in less than an hour but. . . ."

"Yes," Jessie said, "you started to tell me . . . the man in your mother's complex . . . the Zen-Buddhist-but-he's-Jewish?"

"Oh, yes, the Celestial Seasonings guy. . . . Zhirac. A Jerk. Generic esoteric jerk. I can't believe he had me fast first, then dress in all-white pure nonsynthetic fibers. I went up to his grand-mother's apartment, 24P."

"How was it? Spacious?" Martha wanted to know.

"It was a studio," Nina said. "He had it all fixed up. His grand-mother had died and left it to him, and he furnished it with all Chinese and Indian imports. He was wearing some kind of white gauze garment, it looked like a big diaper. I tell you, if I hadn't been taking care of my mother, and going a little crazy, I wouldn't have even walked in. But I was and I did. . . ."

"And it was a disaster?" Martha asked.

"What do you think? We weren't suppose to talk, so we just kind of nodded at each other. Then Zhirac, his real name is Stan, led me over to a futon. We were just about to start . . . he said he could see my 'aura'—it was like a little yellow cloud over my head—when the doorbell rang. Stan asked, 'Who's there?' and the guy answered, 'Exterminator.' And the Jerk turned to me and said, 'Would you mind? I've been waiting a month?' So the extermina-tor came in, and we made love in a cloud of roach spray."

"How was it?" Sue Carol asked.

Nina pantomimed a dead roach, hands curled to her chest, and fell flat on her back on the floor of the loft. "I died," she said. She laughed, but she was recalling what she could never relate out loud: how charmless the encounter had turned. It was as if he had, in fact, let in the exterminator of all hope and dreams. He had killed the frayed fantasy of civility—that two people could mate and end up being polite to each other. But no: she had been left with this golden man, who, only moments before, had bewitched her with his sensuousness, who had surprised her with his equally golden "lingam."

How she had gasped at the sight of that male organ—she, who imagined she had seen them all. The Zhirac lingam had been of unusual width and curvature, it had grown thicker at the center, like an exotic yam. *Damn.* Nina had fallen in love with the lingam at first sight; she'd felt as if she'd uncovered buried treasure; the rare jungle fruit that she might be forbidden to taste. Nina wondered if every sexual act contained one sacred second? Because she could have sworn that they had both been moved, when they had dropped their clothes, and stood naked and surprised. She had not somehow expected this, with Zhirac—she had walked in with her eyes open, as they say. She expected only biology, no more, no less. And then, she had found awe, what she had needed: life, instead of what waited upstairs in Tower A, in her mother's bedroom, where the attendants waited for her to return and death to arrive.

"Exterminator." Yeah, the exterminator could come in. He was expected.

So Zhirac Macklis, the exotic, who mumbled of mantras and auras, was a man who wanted to get rid of his roaches. Okay. But he'd layered more charmlessness on top of that. The charade fell apart fast. It had in fact not been very successful—the apartment had been poorly disguised as a bachelor haunt. His grandmother's salmon Formica and lime wallpaper was still in evidence, as was her framed *Reader's Digest* "Laughter Is the Best Medicine" column.

In this inauspicious setting Zhirac, aka Stan, had walked across the room, not bothering to obscure the fact that he was passing his own gas, into the now pesticide-clouded atmosphere of 24P. The bad odor drafts numbed her. She didn't know what to say, or do. What was he trying to prove? He went to the bathroom, left the door open and the lid up. Burped as he emerged, and told her he had a girlfriend, whom he really cared about, back in Sri Lanka. The girlfriend was an American, too.

Nina mentioned the uncouthness of the trip to the bathroom to her girlfriends, but she could not bring herself to add that he had, in the same odiferous moment, also breathed the name of another woman, who was called, of all things, Tiffany. Had he been trying to offend her on every possible level? Employ all male faux pas in one stinker blast?

The women all laughed, but Jessie could hear the wind howl louder. The predicted "storm of the century" seemed about to arrive. She heard a roar down her chimney as the flames leapt up and encountered greater suction. Even through the heat of the fire, she could feel a draft of cold air. She looked at her window, at that view that somewhat scared her, and she caught her breath—the glass *was* bending inward. What if it shattered? Outside, the cityscape hardened, grew icier, more dangerous, brilliant. Jessie picked up her afghan throw and wrapped it round herself as she walked closer to the window, to touch the glass, and test its resistance.

Claire jumped up. "It's going to really storm," she said. "I better go before it gets worse."

"Sit down," Martha ordered her. "You'll get phlebitis."

Something hissed against the window, and there was a sudden *ping*—sleet or hail, starting.

Chapter Fifteen

In which Martha takes the throne,
and the storm of the century strikes NoHo. . . .

Just Desserts

Martha, fuming, settled herself on the potty Jessie had installed. She peed for it seemed an eternity, giving back the wine, the water, the fluids of the day. And what a day it had been, beginning in triumph with the penthouse triplex closing, the mucho million dollaros, passing through the humiliation of the fertility doctor's office, the inconvenience of this descent to NoHo. And now what? A debacle, with her fiancé, turning forty alone, at a table for two, reservation twice confirmed, at the city's restaurant of the hour, Vert.

Martha's heart hammered. Sweat broke out on her brow. Damnit. How could she have forgotten? She had eaten the apricot sauce off that blasted little Cornish hen. The carbohydrate of that apricot must be double that of the orange juice that had caused her fibrillation this afternoon. Here goes my mitral valve prolapse, Martha thought, sagging as she almost slid off the toilet seat. And to top it off, she was locked in with a long-haired cat.

Had she brought her pills? She cracked open the Kate Spade purse and cursed. Where was her brain today? She had left her little compact of dial-a-pills up at Ph43. Her heart skipped. Her stomach dropped, like an elevator missing floors. Damn, she could faint, hit her head on the improperly installed tiles, and die right here in Jessie's substandard renovation.

Martha stared into her purse and noticed the twisted joint she had confiscated from Sue Carol. Martha had sometimes smoked marijuana socially, to be polite. Donald had friends that liked this. She recalled some relaxation that had occurred, in the past, and also reminded herself of the weed's touted medicinal properties. There was such a thing as "medical marijuana," she thought, hunting for a match to light it.

Anything in a pinch, she thought. If I can just stabilize. Slow and regulate my heart; the symptoms will disappear, the confusion between heart palpitations and fear can be corrected.

I have to get it together, Martha reprimanded herself, no matter what it takes. . . .

Thank goodness, there was a bent pack of matches, next to a candleholder set by Jessie's tub: so Jessie was another of these bathers-by-candlelight, Martha realized. She noted the candle had been wedged into its holder with a crunched scrap of tinfoil—a sudden improvisation as Jessie descended into suds, as Claire had done?

Martha had never made love while wet. Donald complained their skin "squeaked." Once, Martha had asked him to have sex in the gilded shower stall, and he had said, "Dry off."

He was an efficient lover, Martha thought, striking the match and watching the little joint ignite, but he was not experimental. So the sex life they had was the way it would be. . . . She shut her eyes as she inhaled. Don't think about his "peni" problem, she reminded herself. It won't help you get through this present situation.

Martha knew her responsibility was to correct her physical instability and resume her efforts to help her friends, if their lives were salvageable.

Toward this goal, she held her breath, keeping down a great gust of Maui Wowee that Bob had brought home from a TV shoot in Hawaii, and which Sue Carol had swiped from his stash before abandoning him and 11H, and her marriage. Whatever Bob's failings, Martha reflected as she refrained from exhaling, he bought some good stuff.

The grass seemed to still the arrhythmia and quiet her nerves. It also conversely cleared her head, and she was stunned to confront an observation that had disturbed her earlier in the evening: *there had been only five Cornish hens.*

Six women, five hens. Martha did the math several times. Someone had been left out of the menu for the evening. True, Nina was dieting; but had Jessie known that when she planned the meal?

Five hens, and all that rush to push her out the door. Was there a plot against her? Was she the subject of a conspiracy? Martha allowed the thought to emerge on the exhalation of aromatic smoke.

They were her best friends, she reminded herself. Were they all against her?

L isbeth, too, was thinking of smoke. She needed to have one of the Gauloises . . . now. Clutching her cobalt blue lighter and the blue pack of unfiltered French cigarettes, she tiptoed past the kitchen area as Nina and Jessie tackled a bit of the mess.

Martha was in the john, and Sue Carol seemed semiconscious, slumped against a sofa. Claire was reading one of the baby care books Martha had given her, and she seemed riveted. With any luck, Lisbeth would be able to slip out the fire door, up the escape ladder to the nice little roof access area, where she had smoked the last time she visited Jessie.

She did not bother with her coat—she'd only be gone a few minutes. The fresh air would clear her head, she thought. The vodka had both invigorated and confused her. She was still worrying over her date with the DCHR. In her excitement in seeing Steve on the subway, she had forgotten to stop at Pennsylvania Station to mail the required response. Now, she would have to plan on going to Gertz Plaza, in Jamaica, Queens, in the morning, after all.

Maybe she should just skip it, let go of 2A after all. Let Feiler have it and move his fat son into her space. The pressure at the wall had become too great, she thought, maybe it was not worth it.

But the ghosts of her parents accosted her as Lisbeth climbed the metal ladder and the chill wind smacked her face. *Wake up, she could never get another place, not that nice, not in the heart of Manhattan.*

That apartment had been an annuity of sorts, that allowed her parents to stay in the arts. Lisbeth conceded she had always loved the place, too: she had left only briefly, when she moved to Theresa House, for her "privacy." At twenty, she had not wanted to remain at home with her parents, much as she had loved them. She had imagined more love affairs than occurred; anyway, it had been time. Time to grow up, live away from home.

And six years ago, when her parents had died together in a car crash on tour with *Carousel,* it had also been time for Lisbeth to return. 2A was her birthright, the legacy from her gypsy family. It was the only place where she and Steve had been together; it was in a sense a home they shared.

No, she should keep the apartment, but would it be too late to file her documents? Don't think, Lisbeth thought, bracing herself against the wind, which now bore an invisible needling sleet. The cold cut through her sweater; she might as well have been out there in the nude. Lucky, she had her lighter; a match would never have stayed lit. She bent over her cigarette, flicked the flame on, and inhaled the raw flavor of the French cigarette.

Ah. Life's immediate pleasures were worth any penalty. Lisbeth sighed, smoked. She was so lost in thought, and in the simple act of smoking, that she did not hear someone climbing the fire stair.

Of course, Jessie had seen Lisbeth sneak out the fire door. Was she insane, going out in the freezing cold, without a coat? Was she going to smoke or kill herself? Was there a difference?

Jessie did not bother with her own coat: she raced after her friend and began climbing the rusted metal fire ladder. It was a single-rung affair, running up alongside the old brick building. She supposed it was anchored securely but it shook, now, in the bitter wind, and Jessie recalled the expression "metal fatigue" as she climbed.

She could see Lisbeth's feet, elegantly shod in the kid leather boots, as Jessie ascended. Lisbeth was perched on the roof inset, a place where workmen could pause as they installed antennae, cable, or other maintenance equipment.

From where she climbed, Jessie could see the lights of SoHo and the glitter of the Christmas decorations on the stores and atop some office buildings. She could also see the mountains of uncollected trash, the molded Everest of the plowed snow from the previous blizzard, that had now hardened into a blackened berg, studded with bits of garbage and stained with dogs' and derelicts' yellow urine. The trash cans had blown over and rolled down the empty street, clanging alarm: the storm was coming, fast and hard.

"Lisbeth?" Jessie said, almost saying her friend's name as a gasp. Jessie was winded from the climb, the struggle, the wine, the stress of the party, and the apparently futile wait for the phone call.

"Lisbeth," she said, in lieu of a criticism such as Are you nuts? or What are you doing up here, in this cold and wind?

Their eyes met. "I was worried about you," Jessie said, but the wind whipped away her words, and Lisbeth was looking down, saying, "What? I can't hear?"

Jessie wanted to say: Stop smoking that; you're killing yourself, cell by cell, but she knew Lisbeth knew, maybe that was what she wanted. "Come back down," Jessie invited. "We're going to have dessert."

"I'll be down in a minute," Lisbeth said, loud enough to be heard. The storm sounded now like a train that was approaching in the gray black skies above them.

Jessie suddenly felt like crying but she didn't. Instead, she said, "Come on . . . come back down. . . ."

Lisbeth shook her head, and puffed on her Gauloises. She was smiling like a child in a treehouse, knowing she was beyond reach.

Jessie, looking up, flashed on a memory of fifteen years before, when they had both climbed a tower atop Theresa House and stolen the clangor of the building's bell. They had never been caught. After their giggle over the success of the prank, they had returned the metal part, and rung the bells.

She remembered how they had laughed until they had to cross their legs to keep from peeing as they stood, in pajamas, in the night tower, with all Manhattan atwinkle below them. They had been best friends from that night forth, and now Jessie feared Lisbeth was nearing some more definite end. She was too fragile; she lived too close to an edge that dropped into an abyss that Jessie did not even want to imagine.

"You're coming down," Jessie said. She climbed another rung and reached for the other woman's hand, the one that held the lit cigarette. "Drop that thing and get back inside."

She was surprised by the force with which she had spoken. Jessie was not in the habit of telling anyone what to do. But she was not going to stand by and ignore her friend, killing herself one way or another, up above her head. Jessie was surprised by what she herself said and did—trying to force Lisbeth to let go—but she was even more startled by the way she lost her footing in that motion. For a moment, she slipped, only one foot remaining on the ladder, her hand still reaching upward toward Lisbeth.

What would have happened next? Jessie and Lisbeth would never know. Perhaps Jessie would have caught her balance, a foothold, her one hand sufficient to maintain her on the ladder . . . or maybe not, and she would have fallen the twelve stories to Butane Street, and landed beside her shattered cell phone.

But that did not happen because Lisbeth's fine-boned hand, thin and gloveless, the size of a child's, seized Jessie's and held her fast. Jessie scrambled, her foot finding the next rung. It could only have been an instant that she had dangled that way. . . .

Oh my God, Jessie thought, I meant to save *her.* In that instant, Jessie was impressed by the strength in Lisbeth's grip. Who was frail, then, and who foolish?

They didn't say anything; they were never going to talk about this. Jessie could tell. She felt tears start in her own eyes. Lisbeth smiled, and her tears could be explained by the cold, which was now knife sharp. She carefully, against the pressure of the oncoming storm, hunched over and lit a second cigarette. Her porcelain features were illuminated, blue, by the flare of the lighter.

"A last one," she said, and nodded for Jessie to go back inside.

"Last one?" Jessie confirmed.

"Oh, yeah," Lisbeth answered, "last one."

Chapter Sixteen

*In which Nina checks in with her mother and the ghosts of the
Confederated Project.*

"Holding Her Own"

As soon as Jessie vanished to climb the fire stair, Nina began to contemplate the wall phone in the kitchen area. She was soaping the dirty dinner plates—Jessie's dishwasher did not work; it had been incorrectly hooked up, like almost everything in the loft. Jessie had apologized, saying they would have to do the dishes by hand. "If we turn the machine on, the rinse water will overflow," Jessie had warned. So Nina had set up one half of the double sink to wash, while she rinsed the dishes under a hot faucet over the other section of the sink. It was amazing how many dishes they had already used, and they would still need the dessert plates.

Nina was washing the dishes and wondering if she should call and check on her mother up in the far north Bronx. She knew Flo and Basha Belenkov were there, that the two women had instructions to call if her mother worsened, or her pulse registered below fifty-five. But maybe they did not want to disturb Nina; maybe matters had deteriorated so much, there was no point. Nina felt an irresistible urge to call.

Ever since this afternoon, she had been mentally berating herself for taking the small sexual hiatus with Zhirac. What if her mother had died, or as they said in the Confederated Project, "passed away" while she was engaged in that silly sexual encounter? She would have lost the one person on the earth who loved her most while spending time with someone who cared the least. Yet, she had felt, when she went to him, that she had to, to save her own life, or something more complex, her reason for living. A future without men, or physical love, did not beckon. . . . What good would it be? At least she knew what mattered to her. The life force, in her favorite form. Her mother would have urged her to go. "Have some fun, Nina, you're too good to me," she was always saying. "What did I do to deserve you?"

"I don't remember" was Nina's gag answer, but she did remember. Mira had never shown her anything but kindness. Maternal love, Nina had been given, in abundance. Without limits or conditions. But now, as she scrubbed Cornish hen gravy from Jessie's china plates, she had to wonder why she had never been given the other kind of love.

Her mother and father had loved her; they found her nice and attractive, too. But no man had ever said he was "in" love with Nina; no one had proposed even a temporary living arrangement. She had been desired, maybe even adored for a few minutes, each time she was with a man, but none had been moved to, as they said in the Confederated Projects, "pop the question" or "commit."

The closest she had come to a steady had been an older man, a lingerie salesman, who lived in Arizona but visited New York for buying trips, twice a year. He had slept with her twice a year for the past six years and smacked her on the rump, like a good pony, after every time. "What I like," he always said.

Even he had not said "love."

No, all the love meant for Nina Moskowitz on this planet was contained in the failing body of the woman who had given her life.

Who might even now, Nina thought, setting down the scrungee pad, be dead. Nina thought of that other constellation of women, the three women up in the tower near Riverdale, and she almost threw herself onto the phone and called home.

Flo answered in the musical rhythms of the West Indies. "Oh, yes, your mother, she is doing fine."

"May I speak with her?" Nina asked. She imagined the beautiful black Flo walking, her stately hips swaying, as she made her way to Mira's room and handed the smaller woman the portable phone.

"Well," Flo answered, a chuckle in her deep voice, "she is talking to someone named Saul. . . ."

Nina seized the receiver. Saul. Her father. He had died four years ago. As if in a hallucination, Nina could read the font of the scripted booklet "Warning Signs of Impending Death." Number five was "Visitations"—the dying person will be "visited" by the loved dead. They will "see" and "hear" deceased relatives.

"Saul is there?" Nina asked.

"Well, I can't see him," Flo conceded "but Mira is just so glad he's here. She is laughing and smiling. Don't you worry."

Nina immediately asked for Basha Belenkov to get on the phone. "Basha," she begged, "please tell me the truth. Is Mama dying . . . now . . . tonight?"

There was a long pause in which Nina could envision Basha Belenkov, in her housedress, a plaid duster with a giant zipper front and the kerchief she wore indoors to replace the spangled knit cap that was for outside. Her thick knotted hands were always busy, knitting, stirring soup, massaging her mother's legs . . . encouraging the blood, so slowed, to travel backward to the tired heart.

"Please, Basha," Nina said. "I have to know . . . the truth. I can come home . . . I don't want her to die while I am gone."

There was another pause. There was something. Something wrong. Basha to hesitate was a Basha with bad news.

"Your mother has traveled tonight," Basha said finally. "She shut her eyes and was gone but . . ."—Nina's own heart stopped— "then she returned, and she has been talking to Saul and her own parents ever since."

"How is her color?" Nina wanted to know. "Her pulse?"

The answers—"fair" and "fifty-seven"—were indefinite. "Put her on the phone please," Nina asked. "I want to talk to her myself."

There was the longest pause. Was Mira dead, unconscious? Would Basha lie to her? At last the other old woman confessed the truth. "Now, she speaks only Russian."

So her mother was gone, not to the next world yet but back in time, back to Odessa. "Put her on," Nina insisted. "I must hear her voice." There was the sound of Basha's heavy tread on the parquet floors, a shuffling sound as the phone was passed into the bed.

"Mammala?"

There was no reply. Nina racked her memory for the few Russian words she knew, other than *das videnya,* which would never do.

At last she recalled it, and proudly enunciated it into the receiver, to beam the word from NoHo to the edge of the city: *"Marougina."* Ice cream.

"I will come home," she promised her mother, "and I will bring you ice cream."

She felt sure then that her mother would wait before "traveling" again, as Mira stated her preference: "Vanilla."

Nina set down the phone in relief, and almost threw herself into Jessie's arms as the other woman appeared, in the fire door, looking pale and frozen but announcing: "Let's finish that cake already." Then Nina stared at the counter, stricken: she had devoured two entire pieces.

Claire appeared, holding her back in that new way she had. "Look, I really better leave before it's too late."

"It's too late now," Jessie said. *"You've all got to stay. . . . Look."* She pointed at the expanse of her "picture" windows. An unidentified shape flew by. Lisbeth, watching, recalled the twister in *The Wizard of Oz.* At this height, she felt they were all almost airborne, and anything might appear as a projectile.

"It's a garbage storm," Martha declared. "The wind is blowing the crud all over the place."

Jessie touched the glass—it was cold and had a sick give to it, as if it might tremble and surrender to the elements. "You can feel it," she told the others. She bundled the afghan tighter and turned and tossed another of her logs onto the fire; it crackled, and the orange flames leapt up, eager to escape as sparks into that frigid night sky above NoHo.

She paced in front of the fire, remembering something she'd long forgot. "You know, when I was little, on winter nights like this, my father would build a fire and lie down on the floor in front of it. My mother would lie down on his back . . . and I'd climb onto hers. We were a family pyramid. We spent whole nights like that. It was quiet. When I think of that, I know what we had—peace."

"Well, you lived in an isolated place," Martha commented. "I love Vermont but it's bleak."

"No," Jessie said. "It was wonderful. I always thought I'd live like that. . . ."

"On a husband's back, with a little kiddie?"

"Oh, yes," Jessie said. "I was so sure. I had ten dolls and no doubts. When I was seven, I remember thinking, I can get married and have babies when I'm eighteen, only eleven years to go. . . ."

"So?" Martha wanted to know.

"So . . . I haven't found what my parents had . . . and if it isn't like that, I don't want it. I need . . . I need . . . that sacred silence."

Martha was suspicious. "And so now you've found it?"

"For a minute," Jessie admitted, "but I guess I was mistaken, because he was supposed to call me tonight, and he hasn't."

The window now seemed to bend, as if the entire city had gone into a warp. Another piece of trash glanced off the surface before spinning off into space. Jessie could not help but think of Lisbeth's neutrinos. It was all just molecules, matter, the spinning went off into infinity.

Oh, God, why did she fight it? Maybe she should just run out there and grab the first person she could stand. As if sensible decisions were being made. Sensible decisions on freezing nights in NoHo. Who had a choice? Who could stay out in the weather?

Jessie went to Claire, and gave her the afghan. "I think you're going about this the right way. Grow your own. . . ."

"The baby generates a lot of heat," Claire said, handing the afghan back to Jessie. "This is the first winter I've been in the city, that I haven't felt the cold."

"And I've never felt such a chill," Jessie admitted. "It's a cold spot here, in the center of me. Sometimes, I have to ask myself, Why am I here? Why am I here at all?"

"You mean in New York? Or Downtown?" Martha asked.

"I meant on earth," Jessie said.

"Well, I could see how you'd feel hopeless," Martha said.

The wind was negligible compared to the current that whipped through the women; there was near whiplash as they turned toward Martha in a collective defense: "Hopeless?"

Chapter Seventeen

In which Martha detonates, and the evening is officially called a disaster.

The Walpurgisnacht

"Sweeties," Martha addressed them, "I'm not an insensitive person: I can see you're all running on empty. Believe me, I feel sorry for all of you."

"Sorry?" They spoke in one voice.

Jessie saw Claire pale and reach out to touch the wall. She must have anticipated what would happen, she had tried so hard to stop it.

"Sorry for us?" Jessie said to Martha. "I would not go down that line of thought if I were you." She went closer to Claire. "This is a festive occasion," she reminded Martha.

"This is a disaster. I can't believe what I am seeing and hearing here tonight. Somebody has to talk some sense into you all." Martha mentioned the foundation of her philosophy. "The verities. There are certain verities, and you cannot deny those verities and expect to be happy. You have to make a living, get married, and have children." Martha was on her feet, moving among the women, who were lying on the couches or the floor, except for Claire, who had moved nearer the door, and Jessie, who was following Martha, as if she could bodily stop her from what she would say next.

"What kills me," said Martha, "is that this was all unnecessary. Here you all are, practically middle-aged—"

"Middle-aged," screamed Sue Carol, who was supine by the sofa.

"Middle-aged," Martha continued, and still as confused and goopy as you were twenty years ago."

"Early thirties . . . isn't so old," Lisbeth defended from the Jolly Jumper.

"Early thirties?" Martha almost spat. "There are no early thirties." She stalked among them, as if she might drill them into a better action. "What is this fairy tale—sleeping beauties, plural? Wake up, girls . . . your lives, the productive part of them anyway, are almost over. You can't daydream for tomorrow the way you did in school. You're still doing it, as if your future was up ahead; your future's almost past, ladies."

"Maybe that's good," Jessie said, coming to their defense. "Maybe some of us are still looking for. . . ." She couldn't quite grasp the words but was aware the lights had flickered, in that fluctuant way that could warn of a power outage.

"Okay," she continued, building steam, "maybe some of us are still looking for whatever it is that you look for . . . when you don't like what you are looking at."

"What were we supposed to do?" Sue Carol asked.

"I would have introduced you to my male cousins."

There was a mass laughter. "Pass," someone said. "I've seen them."

"Go ahead, laugh at me," Martha challenged them.

They did. Martha went after Nina first, and Jessie realized that she must have wanted to do this for some time.

"Oh, you're laughing at me? You. Who come down here, straight from this sordid situation with a man in diapers? Still reeking from his roach spray?"

"That's *my* fault?" Nina cried.

"Yes, it's your fault!" Martha said. "You sleep with them too soon."

"Oh, if I waited, he would not have let in the exterminator?"

"Absolutely not. You set yourself up. (A) I would not have gone up to his apartment. (B) I would have insisted he take me to a good restaurant. Roach spray would never have entered into it."

"It wasn't her fault," Lisbeth said.

"Oh, and you'd know? You're home, talking to a sofa."

"Good Lord," Sue Carol said. "I've never seen a mouth grow meaner. . . ."

"And you," Martha said, spinning to take aim at the recumbent Sue Carol, "waltz in here with a three-dollar-and-ninety-nine-cent bag full of cheap vegetables and a Baggie with another woman's hair . . . upstaging the guest of honor with your own self-absorbed needs and the neurotic drama of your charade of a marriage."

"What?" Sue Carol said. "What did you just say?"

"You heard me."

Oh, it has hit the fan, Jessie thought. "Cut it out, Martha."

"Why?" Martha spun to face her. "So you can sit around waiting for a sacred silence? It's going to get real quiet for you up ahead. You'll be alone in here, in this unfinished industrial space that I wouldn't call a human habitation, and isn't worth, in real value, a centime! You'll be alone in here, with . . . with a frozen fish head."

Claire went to the elevator door, reached out to press the button. "I can't take any more of this," she said. "I'm sorry, Jessie, but I have to go."

Martha blocked her. "And you," she said in a tender tone, "you who I am so crazy about, you disappoint me by coming down here on a bicycle, totally unprepared to be a mother."

"It's not true," Jessie assured Claire.

"All of you drinking this rotgut wine that will cause a furry baby. And I try; I try to be sympathetic and helpful. I won't even mention how much money I spent. And to add insult to injury, you all treat me as if I'm a fool."

"Martha, you are over the line!" Jessie said.

"No," Martha said. She wasn't screaming; she had a sibilant hiss. Her eyes were shining, but the whites were red. "No, let's clear the air. All night long, you've all been talking about me, behind my back."

Sue Carol half-rose and crawled over to Martha and eyed her through the one good eye. "She's stoned." Sue Carol diagnosed. "Look at her. It's the grass. She took that joint I had. Now, she's paranoid on top of her personality. . . . Some people go that way."

"Some people," Martha said with that hiss that was now accompanied by the steady sting of the sleet at the windowpane. "Some people not me." She went on then, how she had heard them giggling, how she'd felt their contempt for years, through all the phone calls and the movies, the dinners and the lunches. "You only see me because it would be harder to stop seeing me, than just see me once in awhile."

No one said anything. The barometric pressure in the room rose with every silent second. Oh, so she had been right all along. Martha knew, she knew what was behind it. The obvious jealousy. Even though she had had the sense to downplay her achievements, they could not stand her success. Underneath, they hated her for it and they did not even know.

"I spared you, you know," Martha said. "I did not want to rub this in your wounds. I worried how it would affect you, that's only human, that I reached the top. I was voted: Realtor of the Year."

After a stunned second, the women reacted, laughing.

"See," Martha said. "I'll have a family, I'll be happy, and none of you want to see it. I talk about Donald, my wedding, the honeymoon, and you should see your faces . . . *contort.*"

"It'd make anyone want to puke," Sue Carol said.

"Woooooo. Finally. It's coming out. *Admit it. Admit it. You're sorry you invited me.*" She moved to the crib, with its stack of gifts.

"Look at these gifts!" she said. "You all talk a good game but none of you can stand the truth. Who does the most? Who actually does the most for Claire? I put my money where my mouth is."

"I'm sorry . . . I can't stay," Claire said as the automatic door opened.

"No," everyone screamed. "You can't go."

Claire grabbed her bike wheel. "I just want to go home, I just want to go home." She vanished into the freight elevator.

"Oh, no," Jessie said to the closing elevator doors. "You can't go. This party is for you."

They all stood, listening to the groan of the elevator cables and the rising screech of the storm outside.

"Well, thank you, Martha," Jessie said. "This is a complete fiasco. Tonight was supposed to be . . . about kindness. And now look. . . ."

She gave up. Jessie looked around the loft, at the crumpled wrappings, the exposed gifts, the refuse of the meal she had cooked that had gone half-uneaten: she eyed with special grief the stacked remains of the Cornish hens, which Nina had scraped back onto the serving platter. The little hens had barely been picked on; here and there, a breast was exposed, shredded: the tiny drumsticks poked up, untouched. Only Martha and Claire had truly eaten theirs. Even Jessie had only eaten the crisped skin and the sauced vegetables. Everywhere, the empty glasses, bottles, crushed gift boxes, torn wrapping.

Lisbeth lit up a Gauloise.

"Last one," she whispered. "Claire's gone, so it doesn't matter. . . ."

"Oh for God's sake," Jessie said, feeling her lower lip tremble. She suddenly felt her exhaustion, the flight from Colorado, the staggering return from Dean & DeLuca, the effort of cleaning the loft. She could not resist mentioning that she didn't have to have spent over $300 so this event could take place, and that she had had to hit the ground running, and had not even time enough to properly pee. "I don't want to make like a martyr, but my vacuum cleaner broke, and I clawed out that dust from the old dirt bag by hand."

"You busted your hump," Sue Carol said.

"Yes, I did." Jessie was smarting now, the tears hot at her eyelids. "And you know what? I'm sorry. I'm sorry I bothered. I feel like an idiot for even trying . . . to make the effort. I wanted tonight to be perfect, and no one has shown the least bit of consideration for me. Except Claire." Jessie picked up the hunk of the Wailing Wall. "Whatever you say about Claire, she cares."

Jessie went for her own coat. "I'm going after her. She can't go out alone tonight."

"I'll call for my car," Martha offered.

"Oh, you've done enough," Jessie said. "Just go." She handed her the shahtoosh cape. And could not resist adding, "You're wearing the wool of one of the most endangered species in the world. There are only two thousand shahtoosh left alive, and several of them died so that you could look chic."

"They were dead already," Martha said, donning the cape and pressing for the elevator.

The doors parted, and to their shock there stood Claire, holding her bike wheel, the lock, and the NO STANDING sign. Her face was screwed into an expression of utter rage. Jessie pulled her into the loft, whispered, "Don't talk to her . . . she's leaving. Thank God you came back—"

"My bike was stolen," Claire said.

"See," said Martha.

"See," Claire said. She did not raise her voice, she did not have to. "I'm not taking this." She slammed the signpost down with such a thud, Jessie feared for the floor. "No. I am not taking this from you, Martha. You have a lot of nerve coming down here . . . like a SAC missile. You hit every weak spot, you're unerring."

"Thank you," Martha said. "I just wanted you to face reality."

"Reality will have to face me," Claire said. "I haven't been so mad since my stepmother told me to forget medieval music and teach math. Well, I fought her, and I'll fight you."

"What's wrong with being a math teacher?" Martha wanted to know. "At certain points in life, you must make certain compromises."

"Well, I don't intend to end up looking mine in the eye. Keep it up, Martha, keep droning on about orthodontia and IRAs. You only make me fight harder. I sense a miracle upon me, and I refuse to let you make it . . . mundane. Don't infect me with your fear. I have my own."

"It's not enough," Martha insisted.

"Oh, yes it is." Claire came deeper into the room. The others circled her, and Martha tried to break into their ranks.

Claire told them then what it was like . . . that now, she felt she had boarded some express, without stops, until some unknown and terrifying destination. "I wake up at four A.M.," she admitted, "I hear two pounding hearts. I sleep all day and I lie awake all night. I go grocery shopping at four A.M."

"That's foolish," Martha said. "Why don't you call and ask for delivery?"

"That's the way it is now, for some of us, Martha. It's getting stranger and stranger out there. A trip to the Safeway is like a visit to Mars. Working the ATM machines, like the slots, but you never win. A hundred dollars last night, and I don't know what I bought . . . a lightbulb and some juice . . . some food for a day or two . . . so yes, how am I going to manage? How will I live with my baby in one room? But you know what? I do believe in miracles, I do believe in love . . . and I don't care at all that you find me unfit. I don't even care that I'm broke . . . sometimes you have to go broke to get paid; the sucking void primes the pump."

Lisbeth nodded and outed her cigarette in the dregs of El Conquistador.

"I have new life in me," Claire concluded, "and only a child can lead us out of this. . . . Children are our guides to this future. This is a world my baby will explain to me. Children know how to bring joy to this terrible place. I saw a little boy last night, in a subway arcade. He was laughing and winning a war at a machine that led him into outer space."

"You're having a child so that you can play video games?" Martha tried to comprehend.

"Yes, in a way," Claire said, "because otherwise it will get worse, there's a bad wind blowing and a new cold is creeping toward us. . . . Each day, something new and awful happens. We have worse enemies than ourselves."

She stood, holding the NO STANDING sign to which her bike had been chained.

"Let me buy you a new bicycle," Martha offered.

"That's the least you can do," Nina said.

"I don't want what you can buy me," Claire said.

"Well then. . . ." Martha sagged, her shahtoosh cape seeming to go limp along with her. "I guess I should go." She reached down to pick up her purse, and in her confusion, literally lost it—the purse dropped, cracked open, spilled its profusion of keys, credit cards, lipsticks. Martha stooped to collect herself and her belongings. "What do you want me to do?" she whispered. "I'll do it. Do you want me to have a . . . a brunch?" She looked from one woman to the next.

"My treat," she said, a final plea.

When they did not answer, she was forced to go on. "I was having a good time."

"You were having a ball," Nina said.

"I thought it was a wonderful party . . . considering the location."

"Thank you," Jessie said, "so glad you could come."

Martha was left with nothing but the truth, so she told hers, too. It was midnight, and she had no other recourse. The truth is infectious; one confession begets another. She didn't want to leave; she had never wanted to leave. All she wanted was what she had enjoyed when they had all lived at Theresa House.

It was not, she reported, as good as it appeared with Donald. She did not, in fact, like the terms of the prenup nup. "He says all his money is tied up," she told them. "Ha, in his sock. So our 'liquid' cash is really mine. . . ."

"You pay the bills?" Sue Carol asked, in sincere horror. This was worse than she could have hoped.

"Yes, you will all be happy to hear—I pay all the bills, make all the reservations. He barely speaks to me. He's locked in the back, playing with his . . . his computer . . . I guess. He says he's a day trader, but I don't see any profit. And the sex is . . . well, getting problematic. He only makes love to me really—on my birthday. The rest of the time is, well, my concerted effort to get him going." She made a face. "I have to get on top and do all the work.

His thing is not as strong as it used to be, it . . . folds . . . like an accordion. It's pleated, for God's sake. . . . I don't know if that can be fixed in time for the wedding." She told them all of it, her experiments with Viagra. "There's no free lunch," she informed them. "These Viagran erections are odd—and there are side effects. If his hard-on lasts more than four hours, he has to go to Mt. Sinai emergency room. And sometimes, he sees blue."

"Do you love him?" Lisbeth wanted to know.

"Sweetie, his pupils don't even focus. There's no one home. Yes, of course I love him. I've just had to privately acknowledge that he is, well, almost useless."

"So why the big wedding?" Sue Carol asked. "Why do we all have to appear with the hydrangeas in the ecru gowns?"

"Because," said Martha with a heavy sigh, "it's easier."

Than what? Jessie wondered.

"I can still go to a great restaurant," Martha concluded. "I love lobster places. Can you imagine me, alone in a bib? I'd feel absurd. Where am I supposed to go? To coffeeshops where the plates are chipped and the glasses spotty? So some waitress can plunk down my dinner and say, 'There you go?' "

"Hey," said Sue Carol.

"You all hate me," Martha summed up, "and you're my best friends."

She picked up her shopping bags, and went toward the elevator door. No one knew what to do. It was Claire who stopped her from leaving.

"Look," she said, "all friends have arguments, little ripples, undercurrents. It doesn't mean we don't care." She led Martha back to the sofas and sat down, patting the seat beside her. "Listen," she said to Martha, "a lot of what you said made sense, I've grown old but I know . . . I haven't grown up."

"I didn't mean that personally," Martha said. She looked as if she might cry. "We're still young, but we've been young for such a long time. . . ."

"God, you just put things so . . . bluntly. But in a way, I ought to thank you."

"You're welcome," Martha murmured.

Everyone laughed.

"You made me so mad, it cleared my head," Claire confided. "You lit a fire under me. Running out and running back in here is the most action I've seen since the fruit store. God, there may not be a right way, or a wrong way, to do this"—she touched her belly—"but this is my way. I'd rather have the child of that night than the offspring of some lifelong accommodation. I don't want my life to be some long shlep to the finish."

"Thanks," Martha said.

"I think it's just as scary to play it safe. . . . If I lose, I lose big."

Martha looked at Claire then, and finally saw her. "I envy you," she said, "and believe me, I wish you well."

"I know you do," Claire said. "We don't hate you. We do talk about you—but it is with . . . affection. In fact"—she looked around the room—"I think I can speak for everyone when I say— we don't know what we would do without you."

"You're basically a good person," they said in the ritual drone.

"I'm sorry, I'm sorry," Martha sobbed. "I'd never hurt you. . . ."

Claire began to cry next. "I'm not such a ninny as you think either. I have been going to a clinic. I just have to do things on my own. I don't quite fit, with the women execs in maternity suits, or with the Earth shoe girls who want to give birth in the bathtub. But I had the test, the amniocentesis, and I know, I know . . . the baby will be all right and"—the tears broke through—"it's a girl."

They fell into a weeping huddle, crying as they never had . . . not even twenty years before, at Theresa House.

"I'm so glad," Jessie wailed, "that I had the party here."

As a watched pot won't boil, neither will a listened-for telephone ring. At 2 A.M., while all the other women slept, Jessie was roused by the shrill electronic buzz of her wall phone. She had been so absorbed by the evening and her friends that she could not for an instant register the deep voice on the other end, then through the haze of fatigue, she did. . . .

"Well, you," she greeted him. "I hope you have a good excuse. What happened to 'my time is your time'?"

"I was arrested," he said.

She laughed in relief. "Thank God." Then, "Hey, you're allowed one call?"

"I called my mother," he said. "She was expecting me for dinner, and the demonstration got out of hand. I've been sitting in a cell all night."

So have I, she thought. So now what? To believe him or not?

They spoke softly, so she would not wake the others. "Look," she said, "I don't have domestic fantasies anymore . . . I don't need to get involved with . . . your laundry."

"Why are you talking about my laundry?" he asked.

"I don't know," she said, "because I feel strongly that I don't want to really live with you. I just . . . want to visit you sometimes and you visit me, too . . . I just"—oh, damn, she could not keep from saying it, could she?—"love you so much. . . . You're wild and angry, and I would never leave New York, permanently."

"I know," he said. "We know. When do you come back to Colorado?"

"Soon," she said.

"Can you stay?"

"Till the story is over," she said, "till I have what I need."

"I hate to tell you," he confessed, "I think my ancestors did it. I think they were cannibals. I just want to defend their reputation, and I don't like a case that depends entirely on scientific evidence. There are other explanations. . . ." They spoke, simultaneously—"Always."

And hung up.

Who was that?" whispered Nina, from her position, curled on one of the couches.

"Just a guy," Jessie answered.

Chapter Eighteen

Let the Circle Be Unbroken

Jessie stayed awake, attending to her guests, till dawn. She distributed every blanket she had, and found the extra pillows. The women lay, more or less, where they had fallen asleep. . . . One or two leaned, like cats, into each other—Sue Carol against Lisbeth on one sofa, Nina on the other couch. Martha, covered in her own cape, took up the center space on the floor, the baby quilts and crib bunting around her. Claire had curled up, her back against Martha's, her arms around a cylindrical sofa bolster. Even in unconsciousness, Martha had tried to prevail, and draped part of the shahtoosh cape across her friend, who continued to kick off her covers. And so they rested, resisting yet depending on each other. Martha snored slightly; every once in awhile, her nose twitched, as if she sniffed some possibility.

Claire was oblivious; she was dreaming of babies, not just the one within her, but an infinite number of them. In her sleep, she gasped at some wonder glimpsed, some secret of birth that is learned, then forgotten, in the oblivion of infancy: it was the sensation of leaving the womb, of tunneling downward, parting the boned gates of the body to escape into free air and light. *So that's how we get out . . . ,* Claire thought, in the underwater way of the dreamer who can grasp at truth, even as it eludes her. Claire could not recapture the secret, any more than one could repair a bubble, but felt privileged to have known, for a moment, something sacred. In her sleep, she murmured, "Oh, that's *it.*" Maybe it was enough, to have that glimpse, to catch the iridescence even as it dissolved. Within her dream, the babies tumbled, headfirst, somersaulting themselves into space. Inside her body, Claire's baby turned.

As she surveyed her loft at 4 A.M., Jessie strained to recall the origins of the old expression "the city never sleeps." Was it some noir cop series, from the "golden age" of television? Now, the "city never sleeps" had been co-opted and corrupted by a bank, and it meant those chattering ATM machines were spitting sharp twenties in Times Square even under a full moon. "The city never sleeps" could mean continual alertness and a protective awareness, as it had in the past, or it could mean the insomniac pace of our world out of wack, ticking and totaling the charges.

Whatever it meant, Jessie thought, walking on tiptoe to her great windows, this night, the city did sleep. It closed its eyes, just for a little while, for those final moments before the dawn, during the blizzard that would later be classified as "the storm of the century."

By 5 A.M., looking at her view, the "storm of the century" did not seem like a storm at all, but like a respite from all other storms. The snow covered the city's wounds as a bandage. Where there had been dirt, disorder, ugliness of all kind, there was now only whiteness, thickening and soft, and the violet light that illuminated it.

On the twelfth floor, at 16 Butane Street, this light shone on the women, still in their circle, surrounded by the debris of the party. Not everyone stayed fast asleep; some spoke, in murmured stops and starts, calling out to each other as they drifted between this world and another.

Acknowledgments

I must always begin with my mother, Rosie, whose courage and romantic spirit set the standard. Though gone from my life, she is forever my inspiration. My gallant uncles, Ben and Abe, great friends to one another as well as brothers; more than parents to me— they too have my unending gratitude and love. Now my little girls, Alexandra Rose and Jasmine Sou Mei, provide joy and motivation.

This novel being the story of friendship, I must thank my oldest and dearest friends—starting with Diana and Susan, of my own childhood, and in enduring love for Suzanne Watson, whose spirit illuminates this book. Along the way, I celebrate continuing friendship with Tamara DiMattio (from age six) and the ongoing perspective and wit she brings to every situation. Gratitude, too, to Francine Shane—whose strength and generosity also inform these pages and, without whom, I would not have my darling daughter, Jasmine.

I have been fortunate indeed to be warmed by my "other" families, Frank and Ruth Gilroy and the Clan of Gilroy; Stephen and Tina Lang, and the House of Lang; and my kissing cousins, Richard and Betsy Weiss and Anna, Maggie and Peter Weiss.

I especially thank the lovely and exemplary Rosemary Ahern, who graces my life as an editor over many years, and also as a dear friend. Her integrity and perseverance, loyalty and good heart inspire me on a daily basis, and she is in so many ways responsible for whatever virtues this book may have.

Over the many years I have been writing, I've been privileged to work with editors who continue to influence me and raise the barre—the wonderful writer and editor Daniel Menaker; Deborah Garrison, brave editor and poet, whose editing of "A Place in the Country" at the *New Yorker* had such a salutary effect on my life. I thank Joe Kanon, now also a marvelous novelist, whose zest and literary intelligence continue to guide me. A bouquet, too, to my writers group, whose members Ron Nyswaner, Nina Shengold, John Bowers, Rebecca Stowe, Zachary Zklar, Casey Kurtti, Mary Louise Wilson, and Scott Spencer continue to meet over these now several years and support one another. The extra time Ron Nyswaner, Rebecca Stowe, Nina Shengold, and John Bowers spent on various drafts of this manuscript is very much appreciated.

For the kindly and talented Ron Nyswaner, an added thank you does not suffice—his generosity in sharing work and encouragement truly helped me get on with this book and my life. John Patrick Shanley, too, inspires and aids and abets, while raising the barre with his fearless and funny work—he is as generous as he is talented. Suzanne Watson and Nina Shengold, Jane Margesson (my giggle twin) added thank yous, and a deepening love for keeping my body and soul together through the grueling times, as well as sharing so many pleasurable get-togethers. To my first friend and comrade-in-arms in cyberspace, Ben Cheever, I am grateful for the exchanges that have entertained and guided me, while helping me stay the course. And bouquets to Karen Williams, without whom, we all know, I would be lost in cyberspace. Also, my daily appreciation to Toni Ahearn for bringing beauty and order to my home.

And, of course, my appreciation of marvelous Molly Friedrich's energetic endeavor and the momentum she brings to my life and work. Thank you also to Paul Cirone for his warmth and understanding.

There is special thanks, in regard to this tale, to Maria Cellario, Karen Allen, Caroline Aaron, Jayne Haynes, Amy Van Nostrand, Ellen Foley, Olympia Dukakis, and the many other women whose paths intersected with mine in the long course of writing this story. And hats off to that great gentleman, Kip Gould, whose friendship and faith stand the test of time.